JACK HIGGINS

Jack Higgins lived in Belfast till the age of twelve. Leaving school at fifteen, he spent three years with the Royal Horse Guards, serving on the East German border during the Cold War. His subsequent employment included occupations as diverse as circus roustabout, truck driver, clerk and, after taking an honours degree in sociology and social psychology, teacher and university lecturer.

The Eagle Has Landed turned him into an international bestselling author, and his novels have since sold over 250 million copies and have been translated into fifty-five languages. Many of them have also been made into successful films. His recent bestselling novels include *Pay the Devil, Day of Reckoning, Edge of Danger*, *The Keys of Hell* and *Bad Company*.

In 1995 Jack Higgins was awarded an honorary doctorate by Leeds Metropolitan University. He is a fellow of the Royal Society of Arts and an expert scuba diver and marksman. He lives on Jersey.

JACK HIGGINS

A FINE NIGHT FOR DYING

MIDNIGHT RUNNER

Grafton

HarperCollins*Publishers*
77–85 Fulham Palace Road,
Hammersmith, London W6 8JB

www.harpercollins.co.uk

This omnibus edition published in 2005
by HarperCollins*Publishers*

A Fine Night for Dying
Copyright © Martin Fallon 1969

Midnight Runner
Copyright © Harry Patterson 2002

Jack Higgins asserts the moral right to
be identified as the author of these works

ISBN 0 00 773412 3

Set in Sabon by Palimpsest Book Production Limited,
Polmont, Stirlingshire

Printed and bound in Great Britain by
Clays Ltd, St Ives plc

A FINE NIGHT
FOR DYING

PUBLISHER'S NOTE

A FINE NIGHT FOR DYING was first published in the UK by J. Long, London, in 1969 under the authorship of Martin Fallon. The author was, in fact, the writer familiar to modern readers as Jack Higgins. Martin Fallon was one of the names he used during his early writing days. The book was later published in paperback by Arrow – under the authorship of Jack Higgins – but it has been out of print for several years.

In 2003, it seemed to the author and his publishers that it was a pity to leave such a good story languishing on his shelves. So we are delighted to be able to bring back A FINE NIGHT FOR DYING for the pleasure of the vast majority of us who never had a chance to read the earlier editions.

ENGLISH CHANNEL

1969

1

There were times when Jean Mercier wondered what life was all about and this was very definitely one of them. Somewhere beyond the boat in the darkness was a shoreline that he could not see, hazards at which he could only guess, and the lack of navigation lights wasn't helping.

A wind that came all the way from the Urals spilled out across the Golfe de St-Malo, driving the waves into whitecaps, scattering spray against the windscreen of the launch. Mercier throttled back the engine and adjusted his steering slightly, straining his eyes into the darkness, waiting for a light like some sign from heaven.

He rolled a cigarette awkwardly with one hand, aware of a trembling in the fingers that would not be stilled. He was cold and tired and very scared, but the money was good, cash on the barrel and tax-free – more than he could earn from three months of fishing. With an ailing wife on his hands, a man had to take what came and be thankful.

A light flashed three times, and then was gone so quickly that for a moment he wondered whether he had imagined it. He ran a hand wearily across his eyes and it flickered again. He watched through a third repetition, mesmerized, then pulled himself together and stamped on the floor of the wheelhouse. There were steps on the companionway, and Jacaud appeared.

He had been drinking again and the smell, sourly sharp on the clean salt air, made Mercier feel slightly sick. Jacaud shoved him to one side and took the wheel.

'Where is it?' he growled.

The light answered him, ahead and slightly to port. He nodded, pushed up speed and turned the wheel. As the launch rushed into the darkness, he took a half-bottle of rum from his pocket, swallowed what was left and tossed the empty bottle through the open door. In the light from the binnacle, he seemed disembodied, a head that floated in the darkness, a macabre joke. It was the face of an animal, a brute that walked on two legs with small pig-eyes, flattened nose and features coarsened by years of drink and disease.

Mercier shuddered involuntarily, as he had done many times before, and Jacaud grinned. 'Frightened, aren't you, little man?' Mercier didn't reply and Jacaud grabbed him by the hair, one hand still on the wheel, and pulled him close. Mercier cried out in pain and Jacaud laughed again. 'Stay frightened, that's how I like it. Now go and get the dinghy ready.'

With a heave, he sent him out through the open door and Mercier grabbed at the rail to save himself. There were tears of rage and frustration in his eyes as he felt his way along the deck in the darkness and dropped to one knee beside the rubber dinghy. He took a spring knife from one pocket, feeling for the line that lashed the dinghy into place. He sawed through it, then touched the razor edge of the blade of his thumb, thinking of Jacaud. One good thrust was all it would take, but even at the thought his bowels contracted in a spasm of fear, and he hastily closed the knife, got to his feet and waited at the rail.

The launch rushed into the darkness and the light flashed again. As Jacaud cut the engine, they slowed and started to drift broadside-on to the beach marked by the phosphorescence of the surf a hundred yards away. Mercier threw the anchor over as Jacaud joined him. The big man heaved the dinghy into the water on his own and pulled it in by handline.

'Off with you,' he said impatiently. 'I want to get out of here.'

Water slopped in the bottom of the dinghy, cold and uncomfortable, as Mercier mounted the two wooden oars and pulled away. He was afraid again, as he always was these days, for the beach was unknown territory in spite of the fact that he had visited it in identical circumstances at least half-a-dozen times before. But there was always the feeling that, this time, things might be different – that the police could be waiting. That he might be drifting into a five-year jail sentence.

The dinghy suddenly lifted on a wave, poised for a moment, then dropped in across a line of creamy surf, sliding to a halt as she touched shingle. Mercier shipped his oars, slipped out and pulled her round, prow facing out to sea. As he straightened, a light pierced the darkness, dazzling him momentarily.

He raised a hand defensively; the light was extinguished, and a calm voice said in French, 'You're late. Let's get moving.'

It was the Englishman again; Rossiter. Mercier could tell by the accent, although his French was almost perfect. The only man he had ever known Jacaud touch his cap to. In the darkness he was only a shadow, and so was the man with him. They spoke together briefly in English, a language Mercier did not understand, then the other man stepped into the dinghy and crouched in the prow. Mercier followed him, unshipping the oars, and Rossiter pushed the boat out over the first wave and scrambled across the bow.

Jacaud was waiting at the stern rail when they reached the launch, his cigar glowing faintly in the darkness. The passenger went up first and Rossiter followed with his suitcase. By the time Mercier had reached the deck, the Englishman and the passenger had gone below. Jacaud helped him to get the dinghy over the side, left him to lash it to the deck and went into the wheelhouse. A moment later, the engines rumbled softly and they moved out to sea.

Mercier finished his task and went forward to make sure that all was secure. Rossiter had joined Jacaud in the wheelhouse and they stood together at the wheel, the Englishman's thin, ascetic face contrasting strongly with Jacaud's – opposite sides of the coin. One an animal, the other a gentleman, and yet they seemed to get on with each other so well, something Mercier could never understand.

As he moved past the wheelhouse, Jacaud spoke in a low voice and they both burst into laughter. Even in that, they were different, the Englishman's lively chuckle mingling strangely with Jacaud's throaty growl, and yet somehow they complemented each other.

Mercier shuddered and went below to the galley.

For most of the way the passage was surprisingly smooth, considering what the Channel could be like at times, but towards dawn it started to rain. Mercier was at the wheel, and as they started the run-in to the English coast, fog rolled to meet them in a solid wall. He stamped on the deck, and after a while Jacaud appeared. He looked terrible, eyes swollen and bloodshot from lack of sleep, face grey and spongy.

'Now what?'

Mercier nodded towards the fog. 'It doesn't look too good.'

'How far out are we?'

'Six or seven miles.'

Jacaud nodded and pulled him out of the way. 'Okay – leave it to me.'

Rossiter appeared in the doorway. 'Trouble?'

Jacaud shook his head. 'Nothing I can't handle.'

Rossiter went to the rail. He stood there, face expressionless, and yet a small muscle twitched in his right cheek, a sure sign of stress. He turned and, brushing past Mercier, went below.

Mercier pulled up the collar of his reefer jacket, thrust his hands into his pockets and stood in the prow. In the grey light of early dawn the launch looked even more decrepit than usual and exactly what it was supposed to be – a poor man's fishing boat, lobster pots piled untidily in the stern beside the rubber dinghy, nets draped across the engine-room housing. Moisture beaded everything in the light rain and then they were enveloped by the fog, grey tendrils brushing against Mercier's face, cold and clammy, unclean, like the touch of the dead.

And the fear was there again, so much so that his limbs trembled and his stomach contracted painfully. He wiped his mouth with the back of one hand and started to roll a cigarette, fighting to keep his fingers still.

The launch slipped through a grey curtain into clear water, and the cigarette paper fluttered to the deck as Mercier leaned forward, clutching at the rail. Two hundred yards away through the cold morning a sleek grey shape moved to cut across their course.

Jacaud was already reducing speed as Rossiter appeared on deck. He ran to the rail and stood there, one hand shielding his eyes from the rain. A signal flashed through the grey morning and he turned, face grim.

'They're saying "Heave to, I wish to board you." It's a Royal Navy motor torpedo-boat. Let's get out of here.'

Mercier clutched at his sleeve, panic rising to choke him. 'Those things can do thirty-five knots, monsieur. We don't stand a chance.'

Rossiter grabbed him by the throat. 'Seven years, that's what you'll get if they catch us with him on board. Now get out of my way.'

He nodded to Jacaud, ran along the deck and disappeared below. The engines roared as Jacaud gave them full throttle, spinning the wheel at the same time, and the launch heeled over, almost coming to a dead stop, then surged forward into the fog.

The grey walls moved in, hiding them from sight, and the door to the companionway banged open and Rossiter appeared with the passenger. He was a black man of middle years, tall and handsome, and wore a heavy overcoat with a fur collar. He looked around in bewilderment and Rossiter spoke to him in English. The man nodded and moved forward to the rail and Rossiter pulled out an automatic pistol and struck him a heavy blow at the base of the skull. The man lurched to one side and fell to the deck without a cry.

What happened next was like something out of a nightmare. The Englishman moved with incredible speed and energy. He grabbed a heavy chain from the stern deck and wound it around the man's body several times. He gave it a final turn about the neck and hooked the two loose ends together with a spring link.

He turned and shouted to Mercier above the roaring of the engine, 'Okay, grab his feet and over with him.'

Mercier stood there as if turned to stone. Without hesitation, Rossiter dropped to one knee and heaved the man into a sitting position. The man raised his head painfully; the eyelids flickered, then opened. He glared at Mercier, not in supplication, but in hate; his lips parted and he cried out in English. Rossiter stooped and manoeuvred him across his shoulders, then straightened and the man went over the rail, headfirst into the sea, and disappeared instantly.

Rossiter turned and struck Mercier heavily in the face, sending him sprawling to the deck.

'Now pick yourself up and get to work on those nets or I'll send you after him.'

He went into the wheelhouse. Mercier lay there for a moment, then got to his feet and stumbled along to the stern. It couldn't have happened. Oh, God, but it couldn't have happened. The deck slanted suddenly as Jacaud spun the wheel again, and Mercier fell on his face in the pile of stinking nets and started to vomit.

It was the fog that saved them, spreading out halfway across the Channel, shrouding them from view on the run back to the French coast.

In the wheelhouse, Jacaud swallowed rum from the bottle Rossiter passed and chuckled harshly. 'We've lost them.'

'Your luck is good,' Rossiter said. 'You must live right.'

'Pity about the package.'

'That's life.' Rossiter seemed completely unconcerned and nodded to where Mercier crouched by the nets, head in hands. 'What about him?'

'A worm,' Jacaud said. 'No backbone. Maybe he should go for a swim, too.'

'And what would you tell them in Ste-Denise?'
Rossiter shook his head. 'Leave it to me.'

He went along the deck and stood over
Mercier with the rum bottle. 'You'd better have
a drink.'

Mercier raised his head slowly. His skin was
like the belly of a fish, the eyes full of pain. 'He
was still alive, monsieur. Still alive when you put
him into the water.'

Rossiter's pale flaxen hair glinted in the early
morning sun, making him look strangely age-
less. He stared down at Mercier, his face full
of concern. He sighed heavily, crouched and
produced an exquisite Madonna from one of
his pockets. It was perhaps eight inches long
and obviously extremely old, carved by some
master in ivory the colour of his hair, chased
with silver. When he pressed her feet with his
thumb, six inches of blue steel appeared as if by
magic, sharp as a razor on both edges, honed
with loving care.

Rossiter kissed the Madonna reverently, without even a trace of mockery, then stroked the
blade against his right cheek.

'You have a wife, Mercier,' he said gently,

and his face never lost its peculiarly saintly expression for a moment. 'An invalid, I understand?'

'Monsieur?' Mercier said in a whisper, and the heart seemed to stop inside him.

'One word, Mercier, the slightest whisper, and I cut her throat. You follow me?'

Mercier turned away, stomach heaving, and started to be sick again. Rossiter stood up and walked along the deck and stood in the entrance of the wheelhouse.

'All right?' Jacaud demanded.

'Naturally.' Rossiter took a deep breath of fresh salt air and smiled. 'A fine morning, Jacaud, a beautiful morning. And to think one could still be in bed and missing all this.'

2

Fog rolled in across the city, and somewhere in the distance ships hooted mournfully to each other as they negotiated the lower reaches of the Thames on the way out to sea. Fog – real fog of the kind that you seemed to get in London and nowhere else on earth. Fog that killed off the aged, choked the streets and reduced one of the world's great cities to chaos and confusion.

Paul Chavasse abandoned his taxi at Marble Arch and whistled softly to himself as he turned up the collar of his trenchcoat and passed through the gates of the park. There was only one thing he liked better than fog and that was rain. An idiosyncrasy with its roots somewhere in youth, he supposed, or perhaps there was a simpler explanation. After all, both rain and fog enclosed one in a small private world, which could be very convenient at times.

He paused to light a cigarette, a tall handsome man with a face as Gallic as the Pigalle on a Saturday night, and the heritage of his Breton father was plain to see in the Celtic cheekbones. A park keeper drifted out of the shadows and faded without a word, a thing which, considering the circumstances, could only have happened in England. Chavasse went on his way, unaccountably cheered.

St Bede's Hospital was on the far side of the park, a Victorian Gothic monstrosity in spite of its worldwide reputation. They were expecting him, and when he called at Reception, a porter in a neat blue uniform escorted him along a series of green-tiled corridors, each one of which seemed to stretch into infinity.

He was handed over to a senior lab technician in a small glass office, who took him down to the mortuary in a surprisingly modern lift. Chavasse was conscious of two things the moment the doors opened – the all-pervading smell of antiseptic so peculiar to hospitals, and the extreme cold. The vast echoing chamber was lined with steel drawers, each one presumably holding a corpse, but the object of his visit waited for him on an operating trolley covered with a rubber sheet.

'We couldn't get him into one of the boxes, worse luck,' the technician explained. 'Too bloated. Stinking like last year's fish, or worse.'

At close quarters, the smell was quite over-powering, in spite of the preventive measures which had obviously been taken. Chavasse pulled out a handkerchief and held it to his mouth.

'I see what you mean.'

He had looked on death many times in most of its variations, but this monstrosity was something new. He stared down, a slight frown on his face.

'How long was he in the water?'

'Six or seven weeks.'

'Can you be certain of that?'

'Oh, yes – urine tests, the rate of chemical breakdown and so on. He was Jamaican, by the way, or did you know that?'

'So they told me, but I'd never have guessed.'

The technician nodded. 'Prolonged immersion in salt-water does funny things to skin pigmentation.'

'So it would appear.' Chavasse stepped back and replaced the handkerchief in his breast pocket. 'Thanks very much. I think I've seen all I need.'

'All right for us to dispose of him now, sir?' the technician enquired as he replaced the sheet.

'I was forgetting.' Chavasse took out his wallet and produced a printed disposal slip. 'Cremation only, and all documents to the Home Office by tomorrow.'

'They'd been hoping to have him in the Medical School for dissection.'

'Tell them to try Burke and Hare.' Chavasse pulled on his gloves. 'Ashes to ashes for this boy, and no funny business. I'll see myself out.'

When he had gone, the technician lit a cigarette, a slight frown on his face. He wondered about Chavasse. There was a foreign look about him, but he was obviously English. A nice enough bloke – a gentleman, to use an old-fashioned word, but something wasn't quite right. It was the eyes, that was it. Black and completely expressionless. They seemed to look right through you and beyond, as if you weren't there at all. The kind of eyes that

Jap colonel had had, the one in the camp in Siam where the technician had spent the worst three years of his life. A funny bloke, that Jap; one minute full of the milk of human kindness, the next smoking a cigarette without turning a hair, while they flogged some offender to death.

The technician shuddered and unfolded the slip of paper that Chavasse had given him. It was signed by the Home Secretary himself. That did it. He carefully stowed it away in his wallet and pushed the trolley through into the crematorium next door. Exactly three minutes later, he closed the glass door of one of the three special ovens and reached for the switch. Flames appeared as if by magic, and the body, bloated with its own gases, started to burn at once.

The technician lit another cigarette. Professor Henson wouldn't be too pleased, but it was done now, and after all he did have it in writing. He went next door, whistling cheerfully, and made a cup of tea.

*   *   *

It was almost two months since Chavasse had visited the house in St John's Wood, and returning was like coming home again after a long absence. Not so strange, perhaps, when one considered the kind of life he had led for the twelve years he had been an agent of the Bureau, the little-known section of British Intelligence that handled the sort of business no one else seemed to know what to do with.

He went up the steps and pressed the bell beside the brass plate that carried the legend *Brown & Co – Importers & Exporters*. The door was opened almost immediately by a tall greying man in a blue serge uniform, who positively beamed a welcome.

'Good to have you back, Mr Chavasse. You're nice and brown.'

'Glad to be back, George.'

'Mr Mallory's been asking for you, sir. Miss Frazer's been phoning every few minutes.'

'Nothing new in that, George.'

Chavasse went up the curving Regency staircase quickly. Nothing changed. Not a thing. It was just like it had always been. Lengthy periods in which damn-all happened, and then something broke through to the surface and the day needed twenty-seven hours.

When he went into the small outer office at the end of the narrow corridor, Jean Frazer was seated at her desk. She glanced up and removed her heavy reading glasses with a smile that was always a shade warmer for Chavasse than for anyone else.

'Paul, you're looking fine. It's wonderful to see you again.'

She came round the desk, a small heavy-hipped woman of thirty or so, but attractive enough in her own way. Chavasse took her hands and kissed her on the cheek.

'I never did get around to giving you that evening out at the Saddle Room. It's been on my conscience.'

'Oh, I'm sure it has.' There was a look of scepticism on her face. 'You got my message?'

'My flight was delayed, but the messenger was waiting when I got to the flat. I didn't even have time to unpack. I've been to St Bede's and had a look at the corpus delicti or whatever they call it. Most unpleasant. He'd been in the sea rather a long time. Bleached a whiter shade of pale, by the way, which seemed extraordinary considering what you told me about him.'

'Spare me the details.' She flicked the intercom. 'Paul Chavasse is here, Mr Mallory.'

'Send him in.'

The voice was remote and dry and might have been from another world – a world that Chavasse had almost forgotten during his two months' convalescence. A tiny flicker of excitement moved coldly in his stomach as he opened the door and went in.

Mallory hadn't changed in the slightest. The same grey flannel suit from the same very eminent tailor, the same tie from the right school, not an iron-grey hair out of place, the same frosty, remote glance over the top of the spectacles. He couldn't even manage a smile.

'Hello, Paul, nice to see you,' he said, as if he didn't mean a word of it. 'How's the leg?'

'Fine now, sir.'

'No permanent effects?'

'It aches a little in damp weather but they tell me that will wear off after a while.'

'You're lucky you've still got two legs to walk around on. Magnum bullets can be nasty things. How was Alderney?'

Chavasse's English mother lived in retirement on that most delightful of all the Channel Islands and he had spent his convalescence in her capable hands. It occurred to him, with a sense of wonder, that on the previous day at this time he had been picnicking on the white sands of Telegraph Bay; cold chicken and salad and a bottle of Liebfraumilch frosted from the fridge and wrapped in a damp towel, strictly against the rules, but the only way to drink it.

He sighed. 'Nice, sir. Very nice.'

Mallory got straight down to business. 'You've seen the body at St Bede's?'

Chavasse nodded. 'Any idea who he was?'

Mallory reached for a file and opened it. 'A West Indian from Jamaica named Harvey Preston.'

'And how did you manage to find that out?'

'His fingerprints were on record.'

Chavasse shrugged. 'His fingers were swollen like bananas when I saw him.'

'Oh, the lab boys have a technique for dealing with that sort of problem. They take a section of skin and shrink it to normal size using chemicals. They arrive at a reasonable facsimile.'

'Somebody went to a lot of trouble over the body of an unknown man washed up after six weeks. Why?'

'In the first place, it didn't happen in quite that way. He was brought up off the bottom in the trawl net of a fishing boat out of Brixham, with about seventy pounds of chain wrapped around him.'

'Murdered, presumably?'

'Death by drowning.'

'A nasty way to go.'

Mallory passed a photo across. 'That's him, taken at his trial at the Bailey in 1967.'

'What was he up for?'

'Robbing a gambling club in Birmingham. The Crown lost, by the way. He was acquitted for lack of evidence. Witnesses failed to come forward, and so on. The usual story.'

'He must have had a lot of pull.'

Mallory helped himself to one of his Turkish cigarettes and leaned back in his seat. 'Harvey

Preston arrived in England in 1938 when he was twenty and joined the Royal Army Service Corps during the Munich crisis. His mother and father followed a few months later, with his younger sister, and Preston fixed them up with a small house in Brixton. He was stationed at Aldershot with a transport regiment as a truck driver. His mother gave birth to another son, whom they named Darcy, on the third day of the war in September, 1939. A week later Harvey's regiment was posted to France. During the big retreat when the Panzers broke through in 1940, his unit was badly knocked about and he was shot twice in the right leg. He made it out through Dunkirk and back to England, but was so badly lamed by his wounds that he was discharged with a pension.'

'What did he do then?'

'At first he drove an ambulance, but then he underwent the kind of personal tragedy so common during the Blitz. The house in Brixton took a direct hit during a raid and the only survivor was his young brother. From then on, things seem to have taken a different turn.'

'What did he do?'

'Take your pick. Black market, prostitution. After the war he ran a number of illegal gaming clubs and became something of a power in the underworld. Moved into organized crime about nineteen-fifty-nine. The police were certain he was behind a very efficient hijacking organization, but could never prove anything. There were several payroll robberies as well and he was very definitely involved in drug trafficking.'

'Quite a character. What happened after his acquittal? Was he deported?'

Mallory shook his head. 'He'd been here too long for that. But the Yard really turned the heat on. He lost his gaming licence for a start, which put him out of the casino business. It seems they breathed down his neck so hard that he hardly dared stir from his house. It was the money from the Birmingham casino robbery they were after. Even if he couldn't be tried again, they could stop him spending it.'

'Was he married?'

'No, lived on his own. A different girl a night by all accounts, right up to the end.'

'What about the brother, the one who survived the bombing?'

'Young Darcy?' Mallory actually grinned. 'Funny thing happened there. Harvey kept the boy with him. Sent him to St Paul's as a day-boy. Must have been an extraordinary life for him. Mixing with the sons of the upper crust during the day and the worst villains in London by night. He decided to go in for the law, of all things, passed his bar finals three years ago. Cleared off to Jamaica after Harvey's trial.'

'And what did Harvey do?'

'Left the country on a plane to Rome two months ago. They just about took him to pieces at the airport, but there wasn't a thing on him. They had to let him go.'

'Where did he go from Rome?'

'Interpol had him followed to Naples, where he dropped out of sight.'

'To re-emerge two months later in the bottom of a fishing net off the English coast. Intriguing. What do you think he was playing at?'

'I should have thought that was obvious.' Mallory shrugged. 'He was trying to get into the country illegally. As long as the police didn't know he was here, he could recover his money at leisure and leave by the same way he came, whatever that was.'

Chavasse was beginning to see a little light. 'Someone put him over the side in the Channel, that's what you're suggesting?'

'Something like that. There's a lot of money in this passage-by-night business since the Commonwealth Immigration Act. Pakistanis, Indians, West Indians, Australians – anyone who can't get a visa in the usual way. There's good money in it.'

'There was a case in the paper the other day,' Chavasse said. 'The navy stopped an old launch off Felixstowe and found thirty-two Pakistanis on board. That's a fair night's work for someone.'

'Amateurs,' Mallory said. 'Most of them don't stand a chance. It's the professionals who're getting away with it, the people with the organization. There's a pipeline running all the way through from Naples. The Italian police have been doing some checking and they've come up with an interesting report on a boat called the *Anya* that makes the Naples – Marseille run regularly under a Panamanian registration.'

Chavasse reached for the file, turned it round and went through the photos it contained. There were several of Harvey Preston taken through the years, one on the steps of the Old Bailey after his trial, an arm around the shoulders of his young brother. Chavasse leafed through the reports, then glanced up.

'This is police work. Where do we come in?'

'The Special Branch at Scotland Yard have asked us to help. They feel this job requires the kind of talents more appropriate to one of our operatives.'

'The last time they asked for help, it involved me spending six months in three of the worst jails in Britain,' Chavasse said, 'plus the fact that I nearly got my leg blown off. Why can't they do their own dirty work?'

'We've worked out a suitable background for you,' Mallory said impassively. 'Use your own name, no reason not to. Australian citizen of French extraction. Wanted in Sydney for armed robbery.' He pushed a folder across. 'Everything you need is in there, including a newspaper clipping confirming your criminal background. Naturally, you're willing to pay any price to get into Britain, and no questions asked.'

Chavasse felt, as usual, as if some great sea was washing over him. 'When do I go?'

'There's a three-thirty flight to Rome. You should make it with quarter of an hour to spare if you leave now. You'll find a suitcase waiting for you outside. I had one brought over. A good job you didn't have time to unpack.' He stood up and held out his hand. 'The best of luck, Paul. Keep in touch in the usual way.'

Mallory sat down, replaced his glasses and reached for a file. Chavasse picked up his folder, turned and went out. He was chuckling when he closed the door.

'What's so funny?' Jean Frazer demanded.

He leaned across her desk and chucked her under the chin. 'Prettiest-looking Sheila I've clapped eyes on since I left Sydney,' he said, in a very fair Australian twang.

She stared at him in amazement. 'Are you mad?'

He picked up his suitcase and laughed. 'I must be, Jean. I really must be,' he said, and went out.

NAPLES – MARSEILLE

3

The woman was an Indian and very young – no more than sixteen, if Chavasse was any judge. She had a pale, flawless complexion and sad brown eyes that were set off to perfection by her scarlet sari. Chavasse had seen her only once during the two-day voyage from Naples and presumed they were bound for the same eventual destination.

He was leaning against the rail when she came along the deck. She nodded a trifle uncertainly and knocked on the door of the captain's cabin. It opened after a moment or so, and Skiros appeared. He was stripped to the waist and badly needed a shave, but he smiled ingratiatingly, managing to look even more repulsive than usual, and stepped to one side.

The girl hesitated fractionally, then moved in.

Skiros glanced across at Chavasse, winked and closed the door, which didn't look too good for Miss India. Chavasse shrugged; it was no skin off his nose, he had other things to think about. He lit a cigarette and moved towards the stern of the old steamer.

Pavlo Skiros had been born of indeterminate parentage in Constantinople forty-seven years earlier. There was some Greek in him, a little Turk, and quite a lot of Russian, and he was a disgrace to all three countries. He had followed the sea all his life and yet his right to a master's ticket was uncertain, to say the least. But he possessed other, darker qualities in abundance that suited the owners of the *Anya* perfectly.

He sat on the edge of the table in his small cluttered cabin and scratched his left armpit, lust in his soul when he looked at the girl.

'What can I do for you?' he asked in English.

'My money,' she told him. 'You said you would return it when we reached port.'

'All in good time, my dear. We dock in half

an hour and you'll have to keep out of the way until the customs men have finished.'

'There will be trouble?' she asked in alarm.

He shook his head. 'No trouble, I promise you. It is all arranged. You'll be on your way within a couple of hours.'

He got up and moved close enough for her to smell him. 'You've nothing to worry about. I'll handle everything personally.'

He put a hand on her arm and she drew back slightly. 'Thank you – thank you very much. I will go and change now. I don't suppose a sari would be very practical on the Marseille waterfront at night.'

She opened the door and paused, looking towards Chavasse. 'Who is that man?'

'Just a passenger – an Australian.'

'I see.' She appeared to hesitate. 'Is he another like myself?'

'No, nothing like that.' He wiped sweat from his face with the back of a hand. 'You'd better go to your cabin now and stay there. I'll come for you later when everything is quiet.'

She smiled again, looking younger than ever.

'Thank you. You've no idea what this means to me.'

The door closed behind her. Skiros stood staring at it blankly for a moment, then reached for the bottle of whisky on the table and a dirty tin mug. As he drank, he thought about the girl and what he would do with her when things were nice and quiet and they were alone. The expression on his face was not pleasant.

They reached Marseille on the evening tide and it was already dark when they docked. Chavasse had gone down to his cabin earlier and lay on the bunk, smoking and staring up at the ceiling, on which the peeling paint made a series of interesting patterns.

But then the whole boat left a great deal to be desired. The food was barely edible, the blankets were dirty and the general appearance of the crew, from Skiros down, was pretty grim.

Using the information obtained by the Italian police, Chavasse had approached Skiros in a certain café on the Naples waterfront, flashing a roll of fivers that had set the good captain's eyes gleaming. Chavasse had not used the criminal background part of his story – he had preferred to allow Skiros to discover that for himself. He had simply posed as an Australian anxious to get into the Old Country but denied a visa, and Skiros had swallowed the story. For the money, Chavasse would be taken to Marseille, landed illegally and sent on his way to people who would see him safely across the Channel.

Once on board, he had deliberately left his wallet around, minus his bank roll, but containing, amongst other things, the bogus clipping from the *Sydney Morning Herald* which spoke of the police search for Paul Chavasse, wanted for questioning in connection with a series of armed robberies. There was even a photo, to make certain, and the bait must have been taken, for the cabin had been searched – Chavasse had ways of knowing things like that.

He was surprised he had got this far without some attempt to relieve him of his cash and drop him overboard, for Skiros looked like the kind of man who would have cheerfully sold his sister in the marketplace on very reasonable terms.

Chavasse had slept with the door double-bolted each night and his Smith & Wesson handy under the pillow. He took it out now, checking each round carefully. As he replaced it in the special holster that fitted snugly against the small of his back, there was a knock at the door, and Melos, the wall-eyed Cypriot first mate, looked in.

'Captain Skiros is ready for you now.'

'Good on you, sport.' Chavasse picked up a black trenchcoat and reached for his suitcase. 'It's me for the open road.'

Outside it was raining and he followed Melos along the slippery deck to the captain's cabin. When they went in Skiros was seated at his table, eating his evening meal.

'So, Mr Chavasse, we arrive safely.'

'Looks like it, sport,' Chavasse said cheerfully. 'Let's see now, I gave you five hundred in Naples. That's another five I owe you.'

He produced the roll of fivers and counted a hundred out on the table. Skiros gathered them up. 'Nice to do business with you.'

'Where do I go from here?' Chavasse demanded.

'There is no watchman on this dock. No one will stop you when you pass through the gate. Catch the 9:30 express for Paris. Wait at the bookstall on the platform at the other end and you will be approached by a man who will ask you if you are his cousin Charles from Marseille. Everything is arranged from then on.'

'That's it, then.' Chavasse still kept the bonhomie going as he pulled on his trenchcoat and picked up the suitcase. 'Didn't I see an Indian girl about the place?'

'What about her?' Skiros demanded, his smile fading.

'Nothing special. Just thought she might be on the same kick as me.'

'You are mistaken.' Skiros rose to his feet, wiped his moustache and held out his hand. 'I would not delay, if I were you. You've just got time to catch that train.'

Chavasse smiled at both of them. 'Can't afford to miss that, can I? That would really throw a spanner into the works.'

He went out into the rain, moved along the deck and descended the gangway. At the bottom

41

he paused under the lamp for a moment, then moved into darkness.

Melos turned enquiringly to Skiros. 'A great deal of money in that roll.'

Skiros nodded. 'Get after him. Take Andrew with you. The two of you should be enough.'

'What if he kicks up a fuss?'

'How can he? He's in the country illegally and the Sydney police want him for armed robbery. Use your intelligence, Melos.'

Melos went out. Skiros continued to eat, working his way through the meal methodically. When he had finished, he poured himself a very large whisky, which he drank slowly.

When he went out, the rain was falling more heavily, drifting down through the yellow quarterlights in a silver spray. He moved along the deck to the girl's cabin, knocked and went in.

She turned from the bunk to face him, looking strangely alien in a blue sweater and pleated grey skirt. There was something close to alarm on her face, but she made a visible effort and smiled.

'Captain Skiros. It is time, then?'

'Most certainly it is,' Skiros said and, moving with astonishing speed, he pushed her back across the bunk and flung himself on top of her, a hand across her mouth to stifle any sound.

Melos and the deckhand, Andrew, hurried along the dock and paused by the iron gates to listen. There was no sound, and Melos frowned.

'What's happened to him?'

He took a single anxious step forward and Chavasse moved out of the shadows, turned him round and raised a knee into his groin. Melos sagged to the wet cobbles and Chavasse grinned across the writhing body at Andrew.

'What kept you?'

Andrew moved in fast, the knife in his right hand glinting in the rain. His feet were kicked expertly from beneath him and he hit the cobbles. He started to get up and Chavasse seized his right wrist, then twisted the arm around and up in a direction it was never intended to go. Andrew screamed as a muscle ripped in his shoulder, and Chavasse ran him headfirst into the railings of the gate.

Melos had managed to regain his feet and was being very sick. Chavasse stepped over Andrew and grabbed him by the shirt. 'Was I really being met at that station bookstall in Paris?'

Melos shook his head.

'And the Indian girl? What's Skiros playing at there?'

Melos didn't answer. Chavasse pushed him away in disgust, turned and ran back towards the ship.

The girl's teeth fastened on the edge of the captain's hand, biting clean to the bone. He gave a grunt of pain and slapped her across the face.

'By God, I'll teach you,' he said. 'You'll crawl before I'm through with you.'

As he advanced, face contorted, the door swung open and Chavasse stepped in. He held the Smith & Wesson negligently in one hand, but the eyes were very dark in the white devil's face. Skiros swung round and Chavasse shook his head.

'You really are a bastard, aren't you, Skiros?'

Skiros took a step forward and Chavasse slashed him across the face with the barrel of the gun, drawing blood. Skiros fell back across the bunk and the girl ran to Chavasse, who put an arm around her.

'Don't tell me, let me guess. You're trying to get to England, but they won't give you a visa.'

'That's right,' she said in astonishment.

'We're in the same boat, then. How much did he charge you?'

'He took all my money in Naples. He said he would keep it safe for me.'

'Did he, now?' Chavasse pulled Skiros up and shoved him towards the door. 'Get your case and wait for me at the gangway. The good captain and I have things to discuss.'

When he pushed Skiros through the door of his own cabin, the captain turned angrily, blood on his face. 'You won't get away with this.'

Chavasse hit him across the face with the gun twice, knocking him to the floor. He squatted beside him and said pleasantly, 'Get the girl's money, I haven't got much time.'

Skiros produced a key from his trouser pocket,

dragged himself to a small safe beside his bunk and opened it. He took out a bundle of notes and tossed them across.

'You can do better than that.'

Chavasse pushed him to one side, reached into the safe and picked up a black cashbox. He turned it upside-down and three bundles of notes flopped to the floor. He stuffed them into his pocket and grinned.

'There's a lesson in this for you somewhere, Skiros, and worth every penny.' He tapped him on the forehead with the barrel of the Smith & Wesson. 'And now the address – the real address where we can catch a boat for the Channel crossing.'

'Go to Ste-Denise on the Brittany coast near the Golfe de St-Malo,' Skiros croaked. 'St-Brieuc is the nearest big town. There's an inn called the Running Man. Ask for Jacaud.'

'If you're lying, I'll be back,' Chavasse said.

Skiros could barely whisper. 'It's the truth, and you can do what the hell you like. I'll have my day.'

Chavasse pushed him back against the wall, stood up and went out. The girl was waiting anxiously at the head of the gangway. She had a scarf around her head and wore a plastic mac.

'I was beginning to get worried,' she said in her soft, slightly sing-song voice.

'No need.' He handed her the bundle of notes he had taken from Skiros. 'Yours, I think.'

She looked up at him in a kind of wonder. 'Who are you?'

'A friend,' he said gently, and picked up her suitcase. 'Now let's get moving. I think it would be healthier in the long run.'

He took her arm and they went down the gangway together.

FRANCE

4

They caught the night express to Brest with only ten minutes to spare. It wasn't particularly crowded. Chavasse managed to find them an empty second-class compartment near the rear, left the girl in charge and ran to the station buffet. He returned with coffee, sandwiches and half-a-dozen oranges.

The girl drank some of the coffee gratefully, but shook her head when he offered her a sandwich 'I couldn't eat a thing.'

'It's going to be a long night,' he said. 'I'll save you some for later.'

The train started to move and she stood up and went into the corridor, looking out over the lights of Marseille. When she finally turned and came back into the compartment, a lot of the strain seemed to have left her face.

'Feeling better now?' he asked.

'I felt sure that something would go wrong; that Captain Skiros might reappear.'

'A bad dream,' he said. 'You can forget it now.'

'Life seems to have been all bad dreams for some time.'

'Why not tell me about it?'

She seemed strangely shy, and when she spoke, it was hesitantly at first. Her name was Famia Nadeem and he had been wrong about her age. She was nineteen, and had been born in Bombay. Her mother had died in childbirth and her father had emigrated to England, leaving her in the care of her grandmother. Things had gone well for him, for he now owned a thriving Indian restaurant in Manchester and had sent for her to join him three months earlier after the death of the old woman.

But there had been snags of a kind with which Chavasse was only too familiar. Under the terms of the Immigration Act, only genuine family dependants of Commonwealth citizens already in residence in Britain could be admitted without a work permit. In Famia's case, there was no formal birth certificate to prove her identity conclusively. Unfortunately, there had been a great many false claims and the authorities were now sticking rigorously to the letter of the law. No absolute proof of the claimed relationship meant no entry, and Famia had been sent back to India on the next flight.

But her father had not given up. He had sent her money and details of an underground organization which specialized in helping people in her predicament. She was disconcertingly naïve, and Chavasse found little difficulty in extracting the information he required, starting with the export firm in Bombay where her trip had commenced, passing through Cairo and Beirut, and culminating in Naples with the agents who controlled the *Anya*.

'But why did you give Skiros all your money?' he said.

'He said it would be safer. That there were those who might take advantage of me.'

'And you believed him?'

'He seemed kind.'

She leaned back in her seat, head turned to look through her own reflection into the darkness outside. And she was beautiful – too beautiful for her own good, Chavasse decided. A lovely vulnerable young girl on her own in a nightmare world.

She turned and, catching him watching her, coloured faintly. 'And you, Mr Chavasse? What about you?'

He gave her his background story, cutting out the criminal bit. He was an artist from Sydney who wanted to spend a few months in England, which meant working for his keep, and there was a long, long waiting list for permits. He wasn't prepared to join the queue.

She accepted his story completely and without any kind of query, which was bad, considering that it was so shot full of holes. She leaned back again and gradually her eyes closed. He reached for his trenchcoat and covered her. He was beginning to feel some kind of responsibility, which was really quite absurd. She was nothing to him – nothing at all. In any case, with any kind of luck, things would go through pretty smoothly once they reached Ste-Denise.

But what would happen when they arrived

on the English coast and Mallory acted on his information? She'd be on her way back to Bombay for good. They'd never allow her into the country again after an attempt at illegal entry. Life could be very difficult at times. Chavasse sighed, folded his arms and tried to get some sleep.

They reached St-Brieuc just before five o'clock in the morning. The girl had slept peacefully throughout the night and Chavasse awakened her just before they arrived. She disappeared along the corridor, and when she returned, her hair was combed neatly into place.

'Any hot water down there?' he asked.

She shook her head. 'I prefer cold in the morning. It freshens you up.'

Chavasse ran a hand over the hard stubble on his chin and shook his head. 'I'm not too fond of being skinned alive. I'll shave later.'

The train glided into St-Brieuc five minutes later. They were the only passengers to alight. It was cold and desolate and touched with that atmosphere peculiar to railway stations the world over in the early hours of the morning. It was as if everyone had just left.

The ticket-collector, well protected against the chill morning air by a heavy overcoat and scarf, looked ready for retirement. He seemed indifferent to everything, even life itself, and the pallor of his skin, coupled with his constant, repetitive coughing, boded ill. He answered Chavasse with a kind of frigid civility, as if his attention was elsewhere.

Ste-Denise? Yes, there was a bus to Dinard which would drop them within a mile of Ste-Denise. It left at nine o'clock from the square. They would find a café there which opened early for the market people. Monsieur Pinaud was not one to miss trade. He subsided once more into his own cheerless world, and they moved on.

Rain drifted across the square as they went down the steps and crossed to the lighted windows of the café. It was warm inside, but not busy. Chavasse left the girl at a table by the window and moved to the zinc-topped bar.

A middle-aged balding man in striped shirt and white apron, presumably the Monsieur Pinaud referred to by the ticket-collector, was reading a newspaper. He pushed it to one side and smiled. 'Just off the train?'

'That's it.' Chavasse ordered coffee and rolls. 'They tell me there's a bus to Dinard at nine o'clock. That's definitely the earliest?'

Pinaud nodded as he poured the coffee. 'You want to go to Dinard?'

'No, Ste-Denise.'

The coffee-pot froze in mid-air and the man glanced across warily. 'Ste-Denise? You want to go to Ste-Denise?'

His reaction was more than interesting and Chavasse smiled amiably. 'That's right. My girl-friend and I are spending a few days' holiday there. I've arranged to stay at an inn called the Running Man with a Monsieur Jacaud. You know him?'

'Perhaps, monsieur. A lot of people come in here.' He pushed the coffee and rolls across.

Chavasse took the two cups and the plate of rolls across to the table. As he sat down, Pinaud wiped the zinc top of the bar carefully, then moved to a door which obviously led to the rear, and vanished.

'I'll only be a minute,' Chavasse told the girl, and went after him.

He found himself in a deserted, stone-flagged corridor. A notice at the far end indicated the lavatory. There was no sign of Pinaud. Chavasse started forward cautiously and paused. A door on his right was slightly ajar. From the sound of it, Pinaud was on the telephone. The interesting thing was that he was speaking in Breton, which Chavasse, whose paternal grandfather still presided over the family farm near Vaux in spite of his eighty years, spoke himself like a native.

'Hello, Jacaud. Those two packages you were expecting have arrived. The girl fits the description perfectly, but the man worries me. Speaks French like a Frenchman, or like a Frenchman should, if you follow me. Yes – okay. They're waiting for the bus at nine.'

Chavasse slipped back into the café. Famia was already on her second roll. 'Hurry up,' she said. 'Your coffee will be getting cold.'

'Never mind. I'm just going across to the

station to check on that bus time again. I won't be long.'

He went out into the rain without giving her a chance to reply and hurried across to the station. It was still deserted, but he quickly found what he was looking for, a series of metal lockers, each with its own key, where luggage might be left. He took out his wallet and also the extra money he had taken from Skiros. He pushed the whole lot well to the rear of the locker, closed it quickly and concealed the key beneath the insole of his right shoe.

Famia was looking anxious when he returned to the café. He patted her hand reassuringly and went back to the counter.

'I wondered what had happened to you,' Pinaud said.

Chavasse shrugged. 'I thought there might be a local train or something. It's a hell of a time to wait.'

'Don't worry about that.' Pinaud gave him a big smile. 'You just sit tight and have another coffee. Lots of farmers and market people are in and out of here at this time in the morning. I'll

get you a lift to Ste-Denise. Someone is bound
to be going that way.'

'Very decent of you. Perhaps you'd join me
in a cognac? It's a cold morning.'

'An excellent idea.' Pinaud reached for a
bottle and a couple of glasses and filled them
quickly. 'Your good health, monsieur.' He raised
his glass and smiled.

Chavasse smiled right back. 'And yours.'

The brandy burned all the way down. He
picked up his coffee and returned to the table
to await events.

People came and went, mainly porters from the
nearby market, and Chavasse bought the girl
another coffee and waited. It was perhaps half
an hour later when the old van turned out of a
narrow street on the other side of the square.

He watched idly as it approached, and noticed
a Renault emerge from the same street and halt
at the kerbside. The van came on and braked
no more than a couple of yards from the café
window. Jacaud got out.

The girl reacted immediately. 'That man –

what a terrible face. He seems so – so completely evil.'

'Appearances can sometimes be very deceptive,' Chavasse told her.

Jacaud paused just inside the door, glancing casually around the room as if seeking a friend before proceeding to the counter, and yet he had marked them. Chavasse was sure of it. He purchased a packet of cigarettes and Pinaud said something to him. He glanced over his shoulder at Chavasse and the girl then turned away again. Pinaud poured him a cognac and came round the counter.

'You are in luck, monsieur,' he told Chavasse. 'This man is going to Ste-Denise. He has agreed to give you a lift.'

Chavasse turned to the girl and said in English: 'Our good-looking friend has offered us a lift. Should we accept?'

'Is there any reason why we shouldn't?'

He smiled and shook his head. 'You're really very refreshing, but hopelessly out of date. Still – never look a gift horse in the mouth.'

Jacaud swallowed his cognac and crossed to the door. He paused and glanced down at

Chavasse, face expressionless. 'You are going to Ste-Denise, I understand? I'm on my way there now. You're welcome to a lift.'

'Wonderful,' Chavasse said brightly. 'We'll be right with you.'

Jacaud nodded briefly to Pinaud. 'I'll be in touch about further arrangements,' he said in Breton, and went out.

He was already behind the wheel when Chavasse and the girl joined him. There was room for one passenger. The girl took the only seat, and Chavasse heaved the suitcases into the rear and climbed over the tailboard. The van started at once, bouncing its way across the cobbles, passing the parked Renault. He caught a quick glimpse of the driver, a flash of very fair hair, and then the car pulled away from the kerb and came after them, which was interesting.

Chavasse touched the butt of the Smith & Wesson snug in its holster against his spine, then sat back and waited to see what was going to happen.

*　　*　　*

Within a few minutes, they had left the town and were travelling along a narrow country road. The heavy rain and a slight ground mist reduced visibility considerably, but he caught an occasional glimpse of the sea in the distance beyond a fringe of pine trees.

The Renault stayed so close that he could see the driver clearly, a pale man with extraordinary fair hair who looked more like a priest than anything else. They came to a crossroads at a place where the pinewoods seemed to move in on every side. The van carried straight on, the Renault turned left and disappeared. Chavasse frowned.

The van swerved into a narrow sandy track to the left and moved down through the pine trees towards the sea. A few moments later, the engine coughed a couple of times, faltered, then cut out completely. They rolled to a halt, the door opened and Jacaud came round to the rear.

'Trouble?' Chavasse enquired.

'I've run out of petrol,' Jacaud said. 'But it doesn't matter. I always carry an emergency supply. At the back of the bench there.'

Chavasse found an old British Army jerrycan

that looked as if it had been in use since Dunkirk. It was full, which made it awkward to handle in the confined space, and he had to use both hands, which was obviously exactly what Jacaud had counted on. As Chavasse heaved the jerrycan up on the tailboard with every sign of difficulty, the big man's hand appeared from behind his back and the tyre lever he was holding cracked down.

Only Chavasse wasn't there any longer. He dodged to one side, holding the jerrycan in both hands with negligent ease, and the tyre lever dented the edge of the tailboard. Jacaud was already moving backwards out of harm's way, every instinct that had kept him intact for forty-three years warning him that he had made a very bad mistake, but he was too late. The jerrycan took him full in the chest and he went over. He rolled on his face and started to get up and Chavasse landed on his back.

The arm that clamped itself around Jacaud's throat was like a steel band, cutting off his air supply so efficiently that he started to choke at once.

Chavasse wasn't really sure what happened

after that. He was aware of Famia screaming, calling his name, and then the light was switched off very suddenly. There was no pain – no pain at all. A blow to the base of the neck delivered by an expert – the thought was there and yet was not there, and in the same moment vision returned.

He looked up into the face of a ravaged saint, an Anthony burned clear to the bone by the heat of the wilderness. Beneath the drift of flaxen hair the pale blue eyes were empty. There was no love here, no cruelty either, and he crouched beside Chavasse in a kind of meditation, an exquisite ivory Madonna clasped in both hands.

Chavasse was aware of the Smith & Wesson hard against his back, secure in its spring holster. Famia Nadeem stood beside the van, hands together, terror on her face, and Jacaud stood beside her. Chavasse decided to play it cool for another couple of minutes. He came back to Rossiter, stared at him vacantly and ran a hand across his eyes.

The Englishman slapped him in the face. 'Can you hear me, Chavasse?' Chavasse struggled up on one elbow, and Rossiter smiled briefly. 'I was beginning to think I must have hit you harder than I had intended.'

'Hard enough.' Chavasse sat up, rubbing the nape of his neck with one hand. 'You've heard from Skiros, I presume?'

'Naturally. He gives me to understand that you have in your possession a considerable sum of money belonging to the organization I work for. Where is it?'

'In a safe place back in St-Brieuc. I decided it would make what a poker player might term a good ace-in-the-hole. Who am I talking to, by the way? You're not Jacaud, that's for sure.'

'Monsieur Jacaud you have already met. My name is Rossiter.'

'And he and Skiros work for you?'

'In a manner of speaking.'

'Then I don't think much of the way your organization treats its cash customers. When I reached Marseilles, Skiros sent me on my way to the wrong destination with a couple of goons on my tail to rob me. When I went back to the ship to talk things over, he was doing his best to rape the girl. On top of that, he'd taken her for a lot of money. I don't know how well he's been doing for you, but I'd say his bank account would make interesting reading.'

Rossiter didn't seem to be listening. He had turned to Famia Nadeem, a frown on his face. When he went forward, she glanced down and he put a hand under her chin and tilted it up.

'Is he telling the truth?'

Strangely enough, all her fear seemed to have vanished. She looked up at him calmly and nodded. Rossiter turned abruptly and came back to Chavasse. His eyes were bleak and there was an expression of utter desolation on his face.

'What a world,' he said softly. 'What a filthy, loathsome world.' He took a deep breath, something clicked and he was himself again. 'Get up!'

Chavasse did as he was told, producing the Smith & Wesson at the same time. Jacaud gave a kind of angry cry, but Rossiter waved him to silence. He stood, feet slightly apart, tossing the ivory Madonna high into the air and catching it again in his right hand.

'Now what?'

'Now nothing,' Chavasse said. 'I just want to get to London in one piece and fade into the background.'

'Understandable enough.' Rossiter actually smiled. 'Ten years in an Australian jail can hardly have been an exciting prospect. I believe they still run their penal system on rather old-fashioned lines.'

Chavasse managed to look suitably astonished. 'Is there anything you don't know, sport?'

'Not where clients are concerned.'

Chavasse sighed and put the Smith & Wesson away. 'I've had my bellyful of trouble during the past few months, Rossiter. I don't want any more. Just get me to England, that's all I ask. I'll pay whatever is necessary. That business in Marseille was all Skiros, believe me.'

Rossiter slipped the Madonna into his right pocket. 'The money? Where is it?'

Chavasse told him. He also took off his right shoe and produced the key, which Rossiter immediately tossed to Jacaud. 'We'll wait for you here. You can take the Renault.'

Jacaud moved away through the trees without a word and Chavasse lit a cigarette. So far so good. He looked down through the pine trees towards the sea, and smiled.

'Nice country. I was looking forward to this

bit of the trip. My father came from Brittany, you know.'

'I was wondering about your French,' Rossiter said. 'It's really quite excellent.'

'My mother was English, of course, but we've never used anything else but French in the house since I can remember. My old man wouldn't have it any other way.'

Rossiter nodded, produced a slim leather case from his breast pocket and selected a thin black cheroot, which he lit carefully. 'Tell me something about the girl.'

She was sitting in the passenger seat, watching them. Chavasse threw her a smile. 'I only know what she's told me.'

He went through her story quickly, and when he had finished, Rossiter nodded briefly. 'She's very young to have gone through so much.'

He said it as if he meant it, with real sympathy in his voice, and moved towards her. Chavasse sat down on a fallen log and watched them. Rossiter was speaking, the girl answered. Suddenly she was smiling, and a few moments later, laughed out loud. And Rossiter laughed with her, that was the strangest thing of all, so that for a short time he seemed to be an entirely different person. Curiouser and curiouser . . .

Chavasse gave up for the moment, got to his feet and walked to the edge of the clearing, breathing in the scent of damp pines, the good salt air from the sea, the smell that always brought the Brittany of his boyhood back to him, wherever he was. It would have been nice to have surprised his grandfather at Vaux. The old man would have loved that – an unexpected visit from his clever half-English grandson who lectured at a university whose name he could never remember. A little bit too much of the scholar with his doctorate in modern languages, but still a Chavasse for all that.

Chavasse stared down through the trees towards the sea remembering boyhood a thousand years ago and all its wonderful dreams. And now he had returned to Brittany and he could not go to Vaux . . .

A horn sounded through the trees. Jacaud had arrived, and he sighed and came back to the present as Rossiter called to him.

BRITTANY

5

Ste-Denise was twenty or thirty granite cottages amongst pine trees fringing a horseshoe cove that was a natural harbour. There was a wooden jetty of sorts, with an old thirty-foot launch moored to it that looked as if it had seen better days. The tide was turning, and four clinker-built fishing cobles moved out to sea in line astern. A similar boat lay stranded on the beach above the high water mark and two men worked on her hull.

Chavasse took it all in as the van moved out of the trees along the narrow road that merged into the High Street of the village. The only sign of life was a stray dog sitting mournfully in the rain outside a cottage door.

The van left the village behind, and almost stalled as Jacaud dropped two gears to negotiate a steep hill. The Running Man was at the top, a two-storeyed granite house sheltering behind high walls. Jacaud turned through an archway and halted in the cobbled courtyard inside. Chavasse got out and looked around with interest. The whole place had a strangely forlorn look about it and badly needed a coat of paint. A shutter banged to and fro in the wind, and when he glanced up, a curtain moved slightly at a window, as if it had been pulled to one side while someone glanced out.

The Renault entered the courtyard and pulled up just behind the van. Famia got out and stood there, looking uncertain. Rossiter came round from the other side, picked up her suitcase and took her elbow. She looked tired, ready to drop at any moment. He leaned over her solicitously, murmured something and took her inside.

Chavasse turned to Jacaud. 'What about me?'

'If I had my way, you could sleep in the pig-sty.'

'Careful,' Chavasse said. 'You'll be making sounds like a man next. Now let's try again.'

Jacaud went inside without a word and Chavasse picked up his suitcase and followed him. He paused to glance up at the painted sign above the door. It was obviously very old and showed a man running, apparently some kind of fugitive, a pack of hounds at his heels. A pleasant sight indeed, the terror in the poor wretch's eyes frozen into place for all eternity.

Inside was a large square room with a low-beamed ceiling and a tiled floor. There was a scattering of chairs and tables, a large open hearth in which a fire burned, and a marble-topped bar.

Jacaud had gone behind it and was pouring himself a large cognac. He rammed the cork into the bottle and Chavasse dropped his case. 'I'll join you.'

'Like hell you will. Let's see the colour of your money.'

'Rossiter's got it all, you know that.'

'Then you can go thirsty.' He replaced the bottle on the shelf and raised his voice. 'Hey, Mercier, where are you?'

A door at the back of the bar opened and a small, worried-looking man of forty or so came in. He wore a fisherman's patched trousers and was wiping his hands on a grimy towel.

'Yes, monsieur, what is it?'

'Another passenger for the *Leopard*. Take him upstairs. He can share with Jones.'

He glared at Chavasse like some wild animal, turned, kicked open the door and vanished into the kitchen.

'Quite a show,' Chavasse said. 'Is he always like this or is today something special?'

Mercier picked up the suitcase. 'This way, monsieur.'

They mounted some stairs to the first floor and moved along a narrow whitewashed corridor past several doors. Mercier knocked on the one at the far end. There was no reply and he opened it.

The room was small and bare, with whitewashed walls, two narrow truckle beds standing side by side. There was a crucifix on one wall, a cheap colour reproduction of St Francis on the other. It was clean – but only just.

Mercier put down the case. 'Monsieur Jones will probably be back shortly. He is, by the way, Jamaican. A meal will be served at twelve-thirty. If there is anything else you wish to know, you must see Monsieur Rossiter.'

'And who does Monsieur Rossiter have to see?'

Mercier frowned, looking genuinely bewildered. 'I don't understand, monsieur.'

'Let it go,' Chavasse told him.

Mercier shrugged and went out. Chavasse put his suitcase on one of the beds, moved to the window and looked out. So this was the Running Man? Not a very prepossessing sight.

Behind him, someone said, 'Welcome to Liberty Hall, man.'

A gull cried high in the sky and skimmed the sand dunes. Down by the water's edge, Jones threw stones into the sea. He turned and moved back towards Chavasse, tall, handsome, the strong angular face and startling blue eyes evidence of that mixture of blood so common in the West Indies. *Jack Jones?* Well, that was as reasonable a name as any. He had the shoulders of a prizefighter and looked good for ten rounds any day of the week, or Chavasse was no judge.

He flung himself down on the sand, produced

a packet of Gauloises and lit one. 'So you're from Australia?'

'That's it – Sydney.'

'They tell me that's quite a town.'

'The best. You should try it some time.'

The Jamaican stared at him blankly. 'You must be joking. They wouldn't even let me off the boat. They like their immigrants to be the pale variety, or hadn't you noticed?'

It was a plain statement of fact, without any kind of rancour in it, and Chavasse shrugged. 'I don't make the laws, sport. Too busy breaking them.'

The Jamaican was immediately interested. 'Now that explains a lot. I was wondering why a free, white, upstanding Protestant like you was having to use the back door into the old country like the rest of us.'

'Catholic,' Chavasse said. 'Free, white, up-standing Catholic – just for the record.'

Jones grinned, produced his packet of Gauloises for the second time and offered him one. 'And just how badly does the law back home want you?'

'About ten years' worth. That's if I'm lucky

and the judge isn't feeling too liverish on the great day.'

Jones whistled softly. 'Man, you must be a real tiger when you get going.'

'A weakness for other people's money, that's my trouble.' Chavasse looked across the sand dunes to the small harbour and the sea beyond. 'This is all right; about the nicest beach I've touched since Bondi.'

'That's what I thought five days ago – now it's just a drag. I want to get moving.'

'What are you going to do when you get over the Channel?'

Jones shrugged. 'I've got friends in the right places. They'll fix me up with something.'

'But for how long?'

'As long as I need. Once I hit London, I can't go wrong. I'll just merge into the scenery. After all, one black face is the same as another, or hadn't you noticed?'

Chavasse refused to be drawn. 'What about the rest of the clientele?'

'If you turn your head a couple of points to starboard, you'll see them now.'

The old man who appeared over a sand dune

a few yards away wore a blue overcoat two sizes too large that gave him a strangely shrunken look, and his brown, wrinkled skin was drawn tightly over the bones of his face. He wasn't too steady on his feet, either. Chavasse got the distinct impression that if it hadn't been for the woman who supported him with a hand under his left elbow and an arm around his shoulders, he might well have fallen down.

'Old Hamid is seventy-two,' Jones said. 'A Pakistani. He's hoping to join his son in Bradford.'

'And the woman?'

'Mrs Campbell? Anglo-Indian – a half-and-half. What they used to call chi-chi in the good old days of Empire. A fine Scots name, but she can no more get away from the colour of her skin than I can. Her husband died last year and her only relative is a sister who married an English doctor years ago and went to live in Harrogate, of all places. Mrs Campbell tried to get an entry permit to join her, but they turned her down.'

'Why?'

'She doesn't qualify as a dependant under

the Immigration Act, she's an Indian national and she's got tuberculosis. She was born in India, never been to England in her life and yet she talks about it as going home. Funny, isn't it?'

'Not particularly.'

Mrs Campbell was about fifty, with sad dark eyes and a skin that was darker than usually found amongst Eurasians. She seemed cold and wore a shabby fur coat, a heavy woollen scarf wrapped about her neck and head.

They paused, the old man gasping for breath. 'A cold day, Mr Jones, don't you agree?'

Jones and Chavasse stood up and Jones nodded. 'This is Mr Chavasse, a new arrival. He'll be going with us.'

The old man showed no surprise. 'Ah, yes, Miss Nadeem spoke of you.'

'You've met her?' Chavasse said.

'Just before we left for our walk,' Mrs Campbell put in.

Hamid held out a soft, boneless hand, which Chavasse touched briefly before it slipped from his grasp as easily as life would slip from the frail old body before very much longer.

Mrs Campbell seemed curiously embarrassed and tugged at the old man's sleeve. 'Come now, Mr Hamid, we mustn't dawdle. Lunch soon. So nice, Mr Chavasse.' Her English was quaint in its preciseness, and the way in which she spoke was an echo of a bygone age. Chavasse watched them stumble away across the sand dunes, strange, shadowy creatures with no substance to them, adrift in an alien world, and was conscious of an indescribable feeling of bitterness. Men made laws to protect themselves, but someone always suffered – always.

He turned and found Jones watching him enigmatically. 'You look sorry for them, too sorry for any Sydney duck with the law on his tail.'

There was a curious stillness between them. Chavasse said in a harsh, unemotional voice, 'I don't know what in the hell you're talking about.'

'Neither do I, man.' Jones grinned, and the moment passed. 'You want to eat, we'd better move.'

They made their way through the sand dunes and started across the beach above the wooden jetty. Chavasse pointed towards the motor launch moored beside it. 'Is that the boat?'

Jones nodded. 'It kind of fits in with Jacaud, wouldn't you say?'

'What do you make of him?'

Jones shrugged. 'He'd sell his sister or his grandmother for a bottle of rum at the right time. He's on two a day at the moment and escalating.'

'And the man who works for him – Mercier?'

'Frightened of his own shadow. Lives in a cottage on the other side of the village. Just him and his wife. She's some kind of an invalid. A walking vegetable. He jumps when Jacaud roars.'

'And Rossiter?'

Jones smiled softly. 'You like the question bit, don't you?'

Chavasse shrugged. 'Suit yourself.'

'Okay, I will. You know what a zombie is?'

Chavasse frowned. 'Something to do with voodoo, isn't it?'

'To be precise, a dead man brought out of his grave before corruption's had a chance to set in.'

'And given life, is that what you're trying to say?'

'A kind of life, to walk the night and do his master's bidding – a creature of pure, mindless evil.'

'And that's Rossiter.'

'That's Rossiter.' The Jamaican laughed harshly. 'The funny thing is, he used to be a priest – a Jesuit priest.'

'And how would you know that?'

'Ran out of matches one night, so I knocked on his door. He didn't seem to be around.'

'And your natural curiosity got the better of you?'

'What else, man? There were a couple of interesting photographs in the bottom right-hand drawer of his dressing table. He hasn't changed much. There's a nice one dated 1949 of about twenty of them in a group – looks like graduation day at the seminary. The other was taken in 1951 in Korea. Shows him with half-a-dozen kids at the gate of some mission or other.'

Nineteen-fifty-one. The year the Korean War had started. Was that where Rossiter had lost his faith? Chavasse frowned, remembering that tortured, ascetic face. The priest he could see, but the murderer . . . it just didn't seem possible.

He was still thinking about it as they turned into the courtyard of the Running Man.

ENGLISH CHANNEL

6

The main room of the inn was deserted when they entered, and Jones went behind the bar and took down a bottle of cognac and two glasses from the shelf.

'Join me?' he said.

Chavasse nodded. 'Why not?'

There was a sudden bellow of anger as Jacaud appeared through the rear door. 'Put those down. You hear me, you black ape?'

Jones looked him over calmly, not a flicker of emotion on his face. 'Sure I hear you,' he observed, in very reasonable French.

He uncorked the bottle and filled both glasses. Jacaud took a quick step towards him, grabbed him by the shoulder and spun him around.

'Jacaud!' Rossiter spoke from the doorway, his voice full of steel, brooking no denial.

Jacaud turned reluctantly. 'They don't even pay,' he muttered lamely.

Rossiter ignored him and came forward. He was wearing grey trousers, a hand-knitted fisherman's sweater and steel-rimmed spectacles. He carried a slim book in one hand, a finger marking his place.

'Be my guests, gentlemen.'

'Are you going to join us?' Chavasse enquired.

'Mr Rossiter don't drink,' Jones said. 'We're on our own, man.'

He saluted Chavasse, emptied his glass in a single swallow and filled it again. Jacaud, scowling, took down a bottle and glass for himself and retired to the other end of the bar.

'You've been for a walk, I see,' Rossiter said.

Chavasse nodded. 'That's right. It's quite a spot. They must do well in the tourist season round here.'

'Too far off the beaten track and they don't encourage strangers.'

'I was wondering when we make our move.'

'I can't be certain. We have one more passenger. It depends when he arrives. It could be today or tomorrow.'

'And what's the form when we do go?'

'You'll be told at the appropriate time. No need to worry. We know what we're doing.'

Behind them a soft voice said hesitatingly, 'May I come in?'

Famia stood in the doorway, her flawless complexion set off to perfection by a scarlet sari. There was a silver rope necklace about her neck, gold bracelets on her wrists. It was the reactions of his companions that interested Chavasse most. Jones was giving her the kind of appraisal you saw on the face of a connoisseur in an art gallery when confronted with something of value. Jacaud gazed at her with ill-concealed lust. And Rossiter? Rossiter seemed transfixed. His face had turned very pale, which made the eyes seem bluer than ever, and then a strange thing happened. He smiled, and it was as if something had melted inside.

He went forward and gave her his arm. 'They should be ready for us. Shall we go in?' he said, and took her through into the dining room.

He had left his book on the bar counter and Chavasse picked it up. It was the Everyman edition of *The City of God* by St Augustine.

There were times when Chavasse got the distinct impression that he was the only sane person in a world gone mad. This was very definitely one of them. He emptied his glass, nodded to Jones, and went after them.

There was a large walled garden behind the inn, a sad sort of place with gnarled apple trees long since run to seed from lack of proper attention. There were no flowers as yet, for it was still too early in the season and last year's grass overflowed onto the narrow paths, still uncut.

Famia walked there, Rossiter at her side, a figure from Brueghel in her scarlet sari, vivid against that grey-green landscape. She laughed, and the sound rose on the quiet air to the window of Chavasse's room, where he sat with Jones, watching from behind the curtain.

'First time I've seen him smile,' the Jamaican said.

'She's certainly touched something,' Chavasse replied. 'But I'm not sure what.'

Rossiter murmured to the girl, turned and went away. She walked on by herself, pausing to look up at a blackbird on a branch above her head. A moment later, Jacaud appeared.

He was obviously drunk, and swayed slightly as he moved forward, staring at her unwinkingly. She failed to see him, still intent on the blackbird, until he reached out and touched her shoulder. She turned, recoiling immediately, but he caught her by the arm, pulled her close and kissed her. Perhaps he meant no more than that, for as she cried out, struggling to be free, he laughed.

Jones beat Chavasse to the door by a short head. They went down the stairs, along the passage and out through the kitchen. Already they were too late.

Rossiter stood halfway between them and Jacaud, an arm around the girl. Very gently, he put her to one side, his hand slipped into his pocket and came out holding the ivory Madonna.

Jacaud didn't even try to escape, that was the strangest thing of all. He fell on his knees, his great face working as Rossiter slowly advanced, grabbed the Breton by the hair and pulled back his head. There was a sharp click, and steel flashed. Very deliberately, Rossiter drew the point of the razor-sharp blade across Jacaud's forehead; the flesh opened and blood oozed in a crimson curtain.

Jacaud rolled over without a sound and Rossiter wiped the knife mechanically. Famia stood looking at him, a dazed expression on her face. He went to the girl, put an arm around her shoulders and led her past Chavasse and Jones without a glance.

Chavasse turned Jacaud over and dropped to one knee. He took out his handkerchief and wiped the blood away from the great ugly face.

'How is he?' Jones asked.

'Fainted dead away – fright, I expect. Rossiter knew what he was doing. He's marked him badly – no more than that. Sticking plaster should be enough.'

'Did you see his face?'

'Rossiter's?' Chavasse nodded. 'Reminded me of something in Marlowe's play *Faustus*.'

'This is hell, nor am I out of it?' Jones said. 'More than apt.'

Chavasse grinned. 'One thing about the

Jamaican educational system – they certainly must have encouraged you to read.'

'And write, man. And write. Hell, it's the coming thing.'

The Jamaican got a shoulder under Jacaud's arm and raised him. Together they took him inside.

Later in the afternoon, the rain came again with a sudden rush, shrouding everything in a grey curtain. The old woman who did the cooking came in from the kitchen and lit an oil lamp, retiring immediately without a word. Mrs Campbell and Hamid sat as close to the fire as possible and talked quietly with Famia. Jones was reading a book, and Chavasse sat with a week-old copy of *Le Monde*.

He dropped it to the floor and went to the door which led to the bar. Rossiter and Jacaud sat at a table, talking in low tones, a bottle of cognac between them. Otherwise the place was empty, except for Mercier, who stood behind the bar counter polishing glasses. It seemed as good an opportunity as Chavasse was ever likely to get, and he turned, strolled across the room and went into the passage.

He went up the stairs two at a time, moved along the corridor and paused outside Rossiter's room. The lock was child's play, an old mortice that opened smoothly with the first skeleton key he tried, and he went inside.

The room was almost exactly the same as his own, small and bare, with a single bed and an old chest of drawers. It was a place of shadows with the grey light of late afternoon seeping in through the narrow window, but two tall candles burning steadily on either side of a statue of the Virgin gave all the additional illumination that he needed.

There was a suitcase under the bed that contained nothing but clothes. He replaced them neatly and pushed it out of sight again. He went through the drawers next and found the photographs Jones had mentioned, exactly as described. Chavasse examined them in the flickering light of the candles and Rossiter's face jumped out to meet him, clear and quite unmistakable.

He replaced them carefully and searched the other drawers. There was nothing more of interest, which left only the books standing in a neat row on the window ledge. The Bible, a *Life of St Ignatius Loyola*, *The City of God* and various commentaries. There were also copies of *The Sayings of Chairman Mao* and *Das Kapital*, which certainly made for a most Catholic collection in more senses than one.

He checked that everything was as he had found it, opened the door cautiously and stepped out. Jones moved from the shadows of an alcove almost immediately opposite, and smiled.

'Was I right?' he demanded coolly.

Chavasse nodded. 'On the nose.'

'The story of my life. I'm right so often, it's sickening.'

There was the sound of a car pulling up outside. They moved to the window at the end of the passage and peered out. A Mercedes was parked at the entrance and Rossiter and Jacaud stood beside it. Jacaud opened the rear door and a man emerged, wearing a heavy overcoat with an astrakhan collar and a black, old-fashioned trilby. He was Chinese and built like a fort, with a round, smooth, enigmatic face that made his age difficult to judge.

'Man, this gets more like the United Nations every minute,' Jones whispered.

Chavasse nodded, as the Mercedes drove away and Jacaud picked up the newcomer's bags. 'The other passenger, presumably. We'd better get down and see what the form is.'

In the living room Rossiter was already making introductions, and when Chavasse and Jones appeared, he turned with a pleasant smile. 'Ah, now we are all here. Gentlemen, Mr Cheung.'

The Chinese came forward to shake hands. Close up, he was perhaps forty-five, with a smile of exceptional charm. 'So, an Australian?' he said to Chavasse. 'I have had many dealings with firms in your country. I am from Hong Kong.'

He shook hands with Jones rather formally and with considerably less enthusiasm, and then disappeared with Rossiter and Jacaud, who at close quarters looked white and ill, a great strip of surgical tape pasted across his brow.

'At least he shook hands,' Jones observed. 'They don't like my kind of people, man, or did you know that already?'

'To the Chinese, a person of any other race is

naturally inferior,' Chavasse said. 'So don't start feeling sorry for yourself. I'm in there too.'

He went out into the passage and helped himself to one of the old oilskins hanging from the wooden pegs. Jones leaned in the doorway and watched him. 'Going somewhere?'

'I feel like some air.'

'Mind if I tag along?'

'Suit yourself.'

The Jamaican took down an oilskin and they went out into the rain. It fell straight from sky to earth, for there was no wind, and when they went out through the archway Ste-Denise was almost hidden from view. Chavasse went down through the pine trees and moved along the beach into the sand dunes, thinking things over.

There was the organization, apparently simple enough in its aims, which were to get you across the Channel and into the UK, no questions asked, for cash on the barrel. Except that they were also willing to put you over the side in chains in the right circumstances. Having met Jacaud and Rossiter, that fact was becoming easier to accept by the minute.

And what about Rossiter? The Jesuit who

had lost his faith, presumably in Korea where a vicious and bloody confrontation with China had dragged on for years. Hamid, Famia and Mrs Campbell were easy enough to accept, and Jones, of course, fitted neatly into place, but Mr Cheung from Hong Kong? Now he really was an interesting piece of the jigsaw.

He paused on top of a sand dune and looked out over the grey sea. Jones nudged him in the ribs. 'You see what I see? They showing the latest customer over the boat.'

Chavasse squatted, pulling Jones down beside him. Rossiter and Cheung were walking along the wooden jetty towards the *Leopard*. As he watched, they scrambled onto the deck and disappeared down the companionway.

'I wonder what they're up to?' Jones said.

'Only one way of finding out.'

Chavasse got to his feet and went down towards the water, keeping to the cover of the sand dunes, and Jones followed him. The small fishing fleet had long since returned from the day's work, and the boats were drawn up on the beach in a neat row that gave excellent cover.

Within a few moments they had reached the

shelter of the jetty. Chavasse paused and Jones said, 'What exactly did you have in mind?'

'God knows – just my curiosity. I'd like to know what they're doing.'

He worked his way along the heavy timbers, climbing to the next level at the point where grey-green water slopped in lazily. The heavy smell of the sea hung over everything, salt-water, seaweed, dead fish, harsh and pungent, but not unpleasant. He crouched in a cross-piece, Jones right behind him. There were footsteps on the deck above their head.

Rossiter and Mr Cheung were talking together in Cantonese. Chavasse strained every nerve to hear what was being said, but could only catch odd words and phrases. There was a sudden burst of laughter and then the footsteps drummed on the boards overhead as they walked away.

'What were they talking about?' Jones said.

Chavasse shook his head. 'I couldn't catch everything. Putting it together, it seems that Cheung has been sent from a place called Hellgate by a man named Montefiore. Does that make any kind of sense to you?'

Jones nodded. 'Montefiore is something new,

but Hellgate I've come across before. I overheard a conversation between Rossiter and Jacaud.'

Chavasse scrambled up the cross-ties and looked down at the deck of the *Leopard*. It was a depressing sight, shabby and uncared for, festooned with nets and cluttered with lobster pots. The rubber dinghy had been inflated and a powerful outboard motor was attached to its stern.

'One thing's certain,' he said. 'If anything goes wrong, some of us will be swimming. That thing won't hold more than four and make progress. Come on, we'd better get out of here.'

They scrambled back along the timbers and reached the beach again. As they moved up through the sand dunes, Jones chuckled.

'What's so funny?' Chavasse asked.

'You are.' Jones contrived to look innocent. 'Man, you're the only Australian I've ever met who could speak French and Chinese as well as English. Those Sydney schools must really be something.'

'You go to hell,' Chavasse said, and moved on through the pine trees towards the inn.

*   *   *

When they entered, Rossiter was standing alone at the bar and Mercier was in the act of pouring him a brandy. The Englishman turned and smiled. 'Ah, there you are. We were looking for you.'

'We felt like a breath of air,' Chavasse said. 'Anything important?'

'I think so. You'll be pleased to know we're leaving tonight at approximately nine o'clock.'

'How long will the crossing take?'

'About seven hours. If the weather holds, you'll be landed on a beach near Weymouth.'

'Will we be met?'

'Naturally. My colleagues on the other side will have you in London by nine a.m. at the latest. After that you are on your own.'

'And what happens if something goes wrong?' Jones said.

Rossiter looked faintly surprised. 'But it never does, I can assure you. I'll see you later.'

He went out, closing the door, and a small, trapped wind scuffled in the corners and died.

Jones sighed. 'Wish I had his confidence. You think this thing is going to work?'

'Do you?' Chavasse said.

They challenged each other, each man's thoughts unspoken. Jones broke first, his face creasing into a smile. 'I know one thing. It's certainly going to be an interesting night.'

7

The jetty at night was a lonely place, a lantern on a six-foot pole the sole illumination. In its harsh light, the *Leopard* looked less of a bargain than ever, old and ugly like a whore who has seen better days, caught without her make-up on.

Mercier was there, and Jacaud, working on deck when the party from the Running Man arrived. Rossiter led the way, carrying Famia's suitcase. Where the girl was concerned, he was all solicitude, helping her to the deck and handing her down the companionway. The others followed, Chavasse and Jones taking old Hamid and Mrs Campbell between them in turn.

Rossiter held Chavasse back, a hand on his sleeve. 'A word before you go below.'

'Something troubling you?' Chavasse enquired politely.

'Your gun.' Rossiter held out his hand. 'No nonsense, now. There's a good chap.'

Chavasse shrugged, produced the Smith & Wesson and handed it over. 'You're the boss.'

'For a few hours more. Now let's join the others.' He nodded to Jacaud. 'Any time you're ready.'

Chavasse went down the companionway to the cabin and found the rest of them already seated on either side of a central table, looking absurdly formal, as if it was some kind of board meeting and they were waiting for the chairman. Jones pushed up to make room for him on the padded bench and smiled.

'What kept you?'

Before Chavasse could reply Rossiter appeared. He leaned on the end of the table, his hands taking his weight. 'Ladies and gentlemen, we're about to commence the final leg of your journey. If the weather holds, and I can assure you that the forecast is a favourable one, you will be landed approximately seven hours from now in a creek near a small village not far from

Weymouth on the English coast. A member of our organization will be waiting there to take you on to London by road. For the rest of the voyage, I must ask you to stay in your cabin. Are there any questions?' No one spoke, and he smiled. 'You'll find sandwiches through there in the galley, if anyone feels hungry, and a small stove on which you can make coffee. I'll see you later.'

He left, and almost immediately the engines coughed into life and the boat started to move. Chavasse peered out of the nearest porthole and saw Mercier standing under the lantern on the jetty as the *Leopard* moved out to sea. He walked away and Chavasse sat down again.

Jones offered him a cigarette. 'Well, what do you think now?'

'They seem to know what they're up to.' Chavasse leaned across to Famia. 'Everything okay?'

She smiled brightly. 'Fine, just fine. Mr Rossiter has been so kind. He gives one such a feeling of confidence. I'm sure everything is going to be all right now.'

'Let's hope so.'

Chavasse leaned back. The business with the Smith & Wesson had given him something to think about. There could well be some sinister motive behind it. On the other hand, it was perfectly possible that Rossiter was simply taking every precaution. Not that it mattered, for Chavasse, who had long ago learned by bitter experience never to leave anything to chance, still had his Walther PPK automatic, which before leaving, he had strapped to the inside of his left leg just above the ankle with a piece of surgical tape.

He sat back, eyes half-closed, and watched Cheung, who was reading a book at the far end of the table on the opposite side next to Mrs Campbell. Chavasse wondered what it was, and in the same moment remembered two things: Rossiter's excellent Chinese and the copy of *The Sayings of Chairman Mao* he had seen in his room. Yes, indeed, the more he thought about it, the more interesting Mr Cheung became.

With a love of the sea not unnatural in a man whose Breton ancestors had been voyaging to the coast of Newfoundland to fish long before Columbus had discovered the New World, Chavasse had been running a thirty-foot motor yacht out of Alderney for eight years and knew the Golfe de St-Malo and the general area of the Channel Islands like the back of his hand.

Because of this, he was able to keep a reasonably accurate check on their progress, not only from an estimate of the boat's speed, but by direct observation of various lights which were familiar to him.

Although the weather remained fair, the boat pitched considerably in the turbulence common to the area because of the great tidal surge which drives in through the Channel Islands, raising the level of the water in the Golfe by as much as thirty feet. Both Hamid and Mrs Campbell were suffering from sea-sickness in spite of the pills which Rossiter had handed round at the inn before leaving, and the old man didn't look at all well.

It wasn't just the pitching of the *Leopard* which was causing the trouble. There was an all-pervading stench of petrol, which seemed to have got steadily worse for the last hour.

Chavasse looked out of the porthole as they rounded Les Hanois lighthouse on the western tip of Guernsey.

He told Jones, 'A clear run from here. Shouldn't take more than a couple of hours, if the weather holds.'

Jones made a wry face. 'Much more of this and I'll be sick myself. That petrol sure stinks.'

Chavasse said in a low voice, 'I'm not too happy about it. Think I'll go on deck and have a word with our friend.'

The door at the top of the companionway was locked. He hammered on it with his clenched fist. After a while, it opened and Rossiter peered in.

'What do you want?'

'We're getting one hell of a whiff of petrol down here,' Chavasse told him. 'Old Hamid's been sick several times now. He doesn't look too good.'

Rossiter crouched down and sniffed. A frown appeared on his face. 'I see what you mean. Better bring him up for a breath of air while I get Jacaud to check the engine.'

Jones and Chavasse took the old man up

the companionway between them. There was a fair sea running, and a strength three wind, if Chavasse was any judge, but the old boat was coping nicely. The masthead light swung rhythmically from side to side. Jacaud crouched beside the hatch which gave access to the engine. He disappeared from view, and Chavasse left Jones to look after Hamid and crossed to the open hatch.

There was only four feet of headroom inside, and Jacaud had to squat at the bottom of the short ladder while fumbling for the light switch in the dark. He found it, and in the sudden illumination the trouble was plain enough to see, for an inch or so of petrol slopped around his feet.

He edged forward and disappeared from view, reappearing almost immediately. 'How bad is it?' Chavasse asked, as he came up the ladder.

Jacaud ignored him, replaced the hatch and went to the wheelhouse. Chavasse returned to Jones, who stood at the rail, an arm around Hamid.

'What gives?' Jones demanded.

Chavasse shrugged. 'Jacaud wasn't exactly forthcoming. I'd say he has a leak in the fuel tank.'

'Quite correct.' Rossiter joined them, a match flaring in his cupped hands as he lit a cigarette. 'As it happens, we have auxiliary tanks which carry enough fuel for the entire trip in themselves. Jacaud has switched over to them. I think you'll find that things will improve very quickly now.'

'Do we have to return below?' Chavasse asked.

'One of you can stay up here with the old man for another ten minutes or so. He should be all right again by then.'

He went back into the wheelhouse and Chavasse turned to Jones. 'You okay here?'

'Sure.'

'Good – then I'll go below and see how the others are getting on.'

When he went down the companionway to the saloon, the smell of petrol still lingered, but it was nowhere near as strong as it had been earlier. Mrs Campbell looked pale and wan, but Famia seemed fine, and Cheung leaned back in his seat, eyes closed, hands folded across his chest.

Chavasse glanced out of the porthole above his head. In the distance, the green and red navigation lights of a ship following the steamer lane that ran up-Channel from Ushant disappeared, as if a curtain had dropped into place. He peered out, frowning, and there was a step on the companionway.

Jones eased old Hamid into a seat and grinned. 'Not too good out there now. Mist coming in off the water and it's started to rain again.'

At that precise moment, the boat was rocked by a muffled explosion. Mrs Campbell screamed as she was thrown halfway across the table and Chavasse fetched up against the far wall. As he picked himself up, the *Leopard* came to a dead halt and then started to drift.

Chavasse hammered on the door of the companionway. It opened almost at once and Rossiter peered in, a gun in his hand. His face had turned very pale, the eyes glittered, and yet the gun didn't waver in the slightest.

113

'Back you go.'

'Don't be a damn' fool,' Chavasse said. 'If there's trouble, we've got a right to know about it.'

'When I'm good and ready.' Rossiter pushed him back and slammed the door.

'What's wrong up there?' Jones demanded. 'It certainly didn't sound too healthy to me.'

In the stress of the moment his accent had undergone a surprising transformation, replaced by the kind of faultless clipped enunciation common to the products of the English public-school system.

Mrs Campbell was sobbing hysterically and Famia was trying to comfort her. Old Hamid seemed to have come to life in some strange way and was on his feet, an arm around both women. It was Cheung's reactions which were the most interesting. No panic, no hysterics. He sat at the table, face expressionless, eyes watchful.

Chavasse unscrewed one of the portholes and peered out. There was a smell of burning, and Rossiter and Jacaud were arguing in French just above his head.

114

'It's no good, I tell you,' Jacaud cried, and there was panic in his voice. 'The old tub has had it.'

'How far from the coast are we?' Rossiter demanded.

'Five or six miles – maybe seven.'

'Good – we'll continue in the rubber boat. Get it over the side. Our friends at Fixby can run us back to Ste-Denise.'

The rest of the conversation was blown away on the wind and Chavasse turned to face Jones, who knelt on the seat beside him.

'What's going on?' Jones demanded.

'From what they say, the *Leopard*'s had it. They're talking about going the rest of the way in the rubber boat.'

'Can it be done?'

'I don't see why not. It's about six miles to the coast and they've got a good outboard motor on that thing. Of course, there's only room for four passengers, but I shouldn't think that will present much of a problem to Rossiter.'

The door to the companionway was flung open with startling suddenness and Rossiter appeared, the gun in his hand. He waved it at Chavasse and Jones. 'Right, sit down and stay down.'

They did as they were told. Chavasse leaned across the table and groped for the butt of the Walther PPK that was strapped to his leg above the ankle.

Rossiter nodded to Famia. 'All right, Miss Nadeem, on deck.'

She shook her head, complete bewilderment on her face. 'But I don't understand.'

The mask of calmness cracked into a thousand pieces; he grabbed her roughly by the arm and cried wildly, 'You want to die, do you?' He pushed her up the companionway. 'Go on – get on deck.'

Mrs Campbell sagged into her seat as Famia stumbled out of sight, and Chavasse said, 'What do we do? Go down with the ship singing "Abide with me"?'

Rossiter ignored him and spoke to Cheung in rapid Chinese. 'On deck quickly. The boat is sinking.'

The Chinese pushed past Hamid and Mrs Campbell, and Chavasse leaned across the table, his hand fastening around the butt of the Walther. 'I've certainly got to give it to you, Rossiter. It must have taken nerve to see Harvey Preston off the way you did, but this is even better. Four at one go . . .'

Rossiter turned and fired, blindly and in a kind of reflex action, the bullet splintering the bulkhead behind Chavasse and a foot to one side. Mrs Campbell screamed again. Chavasse sent Jones to the floor with a shove in the back and brought the Walther up fast. The bullet caught Cheung on the side of the face, gouging a bloody furrow across one cheek, chipping wood from the doorpost as it went on its way.

Cheung didn't utter a sound. He spun round and flung himself up the companionway, and Rossiter fired three shots wildly. Chavasse went under the table. As the echoes died away, the door was slammed shut and the bolt clicked.

He got to his feet and found Jones already on his way to the companionway. Chavasse got to him just in time and dragged him back as two more shots came through the door.

'Wait, man – wait! He was expecting one of us to do that.'

They flattened themselves against the wall on either side of the companionway, and Jones said softly, 'You know your business, I'll say that for you.'

Chavasse grinned. 'You don't do too badly yourself for a barrister.'

Jones showed no surprise at all. 'You know who I am?'

'Darcy Morgan Preston, aged twenty-nine, profession barrister; in practice in Jamaica since August, 1967. Married, two children. You're trying to find out what happened to your brother Harvey.'

'And you know?'

'Our friends put him over the side, wrapped in about sixty pounds of anchor chain.'

Darcy Preston straightened and moved away from the wall, his face sagging. At the same moment the outboard motor coughed into life outside.

'Let's go,' Chavasse said, and jumped into the companionway.

He fired four times, splintering the wood

around the lock, raised his right foot and stamped hard. The door swung back and he went through to the deck, crouching. He was already too late; the sound of the outboard was fading into the darkness and mist.

8

'Nice people,' Darcy Preston said quietly. 'Now what do we do?'

There was a sudden hiss as if gas were escaping, and a cloud of steam billowed from the engine-room hatch. Already the stern was low in the water and the *Leopard* wallowed sluggishly, hardly lifting as the swell undulated across the sea.

There was a sudden exclamation from the companionway, and when Chavasse turned, old Hamid was standing there. In the diffused yellow light from the masthead lamp, he looked about a hundred years old. He didn't seem afraid in the slightest when he spoke.

'They have gone, Mr Chavasse? They have left us to drown?'

'Not if I can help it,' Chavasse told him. 'How's Mrs Campbell?'

'Not too good, I'm afraid.'

Chavasse turned to Preston. 'Get her up on deck and see if you can find some liquor. Jacaud liked his rum, so there must be a few bottles around. Make her drink as much as you possibly can. Anything to calm her down. I'll see what I can find up here. And hurry, for God's sake. We haven't got long.'

He found three lifejackets in a locker in the wheelhouse and passed one to Hamid. The old man started to unbutton his overcoat and Chavasse shook his head.

'Keep that on, whatever you do. It's going to be cold out there.'

The old man pushed his arms through the straps and Chavasse did a final deck check. The only movable item that might support a person's weight was the aft hatch cover. He got it off and eased it towards the rail, as Preston appeared with Mrs Campbell.

She looked ghastly in the yellow light, eyes dark and fearful, her body shrunken with terror. Chavasse could smell the rum. Preston was holding one bottle in his hand and there were two more under his arm.

He passed one across to Chavasse. 'Stick that in your pocket. It might come in useful.'

Chavasse gave him the two lifejackets. 'The best I can do.'

'And what about you?'

'There's an old cork lifebelt here that will keep me going. Now hurry it up. We've only got a few minutes.'

Suddenly it seemed very quiet, the rain falling in dull steel lances through the light, and they stood by the rail together, ready to go. The sea was already over the stern and slopped in across the deck in a green curtain.

Chavasse glanced at his watch. 'Dawn in another hour. We're between five and six miles off the coast, possibly less, but the tide will start to go in fast soon and we'll go with it. Don't try to swim, that way you'll tire quickly and lose body heat, and don't try to take any clothes off. That would be the worst thing you could do. Mrs Campbell, we're going to put you on the hatch. I want you to just lie still, even if the water breaks over you. The rest of us will hang onto the sides. It's important we try to stay together – any questions?'

The *Leopard* gave a sudden lurch to one side, and Preston lost his balance and went into the water. He surfaced and grabbed for the rail. He even managed a smile.

'We should do this more often. Better get the hatch over fast. Somehow I don't think the boat has much longer to live.'

Strange how one always thought of a boat as a living creature with a soul of its own. Swimming awkwardly, the cork lifebelt under his armpits bumping the side of the hatch as he pushed hard, Chavasse glanced back and watched the *Leopard* slide smoothly under the surface. For a brief moment the green and red navigation lights gleamed above the swell at the masthead, and then they too were dimmed.

It was the darkness that was the real enemy, not the cold, though that was bad enough to begin with. But after a while the bodily temperature adapted itself and the fact that they were all fully clothed helped considerably, as Chavasse knew it would.

But the darkness remained for quite some

time, and Mrs Campbell moaned repeatedly, breaking into terrible fits of crying every so often that no one could do anything about.

Gradually, the dawn came with a kind of grey luminosity because of the mist. Visibility was no more than a hundred yards, and Chavasse noticed with some unease the freshening breeze cold on his left cheek and the whitecaps that were starting to appear all about them.

He turned to Hamid, who hung onto the hatch beside him. The old man was well out of the water because of his lifejacket, but his turban was soaked, his skin shrunken so that every bone showed.

'Are you all right? Can you hang on?'

Hamid nodded without replying and Chavasse pulled his way round to the other side to Darcy Preston, who gave him a tired grin.

'Give me Montego Bay any time. This is no joke.'

'The wind is picking up,' Chavasse said. 'Can you feel it? It'll push us inshore that much faster, but things are going to get rough, so watch out.'

Preston's mouth opened in a soundless cry.

Chavasse turned and saw a grey-green wall of water coming in fast, blocking out the sky. There wasn't a thing he could do about it, nothing anyone could do. This time Mrs Campbell, God help her, didn't even get time to scream. The wave lifted the hatch like a cork chip, turned it over and smashed it down.

Chavasse surfaced in a maelstrom of white water, struggling for breath, still buoyant, thanks to the old lifebelt. Mrs Campbell was twenty or thirty feet away, Darcy Preston swimming after her. Hamid was over to the right, and Chavasse kicked out towards him.

The old man looked badly shaken. He had lost his turban and his long iron-grey hair had come loose and floated on the water as he lay back, obviously exhausted. As Chavasse reached him, the wind tore a gap in the curtain of mist and he saw land low down on the horizon, no more than a mile away at most.

So Jacaud had been over-cautious in his estimate? Either that or they had come in a damned sight faster than he had realized. He turned towards Preston, who was still swimming after

Mrs Campbell, and shouted, 'Land! No more than a mile!'

Preston raised an arm to signify that he understood and continued to swim after Mrs Campbell. The curtain of mist dropped back into place. Chavasse reached the old man and pulled him close.

'Not much longer now. I saw land.'

Hamid smiled wanly, but seemed unable to speak. Chavasse got the bottle of rum out of his pocket and pulled the cork with his teeth. 'Drink some of this.'

He forced the old man's mouth open and poured. Hamid coughed, half-choked, and pulled his head away. 'It is against my religion,' he gasped.

Chavasse grinned. 'Allah will forgive you this once, old man,' he said in Urdu, and swallowed the rest of the rum.

Strangely enough, the old man's only reaction to being addressed in his own language was to reply in the same tongue. 'If I live, it is because Allah wills it. If I am to die – so be it.'

*　　*　　*

Another half-hour and Chavasse was really beginning to feel the cold. He had taken off the belt of his trenchcoat and had used it to secure himself to Hamid, who floated beside him. There was no sign of Darcy Preston or Mrs Campbell – hadn't been for some time now.

Old Hamid was still, eyes closed, his face a death mask, blue with cold. Chavasse slapped him a couple of times and the eyes opened to stare blankly. A kind of recognition dawned. The lips moved, the words were only a whisper.

'Ali – Ali, is it you, my son?' he asked in Urdu.

'Yes, my father.' It took everything Chavasse had to make the correct reply. 'Not long now. Soon we will be home.'

The old man smiled, his eyes closed and suddenly a wave took them high into a sky of lead, holding them above the water long enough for Chavasse to see cliffs through driving rain no more than a couple of hundred yards away. Between lay wave after wave, and white water crashing in to meet the distant shore.

From that moment they moved fast, helpless

in the grip of the current that carried them with it. Chavasse gripped the old man tightly as water broke over them, and then another great wall of water, green as bottle glass, smashed down on them.

Chavasse went deep, too deep, and found himself alone, fighting for life like a hooked fish. His lifebelt had gone, old Hamid had gone, but strangely, no panic touched him. If he was to die, he would die fighting.

There is a behaviour pattern common to all animals and known to psychologists as the critical reaction, a phrase that describes the fury with which any living creature will fight for survival when there is no other way, either backed into a corner by his enemies or alone in a sea of white water, as Paul Chavasse was now.

He broke surface, sucked air into his lungs and went under again, tearing at the buttons of his trenchcoat. He got it off, and then the jacket, and came up for more air. The shoes took a little longer, probably because his feet were swollen from their long immersion in cold salt-water, but suddenly he was free of those too and swimming again, his rage to live giving him strength drawn from that hidden reserve that lies dormant in every man.

And then his foot kicked sand and he went under again. A wave took him forward across a great rounded boulder streaming with water and he found himself knee-deep in seaweed.

Another wave bowled him over. His fingers hooked across a rib of rock, and he held on as the waters washed over him. As they receded, he staggered to his feet and stumbled across the rocks to the safety of a strip of white sand at the base of the cliffs.

He lay on his face, gasping for air, then forced himself to his feet. Hamid – he had to find Hamid. The sea was in his mouth, his ears, his throat, it seemed to sing inside his head as he turned and picked his way through the rocks to the main beach.

He saw Hamid at once, thirty or forty yards away, lying in the shallows, the water breaking over him. Chavasse started to run, calling out in Urdu, 'I'm coming. Hold on! Hold on!'

Stupid, really. The old man would be dead, he knew that. He dragged the body clear of the water, turned it over and, greatest of all miracles, the old eyes opened.

Hamid smiled, all fatigue and pain washed from his face. 'Ali, my son, I knew you would come,' he whispered. 'Bless me now.'

'You are blessed, old man, hold my hand,' Chavasse said in Urdu. 'Blessed and thrice blessed. Go with Allah.'

The old man smiled contentedly, his eyes closed, and the life went out of him.

Chavasse crouched there beside him for quite a while, unaware of the cold, staring blindly into space. When he finally stood up, Darcy Preston was waiting a few yards away, watching him gravely.

Like Chavasse, he was down to shirt and trousers and his lifejacket had gone. There was a cut on his face, another on his left arm.

'What about Mrs Campbell?' Chavasse asked.

Preston shrugged. 'I tried to catch her when that big wave split us all up, but the current was too strong for me. She was still floating when I last saw her. She could still make it.'

Not that he believed that – neither of them

did, and Chavasse said wearily, 'Okay, let's get out of here.'

'Aren't we going to move him?'

'Let's put it like this,' Chavasse said. 'The way things are at the moment, it would make a lot more sense if you and I didn't hang around to be found with him. If we take him higher up the beach, they'll know someone put him there.'

'But what in the hell are we going to do?' Preston demanded.

Chavasse looked at his watch. 'It's a quarter to five. We find the road and the nearest phone box. I put through a call to my people, then we get behind the nearest hedge and wait. You'll be on the way to London in an hour.'

Darcy Preston shook his head. 'Well, one thing's certain. Whatever else you are, you can't be the police.'

'Full marks,' Chavasse said. 'Now let's get out of here,' and he turned and moved towards the cliffs through the grey morning.

LONDON

9

'Montefiore – Enrico Montefiore.' Mallory turned from the window, filling his pipe from an elegant leather pouch. 'One of the richest men in Europe, though very few people have ever heard of him. Doesn't like having his picture taken, but you'll find one or two in his file. He's the kind of big financier who's almost gone out of style. A shadowy figure somewhere in the background, with his finger in so many pies you lose count.'

'And Hellgate?' Chavasse asked. 'What about that?'

Mallory shook his head. 'Doesn't mean a thing. As I recall, Montefiore has a place on Lake Lucerne and a palazzo in Venice. Actually, he's rather dropped out of sight during the past three or four years.' He shook his head. 'This doesn't make any kind of sense at all. Why on earth would a man of Montefiore's background be mixed up in a thing like this?'

There was a knock at the door and Jean Frazer came in. She handed Mallory an envelope. 'More material from S2, sir, courtesy of CIA. China Section.'

She went out and Mallory opened the envelope and took out several record cards, each with a photo pinned to it. 'Better look at these, Paul. See if anyone strikes a chord.'

Cheung was number five, only his name was Ho Tsen and he was a colonel in the Army of the People's Republic of China. It was an excellent likeness and Chavasse passed it across.

'That's our boy.'

Mallory checked through the card and nodded, a slight frown on his face. 'Quite a character. One of their best men, from the looks of this. Rather stupid to pass him off as a Military Attaché in Paris for three years. The CIA was bound to catch on to him.'

The telephone buzzed; he picked it up and listened for just over a minute. When he replaced the receiver, he looked thoughtful.

'That was Travers calling in from this place, Fixby. It's a little village on a creek near Weymouth. There's a broken-down boatyard just outside it run by a man named Gorman. He's missing at the moment. Last seen moving out to sea at about six this morning in a thirty-foot launch he uses to take people big-game fishing.'

Chavasse looked at his watch and saw that it was almost noon. 'They'll be nearly there by now, if the weather holds.'

'Ste-Denise?' Mallory nodded. 'Yes. I'm inclined to agree with you, and our friend from the People's Republic will have returned with them if I'm any judge. For one thing, he's going to need some kind of medical attention, and for another, he won't want to hang around now that things have turned sour. Very practical people, the Chinese.'

'What about Rossiter?'

Mallory picked up a flimsy, and examined it. 'Now he really is an amazing character. I can't get over him. Stoneyhurst, a double first at Cambridge, five years at the English College in Rome and then Korea. The Chinese had him for four years – four years behind the wire. That must have been hell.'

Remembering his own experiences in a similar position for only a week, Chavasse nodded. 'You can say that again. But why did he throw up Holy Orders? What was the given reason?'

'Difficult to discover. The Church doesn't exactly fall over itself to discuss this sort of thing. However, I've pulled a few strings and they've reluctantly given me the address of a priest who was in captivity with Rossiter. His parish is right here in London, which is rather convenient.'

Chavasse examined the card Mallory passed across. Father Henry da Souza. Portuguese, which would probably turn out to mean that his family had been living in England for at least five hundred years. 'Was there ever the slightest suggestion that Rossiter had turned Red?'

Mallory shrugged. 'Anything is possible in this worst of all possible worlds, dear boy. They certainly did a good job on him. Of course, a priest has something to hang on to; something to fight them with. Having said that, there's no question that ministers of religion held by the Chinese for a period and later released have sometimes needed psychiatric help on their return; that's how complete the brainwashing process has been. They've done research into it at Harvard, I understand. Anyway, you go and see Father da Souza and see what you can get out of him.'

'What about Darcy Preston?'

'No problem there, as long as he behaves himself and keeps his mouth shut. We'll put him on a plane for Jamaica tomorrow.'

'Is it all right if he stays at my place in the meantime?'

'I don't see why not.' Mallory shook his head. 'St Paul's by day and Soho by night. What a strange, mixed-up life that boy must have had.'

Chavasse got to his feet. 'He seems to have survived it all rather well. I'll be in touch later this afternoon.'

He was halfway to the door when the phone buzzed again. Mallory called him back with a gesture and picked up the receiver. He put it down again with a sigh. 'The body of a middle-aged woman wearing a lifejacket was pulled out of the sea off Weymouth by a fishing boat an hour ago. Paul, I'm sorry – damned sorry. Especially in view of what you told me.'

'So am I,' Chavasse said, and went out quietly, murder in his heart.

The Church of the Immaculate Conception was not far from the East India Docks, an area that was anything but salubrious. Chavasse parked his car on the opposite side of the road and switched off the engine. He took a cigarette from his case and offered one to Darcy Preston.

'Graham Mallory would hang, draw and quarter me if he knew I'd brought you along. On the other hand, he did tell me to keep an eye on you, and I can't very well be in two places at once.'

'You could try, but I wouldn't recommend it,' Preston said, and he got out of the car.

The church backed onto the river, a small, rather grimy pseudo-Gothic building of a kind which had been built extensively during a certain period of the nineteenth century. They went in through a porched entrance to a place of candles and shadows, incense and quiet peace. It was empty except for the man who knelt by the altar rail in a priest's cassock, white hair flaming like a halo in the candlelight.

Chavasse crossed himself and dipped a knee instinctively, although he had not practised his religion for years, and they moved down the aisle. The priest rose to his feet and was about to move towards the vestry when he saw them and paused, smiling faintly.

'Can I help you, gentlemen?'

His eyes were those of a man who loved the whole world, a rare enough breed. A bad scar ran from the right eye into the hair, but otherwise he had a face as calm and untroubled as that of a two-year-old child.

'Father da Souza? My name is Chavasse. I believe you were expecting me? This is Mr Preston, an associate.'

'Ah, yes.' Father da Souza nodded. 'Something to do with Leonard Rossiter, wasn't it?' He smiled. 'Why don't we go outside? It's rather pleasant at the moment.'

At the rear of the church, a cemetery ran down to the Thames, spiked railings fringing a low wall. There was plenty of activity on the river and the priest had been right – it was pleasant in the pale sunshine.

He sat on a tombstone and accepted a cigarette from Chavasse. 'This is nice – very nice. I often come out here to think, you know. Somehow it has the right atmosphere.' He bent his head to the match Preston held out to him and leaned back with a sigh of content. 'Now then, what was it you wanted to know about Leonard?'

'Before we go any further, Father, I think I should make it clear that this is a serious business and highly confidential. In fact, a matter of national security.'

Da Souza didn't seem perturbed in the slightest. 'Go on.'

'Would you say it was possible that Leonard Rossiter had turned Communist?'

Father da Souza examined the end of his cigarette with a slight, abstracted frown, and sighed. 'As a matter of fact, I shouldn't think there was much doubt about it.'

'I see. Have you ever spoken of this to anyone before?'

'No one ever asked me.'

Chavasse nodded. 'All right, Father, tell me all you can.'

'I was sent to work in Korea just after the Second World War. I was taken prisoner by North Korean forces a few days after the Korean War started.'

'And Rossiter?'

'Oh, I didn't meet Leonard for quite some time – nine months later, when I was moved to a special camp in Manchuria. An indoctrination centre run by the Chinese.'

'And you think Rossiter was brainwashed there?'

Father da Souza laughed gently. 'Good heavens, it isn't as easy as that, you know. They have an extraordinarily simple technique, and yet it works so very often. The original concept is Pavlovian. A question of inducing guilt or rather of magnifying the guilt that is in all of us. Shall I tell you the first thing my instructor asked me, gentlemen? Whether I had a servant at the mission to clean my room and make my bed. When I admitted that I had, he expressed surprise, produced a Bible and read me that passage in which Our Lord speaks of serving others. Yet here was I allowing one of those I had come to help to serve me. Extraordinary how guilty that one small point made me feel.'

'But your faith, Father?' Preston said. 'Wasn't it of any help at all?'

The old priest smiled beatifically. 'My son, my faith was triumphant; it overcame all odds in spite of everything that was attempted with me. I have never felt more certain of God than I did during those dark days.'

'And Rossiter?' Chavasse said. 'What about Rossiter's faith?'

The old priest looked genuinely troubled. 'I am in a difficult position here, gentlemen. I was Leonard's confessor at Nom Bek, and he mine. The secrets of the confessional are sacred. Let me say that he had problems long before he fell into Communist hands. From their point of view he was fruit that was ripe for the picking.'

'What kind of problems?'

'If I may use Marxian terminology, each man has his thesis and his antithesis. For a priest, his thesis is everything he believes in, everything he and his vocation stand for. His antithesis, on the other hand, is his darker side – the side which is present in all of us. Fears and hates, violence, aggression, the desires of the flesh. Leonard Rossiter was racked by guilt long before the instructors at Nom Bek got to work on him.'

'But why did he give up Holy Orders?'

'The official explanation was that he had experienced a crisis of faith – that he could no longer continue. This happened three or four years after his return.'

'But you think he'd fallen for the party line?'

Father da Souza nodded. 'I think it seemed to offer him what he was searching for – a strong faith – a faith which would support him.'

'You say *seemed* to offer him, Father?' Darcy Preston said.

Father da Souza smiled gently. 'One thing I can tell you with certainty. Leonard Rossiter is a soul in torment. He is like the man in Thompson's poem, pursued endlessly by the Hound of God, fleeing from the one certain hope of salvation, hell-bent on destruction because of his own self-loathing.'

Chavasse nodded slowly. 'That's all, Father. I think you've made your point.'

'I hope I've been of help. A pleasure, gentlemen.'

He shook hands and they left him there on the cracked tomb, finishing his cigarette.

'Quite a man,' Darcy Preston said as they got into the car.

'And then some.'

Mallory listened to what he had to say, a strange abstracted look on his face. 'I've spoken to NATO intelligence since you were last here.'

'About Montefiore.'

Mallory nodded. 'It's curiously disturbing, Paul. They haven't got a thing on him. Now that worries me – that really does worry me. I wouldn't mind knowing that he was the most dangerous double-agent in the game as long as one had a hint, but this whole situation smells to high heaven. How do you see it?'

Chavasse stood up and paced backwards and forwards across the room. 'Let's take the two most important strands. Colonel Ho Tsen – a very dangerous Chinese agent – and Leonard Rossiter, who seems to have fallen for the party line during his captivity. That still leaves us with the most puzzling bit of all. Why should a multi-millionaire financier like Enrico Montefiore help to further the cause of militant Chinese-style Communism? And there's another point – the immigration racket. So amateurish.'

'All right, so Rossiter's organization *is* amateurish as you say, but the Chinese don't have a great deal of choice when it comes to friends and allies. They've only got one toehold in Europe, remember – Albania. It's always possible that they just haven't realized how second-rate Rossiter's organization is.'

'You could be right,' Chavasse admitted. 'They certainly can't afford to be too choosy. Any kind of a contact in the European market is better than nothing. I suspect that might be the way they looked at it, and they can be naïve. People are always telling us that we don't understand the Orientals. That may be true, but they certainly don't understand us any better.'

Mallory sat there staring into space for perhaps thirty seconds, then he nodded. 'Right,

Paul, it's all yours. Find them – all three of them. Ho Tsen, Rossiter and Montefiore. I'd like to know what it's all about, but the most important thing is to bring them to a stop.'

'A dead stop?'

'Naturally. Seek and destroy. I can't see any point in taking half-measures. It's completely your baby from now on. Use the usual communication system whenever possible to keep me informed. See Jean on your way out about money. Anything else?'

Chavasse nodded. 'The man you've got keeping an eye on this bloke Gorman at Fixby – pull him off.'

'You're going down there yourself?'

'It would seem as good a place as any to start.'

Mallory reached for the phone. 'I'll see to it now. Good luck.'

Jean Frazer glanced up as Chavasse emerged. 'You look pleased with yourself.'

'I am.'

Chavasse helped himself to a cigarette from the box on her desk. His eyes were like black glass in the dark Celtic face. He looked like the devil himself, and for some reason she shivered.

'What is it, Paul?'

'I'm not too sure,' he said. 'It's been a long time since I felt like this.'

'Like what?'

'Personally involved in something. Me, Paul Chavasse, not just the Bureau. I'm thinking of an old man on his back on a south-coast beach this morning who only wanted to see his son, and a fussy little woman who died alone, utterly terrified. A silly, stupid little woman who never hurt anyone in her life.'

He sighed heavily and stubbed out his cigarette. 'I want revenge, Jean. For the first time, I want to take care of someone permanently for personal reasons. It's a new sensation. What worries me is how happy I feel about the prospect.'

He parted from Darcy Preston with regret, for he had come to like the brilliant, sardonic Jamaican – and not only because of what they had been through together. As he packed one or two things, Darcy sat on the window seat and watched. He was wearing a pair of Chavasse's trousers, a polo-neck sweater and a sports jacket in Donegal tweed.

'Sure you're okay for cash?' Chavasse asked as he locked his suitcase.

Darcy nodded. 'I still have a bank account here.'

Chavasse buttoned an old naval bridge coat that gave him rather a nautical air. 'I don't suppose I'll be seeing you again. By this time tomorrow, you'll be on your way to sunny Jamaica.'

'Land of carefree calypso and shanty towns. Give me Birmingham any day.' Darcy grinned. 'And what about you? Where do you start? At this place, Fixby?'

'Good a place as any.'

The Jamaican held out his hand. 'This is it, then. Good luck, Paul, and next time you see Rossiter, give him one for me. Preferably with your boot.'

Chavasse had the door half-open when Darcy spoke again. 'Just one thing. It's been eating away at me, so I've got to ask. Why did they kill Harvey that way?'

'I can only guess. They were probably in danger of being boarded. In a manner of speaking, they were destroying the evidence.'

Darcy Preston actually laughed. 'You know something, that's really ironic. That's exactly what the blackbirders did with their slaves in the old days when the Royal Navy was on their tail – put them over the side in chains.'

He laughed again, but this time there were tears in his eyes and Chavasse closed the door and left him there, alone with his grief in the quiet room.

Chavasse noticed a jagged scar that stretched from his right ear to his windpipe.

'She's quite a boat.'

'She certainly is. Penta engines, radar, echo-sounder. All that and thirty-five knots. You know boats?'

'A little. Are you Gorman?'

'That's right. What can I do for you?'

'I'd like to take a little trip if your boat is available.'

'Fishing?' Gorman shook his head. 'Too late in the day.'

'I was thinking of rather more than that,' Chavasse said. 'The fact is I want to get across the Channel in a hurry, and a friend of mine told me you might be able to oblige at a price.'

Gorman looked down the creek, whistling softly. 'Who is this friend?' he asked, after a short pause.

Chavasse managed to look suitably embar-rassed. 'To tell you the truth, he wasn't really a friend. Just a bloke I met in a bar in Soho. He said that any time I wanted to get out of the country in a hurry, you were a good man to see.'

Gorman turned abruptly and spoke over his shoulder as he walked away. 'Come up to the office. It's going to rain.'

Chavasse went after him and mounted the rickety wooden stairs to the verandah. At the top he paused and turned his head sharply, aware of some kind of movement down there among the derelict boats. A dog, perhaps, or a rabbit. But it left him with a vague unease as he went into the office.

The place was cluttered with odds and ends of every description. Gorman cleared the table with a sweep of an arm and produced a bottle of whisky and two glasses.

'So you want to get across the water pretty badly?' he said.

Chavasse placed his case on the table and unlocked it. He lifted a shirt and uncovered a thousand pounds made up of several neat bundles of English fivers and French francs. It looked considerably more than it was, and Gorman's bad eye rolled wildly.

Chavasse took out two bundles of fivers and pushed them across. 'That's how badly I want to get across, Gorman. Is it a deal?'

Gorman's smile was so evil as to be almost seraphic. He scooped up the cash and stowed it away in a battered wallet. 'When do you want to leave?'

'The sooner the better, as far as I'm concerned.'

Gorman smiled again, that same seraphic smile. 'Then what are we waiting for?' he demanded, and led the way out.

The boat was called the *Mary Grant* and she was every bit as good as she looked. Chavasse stood at the rail as they moved down the creek towards the open sea and took a few deep breaths of the salt air. It was good to be on the move again, even towards an unknown future. In fact, if he was honest with himself, that accounted for a great deal of the fascination in his work – quite simply the living from day to day, not knowing what lay around the next corner.

Waves started to slap against the hull with strange little hollow sounds that vibrated through the whole boat as they left the shelter of the creek and lifted to meet the Channel swell. He moved to the wheelhouse and paused in the doorway.

'Where were you thinking of putting me down?'

'Anywhere you like,' Gorman said. 'You're the boss.'

'I was thinking of somewhere a little bit off the beaten track. The Golfe de St-Malo or Brittany. I could move on to Marseille from there.'

'Suits me.'

Gorman altered course a couple of points and Chavasse said, 'I'll go below and try to get some sleep.'

'Best thing to do. Could get a little rough in mid-Channel. The glass is falling. You'll find coffee in the big Thermos in the galley.'

Chavasse went below to the main saloon. He was tired – damned tired – which was hardly surprising. He found the coffee in the galley, poured himself a cup and returned to the saloon. He drank slowly, going over the situation point by point. There was nothing to be gained from a confrontation with Gorman just yet; that could come later.

Quite suddenly, his brain almost ceased to function. God, but he was tired. He stretched out on the padded seat and stared up at the bulkhead. The ribs in the roof seemed to undulate slowly, like ripples on the surface of a pond, and his mouth was strangely dry. It was only in the final moment of his plunge into darkness that it occurred to his bemused brain that something might have gone wrong.

He surfaced slowly, for the first few moments, aware only of existing. The saloon was in darkness, that much was obvious, and he was lying face-down on the padded seat. He tried to move, lost his balance and fell to the floor, which was hardly surprising considering that his wrists were securely lashed behind his back.

The *Mary Grant* was still moving, but as he tried to scramble to his feet, the engines were cut and she started to drift. There was a footstep on the companionway, the light was switched on, and Gorman appeared. He squatted so close that Chavasse was aware of the stale smell of sweat from his unwashed body.

'How are you then, matey?' Gorman patted his cheek.

'What's the game?' Chavasse demanded, staying with his role for the time being. 'I thought we had a deal.'

Gorman got up and opened the slim case, which stood on the table. He took out one of the packets of banknotes. 'This is the game, matey – the green stuff. I've always had a fellow-feeling for it. It makes me come out in goose-pimples all over. This little collection, I like so much that I can't bear to be separated from any part of it.'

'Okay,' Chavasse said. 'I won't give you any trouble. Just drop me off at the other end, that's all I ask.'

Gorman's laugh was something to be heard as he pulled him to his feet and pushed him towards the companionway. 'I'll drop you off all right, matey, make no mistake about that. Right into the deep end.'

It was cold on deck, rain drifting down through the yellow light. Chavasse turned to face him. Gorman picked up a length of rusty anchor chain, and Chavasse said calmly, 'Who taught you that little trick – Rossiter?'

It certainly brought Gorman to a stop. He glared at Chavasse, his eye rolling horribly, and when he spoke his voice was the merest whisper.

'Who are you? What is this?'

'It's no good, Gorman,' Chavasse told him flatly. 'My people know where I am. When I end up missing, you'll have some tall explaining to do.'

He had completely miscalculated his man. Gorman gave a cry of rage, and his arm went back to strike, the length of chain cracking out like a leather whip

It never landed. A hand emerged from the shadows and wrenched the chain from his grasp. Gorman spun round and Darcy Preston stepped into the light.

Gorman didn't mess about. His hand went into his pocket and came out clutching a revolver, but he made the mistake of firing too quickly. The bullet ploughed into the deckhouse and Darcy went headfirst into the sea.

Gorman peered into the dark waters and, behind him, Preston pulled himself over the rail, having swum under the keel. There was only one possible weapon, a long-handled gaff used for pulling in game fish, which hung on the side of the wheelhouse in a spring clip. As he pulled it free, the clip twanged musically and Gorman turned.

This time he went by the manual. His arm swung up in a straight line as he sighted along the barrel with his good eye. Chavasse went for him, shoulder down like a rugby forward, sending him staggering against the rail. The revolver discharged harmlessly, and as Gorman straightened, aiming again, Darcy lunged with the gaff, the point catching Gorman in the right armpit. He went over the rail backwards with a cry. By the time Chavasse got there, the dark waters had closed over his head.

'Hold out your hands,' Darcy ordered, and sliced through Chavasse's bonds with the edge of the razor-sharp gaff.

Chavasse turned, massaging his wrists to restore the circulation. 'Now that's what I call a timely intervention. Is it permissible to enquire where in the hell you sprang from?'

'Glad to oblige,' Darcy said. 'After you'd left, I thought about things for at least five minutes, then went downstairs to the garage and helped myself to your car. I left it at Hurn Airport and came the rest of the way by taxi. I was actually in Fixby before you.'

'Then what?'

'Oh, I hung around the boatyard awaiting events, as they say. I heard most of your conversation with Gorman, waited till you'd gone into the office, then came on board and hid in the chain locker.'

'You certainly took your own sweet time about showing up, or was that just your sense of the dramatic?'

'As a matter of fact, I fell asleep. Didn't wake up till Gorman started thumping around and making all that noise.'

Chavasse sighed. 'All right, what are you doing here?'

'It's quite simple. My brother was a criminal by every possible standard. He was a thief and a gangster, but he was good to me. If I said that I loved such a man, could you accept that?'

'Perfectly,' Chavasse told him gravely.

'He didn't deserve to die that way, Paul.

He deserved many things in this life, but not that. When the time comes, I am going to kill Leonard Rossiter personally. We Jamaicans are a religious people, a proud people. An eye for an eye, the Book says, no more, no less. I will have Rossiter's life then, for that is the just thing.'

Chavasse nodded soberly. 'I respect your feelings, I understand them, but between the thought and the deed is often a very wide gap, especially for a man like you. I can kill when I have to, quickly, expertly and without a second thought, because I'm a professional. Can you be that certain?'

'We'll have to see, won't we?'

'Fair enough. I'll get this thing moving, you dry yourself. We'll talk things over later.'

The Jamaican nodded and disappeared into the companionway. Chavasse went along the deck to the wheelhouse and started the engines. They made a fine satisfying growl and he pushed up the throttle and took the *Mary Grant* into the night with a burst of power.

*   *   *

'I always wanted to be a boxer,' Darcy said.

He leaned against the closed door of the wheelhouse, a blanket around his shoulders, a mug of tea in one hand, almost invisible in the darkness.

'What did Harvey have to say to that?'

Darcy chuckled. 'He argued in percentages and he certainly saw no percentage in that. He always said a good fighter was a hungry fighter and I was anything but hungry. Mind you, he indulged me up to a certain point. I had lessons from some of the best pro fighters in the game. He had an interest in a gym in Whitechapel.'

'What made you choose the law?'

'With my background? A hell of a lot of people found that one funny. On the other hand, I knew every crook in Soho, which came in useful when I started to practise.'

'You were constantly in demand?'

'Something like that. I cleared out after Harvey's trial because I realized I simply couldn't continue with the kind of double life I had been leading. Went out to Jamaica and started again. A good move. That's where I met my wife.'

'Time and chance,' Chavasse said.

'As I told your Mr Mallory, Harvey got a letter to me detailing what he intended to do. When he didn't turn up, friends notified me and I decided to follow in his footsteps. It seemed the logical thing.'

'Does your wife know?'

Darcy grinned. 'She thinks I'm in New York on legal business.' He emptied his mug and put it on the chart table. 'And what about you? How did you get into this kind of work?'

'Time and chance again.' Chavasse shrugged. 'I have a language kink. Soak them up like water into a sponge – no work in it at all. I was lecturing in a provincial university and finding it pretty boring, when a friend asked me to help him get his sister out of Czechoslovakia. It had a ring of adventure to it, so I gave it a go.'

'And succeeded?'

'Only just. I was in an Austrian hospital with a bullet in my leg when Mallory came to see me and offered me a job. That was twelve years ago.'

'Any regrets?'

'It's too late for regrets. Far too late. Now

let's come back to the present and discuss what we're going to do when we arrive at Ste-Denise.'

BRITTANY

11

They made such excellent time that it was only nine-thirty in the evening as they approached Ste-Denise. There was a small bay with a deep-water channel marked on the chart about a quarter of a mile to the east, and Chavasse decided to give it a try.

He couldn't have made a better choice. The bay was almost a complete circle, no more than a hundred yards in diameter and guarded by high cliffs which gave excellent cover from the sea. They dropped anchor and went below.

Chavasse put his leather business case on the table, opened it and tossed a couple of packets of francs across to Darcy. 'Half for you, half for me. Just in case.'

'You mean I'm getting paid, too?'

Darcy stowed the money away in an inside

pocket and Chavasse pressed a hidden catch and removed the false bottom of the case to reveal an interior compartment. Expertly packed away inside were a Smith & Wesson .38 Magnum revolver, a Walther PPK and a machine pistol.

Darcy whistled softly. 'What is this, Prohibition?'

'Nothing like being prepared.' Chavasse offered him the Smith & Wesson. 'Guaranteed not to jam. About the best man-stopper I know.' He dropped the Walther into his pocket, and replaced the false bottom in the case and stowed it away in a locker under the table. 'And now for the most interesting act of the evening.'

They rowed ashore in the fibreglass dinghy, beached it and scaled the cliffs by means of a narrow path. The sky was blue-black, and every star gleamed like white fire. There was no moon, yet a strange luminosity hung over everything, giving them a range of vision much greater than might have reasonably been expected under the circumstances. They made rapid progress through the scattered pines and soon came to a point from which they could look down into Ste-Denise.

There was a light here and there in the cottages and several in the downstairs windows of the Running Man.

'How do you intend to play this thing?' Darcy asked.

'By ear,' Chavasse told him. 'Strictly by ear. Let's see how many guests are at the party first.'

They went down the hill, scrambled across a fence and continued along a narrow country lane that soon brought them to the outskirts of the village. Here, the cottages were spaced well apart, each with its own small patch of ground under cultivation.

They passed the first house, and as they approached the second, Darcy placed a hand on Chavasse's sleeve. 'This is Mercier's place, or did you know?'

'Now that is interesting,' Chavasse said softly. 'Let's take a look.'

They moved across the cobbled yard and crouched by the window. Light reached out with gold fingers into the darkness, and through a gap in the curtain they could see Mercier sitting at the kitchen table, head bowed, a bottle of brandy and a tin mug in front of him.

'He doesn't look too happy,' Darcy breathed.

Chavasse nodded. 'Didn't you say something about his wife being an invalid?'

'That's right. Hasn't been out of bed in four years.'

'Then she's hardly likely to interfere if we're quiet. Knock on the door and then get out of sight. I'll handle him.'

Mercier was slow in responding and his footsteps dragged strangely across the stone floor. He opened the door and peered out, took a step forward, an anxious, expectant look on his face. Chavasse touched the barrel of the gun to his temple.

'One cry and you're a dead man, Mercier. Inside.'

Mercier moved backwards and Chavasse went after him, Preston close behind. He closed the door and Mercier looked from one to the other then laughed abruptly.

'This'll be a surprise for Jacaud. He told me you were both dead.'

'Where is he?'

'At the Running Man, entertaining his cronies from the village.'

'And Rossiter?'

Mercier shrugged. 'They came back this morning, just before noon, in the Englishman's boat.'

'That would be a man called Gorman?'

Mercier nodded. 'We've done a lot of business with him in the past. He's always in and out of here.'

'What about the authorities?'

'In these parts, monsieur?' Mercier shrugged. 'People mind their own business.'

Chavasse nodded. 'What happened to Rossiter and the others? Are they still at the Running Man?'

Mercier shook his head. 'Monsieur Rossiter left just after noon in the Renault. He took the Indian girl and the Chinese man with him. The Chinese was heavily bandaged about the face.'

'How did the girl look?'

'How would you expect her to look, monsieur? As beautiful as ever.'

'I don't mean that. Did she seem afraid at all – afraid of Rossiter?'

Mercier shook his head. 'On the contrary, monsieur. She looked at him as if he were . . .'

He seemed to have difficulty in finding the right word. 'As if he were . . .'

'God?' Darcy Preston suggested.

'Something like that, monsieur.'

He was strangely calm and unafraid and the answers came so readily. Chavasse let it go for the moment and carried on. 'Where did they go?'

'I haven't the slightest idea.'

'Come off it, Mercier, you can do better than that. Try Hellgate for a start, and Montefiore – don't tell me you've never heard of them?'

'Of course, monsieur. I have heard those two names on several occasions – snatches of conversation between Jacaud and Monsieur Rossiter, but that is all. To me they are names and nothing more.'

He was speaking the truth, Chavasse was certain, which didn't seem to make any kind of sense.

'What's happened, Mercier?' he said softly. 'You're a different man.'

Mercier turned without a word, walked to a door, opened it and stood to one side. 'Messieurs,' he said, with a small hopeless gesture.

Chavasse and Preston moved to join him and looked into a small, cluttered sitting room. A plain wooden coffin rested on the table, a candle at each end.

Chavasse closed the door gently. 'Your wife?'

Mercier nodded. 'Not a day without pain for four years, monsieur, and yet she never complained, although she knew there could be only one end. I tried everything. Big doctors from Brest, expensive medicines – all for nothing.'

'That must have cost money?'

Mercier nodded. 'How else do you think I came to be working for an animal like Jacaud? For my Nanette – only for Nanette. It was for her that I endured so much horror. For her and her alone that I kept my mouth shut.

'You're saying you went in fear of your life?'

Mercier shook his head. 'No, monsieur, in fear for my wife's life; of what that devil Rossiter might do to her.'

'He made such threats?'

'To keep me quiet. He had to, monsieur, particularly after a trip some weeks ago when I sailed on the *Leopard* as deckhand.'

'What happened then?'

Mercier hesitated, and Chavasse said, 'Let me tell you what happened after we left here last night. The *Leopard* went down in the Channel, did Jacaud tell you that?'

'He said there had been an accident. That the engine had exploded and that the rest of you had been killed.'

'He and Rossiter left us to drown, locked in the saloon,' Chavasse said. 'The woman and the old man died trying to swim ashore.'

Mercier looked genuinely shocked. 'My God, they are animals, not men. Why, only the other week, monsieur, on the occasion I was speaking of earlier, we were sighted off the English coast by a British torpedo-boat. We had only one passenger at the time – a special trip for some reason.' He turned to Darcy. 'A West Indian like you, monsieur.'

Preston's face had tightened and he looked ill. 'What happened?'

'Rossiter said we'd get seven years if we were caught with him aboard. He put him over the side, wrapped in chains – and he was still alive. Still alive. Sometimes in my dreams I can still see the look in his eyes when Rossiter put him over the rail.'

Darcy nodded blindly. 'And he told you he'd kill your wife if you didn't keep quiet.'

'That's right, monsieur.'

Darcy turned abruptly, wrenched open the door and went out. Mercier looked bewildered and Chavasse said quietly, 'His brother – his brother, Mercier. We've come to settle the account. Will you help us?'

Mercier took a reefer jacket from behind the door and pulled it on. 'Anything, monsieur.'

'Good. This is what you will do. Wait by the Running Man and watch the harbour. In a little while, you will see the *Mary Grant* come in. You know her?'

'Of course, monsieur, Gorman's boat.'

'You will enter The Running Man and tell Jacaud that Gorman has returned and is waiting urgently for him down at the jetty. Make sure that other people hear you tell him this.'

'And afterwards?'

'Do you have a boat of your own?'

Mercier nodded. 'An old whaleboat with a diesel engine.'

'Good – when we leave the harbour we will go to a bay called Panmarch. You know it?'

'As I know every inch of this coast.'

'We'll wait for you there.' Chavasse slapped him on the shoulder. 'We will fix him, our brave Jacaud, eh, Mercier?'

Mercier's eyes glowed with fire, the hatred of years boiling over, and they went out together.

There were perhaps a dozen fishermen in the bar when Mercier entered the Running Man, and Jacaud was holding court. They pressed round eagerly as he poured red wine from an earthenware jug, leaving a trail like blood across the counter while the old woman who worked for him looked on with a tight mouth.

'Free,' he roared. 'Everything on me. In the morning, I'll be away and you'll never see old Jacaud again.'

Mercier had difficulty forcing his way through to the bar, but when Jacaud noticed him, he greeted him effusively.

'Mercier, old friend, where have you been hiding?'

His speech was slurred and he gave every appearance of being drunk. Mercier was instantly suspicious, never having seen him the worse for liquor in his whole life.

'I've got a message for you,' he said loudly. 'From Monsieur Gorman.'

Several heads turned in interest and Jacaud frowned, instantly sober. 'Gorman? He is here?'

'At the jetty. He just came in on the *Mary Grant*.'

Jacaud put down the jug and nodded to the old woman. 'It's all yours.' He came round the bar and brushed past Mercier. 'Let's go.'

Outside, a slight wind moved in from the sea and stirred the pines. 'Did he say what he wanted? Is it trouble?'

Mercier shrugged. 'Why should he talk to me, Monsieur Jacaud, a person of no importance? He told me nothing.'

Jacaud glared at him in surprise, aware of a new belligerency in his tone, but there was no time to investigate now. At the end of the street, Mercier paused.

'I leave you here, monsieur.'

'You are going home?'

'That's right.'

Jacaud tried to inject a little friendliness into

his voice. 'I'll drop in later, if I may, after I've seen what Gorman wants. I'd like to talk things over with you now that I'm leaving.'

'As you wish, monsieur.'

Mercier faded into the night and Jacaud continued on his way, walking quickly, without even the slightest hint of drunkenness in his manner. If anything, he was worried, for he was not over-endowed with intelligence. Rossiter had left him strict instructions as to what he was to do and Gorman hadn't entered into them at all.

The *Mary Grant* waited at the jetty, her engines whispering quietly. He went down the ladder to the deck and paused uncertainly. There was a movement in the wheelhouse and he went towards it quickly.

'Gorman?' he demanded hoarsely.

He reached the door, and the heart in him seemed to stop beating, for the face that stared coldly at him from the darkness, disembodied in the light from the binnacle, was one which he had never expected to see again in this life.

Chavasse smiled gently. 'Come right in, Jacaud.'

Jacaud took a step back and the muzzle of a revolver touched him on the temple. He turned his head involuntarily and found himself looking straight at Darcy Preston.

Sweat sprang to his forehead, cold as death, and he started to shake, for what he was seeing simply could not be. He sagged against the wheelhouse door with a groan, and the *Mary Grant* left the jetty and moved out to sea.

By the time they had anchored in Panmarch Bay, Jacaud no longer believed in ghosts, only in miracles, and a miracle was something which could happen to anyone. His awe had been replaced by anger and he awaited his chance to strike. It came when Mercier arrived and tied up alongside in his old whaleboat. Preston went to catch the line he threw, leaving Chavasse in charge, who suddenly seemed to get careless. Jacaud grabbed for the gun he was holding; Chavasse, who had been anticipating just such a move, swayed to one side and clouted him over the head.

JACK HIGGINS

The blow would have dazed any other man, sending him to his knees for several minutes. Jacaud simply rolled on one shoulder, came to his feet and dived for the rail. Darcy managed to get a foot under him just in time and Jacaud went sprawling.

When he got to his feet, he found Preston taking off his jacket. 'Come on then, Jacaud,' he said. 'Let's see how good you are.'

'You black ape.'

Jacaud came in like a tornado, great arms flailing, hands reaching out to destroy, and proceeded to get the thrashing of his life as Darcy demolished him with a scientific exactitude that was awe-inspiring in its economy. The Jamaican in action was something to see, and hatred gave him an additional advantage.

Jacaud landed perhaps three or four punches, but everything else he threw only touched air. In return, he was subjected to a barrage of punches that were devastating in their effect, driving him to his knees again and again until a final right cross put him on his back.

He lay there sobbing for breath, and Darcy dropped to one knee beside him. 'And now,

Jacaud, you will answer some questions, quickly and accurately.'

Jacaud spat in his face.

Chavasse pulled Darcy up. 'Take a breather. Let me try.' He lit a cigarette. 'We all hate you here, Jacaud. The Jamaican, because you and Rossiter drowned his brother. Mercier, because you dragged him down into the filth with you. Me, because I don't like your smell. You're an animal – something from under a stone – and I'd no more hesitate to kill you than I would to step on a slug. Now that we know where we stand, we'll try again. Where has Rossiter gone?'

Jacaud's reply was coarse and to the point.

Chavasse stood up. 'On your feet.'

Jacaud hesitated and Mercier kicked him in the ribs. 'You heard the gentleman.'

Jacaud got up reluctantly and Chavasse tossed Darcy a coil of rope. 'Tie his wrists.'

Jacaud didn't bother to struggle. 'You can do what you like, you won't make me talk. I'll see you in hell first.'

He raved on for some time, but Chavasse ignored him and walked to the stern, where the swivel seats were fastened to the deck for big-game fishing and the hoist and pulley were rigged ready to haul in tuna or shark.

'Let's have him down here.'

Darcy pushed Jacaud forward, and Chavasse swung him around and looped his bonds over the hook on the end of the pulley line. 'Here, what is this?' Jacaud demanded.

Chavasse nodded to the other two. 'Haul away.'

As Preston and Mercier turned the winch handle between them, Jacaud's feet left the deck, and in a moment he was three feet up in the air. He started to struggle, kicking wildly, and Chavasse pushed the hoist out over the water. Jacaud hung there, cursing, and Chavasse tried again.

'Ready to talk, Jacaud?'

'To hell with you – to hell with all of you.'

Chavasse nodded, Darcy released the winch handle and Jacaud disappeared beneath the surface. Chavasse gave him a full minute, checking his watch carefully, then nodded and Darcy and Mercier cranked him in.

Jacaud hung just beyond the rail, chest heaving as he sobbed for breath. He started to cough, then vomited. Chavasse gave him a moment to collect himself.

'Hellgate, Jacaud, and Montefiore. I want to know about both of them.'

Jacaud cursed him, kicking out wildly. Chavasse turned and nodded, his face cold, and the winch creaked again.

This time he made it one minute and a half, and when Jacaud appeared there was hardly any movement at all. Chavasse swung him in, and after a while the great head lifted and the eyes opened.

'Hellgate,' he croaked. 'It's a house in the Camargue near a village called Chatillon. Monsieur Montefiore owns it.'

'And that's where Rossiter and the others have gone?' Jacaud nodded weakly. 'And Montefiore, is he there now?'

'I don't know. I've never met him. I only know what Rossiter has told me.'

'Why didn't you leave with the others?'

'Rossiter wanted me to take care of Mercier – he thought he knew too much and he wanted me to leave openly so that questions would not be asked. I only had a lease on the inn. It's up in a couple of months anyway, so I made it over to the old hag who works for me. I told everyone I was leaving for Corsica tomorrow. That I'd been left a farm by a distant relative.'

Chavasse nodded slowly. 'So, you were to kill Mercier?'

Jacaud started to cough, then gave a strange choking cry. His body heaved as if he was in pain and Mercier and Darcy lowered him to the deck quickly. Mercier dropped to his knees and put an ear against Jacaud's chest. When he looked up, his face was grave.

'He is dead, monsieur. His heart has given out.'

'Let's hope he told the truth then,' Chavasse said calmly. 'Get the ropes off him and put him in the saloon.'

He turned and Darcy grabbed him by the arm. 'Is that all you can say, for God's sake? We've just killed a man.'

'One way or the other, he was due for it,' Chavasse said. 'So cut out the hearts and flowers. I haven't got time.'

He pulled free and went into the wheelhouse. He was examining the chart when they joined him. 'I need a nice deep channel,' he said to Mercier. 'Deep enough for the *Mary Grant* to sink into without trace.'

Mercier sighed. 'A pity, monsieur. It's a beautiful boat.'

'She's still got to go,' Chavasse said. 'Where would you suggest?'

Mercier considered the chart for a moment or two, then jabbed a finger at a group of rocks marked as dangerous about six miles out.

'The Pinnacles, monsieur, they've taken plenty of ships in their time. They stick up from a trench a thousand feet deep. Anything that goes down there will stay down, believe me.'

Chavasse nodded. 'That's it, then. You lead the way in the whaler. I'll follow. Go with him, Darcy.'

'I'll stay with you.'

Chavasse shook his head. 'No point, this kind of job only needs one.'

'I said I'd stay.' Darcy's voice was bleak. 'What I say, I mean.'

He moved into the prow and stood there with his hands in his pockets, shoulders hunched.

'I don't think he is too happy, monsieur,' Mercier commented. 'Which surprises me. After all, they did as much to his own brother.'

'Which is exactly what's bothering him,' Chavasse said. 'He isn't a hunting animal, Mercier. Now let's get moving. We haven't much time.'

The Pinnacles were first observed as patches of white water in the distance. As the boats approached, the turbulence increased and Chavasse was aware of great plumes of spray that blossomed in the night.

The Pinnacles themselves were a scattered group of jagged rocks, in some cases permanently awash, and in others, twenty or thirty feet above the waves. When Mercier whistled sharply and waved, the agreed signal, Chavasse cut the engines and called to Darcy, who had been waiting by the forward hatch with a fire axe. Now he dropped inside and began to batter a series of holes in the prow. When he reappeared, she was already settling at that end and he was soaked to the skin.

Chavasse unfastened a cork lifebelt bearing the ship's name and tossed it overboard as Mercier came alongside.

'Lost at sea,' he said. 'Sunk with all hands. Nobody will ever see Jacaud again.'

'And Gorman?' Darcy asked. 'What about him?'

Chavasse shrugged. 'Believe it or not, but most people who take a dive into the Channel don't turn up again. Even if somebody does find what's left of him after a few weeks, it'll all fit neatly.'

'You have a naturally tidy mind,' Darcy said.

'Too complicated. I'm a professional, you're not. It's as simple as that.'

The whaleboat closed in and they scrambled aboard. Mercier took her round in a wide circle and they watched. The *Mary Grant* was well down by the head now, her stern lifting out of the water. When she went, she disappeared so quickly that if any one of them had closed his eyes momentarily, he would have missed it. The waters rolled over and Mercier opened the throttle and took the whaler away.

'And now what?' Darcy Preston demanded,

dropping down on one of the wide seats, shoulders hunched against the spray.

'We catch a train,' Chavasse said. 'A train for Marseille, if there is one, or is it still we?'

Darcy nodded slowly. 'I've gone too far now to step back. You needn't worry – I'll be behind you all the way.'

'Fair enough.' Chavasse turned to Mercier. 'Take us to some quiet spot on the coast as near to St-Brieuc as possible. Can you manage that?'

'Certainly, monsieur.'

Chavasse gave him a cigarette and held out a match in cupped hands. 'About Jacaud, Mercier, there could be questions.'

'Perhaps, monsieur, but I doubt it. He was to leave in the morning. Most people will think he left a little earlier. In any case, he was seen to go out in the *Mary Grant*, and where is the *Mary Grant* now? Perhaps in a few days that lifebelt will be found by a fishing boat or drift ashore somewhere, and perhaps not. Henri Jacaud never existed, monsieur.'

'And you? What will you do?'

'I will bury my wife,' Mercier said simply.

FRANCE
THE CAMARGUE

12

It was just before midnight when they reached St-Brieuc. By chance there was a train due out in fifteen minutes to Rennes, and Chavasse decided to take it rather than hang about.

At Rennes they had a delay of an hour and a half before the Marseille train and spent it in a café just outside the station. The Jamaican was still brooding and had little to say for himself. In the end, Chavasse had had enough.

'It's no good going on like this,' he said. 'Either we clear the air now or you drop out.'

'Wouldn't that be something of a problem?' Darcy said. 'I'm not even in this country officially.'

Chavasse shook his head. 'I can contact our Paris office. They'll get you out.'

Darcy looked genuinely troubled. 'I don't

know, Paul. When I first got the idea of following you, it seemed to make sense, and especially later when I heard what they'd done to Harvey. I was bitter and angry, I wanted revenge.'

'So?'

'That business with Gorman, I didn't mind that. After all, he was trying to kill you. There was nothing else I could do. But Jacaud.' He shook his head. 'That sticks in my throat.'

'If that's the way you feel, then you'd better leave,' Chavasse told him. 'Rossiter drowned your brother like a rat and without a qualm, he tried his hand at mass murder when the *Leopard* went down and didn't do so badly when you remember what happened to Mrs Campbell and old Hamid. He won't hesitate to see the both of us off the moment he claps eyes on us and realizes we're still in the land of the living. This isn't the Old Bailey or the Jamaican High Court. There's only one law here – kill or be killed – and I've had direct orders. Ho Tsen, Rossiter and Montefiore – they've all got to go.'

The Jamaican shook his head. 'You know, back there in the old days, living with Harvey in Soho, I met every kind of villain there was, but you – you're in a class of your own.'

'Which is why I've survived twelve years at this bloody game,' Chavasse said. 'Now are you in or out?'

'The way I see it, I don't really have much choice in the matter. I know that once I get anywhere near Rossiter, if I don't get him first, he'll get me. It goes against the grain, that's all, to accept that that's the way it is. I had years of it in Harvey's particular jungle – I don't suppose a psychologist would have much difficulty in working out why I took to the law.' He sighed heavily. 'But you can count on me, Paul. I won't let you down.'

'Good, now I know where I am I'll put a call through to our field agent in Marseille. I'd like him to be ready for us when we arrive in the morning.'

He stood up and Darcy said, 'This place, the Camargue – what is it exactly?'

'The delta area at the mouth of the Rhône,' Chavasse told him. 'About three hundred square miles of lagoons and waterways, marshes, white sand dunes and hot sun, though this isn't the best time of the year for that. It's famous for three things. White horses, fighting bulls and flamingoes. I was there as a boy twenty years ago and I've never forgotten it.'

'But what in the hell are they doing in a place like that?' Darcy demanded.

'That remains to be seen, doesn't it?' Chavasse said and went to make his phone call.

Jacob Malik was Polish by birth and had left the country of his origin for political reasons just before the outbreak of the Second World War. For a couple of years, he had worked for the Deuxième Bureau, the old French secret service organization which had died in 1940. He had spent the war working with the British Special Operations Executive, acting as a courier to French Resistance units. An adventurous career had been brought to an end by an FLN grenade through his hotel bedroom window during the Algerian troubles. He had retired to a small café on the Marseille waterfront with his Moorish wife and three children. He had been acting as Bureau agent in that city for six years and Chavasse had worked with him twice.

He was standing beside a Renault estate-car leaning heavily on his walking stick when they emerged from the station, a thin, elegant-looking man with a spiked moustache who carried his sixty years well.

He limped towards them and greeted Chavasse with enthusiasm. 'My dear Paul, how wonderful to see you. How goes it?'

'Excellent.' Chavasse took his hand warmly. 'And Nerida and your family?'

'Blooming. She still misses Algiers, but we could never go back. I wouldn't last a week. They have long memories, those people.'

Chavasse introduced him to Darcy and they all got into the Renault and drove away. It was warm and rather sultry, the sun hidden from view by heavy grey clouds, and yet there was that intense light common to Marseille, dazzling to the eyes.

'What have you arranged?' Chavasse asked.

'I gave the whole thing a great deal of thought after your phone call,' Malik said. 'At exactly four a.m. I hit upon an idea of some genius, though I say this with all due modesty. To get into the Camargue presents no problem. To stay without being observed is impossible.'

'In three hundred square miles of lagoon and marsh?' Chavasse said. 'I don't follow.'

'Oh, the population is small enough, mainly wildflowers and a few cowboys who tend the young bulls and the horses which run wild in all parts of the area. It is because of the sparseness of the population that it is difficult for outsiders to enter without it being known. What you need is a legitimate reason for being there, a reason which anyone who sees you will accept.'

'And you've found it?'

'Birdwatching,' Malik said simply.

Darcy Preston laughed out loud. 'He can't be serious.'

'But I am.' Malik looked slightly injured. 'The Camargue is famous for its wild birds, particularly its colony of flamingoes. People come to study them from all over Europe.'

'You know, I think you might actually have something there,' Chavasse said.

'More than that, my dear Paul, I have the

equipment to go with it. A small cabin-cruiser and all the extras I could think of. A rubber boat, shooting jackets and waders, binoculars, a decent camera. I checked with S2 in London and got the go-ahead. It seemed pointless to waste time.'

'Marvellous.' Chavasse was aware of a sudden irrational affection for him and clapped him on the shoulder. 'Truly marvellous.'

'No need to overdo it, Paul. For this kind of exercise I get a handsome fee – double if I assist in the field.'

'Do you want to?'

'I know the Camargue and you don't, so it would seem sensible.' He smiled. 'And you really have no idea how boring life is these days. A little action would definitely be good for my soul.'

'That's settled then.' Chavasse turned to Darcy, who was sitting in the rear. 'Nothing like some organization.'

'Oh, I'm impressed,' Darcy said. 'I'd be even more so if someone could remember to fill my belly within the next couple of hours. It's contracted so much it's beginning to hurt.'

'That, too, I have arranged, monsieur,' Malik said. 'My café is a stone's throw from the harbour. There my wife will reluctantly provide you with bouillabaisse, simply because it's the local speciality, but if you have sense, you will choose her stuffed mutton and rice and earn her eternal friendship.'

'Lead on, that's all I ask,' Darcy said, and Malik swung the Renault from one line of traffic to the next, narrowly missing a bus, and turned into a narrow street leading down to the harbour.

The stuffed mutton and fried rice was everything Malik had promised; after eating, they drove down to the old harbour, parked the Renault and walked along a stone jetty. There were boats of all shapes and sizes riding at anchor, and scores of dinghies and tenders of every description were tied close to the jetty. They went down the steps and Malik hauled in a six-man inflatable.

Chavasse did the rowing and, under orders, threaded his way through the crowded harbour until they fetched up alongside a twenty-foot fibreglass cabin-cruiser powered by an outboard motor. She was named *L'Alouette* and was painted white with scarlet trim. Darcy climbed aboard, then turned to give Malik a hand. Chavasse followed, after tying up the tender.

The cabin was small, the two padded side-benches making up into beds at night. The only other accommodation was a lavatory and a small galley.

Malik sat down with a sigh, produced a thin black cheroot and lit it. 'And now to business. You'll find a map in that locker, Paul, as well as a false bottom, under which are a couple of machine pistols and half-a-dozen grenades. It seemed like a good idea.'

The map unfolded to show the Camargue in detail; not only the several mouths of the Rhône, but every lagoon, every sandbank, every waterway.

'You can't go too much by this,' Malik said. 'The action of the tide, and the current from the river combine pretty forcefully. A sand-bank can be there one day and gone the next, and some of the waterways can silt up just as quickly. We shouldn't have too much trouble, though. *L'Alouette* only draws two or three feet.'

'And Hellgate? Have you managed to pinpoint it on the map?' Darcy asked.

'Indeed I have. See, just a little on the Marseille side of the Pointe du Nord. Three or four miles inland is the village of Chatillon. Hellgate is marked there, a couple of miles northeast of the village.'

Chavasse found it at once, an island in a lagoon that was shaped like a half-moon. 'Have you managed to find out anything of the place or Montefiore?'

'Naturally, I've been mainly restricted to Marseille because of the time element, but I've managed to produce some useful information. The house is about seventy years old. Built in the nineties by a Russian novelist called Kurbsky who didn't like the Czar and made it obvious. His novels had quite a vogue at the time in America and Europe generally, and he became a wealthy man. He came across the Camargue on a visit to a bull farm in the area and decided to stay. He had the house built where it was because he had an obsession with privacy. It's a wooden building and very Russian in style.'

'What happened to him?'

'He returned home after the Revolution – a grave error. He didn't like Lenin any more than he did the Czar, only this time he couldn't get out. He died in 1925, or was killed off. None of this required any genius, by the way. There is an excellent library in Marseille. I had a friend in the provincial land records office telephone through to Arles to see who owns the place now. It was used as a base by German troops during the war. Afterwards, it was empty until four years ago, when it was purchased by someone named Leduc.'

'Leduc?' Chavasse frowned.

'That was the name on the register.'

Chavasse nodded slowly. 'All right, I'd better fill you in on the details, then you know where you stand.'

When he had finished, Malik looked thought-ful. 'A strange business. This man Rossiter, for example. On the one hand, a bungling amateur who leaves himself wide open. On the other, a ruthless, cold-blooded killer without the slightest scruples.'

'And Ho Tsen?'

'Nasty – very nasty. What's a real pro doing mixed up with people like that?'

'That's what we've got to try and find out,' Chavasse said. 'Although I've got my own ideas on that subject. You know how difficult it is for the Chinese where espionage is concerned. The Russians don't have anything like the same trouble because they can pass off their own people as nationals of most other countries. The Chinese obviously can't do that, which explains why they're willing to use a man like Rossiter, amateur or no amateur. Mind you, that still doesn't explain how someone like Montefiore fits in.'

Malik nodded. 'And what happens afterwards?'

'Elimination – total and absolute.'

'And the girl,' Darcy put in. 'What about her?'

'If we can, we get her out.'

'But only if we can?'

'Exactly. Now let's get going. With most of the afternoon left, we can get a hell of a lot done before nightfall. Agreed, Jacob?'

Malik nodded. 'I'll take her out of the harbour. I know what I'm doing. With this engine, we should make it in a little over three hours, allowing for the weather of course, which I must say doesn't look too good.'

He went out on deck and Chavasse followed him. He stood at the rail, looking back at Marseille, as they moved out to sea. An old city – they had all been here. Phoenician, Greek, Roman. Beyond Cap Croisette, the sky was dark and ominous, and as they lifted to meet the swell from the open sea, rain spotted the deck in great heavy drops.

From the sea, the Camargue was a line of sand dunes drifting into the distance, and as they moved in, great banks of reeds and marsh grass lifted out of the water as if to greet them. With them came the heavy, pungent odour of the marshes, compounded of salt and rotting vegetation and black gaseous mud, a smell that hinted at a darker, more primeval world, a place that time had bypassed.

The bad weather had not developed as expected and the rain had held off except for intermittent showers. As they moved in towards the land, Malik once more took the wheel and Chavasse and Darcy stood at the rail.

Half-a-dozen white horses stood on a sand-bank and watched them as they went by, and beyond, hundreds of flamingoes paced through the shallows, setting the air aflame with the glory of their plumage.

'What happens now, Paul?' Malik asked. 'Do we stop at the village or keep going?'

'No harm in calling in,' Chavasse said. 'You can visit the local shop, see what you can find out. Darcy and I had better stay in the background, just in case.'

'All right,' Malik nodded. 'To pass *through* without stopping would probably engender an unhealthy interest about our identity and business anyway. Small communities are the same the world over.'

And Chatillon was certainly that: two primitive wooden jetties standing just out of the water, an assortment of small boats and a couple of dozen houses. Malik took *L'Alouette* to the extreme end of one of the jetties and Chavasse tied up. Darcy stayed below.

The Pole limped away and Chavasse lounged in the stern, fiddling with a fishing rod, part of the general equipment Malik had provided. There didn't seem to be a great deal of activity on shore. About fifty yards away a man worked on a boat, and two old men sat on the other jetty mending wildfowling nets.

Malik returned in fifteen minutes carrying a paper bag loaded with various provisions. 'Typical French provincials,' he said, as Chavasse helped him over the rail. 'Suspicious as hell of all strangers, but wanting to know every last detail of your business.'

'And what did you tell them?'

'That I was from Marseille with a friend to do some birdwatching and a little fishing. As I told you before, they get people like that in here all the time.'

'And they accepted your story?'

'Completely. It was an old woman in her seventies and her idiot son. I got out the map and asked her where there was a good place to tie up for the night, which gave me an excuse to put my finger on Hellgate amongst other places.'

'What was her reaction?'

'Nothing very exciting. It's private. Nice people, but they don't encourage visitors.'

'Fair enough,' Chavasse said. 'Let's get moving. It'll be dark soon.'

Thunder rumbled menacingly in the distance and Malik started the outboard as Chavasse cast off. Darcy didn't come on deck until they were well away from the village, moving along a narrow channel, reeds pressing in on either hand.

Chavasse scrambled up on top of the cabin and opened the map. At first it was relatively simple to chart a course, but it became progressively more difficult the deeper into the marshes they went.

They had deliberately avoided staying with the principal waterway that gave direct access to Hellgate and kept to the northeast, so that in the end, they were approaching it from the rear.

It was almost dark when they turned into a

small lagoon, and Chavasse called softly, 'Okay, we'll make this do.'

Malik cut the motor and Darcy heaved the anchor over the side into eight or nine feet of water. Suddenly, it was quiet, except for the croaking of bullfrogs and the occasional stirring of a bird in the thickets.

'How far?' Darcy asked.

'Quarter of a mile, no more,' Chavasse said. 'We'll go on in the rubber boat at first light and take a look at the place.'

'An interesting prospect,' Malik said.

'Oh, it should be that, all right.'

Above them thunder cracked the sky wide open and as darkness fell, rain fell with it in a sudden drenching downpour that sent them running to the shelter of the cabin.

Hellgate

13

It was a cold grey world that Chavasse stepped into when he went on deck at four-thirty the following morning. Rain hammered into the waters of the marsh with a thousand voices and yet life stirred out there in the gloom. Birds called and wild geese lifted into the rain.

He was wearing waterproof nylon waders, a hooded anorak, and a pair of binoculars hung around his neck. Darcy Preston joined him, wearing a similar outfit, and was followed by Malik, who sheltered under a large black umbrella.

'The last place God made.' The Pole shuddered. 'I'd forgotten there was such a time of day.'

'Good for the soul, Jacob.' Chavasse hauled

in the dinghy. 'We shouldn't be long – a couple of hours at the most. I just want to size things up, that's all.'

'Just make sure you know how to find your way back,' Malik said. 'It's not too easy in a place like this.'

Darcy Preston took the oars and pulled away and in a few moments *L'Alouette* had faded into the murk. Chavasse used the map and compass and charted a course for Hellgate that took them in a straight line through mud and reeds and narrow waterways, penetrating deeper and deeper into a lost world.

'This is how it must have seemed at the beginning of time,' Darcy said. 'Nothing's changed.'

There was a rustle in the reeds on their left; they parted, and a young bull ploughed through. He stopped in the shallows and watched them suspiciously.

'Just keep going,' Chavasse said. 'That's a fighting bull with a pedigree as long as your arm. They don't take kindly to strangers.'

Darcy pulled harder and the bull faded from view. 'I certainly wouldn't like to be on foot with one of those things on my tail,' he said.

'What in the name of good sense are they doing running around loose?'

'This is where they raise them. This is bull country, Darcy. They just about worship the damn things. We're the interlopers, not the bulls.'

They emerged into a large lagoon and the towers of the house loomed out of the mist fifty yards away. Chavasse made a quick gesture and Darcy pulled into the shelter of the reeds on the right. There was a patch of high ground beyond and they beached the dinghy and got out. Chavasse crouched and focused the binoculars.

As Malik had said, the house was very Russian in style and constructed of wood, with a four-storey tower at each end and a veranda at the front. The whole was surrounded by pine trees which had probably been specially planted when it was first built, but what had originally been the garden was now an overgrown jungle.

There was something curiously false about the place. It was too much like the real thing – a film set for a Hollywood version of a Chekhov play.

Chavasse couldn't see the landing stage, which presumably was on the other side. From an approach point of view, the house couldn't have had a better strategic situation. The lagoon was crescent-shaped and about a hundred yards wide and two hundred long. There was no possibility of an approach under cover during daylight.

He passed the binoculars to Darcy. 'What do you think?'

The Jamaican had a look and shook his head. 'I don't see how anyone could get any closer during daylight without being spotted.'

At that moment a dog barked and two men came running round the corner of the house. They jumped into view when Chavasse focused the binoculars – two Chinese, each clutching an assault rifle. The dog joined them a moment later, an Alsatian; it ran backwards and forwards, rooting in the undergrowth.

'I don't know what it's looking for, but it won't get much of a scent in this rain, that's for certain,' Darcy said.

'I wouldn't be too sure.' Chavasse watched intently through the binoculars. 'It takes a lot to fool a German Shepherd.'

There was a sudden commotion over on the right, a heavy splashing as something forced its way through the reeds. At first Chavasse thought it might be another bull, but he pulled out the Walther PPK just in case. There was a groan of pain, then a splash followed by a cry for help in French.

Chavasse and Darcy pushed through the reeds and emerged on the other side of the sandbank, as a head broke the water in the channel beyond and a hand clutched feebly at air.

Chavasse plunged forward, the water reaching to his chest, and grabbed for the outstretched hand as the man went under again. Their fingers met and he went back slowly, the thick black bottom mud reluctant to let him go.

Darcy gave him a hand and they laid him on his back in the rain, a thin, grey-haired emaciated man of seventy or so. He wore pyjama trousers and a sleeveless vest and his body was blue with cold. His eyes rolled wildly, he gibbered with fear, then passed out.

'Poor devil.' Chavasse raised one stick-like arm. 'Ever seen anything like that before?'

Darcy examined the multiple tiny scars and

nodded soberly. 'A heroin addict by the look of it, and pretty far gone. I wonder who he is?'

Chavasse started to take off his anorak. 'Last time I saw him was in a photo Mallory showed me, though I must say he was looking considerably healthier.'

'Montefiore?' Darcy said blankly.

'In person.' Chavasse raised the unconscious man, slipped the anorak down over his head and picked him up. 'Now let's get out of here before he dies on us.'

On the return journey, Chavasse sat in the stern, Enrico Montefiore cradled in his arms. He was in a bad way, there was little doubt of that, and moaned restlessly, occasionally crying out, and yet never once did he regain consciousness.

There was the sound of the Alsatian barking uncomfortably close somewhere and then the harsh chatter of an outboard motor shattered the morning quiet.

Chavasse sat with the compass in his free hand, relaying precise instructions to Darcy, who was putting his back into the rowing. At one point they stuck in a particularly thick patch of reeds and he eased Montefiore to the floor and went over the side to push.

It was cold – bitterly cold, for by this time the water had managed to get inside his nylon waders, and without his anorak the upper part of his body had no protection at all.

The dog barked monotonously, much nearer now, the sound of the outboard motor coming in relentlessly. Chavasse pushed hard and scrambled aboard as the dinghy moved again.

A few moments later, they broke from cover and drifted into clear water and *L'Alouette* loomed out of the mist.

'Jacob!' Chavasse called and then, as they moved closer, saw that Malik was sitting in the stern, his black umbrella shielding him from the rain.

The dinghy bumped gently against the side of *L'Alouette*. Chavasse stood up and looked straight into Malik's face beneath the black umbrella, which he now realized was lashed to the stern rail with a length of rope. Malik's eyes were fixed in death, his left ear was missing and there was a small blue hole just above the bridge of his nose.

'Good morning, Chavasse, welcome aboard.'

Rossiter moved out of the cabin, smiling pleasantly as if really delighted to be meeting him again.

Colonel Ho Tsen stood in the background, one side of his face covered in surgical tape. He was holding an AK assault rife and looked grim and implacable, every inch the professional.

'One of my men took a photo of you as you came in last night,' Rossiter said. 'We always like to check on new arrivals in this part of the Camargue. You may imagine my surprise when he showed me the print.'

'You took your time getting here,' Chavasse said. 'You're not too efficient.'

'This wretched weather, old man. We got here just after you left. So we decided to wait. Actually, our time wasn't wasted. Your friend was quite forthcoming after the colonel had a few words with him. Oh, yes, I now realize that you know all about us, Chavasse. On the other hand, we know all about you.'

'How nice for you. And what about Montefiore?'

'A problem. He's done this before, which simply isn't good enough. I must have a word with the person who was supposed to be looking after him.'

He went to the door, produced a whistle and blew three blasts. As he turned, Darcy Preston said harshly, 'Who put him on heroin – you?'

'It keeps him amenable most of the time,' Rossiter said.

'As a living vegetable. Why don't you let him die?'

'But who on earth would sign all the cheques?' Rossiter demanded in a half-humorous manner, as if trying to be reasonable about the whole thing.

Which explained a great deal. And then several things happened at once. Montefiore started to groan, thrashed his limbs wildly and sat up, and a dinghy powered by an outboard motor appeared from the mist carrying two Chinese men and the Alsatian.

The two men came aboard, leaving the dog in the dinghy. Ho Tsen spoke sharply to one of them in Chinese, so rapidly that Chavasse could not hear what was said. The man replied in a low voice, eyes down and Ho Tsen slapped him across the face.

'Have they got a dose with them?' Rossiter demanded in Chinese.

One of the men put down his assault rifle and produced a small leather case. He opened it, took out a hypodermic and a glass ampoule. Rossiter filled the hypo and nodded to the Chinese who held Montefiore down by the shoulders. Rossiter gave him the injection.

'That should hold him.'

Montefiore stopped struggling and went very still, all tenseness leaving him, and then a strange thing happened. His eyes opened and he looked up at Rossiter and smiled.

'Father Leonard?' he said. 'Father Leonard, is that you?'

And smiling, the breath went out of him in a quiet sigh and his head slipped to one side.

There was a sudden silence. Rossiter gently

touched his face. It was Ho Tsen who moved first. He pushed Rossiter out of the way and shook Montefiore roughly. Then he turned, his eyes angry.

'He's dead – do you understand? You've killed him. I warned you – I told you you were giving him too much.' He struck out at Rossiter, sending him back against the other bunk. 'One error after another. You'll have a lot to answer for when we reach Tirana.'

For a moment, all attention was focused on the Englishman. Chavasse sent the other Chinese staggering, turned and jumped for the door. He went over the rail, surfaced and struck out for the shelter of the reeds.

He threw a quick glance over his shoulder and saw Darcy struggling with the two Chinese at the rail. Ho Tsen appeared, clubbed the Jamaican with the butt of his rifle and raised it to his shoulder. As he started to fire, Chavasse went under the water and swam for the reeds.

Safely in their shelter, he turned and looked back. The two Chinese were already in the dinghy and casting off; the dog was howling like a wolf. Chavasse started to push through the reeds, half-swimming, half-wading. And then another sound rent the morning: the motor of *L'Alouette* as she got underway.

He came to a waterway so deep that his feet failed to touch bottom. He swam across to a grey-green wall of palm grass and forced his way through. He paused after a few minutes, treading water. The sound of *L'Alouette* was fading. Presumably it was heading for Hellgate, but the outboard motor of the dinghy was popping away in the vicinity and the Alsatian's mournful howl echoed eerily through the rain like a voice from the grave.

Chavasse started to swim again, pushing his way through the reeds; suddenly the sound of the outboard motor ceased abruptly and the dog stopped barking. Which wasn't good, whichever way you looked at it, because now he didn't have the slightest idea where they were.

His feet touched bottom, and he ploughed through thick black mud and moved out of reeds and grass to relatively firm ground. The compass still hung around his neck, enabling him to check his direction, and he concentrated hard, trying to recapture a pictorial image of the map. It was an old trick and surprisingly effective. The island would be the only one of any size in the vicinity of *L'Alouette*'s anchorage, a couple of hundred yards in diameter and a quarter of a mile southwest of Hellgate.

He started to run, then came to a dead stop as a bull loomed out of the mist to confront him. The animal held its head high and stared him right in the eye. Steam drifted from its nostrils and Chavasse backed away slowly. There was a movement to his right as another bull appeared like a dark shadow, flanks glistening. It pawed the ground nervously, its head dipped, the great curving horns gleaming viciously, and then another appeared beyond the first and yet another, six or seven of the great beasts in all, fighting bulls reared for their courage and heart, bred to fight in the ring.

He took a deep breath and walked through them very slowly, passing so close between two of the outer circle that he could have reached out and touched them. He kept on going, stumbling through tussocks of marsh grass, and emerged on a sandy shore. There was a sharp cry, followed by two shots close together, and sand fountained into the air on his right.

The dinghy drifted out of the mist perhaps twenty yards away. In a single frozen moment of time he saw clearly that the Alsatian was muzzled, but not for long. The AK assault rifle cracked again, and as Chavasse turned to run, the Alsatian took to the water.

He didn't have long – a minute or a minute and a half at the most before it ran him down. He tugged feverishly at his belt as he stumbled on. There was a technique for handling big dogs, but its successful application depended entirely on keeping calm and having a hell of a lot of luck in the first few seconds of attack.

The belt came free; he looped it around each hand, then turned and waited, holding his hands straight out in front of him, the belt taut.

The Alsatian came out of the mist on the run and skidded briefly to a halt. In almost the same moment, it moved in, mouth wide. Chavasse pushed the belt at it and the old trick worked like a charm. The Alsatian grabbed at it, teeth tearing at the leather. Chavasse jerked with all his strength, bringing the dog up on its hind legs and kicked it savagely in the loins.

The Alsatian rolled over and he kicked it again in the ribs and the head. It howled terribly, writhing in the mud, and he turned and moved on as the two Chinese arrived.

Another shot followed him, and from somewhere near at hand there was a roar of pain. *The bulls*. In the heat of the moment he had forgotten about the bulls. There was a sudden trampling and one of them appeared, blood streaming from a wound in the shoulder.

Chavasse dived for the shelter of a clump of reeds and dropped on his face as heavy bodies crashed through the mud. There was a cry of dismay, a shot was fired and someone screamed. When he raised his head, he saw an old bull lurch out of the rain, one of the Chinese hanging across his head, impaled on the right horn. The bull shook the man free and started to trample him.

There were two more shots somewhere in the mist and then a terrible cry. Chavasse had heard enough. He moved out of the reeds quickly and took to the water. A few moments later he reached another patch of dry land, checked his compass and started to move southwest towards Hellgate.

It took him the best part of an hour to reach the vantage point from which he and Darcy had viewed the house that morning. He crouched in the reeds and peered across the lagoon. If anything, the mist had thickened and everything was indistinct, ghostlike, more than ever like a sad Russian landscape.

By now *L'Alouette* would be tied up at the landing stage on the other side of the island at the rear of the house and if anything was to be done, it would have to be from here.

To his left, reeds marched out into the grey water, providing plenty of cover for perhaps half of the distance. The final approach would be in the open – no other way.

He was still wearing the nylon waders Malik had provided, and now he sat down and pulled them off. Underneath he was wearing a pair of trousers so wet that they clung to him like a second skin. He moved round towards the line of reeds and waded into the water, crouching low. For the first time since his jump for freedom on *L'Alouette*, he felt cold – really cold – and shivered uncontrollably as the water rose higher. And then his feet lost touch with the bottom and he started to swim.

He paused at the extreme end of the reeds and trod water. There was about fifty yards of clear water left to cover. He took a couple of deep breaths, sank under the surface and started to swim. When he sounded for air, he was halfway there: He surfaced as gently as possible, turned on his back to rest for a brief moment, then went under again.

In a very short time, his body scraped the black mud of the bottom as he neared the island. He came to the surface and floundered ashore into the shelter of a line of bushes.

He crouched there in the rain, sobbing for breath, then got to his feet and moved on cautiously through the derelict garden to the house. There was no sound, not a sign of life – nothing, and a strange kind of panic touched him. What if they had left? What if Rossiter had decided to get out while the going was good? And then Famia Nadeem appeared at the end of the overgrown path he was following.

She wore rubber boots to the knees and an old naval duffel coat, the hood pulled up. She was the same and yet not the same, in some strange way a different person. She walked on, hands thrust into the pockets of her coat, face serious. Chavasse waited till she was abreast of him, then reached out from the bushes and touched her shoulder.

Her expression was something to see. The eyes widened, the mouth opened as if she would cry out, and then she took a deep shuddering breath.

'I couldn't believe it when Rossiter said you were alive.'

'He's here? You've seen him?'

She nodded. 'They came back in the other boat about an hour ago with Mr Jones, though he isn't Mr Jones any more, is he?'

Chavasse put a hand on her shoulder. 'How bad has it been?'

'Bad?' She seemed almost surprised. 'That's

a relative term, I guess. But we mustn't stand here talking like this. You'll get pneumonia. Through those trees is a derelict summerhouse. Wait there. I'll bring some dry clothes, and then we'll decide what's to be done.'

She faded like a ghost and he stood watching her through the quiet rain, conscious of the stillness, drained of all strength. God knew what Rossiter had done to her, but she had been used harshly, must have been for such a profound change to have occurred so quickly.

The summerhouse reminded him of childhood. The roof leaked and half the floorboards were missing and he slumped down against the wall underneath the gaping window. He used to play in just such a place a thousand years ago.

He closed his eyes, tiredness flooding over him, and a board creaked. When he looked up, Rossiter stood in the doorway, Famia at his side.

Her face was calm, completely impassive, pure as a painting of a medieval Madonna.

14

The cellar into which two more Chinese guards pushed him was so dark that he had to pause for a couple of moments after the door was closed, waiting for his eyes to become accustomed to the gloom.

'Darcy, are you there?' he called softly.

'Over here, Paul.' There was a movement in the darkness and Chavasse reached out.

'What happened when I jumped the boat? Are you all right?'

'A knock on the head, that's all. What about you? I thought you'd be long gone.'

Chavasse told him. When he had finished, the Jamaican sighed. 'He certainly must have got through to that girl.'

Chavasse nodded. 'It doesn't make sense. She knows what happened on the *Leopard*.

How can she possibly believe anything he says?'

'There could be a very simple explanation,' Darcy pointed out.

'She's fallen in love with him, you mean?'

'Could be more than that. Might be one of these strong sexual attractions that some people have for each other. It's possible.'

'I suppose so. Immaterial now, anyway.' Chavasse moved through the darkness, hand outstretched until he touched the wall. 'Have you explored?'

'Not really. I was still unconscious when they first dumped me in here.'

Chavasse moved along the wall, feeling his way cautiously. He touched some kind of flat board, felt for the edge and pulled. It came away with a splintering crash and light flooded in.

The window was barred, the glass long since disappeared. It was at ground level and the view was confined to a section of what had once been the lawn stretching down to the landing stage which Chavasse had been unable to see from the other side of the island.

The landing stage had definitely seen better

days and half of it had decayed into the lagoon. The rest was occupied by a forty-foot sea-going launch which had obviously once been a motor torpedo-boat, and *L'Alouette*.

Four men passed by, carrying boxes between them, and went towards the launch. They certainly weren't Chinese, and Chavasse strained forward and managed to catch the odd word as they passed by.

'Albanian,' he whispered to Darcy. 'Which makes sense. Remember the incident on *L'Alouette* when Ho Tsen took a swing at Rossiter? He told him he'd have a lot to answer for when they reached Tirana.'

'The only European Communist nation to ally itself with Red China rather than Russia. It certainly explains a great deal.'

The men returned from the launch. A few minutes later they reappeared, carrying a couple of heavy travelling trunks. 'Looks as if somebody is moving house,' Darcy commented.

Chavasse nodded. 'Destination Albania. They've got to get out, now that we've been nosing around. They've no guarantee that others won't follow.'

'But why keep us in one piece?' Darcy said. 'I wouldn't have thought they'd want excess baggage.'

'But we aren't. I've had dealings with the Albanians before, and the Chinese. They'd love to have me back. And you might be useful, too. They can't tell until they've squeezed you dry.'

The bolt rattled in the door, it opened and the two Chinese appeared. One of them held a machine pistol threateningly, the other came forward, grabbed Chavasse and pushed him roughly outside. They locked the door and shoved him along the corridor.

They passed through a large entrance hall, mounted a flight of uncarpeted stairs and knocked on the first door. It was opened, after a slight delay, by Rossiter who was wearing a dressing-gown. He looked as if he had just pulled it on and was certainly naked to the waist. He tightened the cord and nodded.

'Bring him in.'

Beyond him another door stood open and Chavasse caught a glimpse of a bed, the covers ruffled and Famia stepping into her skirt in front of a mirror. Rossiter closed the door and turned.

'You do keep popping up, don't you? Of course, now we know what you are, it isn't really surprising.'

'What's happened to the man from Peking?' Chavasse asked. 'Doesn't he want to put his two cents' worth in?'

'Indeed he does, but at the moment he's busy packing. Thanks to you and your friend, we're obviously going to have to leave in something of a hurry.'

'For Albania.'

Rossiter smiled. 'You really are on the ball. They'll love you in Tirana.'

'And all points east?'

'Naturally.' Rossiter produced a cigarette case and offered him one. 'A friendly warning. The colonel will want a few words with you when he arrives. Don't get awkward. You saw what he did to your friend. He only asked him once, then started carving. Your man talked fifteen to the dozen when he had one ear gone. I would have thought you could have done better than him.'

'He was an old man,' Chavasse said. 'Trying to make a little extra money. There was no need to do that to him.'

Rossiter shrugged. 'All over the world, thousands of people die every day. You friend Malik was just one more. If his death helps our cause, then he lived and died to some purpose.'

'Word perfect,' Chavasse said. 'They must have done a good job on you back there at Nom Bek.'

'You just don't understand – your kind never does.' Rossiter was grave and serious. 'I was like you once, Chavasse, until I was helped to find a new answer, a truer answer, a new meaning for life.'

'So now it's all right to kill people, old men and women?'

'For the cause, don't you see that? What's one life more or less – mine or yours? We're all expendable. How many men have you killed in your career? Ten? Twenty?'

'I don't notch my gun, if that's what you mean,' Chavasse said, feeling strangely uneasy.

'Have you ever killed a woman?'

Chavasse's mouth went dry, and for a brief moment, a face floated to the surface, the face of a woman he would have preferred to forget.

Rossiter smiled, the strange, saintly face

touched with something very close to compassion. 'I thought so. The difference between us is only in kind. The first and most important lesson to learn is that it isn't what we do that is so important as why we do it. I serve a cause – freedom for every man, justice, equality. Can you say as much? What do you defend, Chavasse? Imperialism, capitalism, the Church, decay everywhere, the people crushed and strangled, unable to breathe. God, when I think of the years I spent serving corruption.'

'With all its faults I'd rather have my way than yours. How many have the Chinese butchered in Tibet in the last five years? Half a million, give or take a few, all for the sake of the cause.'

Rossiter looked slightly exasperated. 'You just don't see, do you? No one matters – no person or persons. We're working for tomorrow, Chavasse, not today.'

Which, significantly, was the exact opposite of the teachings of the creed which he had been raised and educated to serve. Chavasse knew now that he really was wasting his time, but kept probing.

'So anything goes, even feeding poor old Montefiore heroin?'

'I first met Enrico Montefiore when I returned to Europe after the Korean War was over. My superiors had sent me to Vienna because they had decided that I was in need of psychiatric treatment to overcome the effects of what they were pleased to call Chinese brainwashing. Montefiore had been on drugs for years. One evening we received a call from a private sanatorium where he was a patient. He was extremely ill, and thought he needed a confessor.'

'And you were sent?'

Rossiter nodded. 'The start of a fruitful friendship. He came to – how shall I put it – depend on me? When I finally decided to give up Holy Orders, I persuaded Montefiore that he needed quiet and isolation, so he bought this place, under an assumed name. He was badly in decline by then. I've had to look after him like a baby for the past three years.'

'In between assignments for your bosses in Peking.'

'Tirana, Chavasse, let's get it right. Albania has proved a very useful European foothold for us. Of course the Chinese have found me invaluable, for obvious reasons. They're in rather a difficult position as a rule. An Englishman can pass as a Russian if he speaks the language, but what can a Chinese do?'

'There are plenty of Hong Kong and Malayan Chinese living in Britain these days.'

'Indexed and filed – probably checked regularly by MI6 or Special Branch. Much better to be there and yet not there, if you follow me.'

'Which is where your service for immigrants came in?'

'Exactly, only it wasn't my service – it was Jacaud's. There he was running these people across the Channel by the boatload. West Indian, Pakistani, African, Indian – it was perfectly reasonable to have the odd Hong Kong Chinese in there as well.'

It was a bright idea and Chavasse nodded. 'Full marks for using your wits. So Ho Tsen wasn't the first?'

'If I told you how many, you'd feel rather sick.'

He smiled cheerfully, and Chavasse shrugged.

'But no more. They're not going to be too pleased about that when you get back to head-quarters.'

'Oh, I don't know. It couldn't go on for ever and I do have you, after all – a very useful prize.'

There was nothing Chavasse could say that would erase the faint, superior smile from Rossiter's face, and then for some reason he recalled his conversation with Father da Souza.

'I was almost forgetting – I've a message for you.' He lied with complete conviction. 'From da Souza.'

The effect was shattering. Rossiter seemed to shrink visibly. 'Father da Souza?'

'That's right. He has a parish near the East India Docks in London. When I wanted information about you, he seemed the obvious person to see.'

'How is he?' Rossiter's voice was a whisper.

'Fine. He asked me to let you know that there isn't a day in which he doesn't remember you in his prayers. He was rather particular that I should tell you that.'

Rossiter's face had turned pale and he spoke

through clenched teeth. 'I don't need his prayers, do you understand? I never did and I never will.'

The bedroom door opened and Famia emerged. She was wearing a raincoat and headscarf and carried a small suitcase. She ignored Chavasse and spoke to Rossiter.

'I'm ready. Shall I take this down to the boat?'

For a brief moment they might have been alone, for all the attention they paid Chavasse, trapped by that curious intimacy that only belongs to people hopelessly in love with each other. For Chavasse, this was the most interesting discovery of all – that Rossiter obviously genuinely cared for the girl.

He put a hand on her arm and guided her to the door. 'Yes, you take your case down to the boat. We'll be along later.'

One of the guards opened the door. She looked through Chavasse briefly, her face blank as if he wasn't really there, and went out.

As the door closed Chavasse said calmly, 'What did you do? Put something in her tea?'

Rossiter swung round, the look on his face terrible to see. His hand dipped into his pocket and emerged clutching the Madonna. There was a sharp click and the blade jumped into view. Chavasse crouched, arms up, expecting an attack at any moment. The door opened and Ho Tsen entered.

'Trouble?' he enquired in Chinese.

Rossiter seemed at a loss for words, in some way a different person, the awkward pupil caught out and having to justify himself to the schoolmaster.

A look of contempt appeared on Ho Tsen's face. He walked towards Chavasse, hands behind his back, and kicked him in the stomach when he was close enough.

It was expertly done, the work of someone who knew his karate. Chavasse was able to appreciate that much at least before he keeled over.

He rolled around a couple of times and fetched up against the wall. He lay there concentrating on recovering his breath while the voices droned somewhere in the distance, indistinct, meaningless. The colonel's foot had not caught him in the crotch, where such a blow could have had a permanently crippling effect, but in the lower abdomen, obviously by design.

Chavasse had at least been able to tense his muscles to receive it, and although sick and sore, he was already capable of some kind of movement when the two Chinese guards picked him up.

He played it to the hilt, dragging his feet on the way out and groaning softly. They took him down the stairs, across the hall and descended to the basement. When they reached the cellar, they dropped him to the floor. The one who carried a machine pistol over his shoulder now unslung it, holding it ready in his hands while the other got out a key and unlocked the door.

The man with the machine pistol leaned down and grabbed Chavasse by the collar, pulling him to his feet. Chavasse drove the stiffened fingers of his left hand under the chin into the exposed throat, a killing blow when expertly delivered. The man didn't even choke, simply sagged to the floor like an old sack, dropping his weapon. Chavasse came to his feet and lifted his elbow into the face of the man behind. The surprised

Chinese gave a stifled cry and went backwards into the cell. A strong hand jerked the man around, and Darcy Preston hit him once in the stomach and twice on the jaw.

In the silence, Chavasse picked up the machine pistol and grinned. 'I'd say we're in business again.'

'What's next on the agenda?' Darcy asked.

Chavasse held up the machine pistol. 'Even with this, we don't stand much of a chance against Rossiter, Ho Tsen and those Albanians. If we could get on board *L'Alouette*, things could look a little different. Those hand grenades and the machine pistols Malik hid in the false bottom of that locker could more than even things up.'

'What about the girl?'

'She sold us out, didn't she? As a matter of interest, your hunch was right. She and Rossiter can't keep their hands off each other. As far as I'm concerned, she's had it.'

He cut off any further discussion by leading the way outside and trying the other end of the passage. The first stairs they came to had a door at the top, which was not locked. When

Chavasse opened it cautiously, he looked into the kitchen, a large, square room with a fire burning on an open hearth. At that moment another door opened and two of the Albanians entered. Chavasse closed the door gently, put a finger to his lips and they retreated. At the far end of the passage, more steps took them to a door long disused. Darcy wrestled with the rusted bolt and it finally opened to reveal a small walled garden that was as much a jungle as anything else. They went out through an archway at the far end and ran for the shelter of the trees.

They made it and kept on going, Chavasse in the lead, following one of the overgrown paths, the undergrowth pressing in so close on either side that it brushed against them.

Without warning, the path emptied into a clearing on the edge of the lagoon in which stood the ruins of a fake Greek temple. Famia Nadeem was standing there, staring up at the broken columns, hands in the pockets of her duffel coat.

She swung round, startled, and an expression of real alarm appeared on her face. Chavasse dropped the machine pistol and grabbed her cruelly, clamping a hand across her mouth.

'Listen to me, you silly little bitch. Your boyfriend is an agent of the Chinese Communist Government. He's responsible for the deaths of a great many people, including old Hamid and Mrs Campbell. Do you understand?'

She gazed at him, wide-eyed, and he took his hand away. Immediately she opened her mouth, a scream rising in her throat, and he struck her on the jaw with his clenched fist.

He lowered her to the ground and turned to Preston. 'Sling her over your shoulder and make for the landing stage. Get as close as you can and wait in the bushes.'

'What are you going to do?'

'Create a diversion. If I can draw them off it will give you time to board *L'Alouette* and get moving.'

'What about you?'

'I'll swim out from here and join you on your way past, and if I'm not there in time, don't start getting all heroic on me. Just get out of here.'

'You're in charge.'

The Jamaican picked up the girl, slung her

over one shoulder and moved away into the undergrowth. Chavasse retrieved the machine pistol and hurried back towards the house. He already had a plan of sorts. The house was wholly constructed of timber. With the right encouragement it should go up like a torch, and there was one obvious place to start.

He moved back through the tangled garden and entered the basement again. This time, when he cautiously opened the door at the top of the second flight of stairs, the kitchen was empty.

He went in, removed the glass chimney from the oil lamp on the table and scattered its contents across the floor. He made a brief search through the cupboards and found a half-full can of paraffin in one of them. He emptied it to good effect, then moved towards the fire. Behind him, the door opened and Colonel Ho Tsen entered.

If he was armed, it didn't show, and in any case the machine pistol already had him covered.

Ho Tsen actually smiled. 'No sporting chance, Mr Chavasse?'

'In a pig's eye,' Chavasse said. 'The Breton half of me's in charge at the moment and we always pay our debts. This is for Jacob Malik.'

The first burst caught Ho Tsen in the right shoulder, spinning him around, and the second shattered his spine, driving him out through the open door. As he fell, Chavasse picked a burning log from the hearth and tossed it into the centre of the room. There was a minor explosion and he only just made it to the cellar door, flames reaching out to engulf him.

As he went out through the garden, he could hear cries of alarm from the other side of the house, the Albanians from the sound of it, running to see what had gone wrong, just as he had hoped.

He gave it another minute, then ran for the trees. As he reached their shelter, L'Alouette's motor burst into life. So Darcy had made it after all? Behind him there was a sudden crackling as flames exploded through the windows, blowing out the glass.

A bullet splintered the trees above his head and he swung round, emptying the machine pistol in a wild burst that sent the Albanian who had fired at him in headlong retreat round the corner of the house.

Chavasse ran, head down, and shots chased him through the undergrowth, slicing through the pine trees above his head. He burst from cover and plunged headlong into the lagoon as *L'Alouette* appeared round the point about fifty yards out.

As he started to swim, *L'Alouette* altered course towards him, slewing to a halt broadside on as Darcy spun the wheel and cut the motor.

The Jamaican ran for the rail and pulled Chavasse over with easy strength.

'Get going, for Christ's sake,' Chavasse gasped.

As Darcy vanished into the wheelhouse, a bullet ricocheted from the rail as the first Albanian arrived at the water's edge. Chavasse turned and saw Rossiter appear from the trees with the other three men. The outboard of *L'Alouette* roared, and Darcy took her away in a burst of speed, bullets chopping into her hull.

15

Once around the southern tip of the island they were out of the direct line of fire, and safe. The girl lay on her face near the stern rail where Darcy had dropped her. When Chavasse picked her up she groaned and her eyelashes fluttered.

He took her into the cabin, laid her gently down on one of the seats, then opened the map locker and removed the false bottom. He unbuttoned his wet shirt, stuffed the grenades inside for ease in carrying, picked up the two machine pistols and went on deck.

Darcy was giving the motor all it had and Chavasse shook his head. 'You're wasting your time. That MTB has four times our speed. We've got maybe five minutes to get ready for them, so throttle down.'

'What do we do?'

'Fight the best way we know how. First of all, I'll show you how to use one of these things.'

He went over the finer points of the machine pistol briefly, then quickly primed the grenades. 'I want them to go off in a hurry. Three seconds is all you've got from the moment you release the handle, and don't you forget it. You take three – I'll take three. You can carry them inside your shirt.'

He looked back through the mist to where smoke drifted sluggishly through the heavy rain. 'I shouldn't think there will be much of Hellgate left after that little lot has burned itself out. Cut the motor.'

Somewhere not too far away, the engines of the MTB roared like an angry lion. They had entered a smaller lagoon and *L'Alouette* moved broadside towards the entrance of the narrow waterway at the far end. She drifted to a halt, her prow in the reeds, and Chavasse nodded.

'This is as good a place as any. Now let's have the girl up here and I'll tell you what we do next.'

*　　*　　*

Her speed considerably reduced in the narrow waterway, the MTB was moving slowly when she entered the small lagoon, and the Albanian stationed in the prow, sub-machine gun at the ready, saw *L'Alouette* and cried out.

The engines of the MTB died and she moved on, carried by her own momentum, drifting past the place where Darcy Preston stood waist-deep among the reeds, holding Famia securely, a hand clamped across her mouth.

Chavasse waited on the other side of the lagoon on a piece of relatively high ground, soft black sand surrounded by marsh grass. Two grenades lay on the ground beside him, another was ready in his hand.

He caught a glimpse of Rossiter's flaxen hair in the window of the wheelhouse and then the MTB was abreast. She was perhaps twenty or thirty feet away from him when he tossed the first grenade. It bounced on the stern deck, rolled into the water and exploded. The MTB rocked in the turbulence and there was a cry of alarm as the man in the prow went headfirst into the water.

On the other side of the lagoon, Darcy pushed

the girl away from him, took a grenade from inside his shirt, pulled the pin and tossed it. It had further to go than he had realized and fell short, sending a fountain of water skywards. As he took out another one, the girl screamed and flung herself on him just as he threw it. It fell into the water no more than fifteen feet away and the blast flattened the reeds and blew them both over.

Darcy surfaced, reaching for the girl, and found himself under heavy fire from two of the Albanians who crouched by the rail of the MTB with sub-machine guns. In the wheelhouse Rossiter gave the engines full power and spun the wheel, and in the same instant, Chavasse's second grenade exploded under the boat, blowing most of the stern away and taking the propeller with it. The MTB shuddered and bucked like a live thing. As she slowed, Chavasse tossed his last grenade. It landed amidships and exploded with shattering force.

Rossiter was at that very moment emerging from the wheelhouse and the blast blew him into the water. The MTB heeled over, black smoke pouring from the engine hatch. Two of the Albanians still crouched at the rail, firing towards Darcy. Chavasse moved a few yards to one side, to a place where he could get a clear view, and drove them both over the side with a long burst from his machine pistol.

There was some kind of explosion in the engine room and flames burst through the hatch. The entire boat lurched to one side, rolled over and started to sink.

It was all over. In the sudden quiet the only sound was Famia's hysterical crying as she floundered through the shallows, trying to pull free from Darcy Preston's restraining hand.

Chavasse slung his machine pistol and swam towards them. When he was close enough to their side of the lagoon, he started to wade, reaching for the girl's left hand. She struggled fiercely, with a strength that was frightening in its power. For a moment, the three of them were caught in a mad tableau, Chavasse hanging on to one hand, Darcy Preston the other, at the same time trying to hold his machine pistol out of the water under the mistaken impression that it would cease to function if wet.

And then it happened, like something out of a nightmare. Out of the water, amongst the floating wreckage, Rossiter rose like some terrible phoenix, his clothes soaked in blood. That strange ascetic face was calm, devoid of all expression, the wet flaxen hair plastered into a skullcap.

The girl screamed his name, struggled violently and tried to plunge towards him. In the same moment, his right hand went back, there was a click and a flash of steel in flight.

Everything seemed to happen at once. The girl, still frantically trying to tear herself free, floundered across Chavasse's path and the knife buried itself in her heart, the ivory Madonna protruding from beneath her breasts.

Rossiter gave a terrible cry, reaching out towards her, and Darcy Preston emptied the machine pistol into him, driving him under the surface of the water.

Chavasse caught the girl as she swayed, a look of complete surprise on her face. He held her close to him and gently eased out the knife. In the same moment that it left her body, the life went out of her also. She hung for a moment on his left arm and then he released her and she sank from sight.

He turned and Darcy cried, 'Is this what we came for, this butcher's shop?'

He threw the machine pistol into the water, turned and waded through the shallows to *L'Alouette*. Chavasse went after him, and when he scrambled over the rail, Darcy was already in the wheelhouse.

The boat started to move, pushing its way through the narrow waterway, emerging a few moments later into the main channel. Beyond, through the rain, the smoke drifted up from Hellgate. Chavasse knelt there by the rail, very cold, trembling slightly, drained of all emotion.

And then he realized a strange thing – he was still clutching Rossiter's knife in his right hand. The channel widened as they moved through the estuary out to sea and he stared down at the ivory Madonna.

'And how many men have you killed in your career, Chavasse?'

The words seemed to whisper in his ear as if Rossiter himself had spoken. In a sudden gesture of repugnance, Chavasse flung the knife from him. It glinted once, then sank beneath a wave. Somewhere overhead geese called as they moved out to sea and he rose to his feet wearily and went to join Darcy in the wheelhouse.

JACK HIGGINS

BAD COMPANY

The following pages contain an extract from
Jack Higgins's latest bestselling thriller,
Bad Company, which features his ever-popular
hero, undercover enforcer Sean Dillon.

Available now from HarperCollins

HarperCollins*Publishers*

On the morning of 26 April 1945, two Junkers 52s loaded with tank ammunition managed to land in the centre of beleaguered Berlin on a makeshift runway constructed from a city road. Russian artillery was pounding the city hard, and within a few days it would be the end of the Third Reich and Hitler would be dead by his own hand.

The Junkers were not the only planes to land that way. That same day Luftwaffe General Ritter von Greim flew into Berlin in a Fieseler Storch, accompanied by air ace Hannah Reitsch. Von Greim became badly wounded, however, and Reitsch took over and managed to land the plane on East West Avenue near the Brandenburg Gate. Von Greim, promoted to Field Marshal, left again the following day in an Arado piloted by Reitsch.

There are reports of many other light aircraft at that time leaving Berlin using streets as runways. Legend has it that Martin Bormann, the most powerful man in Germany next to Hitler, escaped to Norway that way to join a U-boat bound for South America.

And there is another legend, one even more extraordinary: the story of SS Sturmbahnführer Baron Max von Berger, who escaped in a Fieseler Storch, taking off from East West Avenue shortly after the Führer's marriage to Eva Braun and carrying with him Hitler's most enduring legacy ...

DAUNCEY VILLAGE
WEST SUSSEX

2002

1

It was raining when they buried Kate Rashid, Countess of Loch Dhu, a rain that swept in across Dauncey Village like a solid curtain, sending people hurrying for the shelter of the church. They were all there, the great and the good, to say farewell, their cars blocking the High Street.

General Charles Ferguson's Daimler had just arrived. He sat there in the rear with Sean Dillon, who took a silver flask from his inside pocket, swallowed a little Bushmills whiskey and lit a cigarette.

'Are we going in?'

'No,' Ferguson said.

'Then why are we here?'

'It's the civilized thing to do, Dillon. It's a great story, after all. The world's richest woman crashing into the sea off the English coast at the controls of her own plane. Her cousin Rupert mysteriously disappeared.' He leaned back. 'You couldn't improve on it if it was a made-for-television movie.'

Dillon took another swig from his flask. 'I've said it before, but it's the cold-blooded bastard you are, General.'

'Really? I thought that was you, Dillon.'

'All right. But I repeat: if we're not going in, what are we doing here?'

'Patience, Dillon. I'm waiting for someone.'

'And who might that be?'

'Well, for starters, a good friend of yours.' A Mercedes rolled in and braked behind them. 'And here he is.'

Blake Johnson emerged, ran through the rain and scrambled into the back of the Daimler.

'Great to see you, General.' He took Dillon's hand. 'And you, my fine Irish friend.'

'And where in the hell have you come from?' Dillon demanded.

'The White House, of course.'

Blake was in his early fifties, his hair still black, and an ex-Marine. He was also Director of the White House's General Affairs Department, though everyone who knew it – which wasn't many – just called it 'The Basement'. In actuality, it was the President's private hit squad, totally separate from the CIA, the FBI, the Secret Service, or any other governmental organization.

Dillon was intrigued. 'But why are you here?'

Ferguson ignored him. 'Is it true? About the Baron?'

'Yep. Just announced. The President ordered me straight to you, General, and here I am.'

'And who's this Baron creature when he's at home?' said Dillon.

'You're about to find out,' Ferguson said.

A Rolls-Royce pulled in at the church gate. A uniformed chauffeur emerged, got an umbrella up, and opened the rear door. A young man in his early thirties emerged, hurried to the other door and waited.

The man who stepped out was very old, wore a black leather overcoat and slouch hat, and carried a silver-topped walking stick. The young man held the umbrella over him, offered his arm and they went up the path to the church.

'There he goes,' Blake said.

Dillon frowned. 'Who is he?'

'Baron Max von Berger,' Ferguson said. 'An exceedingly rich man. And – as Blake has just confirmed – none other than Kate Rashid's silent partner.'

'Rashid?' Dillon said. 'Just a minute. Are you saying Berger as in Berger International?'

'That's right.'

'But they're worth billions.'

'Exactly.'

'And they now have control of Rashid Investments?'

'Unfortunately so.'

'Well,' Dillon said, and paused. '*That* could be a problem.'

The rain hammered on the roof, organ music swelled from the church. Blake said, 'Why does it always rain at funerals?'

'It's the way Hollywood does it,' Dillon said. 'It's life imitating art. Who was the hard man?'

'The one escorting him?' Blake nodded. 'Interesting you should call him that.'

'It's the broken nose. I'd hate to see what was left of the man who did that to him.'

Ferguson joined in. 'The name is Marco Rossi. He studied economics and business at Yale, then joined the Italian air force and flew a Tornado in Bosnia. You'd have a lot in common with him, Dillon. He was shot down and had a very energetic time behind Serb lines. Very unreasonable people, the Serbs, but then you know that. His mother once worked for the Baron. She was born in Palermo and, yes, her uncle, one Tino Rossi, was Mafia in a very big way.'

Dillon said, 'So what's young Marco up to now?'

It was Blake who answered. 'Amongst other things, he's taking over all security operations for Rashid Investments worldwide. Don't kid yourself, Sean. This guy is good. He's not to be screwed with, even on the pavement.' He shrugged. 'I've even met him on the social circuit in Washington. He's charming and civilized, and the women love him.'

'Only don't push him the wrong way,' Ferguson said. 'When he was on the run behind the Serb lines in Bosnia, he killed at least four men, that we know of. He keeps an ivory Madonna in his pocket. When you press the button, the blade jumps out and shears right up under the chin.' Ferguson smiled thinly. 'Your kind of man, Dillon.'

'So if he's taken over all the security operations at Rashid Investments, that means that he can access everything the Rashids ever had on us in their computers.'

'Exactly,' Ferguson said. 'Including how you shot Kate Rashid's three brothers and interfered rather harshly in their oil operations in Hazar. And I do think he's going to find it more than a remarkable coincidence, that Kate Rashid subsequently went into the drink at the controls of her Black Eagle and her dear cousin Rupert vanished off the face of the earth.'

'So they're going to be coming for us.'

'Oh yes, Dillon. I very much think so.'

He reached into his briefcase and extracted a large envelope.

'You'll want to read all of that. Especially the bit about what von Berger did in World War II. That's especially enlightening.'

He leaned back. 'Yes, Dillon, I think we're in for a very, *very* interesting time of it.'

BERLIN
THE FÜHRER BUNKER

---

30 APRIL 1945

2

If there was a hell on earth it was Berlin. It seemed to be on fire, a charnel house, black smoke drifting everywhere. The city was doomed, everyone knew that, and the Russians were already in control of the eastern half.

The people were on the move, refugees from their own city, carrying what they could, a few pitiful belongings, with the desperate hope that they might somehow get to the West and reach the advancing American army.

Groups of SS were stopping anyone in uniform. Those without a pass or some sort of order were shot on the spot. Shells were dropping in, fired at random by Russian artillery. People cried out in alarm and scattered.

Sturmbahnführer Baron Max von Berger sat in the front passenger seat of a *Kubelwagen,* the German equivalent of a jeep. He had an SS corporal driving, a sergeant in the rear seat clutching an MP40 Schmeisser machine pistol. As they moved along the Wilhelmstrasse close to the Reich Chancellery, they saw three SS soldiers with two men in civilian clothes on their knees, about to be shot.

Von Berger told his driver to halt. 'Stop!' he said. 'What is your authority for this?'

The men paused. Their leader, a sergeant, had a brutal unshaven face. He took in von Berger's black leather coat and the young face, and failed to notice the Knight's Cross with Oak Leaves and Swords under the collar of the coat.

'And who the hell are you, sonny?'

'*Sturmbahnführer* von Berger.'

The smell of brandy was powerful. 'At your age? You look about nineteen. I bet you stole the uniforms, you and your mates here.' He cocked his Schmeisser. 'Let's see *your* authority.'

'Oh, I can show you that.'

Max von Berger took a Luger from his right-hand coat pocket and shot him between the eyes. The sergeant in the rear of the *Kubelwagen* sprayed the other two as they turned to run.

The two men who had been faced with death got up in a daze and von Berger waved them away. 'Clear off.' He turned to his driver. 'Carry on.'

The *Kubelwagen* turned out of Wilhelmstrasse and into Vossstrasse and approached the Reich Chancellery, which was, like everything else, a victim of the bombardment, defaced and crumbling. It had long since passed functioning as any kind of headquarters, but under thirty metres of concrete was Adolf Hitler's last command post, the Führer Bunker. It was a self-supporting, subterranean world complete with electricity, fresh water and extensive kitchens; still in touch with the outside world by radio and telephone; and crowded with people like Bormann and Ribbentrop and numerous generals, all trying to avoid the harsh reality that thirty metres over their heads, the Third Reich was coming to a disastrous end.

The vehicle ramp was ruined, but there was room to park the *Kubelwagen* to one side. The SS sergeant got out and opened the door for von Berger. 'Quick thinking, Herr Baron.'

'A reflex, Karl – it's been a long war. You

didn't do too badly yourself.' He got out, reached for a briefcase, turned and walked to the two SS sentries at the Bunker entrance.

They sprang to attention. '*Sturmbahnführer*.'

'One of you deliver this to Major-General Mohnke's aide. It's the report the general wanted on the state of Number Two Brigade's readiness for the final assault.' One of the men took it and went downstairs. Von Berger turned to the other and clapped him on the shoulder. 'Find me a drink. I was shot in the left hip last year, and some mornings it hurts like the devil. I'll be in the garden.'

The boy went off at the double and von Berger said, 'Come on, Karl,' and went round to the once-lovely garden, now a wreck, with some trees uprooted, the occasional shell hole. There was a sadness to the place for what once had been and, for a moment, the artillery seemed like only the sound of distant thunder on the horizon. He took out a cigarette case, selected one, and Karl Hoffer gave him a light. A tough, hard young man of twenty-five, Hoffer was a forester from the Baron's great estate in the forest of Holstein Heath, the *Schwarze*

Platz, the dark place. They'd served together for four years.

'So, my friend, we're in a fine fix, aren't we?'

'We were in Stalingrad, too, but we made it out, Baron.'

'Not this time, Karl. I'm afraid we might have to take up permanent residence. I wonder what it's like at home.'

He was thinking of Schloss Adler above the village of Neustadt. It had been his family home for seven hundred years, a huge expanse of forest, dark and mysterious, dotted with villages, every inhabitant a member of the extended family of which he was the head.

'Have you heard from the Baroness?' Hoffer asked.

'I had that letter four months ago, but nothing since. And you?'

'Just that one from my Lotte in February. She mentioned the Baroness, of course.' Lotte worked as her maid at the Schloss.

Von Berger's father, a major-general, had been killed during the Polish campaign in thirty-nine, elevating Max suddenly to the title of

Baron. His mother had died at his birth. The only woman in his life was his beloved Elsa and they had married early because of the war. Like von Berger, she was twenty-three and the boy, little Otto, was three years of age.

The young SS guard appeared clutching a bottle and two glasses. 'I'm sorry, Herr Baron, it's vodka, I'm afraid.'

Max von Berger laughed. 'I'd say that's rather appropriate, but you've only brought two glasses.'

The boy flushed. 'Well, I did put one in my pocket, *Sturmbahnführer*.'

The Baron turned to Hoffer. 'See how well we train them?' He took the bottle, jerked off the cork, then poured liberally into one of the glasses and tossed it down. He gasped, 'God, that hit the spot. The Russians made this one in the backyard.' He poured another, which went the same way. 'Great. Take that for a moment, Karl.'

'Baron.'

Von Berger removed his leather greatcoat and handed it to Hoffer. 'Suddenly my hip feels fine.' He poured a third vodka and gave the boy the bottle back. 'Now you two.'

He took a cigarette out of his case one-handed, the glass of vodka in the other. Hoffer gave him a light and the Baron walked away, enjoying his smoke and sipping the vodka.

Hoffer and the boy had a quick one and poured another. The boy was fascinated by von Berger. 'My God, his uniform. I've never seen anything like it.'

Hoffer was wearing combat camouflage gear. He shrugged. 'I've got the same thing under this lot. Except for the medals.' He grinned. 'The medals are all his.'

In spite of his youth, Baron Max von Berger had seen action in Poland, France and Holland with the Waffen SS. Afterwards, he'd transferred to the 21st SS Paratroop Battalion, and been wounded at Malame in Crete. Then had come Rommel's Afrika Korps and the Winter War in Russia. He wore a gold badge, which meant he had been wounded five times.

Despite the silver Death's Head badge on his service cap and the SS runes and rank badges on his collar, he was all *Fallschirmjäger,* in flying blouse and jump trousers tucked into paratroop boots Luftwaffe-style, though in field grey.

The gold-and-silver eagle of the paratroopers' qualification was pinned to his left breast above the Iron Cross. The Knight's Cross with Oak Leaves and Swords hung from his throat.

Karl Hoffer said, 'He's special people, the Baron. We've been through four years of hell together and we're still here.'

'Maybe not for much longer,' the boy said.

'Who knows? In Stalingrad, we thought we'd had it, and then right at the end we both got wounded and they put us on one of the last planes out. Three hundred and fifty thousand men went down the drain, and we made it out.'

At that moment, General Mohnke appeared from the garden entrance of the Bunker. He ignored them and moved towards von Berger.

'Baron, the Führer wants to see you.'

Max von Berger turned, puzzlement on his face. 'The Führer?'

'Yes, at once.'

Von Berger paused beside Karl and held out his glass. Karl filled it and von Berger toasted him. 'To us, my friend, and the three hundred and sixty-five men of the battalion who died for whatever.' He tossed the drink back and threw the glass away. 'So, General,' he said to Mohnke, 'Let's not keep the Führer waiting.'

He followed the general down a flight of steps, the concrete walls damp with moisture. Soldiers, mainly SS, were crammed in every nook and cranny of the apparently endless corridors and passageways. There was a general air of despair – more than that, resignation. When people talked, it was in subdued tones against the background of the whirring electric fans that controlled the ventilation system. The soldiers only stopped talking at the surprising sight of Max von Berger in his immaculately tailored uniform, medals aglow.

They passed through the lower levels that housed most of the Führer's personal staff, Goebbels and his family, Martin Bormann, and many generals. Mohnke still led the way, but von Berger knew exactly where he was going, for he had been there before.

In the garden bunker was the Führer's study,

as well as a bedroom, two sitting rooms, bathroom facilities, and a map room, close by and convenient for the constant conferences. Mohnke knocked on the door and went in. Von Berger waited. There was a murmur of voices, then Mohnke returned.

'The Führer will see you now.' He grabbed the young man's hand. 'Your comrades of the SS are proud of you. Your victory is ours.'

A slogan initiated by Goebbels in one of his inspired moments, and the subject of much ribaldry in the ranks of the SS. In any case, von Berger couldn't imagine what he had done to cause such adulation.

'You're too kind, General.'

'Not at all.' Mohnke was sweating and looked slightly dazed. He stood back and von Berger passed into the study.

The Führer sat at his desk, leaning over a map. He seemed shrunken, the uniform jacket too large for him; the face seemed wasted, the eyes dark holes, no life there at all, his cheeks hollow, a man at the end of things. The young woman beside him was an SS auxiliary in uniform. She held a sheaf of documents, which she passed one by one for Hitler to sign with a shaking hand. Her name was Sara Hesser. She was twenty-two years of age and had been pulled in by the Führer himself to act as a relief secretary.

He glanced up at her. 'Deliver these. I'll see the Baron in the sitting room. You can then bring the special file to me. Is it up to date?'

'As of last night, my Führer.'

'Good.' He stood up. 'Follow me, Baron.'

He shuffled ahead, opened the door and led the way into the first sitting room. He sat in an armchair by a coffee table.

'Baron Max von Berger, *Sturmbahnführer* of the SS, you took a holy oath to protect your Führer. Repeat it now.'

Von Berger clicked his heels together. 'I will render unconditional obedience to the Führer of the German Reich and People, Adolf Hitler, Supreme Commander of the Armed Forces, and will be ready, as a brave soldier, to stake my life at any time on this oath.'

Hitler nodded in satisfaction. 'You have a magnificent record for one so young and yet you never joined the Nazi Party. Why not?'

'It didn't seem appropriate, my Führer.'

'A typical response from the head of a great family. The aristocrat to the end – and yet you served me well. Why was that?'

'It's a matter of honour, my Führer. I took the oath.'

'Just what I thought you'd say. You're a remarkable young man. I sensed that when I decorated you with the Swords. That's why I made you an aide. I was saving you. You'd be no use to me dead and that's what would have happened if you'd returned to the front.'

Max von Berger took a deep breath. 'What would you have me do, my Führer?'

'The most important task left to anyone in this Bunker. The Russians are coming. They want to cage me, and I can't have that. My wife and I will commit suicide – no, no, don't look like that, von Berger. The important thing is my work must continue, and you will play a part in that, the most important part.'

By his wife, he was, of course, referring to his mistress, Eva Braun, whom he had married around midnight on the 28th.

'We must see that National Socialism survives, that is essential. We have vast sums of money, not only in Switzerland, but in South American countries sympathetic to our cause. Many of my emissaries are already in the Argentine and Brazil. We must maintain the *Kameradenwerk*, the Action for Comrades.'

There was a knock at the door and Sara Hesser came in, a briefcase in one hand. Hitler waved her to one side. 'I have no secrets from Sara, as you will see.'

'So where do I fit in, my Führer?'

Hitler raised a hand. 'The Führer Directive.'

Sara Hesser opened the briefcase, extracted a sheet of paper and passed it to von Berger, who read it with some astonishment. It was explicit:

> *The Führer Bunker, April 30, 1945.*
> *The bearer of this pass, an aide on my staff, is Sturmbahnführer Baron Max von Berger, on a personal assignment from me. All personnel, civil and military, will render him every assistance.*
> *Adolf Hitler*

'This may help you,' Hitler said.

For Max von Berger, the implications were breathtaking. 'But in what way, my Führer?'

'To get through whatever happens to you in the next few days. To help you get home, to survive and prepare yourself for your inevitable capture by the Americans or British.'

Von Berger was bewildered. 'But there are no Americans here, my Führer, only Russians.'

'You don't understand. Listen. During the last few days, many planes have flown in from Gatow and Rechlin, using streets such as the East West Avenue near the Brandenburg Gate as runways. Field Marshal von Greim came in the other day in a Fieseler Storch.'

Max von Berger struggled to control himself. The only reason for von Greim to come to Berlin was to be promoted to head of the Luftwaffe. The Führer, of course, could have told him on the telephone. Instead, von Greim had flown in from Munich escorted by fifty fighters, and forty of them had been shot down.

He said patiently, 'And how does this affect me?'

'I spoke to the Commandant of the Luftwaffe

base at Rechlin. A pilot has volunteered to fly you out in a Storch. It has already arrived and is waiting in that huge garage at Goebbels' house. The heavy rain and steam from the fires will make it an ideal time to go.'

'But to do what, my Führer?'

Hitler put out a shaking hand and Sara Hesser put the briefcase on the desk. 'When the war is over, industry will collapse and so will your family's company, Berger Steel. Eventually, though, things will start to improve, and especially for you. In here, you will find details of deposits in Switzerland, codewords, passwords, which will give you access to millions. You'll build Berger back into a power.'

Von Berger was speechless.

'That is not all.' Hitler opened the briefcase and produced a book bound in dark blue. 'I have kept a diary for the past six months, a time in which everyone has betrayed me. Goering, Himmler.' He shook his head. 'And no one tried more than me to be reasonable. I even sent Walter Schellenberg to Sweden to meet Roosevelt's representative, did you know that? No, of course you didn't. I offered a negotiated peace to combat the Red menace. Am I the enemy? No. It is that dog Stalin. Together, the US and Germany, we could have smashed him, but, no, my offer was rejected. The Americans will reap the whirlwind, believe me. The Russians will not recognize what they have taken. The damage they will do to Berlin is beyond anyone's comprehension. Yet Roosevelt and Eisenhower have decided to hold back after the Elbe crossing. Patton and his tanks could be here in twenty-four hours, but they've been told to stay where they are in obedience to Stalin's wishes and allow the Reds to take Berlin.'

'My God,' von Berger said.

'Believe me, in the years to come, America and Britain will rue this as their greatest folly. And it is all in my diary. Every day, I have dictated it to Fräulein Hesser. You may notice the trembling in my hand – an unfortunate ailment that has plagued me for some time. But I have signed each entry.'

'So what do I do with the diary, my Führer?'

'There will come a time when it will be of use to advance our cause. I do not know when – but you will, Baron. You will be its keeper. It is a holy book, Baron. I want no copies, your oath on that? Protected at all times. You may read it, if you wish. You will find the account of my dealings with Roosevelt particularly interesting.' He shook his head. 'I have every belief that you will achieve this for me.'

And Baron Max von Berger, a great soldier and a brave man, but who had always despised the Nazi Party, for some reason felt incredibly moved. The young woman put the diary and documents back into the briefcase and handed it to him.

Hitler said, 'So, you will leave within the next hour because of the bad weather.'

'May I take my sergeant with me?' von Berger asked.

'Of course. You can also take Fräulein Hesser.' He glanced up at her.

She said, 'No, my Führer, my place, my duty, is with you.'

'So be it.' Hitler stood and held a shaking hand to von Berger. 'Strange. Not even a Party member, and yet I chose you.'

Von Berger shook his hand strongly. 'I accept the task. It is a matter of honour.'

'On your way. We shall not meet again.'

Sara Hesser went and opened the door. Max von Berger, the briefcase in his hand, paused and turned, and the sight of Hitler, hunched at his desk, was to haunt him for his entire life.

'My Führer.' He gave a military salute.

Hitler gave a thin smile. 'Even now you cannot bring yourself to give me a Party salute. You touch your cap like a British Guards officer.'

'I'm sorry, my Führer.'

'Oh, go on. Just go.' Hitler waved his hand and Sara Hesser closed the door on the Baron.

He found his way back up the crowded passageways and through the garden Bunker, where he found Hoffer and the young SS soldier sitting under a concrete awning in the entrance, drinking the rest of the vodka while it rained relentlessly.

Hoffer stood up. 'Baron?'

'We're getting out, Karl. Believe it or not, but we're going to get out.'

'But how, sir?'

Von Berger took him to one side. 'I've been given a special mission by the Führer. There's a light plane waiting. I'm not saying more, but we're going home, we're going to Holstein.'

'I can't believe it.'

'Well, it's true. Give me my coat and get some weapons.'

He turned and the boy said, 'You're going, *Sturmbahnführer*?'

Von Berger smiled and clapped him on the shoulder. 'What's your name, boy?'

'Paul Schneider.'

'Then I'll tell you what, Paul Schneider. Instead of waiting to face death at the hands of the Russians, you can come with us, fly to the West, and surrender to the Americans.'

'I can't believe it,' the boy gasped.

'Sergeant Hoffer just said that.' He turned to Hoffer. 'Get moving.'

Within forty minutes, von Berger, Hoffer and young Schneider left the Bunker, exiting into Hermann Goering Strasse. They were well armed with military packs containing extra ammunition and grenades. Each one had a Schmeisser machine pistol slung across his chest.

There were people pouring along the Tiergarten in hordes now, a terrible panic having taken over, and the fog, made worse by the smoke, swirled across the city, not even the heavy rain managing to clear it. The rumble of artillery was constant, women with children screamed, terrified.

The three men moved along the Tiergarten on the edge of the crowd, cut across by the Brandenburg Gate to Goebbels' house. It showed evidence of damage, obviously from shell splinters, but the very large garage was intact. There was a Judas gate in the main door and Hoffer opened it gently.

'Hold it,' a voice called, and a light was switched on. A small Fieseler Storch spotter plane appeared, a young Luftwaffe captain standing beside it in uniform and flying jacket. He held a Schmeisser at the ready.

Von Berger moved past Hoffer. 'I'm *Sturmbahnführer* von Berger. Who are you?'

'My name is Ritter – Hans Ritter – and thank God you're here. This is the fourth time I've done this run and it wasn't fun. Could I ask where we're going?'

'To the west, to Holstein Heath in Schwarze Platz. There's a castle, Schloss Adler, above Neustadt. Can we make it?'

'Yes. It's a three-hundred-mile flight and we'll have to refuel somewhere, but I'll tell you what, *Sturmbahnführer*, I'd rather be there than here, so let's get the hell out of this place. Get your lads to open the doors.'

'A sound idea.'

Hoffer and Schneider opened the sliding door and Ritter climbed into the Storch and started the engine. The three men clambered in and Hoffer closed the door.

Outside, the fleeing refugees turned in astonishment, then fled to either side as the Storch bumped over rubble and glass and turned towards the Victory Column. The rain was torrential.

Ritter boosted power and roared down the avenue towards the Victory Column. People scattered, the Storch lifted, and at that moment, Russian artillery opened up, shells exploding on each side. The plane banked to starboard, narrowly missing the Victory Column, and rose up through the fog.

MIDNIGHT
RUNNER

Death is the Midnight Runner.
Arab proverb

In the Beginning

1

Daniel Quinn was a good Ulster name. Belfast Irish Catholic, as a young man, his grandfather had fought with Michael Collins during the Irish War of Independence, and then, a price on his head, he'd fled to America in 1920.

He'd become a construction worker in New York and Boston, but it was as a member of that most secret of Irish societies, the Irish Republican Brotherhood, that he'd begun to gain real power. Employers learned to fear him. Within a year, he was an employer himself and on his way to becoming a millionaire.

His son, Paul, was born in 1921. From an early age, Paul was obsessed with flying, and in 1940, while a student at Harvard, he'd travelled to England on impulse and, using his father's name, joined the RAF as a fighter pilot, an American volunteer.

His father, anti-Brit, was horrified and then proud of him. Paul earned a DFC in the Battle of Britain, and then moved on to the American Army Air Force in 1943 and earned another one there. In 1944, however, Paul Quinn was badly shot up in a Mustang fighter over Germany. Luftwaffe surgeons did what they could, but he would never be the same again.

Released from prison camp in 1945, he went home. His father had made millions out of the war, and Paul Quinn married and had a son, Daniel, born in 1948, though his mother died in childbirth. Paul Quinn never completely regained his health, however, and contented himself as an attorney in the legal department of the family business in Boston, a sinecure, really.

Daniel, a brilliant scholar, also went to Harvard, to study economics and business administration, and by the time he was twenty-one, he had his master's degree. The logical next step would have been to go into the family business, which now numbered hundreds of millions of dollars' worth of property, hotels and leisure, but his grandfather had other ideas: a doctorate, and then a glittering future in politics were what he had in mind.

Strange how life often swings on small things.

Watching TV one evening, seeing the death and carnage in Vietnam on the news, the old man expressed his disapproval.

'Hell, we shouldn't even be there.'

'But that isn't the point,' Daniel replied. 'We are there.'

'Well, thank God you're not.'

'So we leave it to the black kids who never stood a chance, to the working-class kids, to Hispanics? They're getting slaughtered by the thousands.'

'It's not our business.'

'Well, maybe I should make it mine.'

'Damn fool,' the old man said, a little fearful. 'Don't you do anything stupid, you hear me?'

The following morning, Daniel Quinn presented himself at the downtown Army recruiting office. He began with the infantry, and then joined Airborne as a paratrooper. His first tour brought him a Purple Heart for a bullet in the left shoulder and a Vietnamese Cross of Valour. Home on leave, his grandfather saw the uniform, the medals, and cried a little, but Irish pride won the day.

'I still say we shouldn't be there,' he said, looking at his grandson's tanned face, the skin taut over the cheekbones. There was something in his eyes that hadn't been there before.

'And I say again, we are, so we have to do it right.'

'What about a commission?'

'No, Granddad. Sergeant is fine.'

'You're crazy.'

'I'm Irish, aren't I? We're all a little crazy.'

His grandfather nodded. 'How long have you got home?'

'Ten days.'

'Then straight back?'

Daniel nodded. 'I'm going into the Special Forces.'

The old man frowned. 'What's that?'

'You don't want to know, Granddad, you don't want to know.'

'Well, try and have a good time while you're here. See a few girls.'

'I surely will.'

Which he did, and then it was back to the green hell of Vietnam, the constant throbbing of the helicopters, death and destruction all around, all the roads inevitably leading to Bo Din and his own personal appointment with destiny.

Camp Four was deep in the bush north of the Mekong Delta, the river snaking through marshland, great banks of reeds and the occasional village. It was raining that day, a monsoon kind of rain that hung like a grey curtain, making it difficult to see much. Camp Four was a jumping off point for Special Forces deep penetration operations, and Quinn had been ordered there just as they'd lost their master sergeant.

As usual, he'd hitched a lift in a Medevac helicopter, but, things being stretched, this contained only one pilot and a young medic-cum-air gunner named Jackson, who sat at the heavy machine gun and peered out the open door. The helicopter dropped lower as visibility became worse in the rain. There were paddy fields below, the brown line of the river, and Quinn stood, held on, and looked down.

A sudden explosion came over to the right, flames mushrooming, and as the pilot banked, a village emerged from the rain, some of the houses on stilts on the river. Quinn saw canoes and fishermen's flatboats, people crowding into them, some of them already pushing off. He also saw Vietcong in straw hats and black pyjamas, heard the distinctive crack of AK47s, and below him people began toppling from boats into the water.

As the helicopter approached, the VC looked

up in alarm and some of them raised their rifles and fired. Jackson returned fire with his heavy machine gun.

'Christ, no!' Quinn told him. 'You'll get the civilians, too.'

The pilot called over his shoulder, 'We'd better get out of here,' and banked away as a round or two hit them. 'That's Bo Din. Lots of VC activity in this area.'

It was at that moment that Quinn saw the mission on the edge of the village, the tiny church, the small group of people in the courtyard, Vietcong moving up the street.

'It's a nun with a dozen kids,' Jackson said.

Quinn grabbed the pilot by the shoulder. 'We'll have to put down and get them.'

'We'd be lucky to get off again,' the pilot shouted. 'Look down the road.'

There were Vietcong everywhere, at least fifty, swarming between the houses, hurrying to the mission.

'Courtyard's too small. I'd have to land in the street. It won't work.'

'Okay, just drop me off, then get the hell out of here and bring in the heavy brigade.'

'You're nuts.'

Quinn looked down at the nun in her white tropical habit. 'We can't leave that woman or those kids. Just do it.'

He stuffed the pockets of his camouflage jacket with flares and grenades, slung pouches of magazines around his neck, and found his M16. Jackson fired a long burst down the street that scattered the Vietcong and knocked several down. The helicopter hovered just above the ground and Quinn jumped.

'I guess I'm nuts, too,' and Jackson followed him, clutching an M16, a belt of magazines around his neck, a medical bag over his shoulder. There was a storm of firing as the Vietcong started up the street again, and the two Americans ran to the entrance of the courtyard where the nun was coming forward with the children.

'Back, Sister,' Quinn called. 'Get back.' He pulled his grenades out and tossed one to Jackson. 'Together.'

They pulled the pins, counted to three, stepped out and lobbed. The explosions were deafening. A number of Vietcong went down, the rest retreated for the moment. Quinn turned to the nun. She was in her early twenties, with a pale and pretty face. When she spoke, it became clear she was English.

'Thank God you came. I'm Sister Sarah Palmer. Father da Silva is dead.'

'Sorry, Sister, there's only the two of us. The helicopter's gone for help, but God knows how long it will take.'

Jackson fired a burst down the road and called, 'What the hell do we do? We can't hold this place. They'll be all over us.'

The wall at the rear had crumbled over the years. Beyond, great banks of reeds at least ten feet tall faded into the downpour.

Quinn said to Jackson, 'Take them into the swamp, do it now.'

'And you?'

'I'll hold things here as long as I can.'

Jackson didn't even argue. 'Let's move it, Sister,' and she didn't argue either.

Quinn watched them go, the children greatly upset, some crying. They scrambled across the crumbling wall, and he took a grenade from his pocket and pulled the pin. He heard the sound of an engine and when he peered round the wall, a battered jeep was coming up the street, two Vietcong standing up at a machine gun behind the driver. God knows where they'd got it from, but more Vietcong sheltered behind. They started to fire, and Quinn tossed the grenade at the last possible moment. It dropped neatly into the jeep and there was a hell of an explosion, bits of the vehicle and broken men tossed in the air, flames everywhere.

The rest of the Vietcong ran for their lives. A silence descended, with only the rush of the rain. Time to go. Daniel Quinn turned, ran to the crumbling wall, scrambled across, and made for the reeds. A moment later, he jumped into those reeds, pausing only to fit his bayonet to the M16, then he plunged forward.

Sister Sarah Palmer led the way, holding the hand of one child and carrying the smallest, the others following. She spoke softly to them in Vietnamese, telling them to be quiet. Jackson followed at the rear, M16 ready.

They came out into a dark pool and she stood there, thigh deep, her habit hitched up to her belt. The rain thundered down, and there was a kind of white mist. She looked over her shoulder at Jackson.

'If I've got my bearings, there should be a road over to the right.'

'And what good will that do, Sister? They'll run us down, and to be honest, I'm more concerned about Quinn. There hasn't been a shot fired since that explosion.'

'Do you think he's dead?'

'I sure as hell hope not.'

Suddenly, a young Vietcong stepped out of the reeds behind him, a bayonet on the end of his AK, and stabbed Jackson in the back under the left shoulder blade, missing his heart by inches. He cried out and went down on his knees. On the other side of the pool, three more VC emerged, all very young, one of them a girl, clutching AKs.

Jackson tried to get up, using his M16 as a crutch. In silence, the Vietcong watched gravely, then there was a sudden savage cry and Quinn burst out of the reeds, firing from the hip, ravaging all three in a kind of slow motion. The fourth, the one behind, surged forward, too late, as Quinn turned and bayoneted him.

Quinn put an arm around Jackson. 'How bad is it?'

'Hurts like hell. But I'm still here. There are some battle packs in my bag, but I think we'd better get out of here first.'

'Right.' Quinn turned to Palmer. 'Move out, Sister.'

She did as she was told, following with the children. They came to a shallower spot, a knoll sticking out of the water. There was room for all of them. Jackson sat there and Quinn ripped at the jagged rent left by the bayonet, exposing the wound.

'Battle packs in the bag?'

Sister Sarah Palmer reached for it. 'I'll handle it, Sergeant.'

'Are you sure, Sister?'

She smiled for the first time. 'I'm a doctor. The Little Sisters of Pity is a nursing order.'

Behind in the reeds, they heard many voices, like foxes crying. 'They're coming, Sarge,' Jackson said, clutching his rifle and leaning over as she went to work on him.

'Yes, they are. I'll have to put them off.'

'How can you do that?' Sister Sarah asked.

'Kill a few at random.' Quinn took a couple of flares from his pocket and gave them to Jackson. 'If the cavalry make it and I'm not back, get the hell out of here.'

'Oh, no, Sergeant,' Sister Sarah said.

'Oh, yes, Sister,' and he turned and plunged into the reeds.

*   *   *

He could have used his bayonet, a silent killing, but that wouldn't have caused the panic he needed. His first target was providential, two VC standing so that they could survey the marsh, their heads and shoulders above the reeds. He shot both in the head at a hundred yards.

Birds lifted in the heavy rain, voices called to each other in anger from various areas. He selected one and moved in, shooting another man he found wading along a ditch. He got out fast, easing across the reeds, crouched by another pool and waited. Special Forces had developed a useful trick for such situations. You learned a few Vietnamese phrases as fluently as possible. He tried one now and fired a shot.

'Over here, comrades, I've got him.'

He waited patiently, then called again. A few moments later, three more men appeared, wading through the reeds cautiously.

'Where are you, comrade?' one of them called.

Quinn took out his last grenade and pulled the pin. 'Here I am, you bastards,' he cried in English and lobbed the grenade. There were cries as they tried to scramble away and the grenade exploded.

By now there were shouts everywhere, as the panic he had sought for set in. As he moved on, he saw a road, Vietcong scrambling onto it. He eased back into the reeds to get his bearings and became aware of engines throbbing close by, but by then the late afternoon light was fading and it combined with the tropical rain to reduce everything to minimum visibility. A flare shot into the air, disappearing into the murk, a Huey Cobra gunship descended three hundred yards away and he heard others whirling above, but the Huey was too far away, and he plunged forward desperately, already too late.

The flare that Jackson had fired had worked, and two crewmen jumped out of the Huey and bundled the children inside quickly, followed by Sister Sarah.

The black crew chief lifted Jackson by the arms. 'Let's get out of here, man.'

'But the Sergeant's still out there, Sergeant Quinn.'

'Hell, I know him.' Shooting started again from the reeds and bullets thudded into the Huey. 'Sorry, man, we've got to go. It'll be dark any time and we've got to think of these kids.'

He raised Jackson to the waiting hands that pulled him in, followed and called to the pilot at the controls, 'Let's go.'

The Huey lifted. Jackson was actually crying and Sister Sarah leaned over him anxiously.

'But what about the sergeant?' she said.

'There's nothing we can do. He's dead, he's got to be dead. You heard all that shooting and the grenade exploding. He took on all those bastards single-handed.' The tears poured down his cheeks.

'What was his name?'

'Quinn, Daniel Quinn.' Jackson moaned in agony. 'Christ, but it hurts, Sister,' and then he passed out.

But Quinn was still in one piece, mainly because the enemy had assumed he'd escaped in the Huey. He made it to the river as darkness fell, thought about it, then decided that if he was to stand a chance he needed to be on the other side. He approached Bo Din cautiously, aware of the sound of voices, the light of the cooking fires. He slung his M16 around his neck, waded into the water, and with his combat knife sliced the line holding one of the flat-bottomed boats. The boat drifted out with the current, and he held on and kicked, Bo

Din fading into the darkness. He made the other side in ten minutes, moved into the jungle and sat under a tree, enduring the heavy rain.

At first light, he moved out, opening a can of field rations, eating as he went. He hoped for a gunboat on the river, but there was no such luck, so he kept on walking through the bush, and four days later, as if returning from the dead, he arrived at Camp Four on his own two feet.

Back in Saigon, the general attitude was disbelief. His unit commander, Colonel Harker, grinned when Quinn, checked out by the medics and freshly uniformed, reported as ordered.

'Sergeant, I'm at a loss for words. I don't know which is more extraordinary – your heroism in the field or the fact that you made it back alive.'

'That's very kind, sir. May I ask about Jackson?'

'He's in one piece, though he nearly lost a lung. He's at the old French Mercy Hospital. The Army runs it now.'

'He behaved admirably, sir, and with total disregard for his own safety.'

'We know that. I've recommended him for the Distinguished Service Cross.'

'That's wonderful, sir. And Sister Sarah Palmer?'

'She's helping out at the Mercy. She's fine and so are all the kids.' Harker held out his hand. 'It's been a privilege, son. General Lee will see you at headquarters at noon.'

'May I ask why, sir?'

'That's for the General to tell you.'

Later, at Mercy, he visited Jackson, and found him in a light, airy ward with Sister Sarah sitting beside him. She came round the bed and kissed him on the cheek.

'It's a miracle.' She appraised him quickly. 'You've lost weight.'

'Well, I wouldn't recommend doing it the way I did. How's our boy?'

'His left lung was badly injured by that bayonet, but it will heal in time. No more Vietnam, though. He's going home,' and she patted Jackson's head.

He was overjoyed to see Quinn. 'Jesus, I thought you were long gone, Sergeant.'

'Daniel,' Quinn told him. 'Always call me Daniel, and if there's ever anything I can do for you back in the States, just call me. You hear? And congratulations on your Distinguished Service Cross.'

'My what?' Jackson was incredulous.

'Colonel Harker's put you up for it. It'll go through.'

Sister Sarah kissed Jackson on the forehead. 'My hero.'

'This is the hero, Daniel here. What about you, Sarge?'

'Oh, Christ, I don't want any medals. Now settle down. All this fuss is bad for your lung. I'll see you later.' He nodded. 'Sister.' And walked out.

She caught up with him at the rail of the shaded terrace, lighting a cigarette, handsome in his tropical uniform.

'Master Sergeant Quinn.'

'Daniel will be fine for you, too. What can I do for you?'

'You mean you haven't done enough?' She smiled. 'Colonel Harker was kind enough to tell me a bit about your background. With all you have, why did you choose to come here?'

'Easy. I was ashamed. What about you? You're English, dammit. This isn't your war.'

'As I told you, we're a nursing order. We go wherever we're needed – it doesn't matter whose war it is. Have you ever been to London? We're based at St Mary's Priory on Wapping High Street by the Thames.'

'I'll be sure to look you up the next time I'm there.'

'Please do. Now would you like to tell me what's troubling you – and don't try to say you're not troubled. It's my business to know these things.'

He leaned against a pillar. 'Yes.' He shook his head. 'I've killed before, Sister, but never like in the swamp. At least two of them at close range were young women. I was on my own, I had no choice, but still . . .'

'As you say.'

'But still a darkness came over me. I saw only the killing, the death and destruction. There was no balance, no order.'

'If it worries you, make your peace with God.'

'Ah, if only it were that simple.' He glanced at his watch. 'I'd better go. Generals don't like to be kept waiting. May I kiss you goodbye?'

'Of course.'

He touched her cheek with his lips. 'You're a remarkable young woman,' and he went away down the steps. She watched him go, then returned to Jackson.

At headquarters, he was passed through to General Lee with unusual speed, and soon found himself shown into the great man's office by a smiling

Captain. Lee, a large, energetic man, jumped up behind his desk and rushed around. As Quinn tried to salute, Lee stopped him.

'No, that's my privilege. I'd better get used to it.' He clicked his heels and saluted.

'General?' Quinn was bewildered.

'I've had a communication this morning from the President. Master Sergeant Daniel Quinn, I am proud to inform you that you have been awarded the Congressional Medal of Honor.' And he saluted again, gravely.

And so the legend was born. Quinn was sent home, endured many interviews and ceremonies until he could take no more, and finally, with no interest in a permanent military career, he left the Army. He went back to Harvard and studied philosophy for three years, as if trying to exorcise some kind of demon, and carefully kept out of bars so that he would not become involved in any physical arguments. He did not trust himself enough for that.

Finally, he agreed to go into the family business. At least it meant he'd be able to help his old friend, Tom Jackson, who'd received a law degree from Columbia after Vietnam and had risen over the years to head the legal department at Quinn Industries.

He didn't marry until he was in his thirties. Her name was Monica, and she was the daughter of family friends; it was a marriage of convenience. Their daughter, Helen, was born in 1979, and it was around that time that he decided to follow his grandfather's dream, and entered politics. He put all his financial interests into a blind trust and ran for an open Congressional seat, won by a narrow margin, and then by ever greater margins, until finally he challenged the incumbent senator, and won there, too. Congress began to wear upon him after a while, though: the backstabbing and deal-making and constant petty crises, and then, when his grandfather died in a private plane accident, he began to rethink all his priorities.

He wanted out, he decided. He wanted to do something more with his life. And it was at that point that his old friend, fellow veteran and now President, Jake Cazalet, came to him and said that if Daniel wanted to give up his seat, he understood, but he hoped Daniel was not forsaking public service. He needed someone like Daniel to be a troubleshooter, a kind of roving ambassador, someone he trusted absolutely. And Daniel said yes. From then on, wherever there was trouble, from the Far East to Israel, Bosnia, Kosovo, he was there.

Meanwhile, his daughter followed family tradition and went to Harvard, while his wife held the fort back home. When she was diagnosed with leukaemia, she didn't tell him until it was too late – she hadn't wanted to interrupt his work. When she died, the guilt he felt was intolerable. They held a funeral reception at their Boston home, and after the guests had departed, he and his daughter walked in the gardens. She was small and slim, with golden hair and green eyes, the joy of his life, all he had left, he thought, of any worth.

'You're a great man, Dad,' she said. 'You do great things. You can't blame yourself.'

'But I let her down.'

'No, it was Mum's choice to play it the way she did.' She hugged his arm. 'I know one thing. You'll never let me down. I love you, Dad, so much.'

The following year she won a Rhodes Scholarship for two years at Oxford University, at St Hugh's College, and Quinn went to Kosovo to work for NATO on the President's behalf. That was where things stood, until one miserable March day when the President asked to see Quinn at the White House, and Quinn went . . .

WASHINGTON

LONDON

2

Washington, early evening, bad March weather, but the Hay-Adams Hotel, where Daniel Quinn was staying, was only a short walk from the White House.

Quinn liked the Hay-Adams, the wonderful antiques, the plush interior, the restaurant. Because of the hotel's location, they all came there, the great and the good, the politicians and the powerbrokers. Daniel Quinn didn't know where he fitted in on that spectrum any more, but he didn't much care. He just liked the place.

Quinn stepped outside and the doorman said, 'I heard you were here, Senator. Welcome back. Will you be needing a cab?'

'No, thanks, George. The walk will do me good.'

'At least take an umbrella. The rain might get worse. I insist, Sergeant.'

Quinn laughed. 'One old Vietnam hand to another?'

27

George took an umbrella from his stand and opened it. 'We saw enough of this stuff back in the jungle, sir. Who needs it now?'

'That was a long time ago, George. I had my fifty-second birthday last month.'

'Senator, I thought you were forty.'

Quinn laughed, suddenly looking just that. 'I'll see you later, you rogue.'

He crossed to Lafayette Square, and George was right, for the rain increased, sluicing down through the trees, as he passed the statue of Andrew Jackson.

It gave him the old enclosed feeling. The man who had everything – money, power, a beloved daughter – and yet, too often these days, he felt he had nothing. It was what he called his 'what's-it-all-about' feeling. He was coming to the other side of the square, lost in his own thoughts, when he heard the voices. In the diffused light from a street lamp he saw them clearly enough: two street people wearing bomber jackets, wet with the rain, talking loudly. They were identical except for their hair – one had it down to his shoulders, the other had his skull shaved. They were drinking from cans, and as one of them kicked an empty out to the sidewalk, he saw Quinn and stepped in his way.

'Hey, bitch, where do you think you're going? Let's see your wallet, man.'

Quinn ignored him and moved ahead. The one with long hair produced a knife, and the blade jumped.

Quinn closed the umbrella and smiled.

'Can I help you?' he said.

'Yeah, you can give me your money, asshole, unless you want some of this.' He waved the blade in the air.

Shaven-head was next to Longhair now and he laughed, an ugly sound, and Quinn swung the umbrella, the tip catching the man under the chin. He dropped to one knee and Quinn stamped in his face, suddenly thirty years younger, a Special Forces sergeant in the Mekong Delta. He turned to the one with the knife.

'You sure about that?'

The knife swung as Quinn grabbed the wrist, straightened the arm, and snapped it with a hammer blow. The man screamed and staggered back, and as the other started to get up, Quinn stamped in his face again.

'Just not your night, is it?'

A limousine braked hard and the driver came out, producing a Browning from under his left arm. He was very big and very black and Quinn knew him well: Clancy Smith, an ex-Marine and the President's favourite Secret Service man. His passenger, who'd joined him, was just as familiar, a tall, handsome man around Quinn's age, his hair still black, named Blake Johnson. Johnson was the director of the General Affairs Department at the White House, though everyone who knew about it – which wasn't many – just called it the Basement.

'Daniel, are you okay?' Blake asked.

'Never been better. What brings you here?'

'We decided to come pick you up, though I should have guessed you'd be walking, even on a night like this. The hotel told us we'd just missed you.' He surveyed the scene. 'Looks like you've been having a little excitement.'

The two men were on their feet now and had retreated under the trees, a sorry sight. Clancy said, 'I'll call the police.'

'No, don't bother,' Quinn told him. 'I think they've got the point. Let's go.'

He got in the rear of the limousine and Blake followed. Clancy got behind the wheel and drove away.

It was quiet, except for the whimpering of

Shaven-head. 'For God's sake, shut up,' the other one said.

'He broke my nose.'

'So what? It's going to spoil your pretty face? Give me a cigarette.'

Half a block away, another limousine sheltered under the trees. The man who sat behind the wheel was of medium height, around thirty, handsome with blond hair. He wore a white shirt, dark tie, and leather Gucci overcoat. His passenger was of the same age, a very beautiful woman with jet-black hair and fierce, proud features. There was a slightly Arab look to her, which was not surprising, since she was half-Arab, half-English.

'That was a poor showing, Rupert. You have a rather inferior class of employee, I'm afraid.'

'Yes, very disappointing, Kate. Mind you, Quinn was impressive.' Rupert Dauncey pulled on a pair of thin black leather gloves.

Lady Kate Rashid waved the thought aside. 'We'd better get going. We'll just have to try something else.'

'Such as?'

'I understand the President is dining tonight at the Lafayette Restaurant in the Hay-Adams. Perhaps he'd like some company.'

'My God, cousin, you do like your fun.' His voice was very pleasant, with a strong tinge of Boston. 'Excuse me a moment. I'll be back.'

As he got out, she said, 'Rupert, where are you going?'

'My money, sweetie, I want it back.'

'But you've got money, Rupert.'

'It's the principle of the thing.'

He lit a cigarette as he crossed the avenue to the two men huddled under the trees.

'Well, that was very entertaining.'

'You told us he'd be a walkover,' Shaven-head said.

'Yes, life can be a bitch sometimes. But you two screwed up royally, didn't you? I want my money back.'

'Go to hell.' Shaven-head turned to his friend. 'Don't give him nothing.'

'Oh, dear.'

Rupert produced a .25 Colt from his right-hand pocket, a bulbous silencer on the end. He prodded Shaven-head's left thigh and pulled the trigger. The man cried out and went down. Rupert held out a hand and the other got the bills out hurriedly.

Rupert said, 'I noticed you had a mobile phone

when we met earlier. I'd call the police if I were you.'

'Jesus,' the man said. 'And what do I say?'

'Just tell them you were mugged by three very large black men. It's Washington, they'll believe you. Terrible, the crime situation in the city, isn't it?'

He walked back to the car. As he got behind the wheel, Kate Rashid said, 'Can we go now?'

'Your wish is my command.'

3

As they pulled up to the White House, Blake clicked off his cell phone. 'I never heard Cazalet at a loss for words, but he is now. He's shocked.'

'*I'm* shocked,' Quinn said. 'Blake, I'm fifty-two years old. Vietnam was a long time ago.'

'It was a long time ago for all of us, Daniel.'

'But, Blake, what I did to those two back there. Where the hell did that come from?'

'It never goes away, Senator,' Clancy Smith told him. 'It's like being branded for the rest of your life.'

'Is it the same for you? Does the Gulf War still affect you today?'

'Ah, hell, I never think about it,' said Smith. 'We all cut throats on the right occasion, Senator, you just did it with style. That's why you're the legend.'

'Bo Din?' Quinn shook his head. 'It's like a curse.'

'No, Senator, an inspiration,' and they were inside the gate.

When the three of them entered the Oval Office, President Jake Cazalet was seated at his desk, which was littered with papers. The room was in shadows, a table light on the desk. Cazalet, like Blake and Quinn, was in his early fifties, his reddish hair peppered with grey. He jumped to his feet and came round the desk.

'Daniel, what a hell of an experience. What happened?'

'Oh, Blake will tell you. Could I possibly have an Irish whiskey?'

'Of course. Clancy, will you see to it?'

'Mr President.'

Daniel followed him out to the anteroom. He waited as Clancy poured, aware of the murmur of voices from the Oval Office. When he went back, Cazalet turned to greet him.

'A hell of a thing.'

'What? That I've just discovered I'm still a killer after thirty years?'

Cazalet took his hand. 'No, Daniel, that you still have what it takes to be a hero. Those two lowlifes made a mistake. They won't be trying that again for a while.'

'Thanks, Mr President. I hope that's true. Now – what can I do for you? Why did you want to see me?'

'Let's sit down.'

They drew chairs up to the coffee table. Clancy stood against the wall, as always, dark, taciturn, and watchful.

The President said, 'Daniel, you've done a fine job so far in your new role, especially your work in Bosnia and Kosovo. I can't think of anybody who could have done better in the time I've been here, and that's five years now. I know you have another trip to Kosovo coming up, but after that – I was wondering if you could put down roots in London for a while? Completely separate from the London Embassy, just some . . . research it'd be useful to have done.'

'What kind of research?'

Cazalet turned. 'Blake?'

Blake Johnson said, 'Europe has changed, Daniel, you know that. There are terrorist groups all over the place, and not only the Arab fundamentalists. The emerging problem is anarchism. Groups with names like the Marxist League, the Army of National Liberation, a new group called Act of Class Warfare.'

'So?' Quinn asked.

'Before we get into the details,' Cazalet said, 'I must say this goes beyond any security classification you've ever had.' He pushed a document across. 'This is a Presidential Warrant, Daniel. It says you belong to me. It transcends all our laws. You don't even have the right to say no.'

Quinn studied it. 'I always thought these things were a myth.'

'They're real enough, as you see. However, you're an old friend. I won't force you. Say no now and we'll tear this up.'

Quinn took a deep breath. 'If you need me, Mr President, then I'm yours to command, sir.'

Cazalet nodded. 'Excellent. Now – how much do you actually know about what Blake does at the Basement?'

'I must confess, Mr President, not a tremendous amount. It's some kind of private investigative squad, but the White House has done a pretty good job over the years of keeping a lid on it.'

'I'm gratified to hear it. Yes, you're right. Many years ago, faced with the possibility of Communist infiltration at every level of the government, the then-President – I won't even tell you who – invented the Basement as a small operation answerable only to him, totally separate from the CIA, FBI, and the Secret Service. Since then, it's been handed from one President to another, and it's certainly been invaluable to me.'

Blake cut in. 'There's also a similar outfit in London, to which we are very close, run by a man named General Charles Ferguson. He works out of the Ministry of Defence and is responsible only to the Prime Minister of the day, irrespective of politics.' He grinned. 'They're known as the Prime Minister's private army.'

'I can see why you'd like that,' Quinn said.

'His chief assistant is a Detective Superintendent Hannah Bernstein from Special Branch at Scotland Yard. A hell of a woman. Smart as a whip, but she's also killed several men, and been shot several times herself.'

'Good God.'

'The best is yet to come,' Cazalet told Quinn. He passed him a file. 'This is Sean Dillon, for years the Provisional IRA's most feared enforcer.'

Quinn opened the file. The photos showed a small man, no more than five feet five, with fair hair almost white. He wore dark cords and an old black flying jacket. He dangled a cigarette from one corner of his mouth and smiled the kind of

smile that seemed to say he didn't take life too
seriously.

Quinn said, 'He looks like a dangerous man.'

'You don't know the half of it. Several years ago,
Ferguson saved him from a Serb firing squad, and
then he blackmailed him into joining his outfit.
Now he's Ferguson's best man.' Cazalet paused.
'He helped save my daughter a few years ago,
when she was kidnapped by terrorists, he and
Blake together.'

Quinn looked from one to the other. 'Your
daughter? Kidnapped? I – I never knew –'

'Nobody knew, Daniel,' Cazalet said. 'We didn't
want anybody to know. And he saved my life, too.'
He held up his hand as Quinn began to exclaim
again. 'And that brings us back to our original
topic. Blake?'

Blake said, 'Do you remember last Christmas
when you stopped over in London?'

'Of course. It was a chance to see Helen at
Oxford.'

'That's right, and the President asked you to
guest one or two functions through the Ambassador that would be attended by Lady Kate Rashid,
the Countess of Loch Dhu.'

'That's right, and I wondered why. It wasn't

really made clear what I was trying to find out, except that I was to get to know her. So I met the lady briefly, made discreet enquiries, and had a code computer analysis done by my people on the Rashid organization.'

Blake said, 'So you know how much they're worth.'

'I sure do. The latest quotes, including their oil interests in Hazar, indicate about ten billion dollars.'

'And the president of the company?'

'The Countess of Loch Dhu.'

Blake held out a folder. 'This is our file on the Rashids. It's very interesting. For instance, it includes a list of their charitable donations, which include large donations to several education programmes, including the educational programme of Act of Class Warfare, and the Children's Trust in Beirut.'

Quinn said, 'I remember that. But it all seemed kosher to me. Educational charities are common among the truly rich. It's like handing out alms to the poor to assuage your guilt at having so much. I've been there myself.'

Blake said, 'What if I told you the Children's Trust in Beirut is a front for Hezbollah?'

Daniel Quinn was bewildered. 'Are you suggesting she's up to something subversive? Why would she want to do that?'

'You remember how I said Dillon saved my life?' said Cazalet. 'Well, this is where that comes in.'

Blake continued. 'As you know, Kate Rashid is Arab Bedu through her father and English through her mother – that's where the title comes from, the Daunceys. She had three brothers, Paul, George, and Michael.'

'Had?'

'Yes. Last year, their mother was killed in a car accident by a drunken diplomat from the Russian Embassy. But a foreign diplomat can't be brought to court, so the brothers arranged their own punishment, which was permanent. What further infuriated them was that they learned he had been brokering an oil deal in Hazar involving us and the Russians. Hazar was their territory. As far as they were concerned, here were these two great powers swaggering arrogantly over not only their economic rights but over Arabs in general: the West disrespecting the East. So they decided we needed to be taught a lesson.'

'Paul Rashid tried to have me assassinated on Nantucket,' Cazalet said. 'Clancy took a bullet in the back meant for me. Blake personally shot one of the assassins.'

'Mr President, this is – this is astonishing,' Quinn said.

'Unfortunately, it didn't end there,' Blake told him. 'It's all in the file. Suffice it to say that ultimately all three Rashid brothers paid the price for their fanaticism – leaving only their sister, Kate. The richest woman in the world probably, a woman who has everything and lost everything. Three beloved brothers. She wants revenge, I'm sure of it.'

'You mean she couldn't get the President last time, so she might try again?'

'We believe she could be capable of anything. There's one other wild card. The Daunceys had what the English aristocracy call a minor branch, some people who moved to America in the eighteenth century and settled in Boston.'

'They're lawyers and judges now,' Cazalet said. 'Very respectable. I know the family.'

Quinn said, 'Is there something I should know here?'

Blake passed another file across. 'Rupert Dauncey – West Point, Parris Island.'

'Another Marine, eh?'

'Yes, and a good soldier,' Blake said. 'He won a Silver Star in the Gulf, then served in Serbia and Bosnia. There was a suggestion he might have killed Serbs a tad harshly, but nothing came of it, and after a very nasty Muslim ambush, which he foiled, he received the Distinguished Service Medal. He was raised to a quick Captaincy –'

'Which led to a transfer to the Marine Embassy Guard in London,' the President said.

'And I can guess what happened next,' Quinn said. 'Once in London, he introduced himself to the good Countess, is that it?'

'They hit it off immediately, and have been very close ever since,' Blake said. 'He's very good-looking, I gather, especially in his Marine dress uniform. All those medals. I believe, technically, that he's Kate Rashid's third cousin.'

'Ah, well, that would make it legal.'

'Well, no. To put it delicately, Rupert Dauncey is of a different persuasion,' Blake told him.

'You mean he's gay?'

'I'm not sure. He's not into women, we know that. On the other hand, he doesn't cruise bars, and there's no indication of a boyfriend either. Anyway, if we can set that aside – we can't help feeling that between the two of them, they're hatching something. Lady Kate still bears a grudge not only against the President but against me and Sean Dillon and his crew, since we were all involved in the deaths of her brothers.'

Jake Cazalet said, 'That's why I want you to go to London. We'll arrange for you to meet with General Ferguson, Dillon, Superintendent Bernstein. I'll speak to the Prime Minister, who is well aware of the situation.'

'And then?'

'Nose around, use your contacts, see what you can find out. Maybe we're wrong. Maybe she's changed. Who knows?'

'I do,' Blake said. 'She hasn't, and she won't.'

'Fine. I bow to your superior judgment.'

'I'll go as soon as I come back from Kosovo,' Quinn said. 'Quinn Industries has a townhouse in London, I'll stay there. If I remember right, in fact, it's close to the Rashid place.'

'Good.' The President smiled. 'Now, for the more immediate future, let's discuss plans for dinner. I'm going out tonight, to the Lafayette. You should join us.'

'I'd be delighted.'

'Especially because – Blake always being a hundred and fifty percent right on intelligence matters

– I understand that none other than the Countess of Loch Dhu and her cousin, Rupert Dauncey, are booked for dinner there as well.'

'*What?*'

'You know me, Daniel, I always did like to put the cat in amongst the pigeons. Time to stir things up.' He turned to Clancy. 'You've got things in hand, presumably?'

'Absolutely, Mr President.'

'Fine. We'll meet at eight-thirty. Be kind enough to see that Senator Quinn is returned to the hotel.'

'At your orders, Mr President,' Clancy told him.

'And Clancy, if Dauncey is around, don't take any shit. He may be a Marine Major, but as I recall, you were one of the youngest sergeant majors in the Corps.'

'What is this?' Quinn demanded. 'Parris Island? You expect him to kick ass?'.

Jake Cazalet laughed. 'Would you, Clancy?'

'Hell, no, Mr President. I'd more likely put the Major on a seven-mile run with a seventy-five-pound pack on his back.'

'I love it,' Quinn said. 'All right, I'll see you there.' He went out, Clancy following.

'You'll speak to Ferguson?' Cazalet said to Johnson.

'First thing in the morning.'

General Charles Ferguson's office was on the third floor of the Ministry of Defence overlooking Horse Guards Avenue. He was at his desk the next day, the red security phone in one hand, a large, untidy man with grey hair, a fawn suit and Guards tie. He put the phone down and pressed his intercom. A woman answered.

'General?'

'Is Dillon there?'

'Yes, sir.'

'I'll see both of you now.'

Detective Superintendent Hannah Bernstein entered, a woman in her early thirties, young for her rank, with close-cropped red hair and horn-rimmed spectacles. Her black trouser suit was elegant, and looked more expensive than most people could afford on police pay.

The small, fair-haired man with her wore an old black flying jacket. There was a force to him, obvious the moment he entered the room. He lit a cigarette with an old Zippo lighter.

'Feel free, Dillon,' General Ferguson said.

'Oh, I will, General, knowing the decent stick that you are.'

'Shut up, Sean,' Hannah Bernstein told him. 'You wanted us, sir?'

'Yes. I've had interesting news from Blake Johnson concerning the Countess of Loch Dhu.'

Dillon said, 'What's Kate been up to now?'

'It's more a matter of what she might be up to. There are computer printouts on the way. Hannah, would you see if they've arrived?'

She went out. Dillon poured a Bushmills and turned. 'She's back, is that it, General?'

'She promised to get the lot of us, didn't she, Sean? As payment for her brothers?'

'She can try and I love her dearly.' Dillon drained his glass and poured another. He raised it in salute. 'God bless you, Kate, but not after what you tried to do to Hannah Bernstein. Try anything like that again and I'll shoot you myself.'

Hannah came in with fax sheets and printouts.

Ferguson said, 'I'll tell you first what Blake's told me, then you two read what's in here.'

A little while later, they were up to date.

'So she's got herself a man,' Hannah said.

Dillon looked at the printout photo of Rupert Dauncey.

'More or less, anyway.' He grinned.

Ferguson said, 'I'll tell you what disturbs me. The information Daniel Quinn's people got about those donations: the Act of Class Warfare education programme, the Children's Trust in Beirut.'

'Well, she is half Arab, and the Bedu leader in Hazar,' Dillon told him. 'You expect her to give to Arab causes. But I agree. There's more here than meets the eye.'

Ferguson nodded. 'So what do we do?'

'To find out what she's up to?' Dillon turned to Hannah. 'Roper?'

She smiled and said to Ferguson, 'Major Roper, sir?'

'The very man,' Ferguson said.

4

Daniel Quinn was waiting by the entrance of the Hay-Adams when the limousines arrived. Clancy Smith was first out, followed by three other Secret Service men from two escort vehicles. Clancy passed Quinn and nodded as he went in. Blake got out and waited for the President, who went up the steps and shook Quinn's hand.

'Daniel.'

It was all for the cameras, of course. There were, as usual, two or three photographers who'd heard the President would be there. Lights flashed, photos were taken, Cazalet shaking Quinn's hand. Clancy appeared in the entrance. The other Secret Service men flanked the President and Blake as they went in.

Blake, Cazalet, and Quinn were placed by the restaurant manager at a round table in a corner, excellent from a security point of view. All around

51

them, enthralled diners produced a muted buzz of conversation. Clancy organized his men, who stood against the wall. Clancy himself hovered, always the dark presence.

'Drinks, gentlemen?' Cazalet said. 'What about a good French wine?' He turned to the waiter. 'Let's try a Sancerre.'

The waiter, his evening made, nodded eagerly. 'Of course, Mr President.'

'I'll tell you, I can use a drink.' Cazalet turned to Quinn. 'I've been trying to deal with this whole energy thing we've been having. With the prices sky-rocketing, oil demand climbing, those damn rolling blackouts – it's like I'm just waiting for some disaster to strike. And people are starting to notice. Did you see that poll last week? "Why doesn't the government do something about it?" Well, I'm trying, damn it. Some people are starting to smell blood in the water – you know who I mean. If I can't figure out a way to alleviate this mess, the midterms next year are going to be a disaster, and then I can forget about trying to get through any of my programmes. I might as well resign for all the good I could do.'

Quinn started to say something, but Cazalet just waved him off. 'Oh, never mind me. I'm just venting. That's not what this dinner is about.' He smiled. 'We're here for a little entertainment. It's like waiting for the start of a Broadway play.' He glanced toward the door. 'And I believe the curtain is about to go up.'

The Countess of Loch Dhu was at the door. The diamonds at her throat were dazzling, the black silk trouser suit a kind of art form. Beside her, Rupert Dauncey wore an elegant Brioni blazer and trousers, with a white shirt and dark tie. The blond hair was perfectly combed.

The restaurant manager was on to them in a moment and began to lead them through the tables. As they grew closer, the President said, 'Speak to her, Blake, you're the one who knows her.'

Blake stood up as she approached and said, 'Kate. Well, this is serendipity.'

She paused, smiled, then reached to kiss his cheek. 'Why, Blake, how nice.' She turned. 'Have you met my cousin, Rupert Dauncey? No, I don't believe you have. You have a lot in common, you know.'

'Oh, his reputation precedes him,' said Blake.

Rupert Dauncey smiled. 'As does yours, Mr Johnson. And Senator Quinn's here.'

'Thank you,' said Quinn. 'Nice to see you again, Countess.'

She nodded. 'Likewise.'

'Mr President,' said Blake, 'may I present Lady Kate Rashid, the Countess of Loch Dhu.'

Cazalet stood and took her hand. 'We've never met, Countess. Will you and Mr Dauncey join us for a drink? A glass of champagne, perhaps?'

'How could I refuse?'

Blake waved to the waiter and spoke to him. Rupert pulled a chair out, seated her, and turned to Clancy Smith.

'The last time I saw you, Sergeant Major, we were in very deep shit inside Iraqi lines.'

'We surely were, Major. I missed you in Bosnia.'

'A good place to miss anybody.' Dauncey smiled and moved to stand beside him. 'But we're holding things up.'

The waiter poured glasses of Dom Pérignon. Cazalet raised his glass. 'To you, Lady Kate. Rashid Investments is doing extremely well at the moment, I'm told. I'm particularly impressed with your Hazar results.'

'Oil, Mr President. Everyone needs oil.' She smiled. 'As you know yourself.'

'Yes, but the Hazar operations have had remarkable results. I wonder why.'

'You know why. Because I control the Rashid

Bedu in both Hazar and the Empty Quarter. Without me, you and the Russians are nothing. They're the cruellest deserts in the world, you know.' She turned to Blake and smiled. 'But Blake knows that. He was there when my brother George was killed.'

'Yes, I was,' Blake said. 'I was also there the night before, when Cornet Bronsby was killed.' He turned and told the President what he already knew. 'Bronsby was with the Hazar Scouts. They don't have a real army down there, just a regiment. The Rashid Bedu did a very thorough job on him with their knives.' He turned to Kate with a smile, but there was no humour in it. 'But then at dawn, Sean Dillon took his revenge. It was four of you, as I recall, wasn't it? At five hundred metres? A hell of a marksman, Sean.'

'A hell of a bastard,' Kate Rashid said.

'Because one of them was your brother George? He should have thought of that before he started murdering people.'

The air hung thick and cold around the table. Then the Countess smiled. 'Well, murder is something you'd know a lot about, wouldn't you, Mr Johnson? Not to mention the price one must pay for it. Sometimes a very high price.' She leaned close to him. 'Please share that knowledge with your friends, won't you?'

'Don't do it, Kate.' Blake held her wrist. 'Whatever it is you're planning, don't do it.'

'Blake, I can do anything I want,' she said. 'Rupert?'

He pulled her chair back. She stood. 'Mr President, an honour.' She turned and nodded to Dauncey, who said, 'Gentlemen,' and followed.

There was silence for a while after she'd gone. Finally, Quinn said, 'What the hell was all that about?'

'Just read the files, Daniel,' Cazalet said. 'And get to London as soon as you can.' He gazed after her. 'Something tells me we may have less time than we thought.'

Kate Rashid and her cousin sat at another corner of the restaurant. 'Cigarette, Rupert.'

He gave her a Marlboro and flicked a brass lighter made from an AK round.

'There you go, sweetie.'

She reached for the lighter. 'Where did you get this, Rupert? I never asked you.'

'Oh, it's a Gulf War souvenir. I was ambushed,

in a pretty bad situation, and I picked up an Iraqi AK assault rifle. It saved my bacon until help arrived – funnily enough, in the person of Sergeant Major Clancy Smith over there. Afterwards, when I checked, there was one round left in the magazine.'

'That was close.'

'It surely was. I pocketed it and had it made into a lighter by a jeweller in Bond Street.' He took it from her. 'You know the phrase, Kate? *Memento mori?*'

'Of course, Rupert, my darling. Reminder of death.'

'Exactly.' He tossed the lighter up and grabbed it again. 'I should be dead, Kate, three or four times over. I'm not. Why?' He smiled. 'I don't know, but this reminds me.'

'Do you still go to Mass, darling, to Confession?'

'No. But God knows and understands everything, isn't that what they say, Kate? And he has an infinite capacity for forgiveness.' He smiled again. 'If anyone needs that, I do. But then you know that. You probably know everything about me. I should think that it took you all of half an hour after I introduced myself at that reception in London before you had your security people on my case.'

'Twenty minutes, darling. You were too good to be true. A blessing from Allah, really. I'd lost my mother and my three brothers and then there you were, a Dauncey I never even knew existed – and thank God for it.'

Rupert Dauncey felt emotion welling inside of him. He reached for her hand. 'You know I'd kill for you, Kate.'

'I know, darling. You may well have to.'

He smiled and put a cigarette in his mouth. 'I love you to bits.'

'But Rupert, women don't figure on your agenda.'

'I know, isn't it a shame? But I still love you.' He leaned back. 'So where are we?'

'Senator Daniel Quinn over there. It's very interesting how chummy he seems to be with Cazalet. Before when I wanted him dead, it was because his people were finding out too much about my activities. Now, I wonder if he doesn't have some bigger agenda.'

'Such as?'

'I don't know. But I think it would be interesting to find out ... Do you know that he has a daughter, Rupert? Named Helen. She's a Rhodes Scholar at Oxford.'

'Yes? And?'

'I want you to cultivate her.'

'I don't understand.'

'Well, you know about my little charitable works, don't you? I believe in supporting oppressed and minority political groups. People like Act of Class Warfare, the United Anarchist Front, the Army of National Liberation in Beirut. They're a little wild, but . . . well meaning.'

'Well meaning, my backside.'

'Rupert, how unkind. Well, anyway, the Act of Class Warfare education programme operates from my castle, Loch Dhu, in western Scotland, a rather run-down old thing but nice and remote. It provides adventure courses for young people. Teaches them how to handle themselves. And for some of the older ones . . . a little more.'

'Like in Hazar?'

'Very good, Rupert! Yes. The Army of Arab Liberation Children's Trust. That's rather more serious business. Full paramilitary training, run by mercenaries. Some of them are Irish, you know. There are plenty of them around since this whole peace process thing began.'

'So what do you want from me?'

'I want you to oversee Loch Dhu, start keeping an eagle eye out, make sure nobody is snooping around. And I want you to keep close contact with Act of Class Warfare.'

'Why?'

'Because I've got a feeling we'll be seeing Senator Quinn again, and sooner than we think. Did you know, Rupert, that Act of Class Warfare has branches at most of the major universities now? Filled by the children of the affluent who want to destroy capitalism?' She chuckled.

'And what does that have to do with Quinn?'

'Because, my dear Rupert . . . Helen Quinn is a member of the Oxford branch.'

In London the following morning, Major Roper appeared at Sean Dillon's cottage at Stable Mews, a strange young man in a state-of-the-art electric wheelchair. He wore a reefer coat, his hair was down to his shoulders, and his face was a taut mask of the kind of scar tissue that only comes from burns. An important bomb disposal expert with the Royal Engineers, decorated with the George Cross, his extraordinary career had been terminated by what he called 'a silly little bomb' in a small family car in Belfast, courtesy of the Provisional IRA.

He'd survived and discovered a whole new career in computers. Now if you wanted to find out anything in cyberspace, no matter how buried, it was Roper you called.

Ferguson and Dillon were there to greet him.

'Sean, you bastard,' Roper said cheerfully.

Dillon smiled and helped him over the step. 'You look well.'

'Hannah didn't say much. She sent me a file, though. Are we going to war again?'

'I'd say it's a distinct possibility.'

He followed Roper along the corridor and they found Ferguson on the telephone. He replaced it. 'Major, how goes it?'

'Fine, General. You've got work for me?'

Ferguson nodded. 'Indeed we have.'

For the next half hour, they went over the whole background of the case, until finally Dillon said, 'And what we would like you to do first is check out those groups she's been giving money to. If she's got an Achilles' heel, that may be it. I don't know what we're looking for, exactly –' he grinned '– but we'll know when we find it.'

'You realize,' Roper said, 'that if Quinn's people checked her out a few months ago, she knows it. They're bound to have left footprints, which means that she's had time to try to cover her tracks, if she wanted to.'

'Does that mean you don't think you'll find anything?' Ferguson asked.

Roper's scar tissue lifted in what passed for a smile. 'I said she'd try. I didn't say she'd succeed.'

LONDON
———
OXFORD
———
HAZAR
———

5

Roper's apartment in Regency Square was on the ground floor, with its own entrance and a slope to the door to facilitate his wheelchair. The entire place, including the kitchen and bathroom, which had a specialized shower and toilet system, was designed not only for a handicapped person but for one who, as in this case, was determined to fend for himself. In what should have been a sitting room, there was instead a computer laboratory and workbench, and the equipment there was state-of-the-art, some of it classified, obtained not only because he was a Major on the Army reserve list but because Ferguson used his muscle whenever he had to.

Three days after Quinn's meeting with the President, the front doorbell sounded at ten in the morning. Roper pressed a remote control and a moment later, Ferguson, Dillon, and Hannah Bernstein came in.

'So, what have you got?' Ferguson asked Roper.

'Well, as you said, the Rashid Educational Trust pours money into an incredible variety of causes. The list's as long as your arm. Most of them appear legit, but not all of them. This Children's Trust in Beirut, for instance, is definitely Hezbollah. And she's got other trusts scattered around Syria, Iraq, Kuwait, the Oman. I'm still working on them, but I'd bet you anything some of them are terrorist fronts as well.'

'What on earth's she playing at?' Ferguson said.

'She's consolidating her power,' Dillon said. 'Establishing links with all the major Arab leaders. Gaining influence through either peace or violence, depending on what suits her particular needs.'

Roper nodded. 'And don't forget the size of her oil interests in the Middle East. Rashid Investments controls a third of all production there. She could bring down the whole house of cards if she wanted to.'

'Christ,' Ferguson groaned. 'A third of Middle Eastern oil production.'

Dillon turned back to Roper. 'What about here at home? She hasn't made grants to the IRA or the Ulster Freedom Fighters or anything like that?'

'No, but there are a lot of fringe organizations, like

the People's Army, the Socialist Marxist League, the Nationalist Liberation Group, the United Anarchists, and so on – and all the contributions presented as educational grants.'

'And next time there's a riot in London, how many of the members will be there?' Hannah asked.

Roper shrugged. 'She's very clever. Everything is done in the open and above board. Many people would applaud what she's doing.'

'On the surface, maybe,' Ferguson said. 'But she's clever, all right. What about Act of Class Warfare?'

'Despite its name, it seems pretty innocuous. Its biggest feature is a kind of outdoor educational programme for kids from twelve to eighteen. School parties, canoeing, trekking, mountain climbing.'

'I wonder what the older students get?' Dillon asked.

'Its headquarters is in western Scotland, in a town called Moidart, at Loch Dhu Castle. Yes, it belongs to the Countess.'

Ferguson was astonished. 'But I've been there. We all have.'

Even Roper was surprised. 'What do you mean?'

It was Dillon who answered. 'A few years ago, we had to deal with a very bad article named Carl Morgan who'd rented that castle for a few weeks. The General, Hannah, and I took him on from Ardmurchan Lodge on the other side of the loch.'

Hannah turned to Ferguson. 'But Lady Katherine owned it.'

'Actually, it's a little more complicated than that,' said Roper. 'When Sir Paul Dauncey received the title of Earl of Loch Dhu from James the First, it was an old castle even then. It was rebuilt in mid-Victorian style by one of the later Earls, starting in 1850, but the family hardly ever used it – they preferred Dauncey Place. More recently, they leased it to the Campbell family for fifty years. On the death of Lady Katherine Rose five years ago, the lease reverted to the Daunceys.'

'Or since the marriage of Kate's mother to the Rashids,' Dillon said.

'Carl Jung once said there was a thing called synchronicity,' Hannah said. 'An event going beyond mere coincidence that makes you think there's some deeper meaning involved.'

'Yes, spooky, isn't it?' Dillon said. 'Kate Rashid's been waiting for us to turn up all this time.'

'Don't talk nonsense.' It was Ferguson who

interjected. 'But, you know, I think it's time for us to shake the pot a bit.'

'What do you mean, sir?' Hannah asked.

Ferguson turned to Dillon. 'Sean, I think it's time for "we know that they know and they know that we know".'

'And what would that accomplish?' Dillon asked.

'All right. Now, this is top secret and for your ears only, and Whitehall would probably skin me alive for telling you – but for the past couple of years, Kate Rashid's done . . . some work for the government. She's been a secret emissary for the Foreign Office and the Prime Minister.'

'*What?!*' Hannah exclaimed. 'Oh, I can't believe this!'

'Do we get to know who's at the other end?' Dillon asked.

'Saddam Hussein.'

'Good God,' Hannah moaned.

'She knows him well, you see, and he's a great admirer.'

'She can't put a foot wrong, can she?' Roper commented. 'So what you're saying is that she has protectors, that we'd have difficulty getting certain people to think ill of her at the highest levels of government.'

'Yes. But I damn well do,' Ferguson said.

'And you'd like Kate Rashid to know you're on her case?'

'Exactly.' He turned to Hannah Bernstein. 'You and Dillon, I want you to go to Loch Dhu castle, see what you can stir up.'

'When, sir?'

'Right now. Phone Farley Field. Tell Lacey and Parry to get the Gulfstream ready. If I remember right, there's an old abandoned RAF strip by the Loch. It's only four hundred and fifty miles, it should take you an hour and a half.'

'We'd need transport, sir.'

'Then phone the air-sea rescue base at Oban. Tell them to send an unmarked car. Do it now. Go on, Superintendent, you can use your mobile in the car.'

He almost pushed her out of the room, and Dillon smiled at Roper as he followed. 'Now you know how we won the war.'

'Which war?' Roper asked.

At Farley Field, the small RAF installation used for covert operations, they were greeted by Squadron Leader Lacey and Flight Lieutenant Parry.

Both officers were holders of the Air Force Cross, awarded for hazardous operations in various parts of the world on Ferguson's behalf. Both men wore nondescript blue flying overalls with no rank tabs.

Lacey said, 'Nice to see you, Sean. Will it be messy?'

'Probably not – but you never know, do you?'

'We're using the Lear, since it doesn't have RAF roundels, Superintendent. You did say you wanted this business low-key.'

'Of course. Let's get moving.'

She went up the ladder, Dillon behind her, and the pilots followed. Lacey went to the cockpit and Parry closed the door. A minute later, they sped down the runway and took off, climbing fast to thirty thousand feet.

'Why the emphasis on anonymity when Ferguson wants Kate to know it's us?' Dillon asked.

'We're a covert organization, and we want to keep it that way. A plane with RAF roundels and two officers in uniform could form the basis of a formal complaint if the Countess so desired.'

'Ah, Kate would never do that. There are rules, even in our business.'

'You've never obeyed a rule in your life.'

He lit a cigarette. 'The ones that suit me, I do. How are you feeling these days, Hannah?'

The previous year, during the feud with the Rashids, she'd been shot three times by an Arab gunman.

'Don't fuss, Dillon. I'm here, aren't I?'

'Ah, the hard woman you are.'

'Oh, shut up.'

Parry had left a couple of newspapers on the seat. She picked up *The Times* and started to read.

At the same time, other things were happening in the world. In Kosovo, Daniel Quinn entered the village of Leci in a Land Rover owned by the British Household Cavalry Regiment. A trooper stood up behind a mounted machine gun and another drove while Quinn, wearing a combat jacket, sat in the rear beside a Corporal of Horse – the equivalent of a sergeant in other units – named Varley.

It started to rain. There was smoke in the air, acrid in the damp, from houses still burning. There was no sign of the population.

Varley said, 'It looks as if that same Albanian flying column's been here, too.'

'Could we be in trouble?'

'Probably not, as long as we fly that.' Varley nodded to the Union Jack pennant mounted at the side of the engine.

'I noticed you don't fly the UN flag or wear their blue berets.'

'We go our own way. It works better. They don't think of us as taking sides.'

'That makes sense.'

He heard the throb of a helicopter overhead, unseen in the mist and rain. It reminded him at once of Vietnam, and it brought back the unmistakable smell that only came from burning flesh, once experienced, never forgotten. It was almost too much for Quinn as a hundred memories, dormant for years, came flooding back.

The driver braked and switched off the engine. It was very silent in the rain, the sound of the helicopter fading.

'Bodies, Corporal.'

Varley stood and so did Quinn. There were half a dozen of them: a man and a woman and three children, another body face-down some yards away.

'Looks like a family party, all gunned down together.' Varley shook his head. 'Bastards. I've seen bad things in my time, but this bloody place beats the lot.' He turned to the trooper at the machine gun. 'Cover us while we move them. We can't very well drive over them.'

'I'll help,' Quinn told him.

He and Varley and the driver got out and approached the bodies, and for Quinn it really was Vietnam all over again, as if nothing had happened in between. He picked up one of the children, a boy who looked about eight, and took him to the side of the street, laying him down against a wall. Behind him, Varley and the trooper followed with a child each.

Quinn felt dreadful, the darkness creeping into him from deep inside, as Varley and the trooper picked up the man between them, carried him to the wall, then returned for the woman.

He took a deep breath and went to the other body, which was dressed in boots, baggy pants, an old combat jacket, and a woollen hat. It had obviously been shot in the back. He turned the body over and recoiled in horror as he looked into the mud-spattered face of a young woman. The eyes were open, fixed in death. She was perhaps twenty-one or two. She could have been his own daughter.

Varley called, 'You need a hand, Senator?'

'No, I can manage.'

Quinn knelt, picked the girl up and stood. He walked to the wall and sat her down so that she was against it. He took out a handkerchief and carefully wiped the mud from the face, then closed the eyelids, stood up, walked away, leaned against the wall, and was violently sick.

The trooper with Varley said, 'Bloody politicians. Maybe it does them good to see some real shit for a change.'

Varley grabbed his arm and squeezed hard. 'Thirty years ago, while serving with the Special Forces in Vietnam, that "bloody politician" won the Congressional Medal of Honor. So why don't you just button your lip and get us out of here?'

The trooper slid behind the wheel, Varley and Quinn got in the rear, and they moved out. The Corporal of Horse said, 'You know what we do in London, don't you, Senator? The Household Cavalry? We ride around in breastplates and helmets with plumes and sabres, and the tourists love us. The British public, too. They think that's all we are: chocolate soldiers. So why did I serve in the Falklands at nineteen, in the Gulf War and Bosnia, and now this shit heap?'

'So the great British public is misinformed.'

Varley produced a half bottle from his pocket. 'Would you like some brandy, Senator? It's strictly against regimental regulations, but medicinal on occasion. Even though it is rotgut.'

It burned all the way down, and Quinn coughed and handed it back. 'Sorry about what happened back there. I feel as if I let you down.'

'It happens to all of us, sir. Don't worry about it.'

'The thing is, I have a daughter. Helen. That young woman was just about her age.'

'Then I'd say you could do with an extra swallow.' And Varley passed the bottle back to him.

Quinn took another drink and thought about his daughter.

Who at that moment in time was seated in an Oxford pub called the Lion, which was popular with students and just down the street from an old school hall where Act of Class Warfare had its Oxford headquarters. She was sitting in one corner with a young, long-haired student named Alan Grant, drinking dry white wine and laughing a lot. Grant was doing a trick for her. His brother was a security specialist and had sent Grant a new toy – a pen that doubled as a tape recorder. Grant had been amusing himself by recording snatches of conversation and playing them back with appropriately caustic comments. Helen thought it was a riot.

In a booth on the other side of the bar, Rupert Dauncey sat with a minor Oxford professor named Henry Percy, a woolly minded individual fond of just about any kind of cause.

'Thank you for the cheque, Mr Dauncey. We at Act of Class Warfare are incredibly grateful for the continuing support of the Rashid Educational Trust.'

Rupert Dauncey had already decided the man was a hypocritical creep and wondered how much of the cash had actually stuck to his fingers, but he decided to play the game.

'We're glad to be of help. Now what's all this on Saturday? Some kind of demonstration in London? I hear you're going.'

'Indeed we are. Liberty in Europe Day! The United Anarchist Front has organized it.'

'Really? I thought there already was liberty in Europe. Well, never mind. So your rosy-cheeked students are going to take part.'

'Of course.'

'You know the police don't like demonstrations in Whitehall. They can so easily turn into riots.'

'The police can't stop us. The voice of the People will be heard!'

'Yes, of course,' Rupert agreed dryly. 'Are you leading this thing or are you just one of the marchers?'

Percy stirred uneasily. 'Actually, I, uh, I won't be able to be there on Saturday . . . I have a prior commitment.'

I just bet you have, Rupert Dauncey thought, but he smiled. 'Do me a favour. That nice girl over there, I heard her speaking as I passed. I believe she's American. Is she one of your members?'

'Yes on both counts. Helen Quinn. Rhodes Scholar. Charming girl. Her father is actually a Senator.'

Rupert, who knew very well who she was, and even knew the boy's name, said, 'Introduce me on the way out, won't you? I love meeting fellow Americans abroad.'

'Of course.' Percy got up and led the way. 'Hello, you two. Helen, I'd like you to meet Rupert Dauncey, a countryman of yours.'

She smiled. 'Hi there, where are you from?'

'Boston.'

'Me too! That's great. This is Alan Grant.'

Grant obviously saw the whole thing as an intrusion and had turned sullen. He pointedly ignored Dauncey. Rupert carried on. 'You're a student here?' he asked her.

'St Hugh's.'

'Ah, an excellent college, I'm told. Professor Percy tells me you're going to this rally on Saturday.'

'Absolutely.' She was full of enthusiasm.

'Well, take care, won't you? I'd hate to see anything happen to you there. Goodbye. I hope to see you again.'

He walked out with Percy, and Grant said in a cockney accent, 'Posh git, who does he think he is?'

'I thought he was nice.'

'Well, that's women for you.' He touched a button in his pocket, and Rupert's voice rang out: 'I'd hate to see anything happen to you there.'

'I know what *he'd* like to see happen to you,' he grumbled. 'Felt like punching him in the nose.'

'Oh, Alan, stop it!' Honestly, sometimes Alan just went too far, Helen thought.

*　　*　　*

For Hannah Bernstein and Dillon, the flight to Moidart crossed the Lake District, the Solway Firth and the Grampian Mountains, and soon the islands of Eigg and Rum came into view, the Isle of Skye to the north. They descended to an old World War II airstrip with a couple of decaying hangars and a control tower. An estate car was parked outside the tower, a man in a tweed suit and cap beside it. Lacey taxied the Lear toward him and switched off. Parry opened the door, dropped the steps, and Lacey led the way down. The man came forward.

'Squadron Leader Lacey, sir?'

'That's me.'

'Sergeant Fogarty. They've sent me from Oban.'

'Good man. The lady is Detective Superintendent Bernstein from Scotland Yard. She and Mr Dillon here have important business at Loch Dhu Castle. Take them there and do exactly what the Superintendent tells you. You'll bring them back here.'

'Of course, sir.'

Lacey turned to the others. 'See you later.'

* * *

They approached the castle in twenty minutes, still as imposing as they remembered it, and set well back from the road. The walls were ten feet high, and smoke curled up from the chimney of the lodge. The gates were shut. Dillon and Hannah got out, but there were no handles, and when he pushed, nothing happened.

'Electronic. That's an improvement from the old days.'

The front door opened and a man with a hard, raw-boned face appeared. He wore a hunting jacket and carried a sawn-off shotgun under his left arm.

'Good afternoon,' Hannah said.

He had a hard Scots voice. 'What do you want?' He sounded decidedly unfriendly.

'Now then,' Dillon told him. 'This is a lady you're dealing with, so watch your tone. And who might you be, son?'

The man stiffened, as if sensing trouble. 'My name's Brown. I'm the factor here, so what do you want?'

'Mr Dillon and I were here some years ago for the shooting,' Hannah told him. 'We rented Ardmurchan Lodge.'

'We know you're running adventure courses for

young people at the castle these days,' Dillon said, 'but we wondered if Ardmurchan Lodge might not still be available. My boss – General Ferguson – would love to rent it for the shooting again.'

'Well, it isn't, and the shooting season's over.'

'Not the kind I'm interested in,' Dillon told him amicably.

Brown took the shotgun from under his arm. 'I think you'd better leave.'

'I'd be careful with that – I'm a police officer,' Hannah said.

'Police officer, my arse. Get out of here.' He cocked the shotgun.

Dillon raised a hand. 'We don't want any problems. Obviously, the lodge isn't available. Come on, Hannah.'

They went back to the car. 'Drive on just out of sight of the gate,' Dillon told Fogarty.

'What happened back there is an intelligence matter, Sergeant, you understand?' Hannah said.

'Of course, ma'am.'

'Good, then pull in,' Dillon told him. 'I'm going over the wall and you can give me a push.'

They stopped and got out, Fogarty joined his hands together, and Dillon put his left foot in them. The big sergeant lifted, and Dillon pulled himself over the wall, dropped into the trees on the other side and moved towards the lodge.

Brown was in the kitchen, the gun on the table, and dialling a number on the wall phone, when he heard a slight creak and felt a draught of air. Brown dropped the phone and reached for the shotgun and then became aware of the Walther in Dillon's right hand.

'Naughty, that,' Dillon said. 'I might have shot you straight away instead of just thinking about it.'

'What do you want?' Brown said hoarsely.

'You were phoning the Countess of Loch Dhu in London, am I right?'

'I don't know what you're talking about.'

Dillon slashed him across the face with the Walther. 'Am I right?' he asked again.

Brown staggered back, blood on his face. 'Yes, damn you. What do you want?'

'Information. Act of Class Warfare. School parties, right? Kids having a nice week in the country, climbing, canoeing on the loch, trekking. That's what you offer?'

'That's right.' Brown got a handkerchief out and mopped blood from his face.

'And what about the other courses for the older ones?'

'I don't know what you mean.'

'The guys and girls who like to hide their faces with balaclavas and take part in riots. Let me guess. You teach them interesting things like how to make petrol bombs and handle policemen on horseback.'

'You're crazy.'

Dillon slashed him again.

'I can't help you,' Brown said wildly, his face crumbling. 'It's as much as my life's worth.'

'Really?' Dillon grabbed him by the throat, pushed him across the table, and rammed the muzzle of the Walther against the side of his right knee. 'And what's a knee worth? You've got ten seconds to decide.'

'No, no. All right. I'll tell you. It's true. They run training courses, just as you say. They come from all over the country, sometimes even abroad. But I just take care of the house and grounds – that's all I know, I swear it!'

'Oh, I doubt that very much. But that's all right. All I needed was your confirmation. That wasn't too bad, was it? Now if you'll just open the gates, I'll be on my way.' He picked up the shotgun and tossed it through the open door into some bushes. 'Then I suggest you make that phone call to the good Countess. I'm sure she'll be most interested.'

Brown shuffled to the front door, pressed a button in a black box, and opened the door. Outside, the main gates began to part. Dillon stopped and turned.

'Don't forget now. Dillon was here, and give her my love.'

He walked out into the road and half-ran to the car. He got in beside Hannah and said to Fogarty, 'Back to the plane.'

They drove away. Hannah said, 'You didn't leave anyone dead back there?'

'Now, would I do a thing like that? It turns out he was a very reasonable man, our factor. I'll tell you about it on the plane.'

Brown, between a rock and a hard place, took Dillon's advice, of course, and phoned Kate Rashid at her house in London but found that she was out, which made him feel worse. Desperate, his face hurting like hell now, he tried the mobile number he'd been given for emergencies. Kate and Rupert were eating at The Ivy. She listened as Brown poured it all out.

She said calmly, 'How badly are you hurt?'

'I'm going to need stitches. The bastard slashed my face with his Walther.'

'Well, he would, wouldn't he? Tell me again what he said.'

'Something like, say Dillon was here and give her my love.'

'That's my Dillon. Get yourself a doctor, Brown. I'll talk to you later.' She put her mobile on the table.

The waiter had stood back respectfully. When Rupert nodded, he now poured Cristal champagne in both glasses and withdrew.

'To your bright eyes, cousin,' he toasted her. 'Why is it I smell trouble from the little I've heard?'

'Actually, what you smell is Sean Dillon.' She drank a little champagne and then told him what Brown had said. 'What's your opinion, darling?'

'Well, obviously they were there on Charles Ferguson's behalf. They didn't even pretend. Their only reason for visiting Loch Dhu was to let you know that they knew.'

'What a clever boy you are. Anything else?'

'Yes. In a way, he's calling you out.'

'Of course he is. Oh, General Ferguson's in charge, but it always comes down to Dillon. He spent all those years with the IRA, and the Army and the RUC never touched his collar once, the bastard.'

'But a clever bastard. So what now?'

'We'll see him tonight. It's time you two met.'

'And how do we do that?'

'Because, as you said, he's calling me out. It's an invitation, and I know just where to find him.'

6

Later that afternoon at Ferguson's flat, the General sat by the fire, listening to Hannah Bernstein's account of the trip. 'Excellent,' he said. 'You seem to have behaved with your usual ruthless efficiency, Sean.'

'Ah, well, the man needed it.'

'So what happens now?'

'She won't let it go. It's like one of those old Westerns. The villain comes out of the saloon to meet the hero for a gunfight in the street.'

'An interesting parallel.'

'She won't be able to resist a face-to-face.'

'And where will this event take place?'

'Where we've met so often before – the Piano Bar at the Dorchester.'

'When?'

'Tonight. She'll be expecting me.'

Ferguson nodded. 'You know, you could be

right. I'd better come with you.'

'What about me, sir?' Hannah asked.

'Not this time, Superintendent. You've had a strenuous day. You could do with a night off.'

She bridled. 'You know, I did pass a stringent medical exam before Special Branch allowed me to return to duty. I'm fine, really I am.'

'Yes, well, I'd still prefer you to take the night off.'

'Very well, sir,' she said reluctantly. 'If you've no further need of me, I'll get back to the office and clear a few things up. Are you coming, Sean?'

'Yes, you can take me to Stable Mews.'

Ferguson said, 'Seven o'clock about right, Sean?'

'Fine by me.'

She dropped him at his cottage, but Dillon didn't go in. He waited until the Daimler had turned the corner, rolled up the garage door, got into the old Mini Cooper he kept as a run-around, and drove away.

He was thinking about Harry Salter. Salter was a very old-fashioned gangster, now reasonably respectable, but not completely so, and he and his nephew, Billy, had been involved as much as anyone else in the feud that had led to the death of Kate Rashid's brothers.

Traffic was as bad as London traffic usually is, but Dillon finally reached Wapping High Street, turned along a narrow lane between warehouse developments, and came out on a wharf beside the Thames. He parked outside the Dark Man, Salter's pub, its painted sign showing a sinister individual in a dark cloak.

The main bar was very Victorian, with gilt-edged mirrors behind the mahogany bar, and porcelain beer pumps. Bottles ranged against the mirror seemed to cover every conceivable choice for even the most hardened drinker. Dora, the chief barmaid, sat on a stool reading the London *Evening Standard*.

At that time in the afternoon, before the evening trade got going, the bar was empty except for the four men in the corner booth playing poker. They were Harry Salter; Joe Baxter, and Sam Hall, his minders; and Harry's nephew, Billy.

Harry Salter threw down his cards. 'These are no bleeding good to me,' and then he looked up and saw Dillon and smiled.

'You little Irish bastard. What brings you here?'

Billy turned in his chair and his face lit up. 'Hey,

Dillon, great to see you,' and then he stopped smiling. 'Trouble?'

'How did you guess?'

''Cos you and me have been to hell and back more times than I can count. By now, I can tell the signs. What's up?'

There was an eagerness in his voice and Dillon said, 'I've been the ruin of you, Billy. You never used to be so willing to put yourself in danger. Remember when I quoted your favourite philosopher: "The unexamined life is not worth living"?'

'And I said that to me it meant the life not put to the test is not worth living. So what's up?'

'Kate Rashid.'

Billy stopped smiling. They all did. Harry said, 'I'd say that calls for a drink. Bushmills, Dora.'

Dillon lit a cigarette and Billy said, 'Let's hear it.'

'Remember Paul Rashid's funeral, Billy?'

'Don't I just. No mourners, she said, but you had to go anyway.'

'And you said, "Is that it then?" and I said, "I don't think so." And then when we ran into her at the Dorchester, she sentenced us all to death.'

'Well, she can try,' Harry said. 'As I told her

then, people have been trying to knock me off for forty years and I'm still here.'

Billy said, 'Look, what's happened, Dillon? Let's be having it.'

Dillon swallowed his Bushmills and told them everything. They'd worked with him and Blake Johnson in the past, knew all about the Basement, so there was no reason to hide anything. He finished by telling them what had happened at Loch Dhu and what he intended to do.

'So you think she'll be there tonight?' Harry Salter asked.

'I'm certain of it.'

'Then Billy and I will be there, too. We'll have another drink on it,' and he called to Dora.

A little while later, Dillon punched the doorbell at Roper's place. The Major said over the voice box, 'Who is it?'

'It's Sean, you daft sod.'

The electronic lock buzzed, and Dillon pushed open the door. Roper was seated at his computer bank in his wheelchair.

'I've had Ferguson on the line. He told me about Loch Dhu, but I'd like to hear it from you.'

Dillon lit a cigarette and told him. 'So there you are. Pretty much as we thought.'

'So it would appear.'

'What have you got? Anything new?'

'Well, I thought I'd see if I could trace Kate Rashid's travel patterns. She uses a company Gulfstream, so I can access times easily enough – air traffic slots have to be booked – and I can ascertain when she's been on board through Passport Control and Special Branch.'

'Any significant pattern?'

'Not much. She's only been up to Loch Dhu once recently. Used the same old airstrip you did. Here's something that might be interesting, though: she went to Belfast last month.'

'Now that is interesting. Any thoughts on where she went?'

'Yes. She landed late afternoon and had a slot booked back to Heathrow the following after-noon, so that seemed to indicate a hotel for the night. So I started with the Europa, accessed their booking records, and there she was.'

'And why was she there?'

Roper shook his head. 'That I don't know. But if she does it again, I'll let you know. You could fol-low her. Of course, it could be perfectly legitimate.

Rashid Investments has taken a big stake in Ulster since peace broke out.'

'Peace?' Dillon laughed harshly. 'Believe that, you'll believe anything.'

'I agree with you. After all, I was the one who defused a hundred and two bombs. Too bad it wasn't a hundred and three.' He patted the arm of the wheelchair.

'I know,' Dillon said. 'You know, considering I was on the other side, I sometimes wonder why you put up with me.'

'You were never a bomb man, Sean. Anyway, I like you.' He shrugged. 'By the way, if you want a drink, there's a bottle of white wine in the fridge over there. It's all I'm allowed.'

Dillon groaned. 'God help me, but it will do to take along.' He got the bottle from the fridge. 'Jesus, Roper, it's so cheap it's got a screw top.'

'Don't moan about it, pour it. I'm a reserve officer on a pension.'

Dillon obeyed, and put a glass at Roper's right hand while Roper played with the keys. Dillon took a swallow and made a face. 'I think someone made this in the backyard. What are you looking at now?'

'Rupert Dauncey. Quite a character, but nothing

we don't know about him already. There's something about him, though, a ruthlessness, always on the edge. There's a dark side to that one.'

'Ah, well there's a dark side to all of us. Can you tell if he was with Kate on the Irish trip?'

'There are Special Branch regulations regarding passengers on executive jets. He wasn't on board. He's a comparatively new arrival to her entourage, remember.'

'I suppose so.'

Roper drank some wine. 'However, he is on board tomorrow morning at ten o'clock, with the Countess. Would you like to know where they're going?'

'Where?'

'Hazar.'

'Hazar, hmm? That means Hamam airport. You know, the RAF built it in the old days. There's only one runway, but it can take anything, even a Hercules. Check on something for me. Last time I was there, we used an outfit called Carver Air Transport. See if they're still there.'

Roper tapped his keys. 'Yes, they are. Ben Carver? Ex-Squadron Leader in the RAF?'

'The old sod,' Dillon said. 'So what's Kate up to?'

'That's what Ferguson asked when I told him. Of course, there are a dozen different reasons why she could be going down there, but Ferguson said he would contact Tony Villiers, ask him to keep an eye on her.' Colonel Tony Villiers was the Commander of the Hazar Scouts.

'That should help. Villiers is good, and he isn't particularly keen on the Rashids since they skinned his second-in-command, Bronsby.'

'Yes, they do have their little ways. Now go away, Dillon. I've got work to do.'

At that moment, on the border between Hazar and the Empty Quarter, Tony Villiers was encamped with a dozen of his Hazar Scouts and three Land Rovers. A small fire of dried camel dung burned, a pan of water on top.

His men were all Rashid Bedu and all accepted Kate Rashid as leader of the tribe, but the clan spilled across the border as well. There were good men over there in the Empty Quarter and there were bad men, bandits who crossed into Hazar at their own risk, for the Scouts had sworn a blood oath to Villiers. Honour was of supreme importance to them – each one would kill his own brother if necessary, rather than violate his oath.

They sat around the fire, AK assault rifles close at hand, wearing soiled white robes and crossed bandoliers. Some smoked and drank coffee, others ate dates and dried meat.

Tony Villiers wore a head cloth and crumpled khaki uniform, a Browning pistol in his holster. He'd never got used to dates and had just eaten the contents of a large can of baked beans cold. One of the men came across with a tin cup.

'Tea, *Sahb*?'

'Thanks,' Villiers replied in Arabic.

He sat down and leaned against a rock, drank the bitter black tea, smoked a cigarette, and looked out to the Empty Quarter. It was disputed territory there, and utterly lawless. As someone had once said, you could kill the Pope there and no one would be able to do a thing. That's why he kept to his side of the border whenever possible.

Villiers, approaching fifty now, had served in the Falklands and every little war in between up to the Gulf and Saddam, then had ended up on secondment here in Hazar. It was just like in the old days, a British officer commanding native levies, and it was beginning to pall.

'Time to go, old son,' he said softly. As he lit another cigarette, the mobile in his left breast pocket rang.

The Codex Four was not available on the open market. It had been developed for intelligence use in places where strict security was necessary, and Villiers had his courtesy of Ferguson.

'That you, Tony? Ferguson here.'

'Charles, how's every little thing at the Ministry of Defence?'

'Put your scrambler on.'

Villiers pressed a red button. 'Done.'

Ferguson said, 'Where are you?'

'Wouldn't mean a thing to you, Charles. Marama Rocks, just on the border with the Empty Quarter. I'm on patrol here with a few of my men.'

'You've got a new second-in-command, I hear.'

'Yes, another Cornet, from the Life Guards this time, named Bobby Hawk. He's off in the other direction with his patrol. To what do I owe the pleasure?'

'I've just heard that Kate Rashid's flying in tomorrow.'

'Well, that's not unusual. She comes here all the time.'

'I know, but there've been some funny things

going on here. I just have a gut feeling, that's all. Where does she go?'

'Lands at Hamam, then goes to Shabwa Oasis in the Empty Quarter by helicopter. But you know that, you've been there yourself.'

'Is anything going on there, Tony?'

'I wouldn't know. These days I'm forbidden by the Sultan's decree to go over the border into the Empty Quarter.'

'Don't you find that strange?'

'Not really. All right, I know Kate Rashid has the Sultan by the throat, so I assume that it's her order, not his. But she's the leader of the Rashid Bedu and that's Rashid territory. End of story.'

'Could there be something going on out there?'

'Preparing for a revolution, you mean? Come on, Charles, what does she need a revolution for? She's got everything she wants.'

'All right, all right, but be a good chap. Scout around, put the word out.'

'If I do, Kate Rashid will know in five minutes, but all right, I'll do what I can. I'm due down at the port tomorrow anyway.'

'Good man, Tony, keep in touch.'

Villiers sat there thinking about it, then called,

'Selim.' His sergeant came over. 'A big place, the Empty Quarter.'

'Awesome, *Sahb*.'

'A man could hide out there forever.'

'This is true, *Sahb*.'

'In fact, many men?'

Selim looked a little hunted. 'This is possible, *Sahb*.'

'Shabwa is not the only oasis your people use, there are others.'

'All Rashid, *Sahb*.'

'So, if others came, from another tribe for instance, you would know.'

'We would kill them, *Sahb*. Any oasis is ours, the wells are ours.'

'But if such people had permission, say from the Countess?'

Selim was caught and terribly upset. 'Yes, *Sahb*, that would be different.' His face was pale.

'Yes, I thought so.' Villiers patted his shoulder. 'We move out in ten minutes.'

Villiers turned and looked to the Empty Quarter. There was something out there. Ferguson's wild shot had been right. Poor old Selim, so transparent. But what could it be? No way of knowing. If he strayed over the border, he wouldn't last half a day.

The Bedu would know – knew where he was now, come to that. He sighed, took out the Codex Four and dialled Charles Ferguson back, rather sooner than he had intended.

Dillon was at the Dorchester just before seven, dressed in a black Brioni suit, white shirt and black tie. He called it his undertaker look, which was appropriate since he carried a Walther in a special pocket under his left arm. He was greeted by Giuliano, the manager.

'Bushmills,' Dillon said. 'General Ferguson will be joining me, and we'll want a bottle of Cristal then.'

'I'll see to it personally.'

There weren't that many people in. It was too early for the evening rush, and was a Monday evening anyway. Dillon accepted the Bushmills from Giuliano and waited. A moment later, Ferguson joined him.

'So – no sign of the opposition?'

'Not as yet. Champagne?'

'I suppose so.'

Dillon nodded to Giuliano, who smiled and spoke to a waiter who brought the Cristal in a bucket. Giuliano opened the bottle, Ferguson did the tasting.

'Fine.' He turned to Dillon. 'I've had two phone calls with Tony Villiers. Let me tell you about them.'

Afterwards, Dillon said, 'Still nothing concrete. But Tony smells something, too. That's good enough for me.'

Ferguson looked around. 'Still no sign of her. You could be wrong, Sean.'

'It's been known to happen. But not tonight, I think.' He smiled. 'I know what'll bring her.'

He walked over to the pride of the bar, the extraordinary mirrored grand piano that had once belonged to Liberace, sat down, and lifted the lid. Giuliano came over with his glass of Cristal.

'All right with you?' Dillon asked.

'Of course. It's always a pleasure to hear you play. The pianist isn't in until eight.'

Dillon started with a Gershwin melody, just as Harry and Billy Salter appeared at the bar entrance. Harry, who was into Savile Row suits that season, wore a navy blue chalk stripe, the kind of thing beloved of bank presidents. Billy wore an expensive-looking black bomber jacket and black trousers. They crossed to the bar and

Ferguson said, 'Good God, what are you rogues doing here?'

'My idea,' Dillon called.

'And mine, General.' Harry sat down. 'Dillon's filled us in on everything.'

'Damn you, Sean, that's totally out of order,' Ferguson said.

'Come off it, General, as far as the Countess of Loch Dhu is concerned, we're in this together, the four of us, all tarred with the same brush.'

'Dead right,' Harry said. 'So I'll have a glass of champagne with you and await events.'

Dillon called, 'Tell them about Tony Villiers.'

'Oh, all right.' And Ferguson did.

More people had come in, scattered around the room at various tables. Billy walked to the piano and leaned on it. Dillon was playing 'A Foggy Day in London Town'.

'I like that,' Billy said. '"I was a stranger in the city."'

'"Out of town were the people I knew."' Dillon smiled. 'You're looking good, Billy.'

'Never mind the soft soap. What do you think she's playing at?'

'I've no idea. Why don't you ask her? She's just come in.'

Billy turned and found Kate Rashid standing at the top of the steps, Rupert Dauncey beside her. She wore a black trouser suit, her hair tied back, a pair of very large diamond studs, and no other jewellery. Rupert wore a single- breasted navy blue blazer and grey trousers, a scarf at his neck.

Billy turned back. 'Seeing her reminds me: there's something I always wanted to ask you, Dillon. You never married. Are you bent or something?'

Dillon spluttered and then started to laugh. When he was in control, he said, 'It's simple, Billy. I'm always drawn to the wrong women.'

'You mean the bad ones.'

'And the Hannah Bernsteins of this world wouldn't touch me with a bargepole, not with my wicked past. Now if we could postpone this discussion of my sexual proclivity for a while, here she comes.'

Kate Rashid approached and Billy went and stood behind his uncle. She passed the group at the table and moved to the piano. Rupert lit a cigarette.

'Very nice, Dillon,' she said.

'I told you once before, Kate: good bar-room piano, that's all. I take it this is the famous Rupert Dauncey?'

'Of course. Rupert, the famous Sean Dillon.'

They nodded, then Dillon shook a cigarette from a packet of Marlboros and put it in his mouth one-handed. Dauncey offered him a light and Dillon moved into another number. 'You recognize this one, Kate?'

'Of course. "Our Love is Here to Stay."'

'I wanted you to feel at home. Why don't you say hello to the boys?'

'Why not, indeed.' She turned to the table. 'Why, General Ferguson, what a pleasant surprise. I don't think you've met my cousin, Rupert Dauncey.'

Ferguson said, 'No, but I feel I know him well.' He shook Dauncey's hand.

'A pleasure, General.'

'Join us for a glass of champagne.'

'Thank you,' Kate Rashid said, and Dauncey pulled a chair forward and seated her. 'You'll be fascinated by the General's friends, Rupert. Mr Salter here is a gangster, but no ordinary gangster. For years, he was one of the most important guvnors, as they call it, in the East End of London. Isn't that so, Mr Salter? Billy here is his nephew, another gangster.'

Billy didn't say a word but simply looked at her, his face pale, and left it to his uncle.

'If you say so, Countess,' Harry said, and turned

to Rupert. 'We know all about you, son, you do a good act.'

'I'll take that as a compliment, coming from you, Mr Salter.'

Rupert drank some champagne and Dillon came back and joined them. 'So what do you want, Kate?'

'Why, Dillon, nothing – nothing at all. I thought it was you who wanted to see me. You left your calling card, after all, and I wouldn't want to disappoint you, of all people.' She picked up her glass of Cristal and emptied it in a single swallow. 'But I'm hungry, and I don't want to eat here. Where should we go, Rupert?'

'Don't ask me, sweetie, London's your town.'

'Somewhere fresh would be nice, somewhere new.' She turned to Salter. 'Come to think of it, didn't I read in one of the gossip columns that you've opened a new restaurant, Mr Salter? Harry's Place? Hangman's Wharf, isn't it?'

'Going a bomb,' he said. 'Booked up for weeks.'

'What a shame, Rupert, and I so wanted to try Mr Salter's cooking.'

'We can make room,' Harry said. 'Call the restaurant, Billy.'

Billy's face was almost bone white now. He glanced at Dillon, who nodded slightly. Billy took out a mobile and dialled. After a few moments, he said, 'All right, it's done.'

Kate Rashid said, 'How kind. So, we'll be on our way, Rupert.' He pulled out her chair and she got up. 'We'll see you gentlemen there.'

'You can count on it,' Dillon told her.

She kissed his cheek. 'Later, then, Dillon.'

She turned and went. Rupert said, 'Gentlemen,' and followed her.

'There's something about that bastard,' Billy said. 'And I just don't like it.'

'That's because you have good taste, Billy,' Dillon said. He drained his glass. 'Let's go.'

As the Bentley drove away from the Dorchester, Kate Rashid pulled the partition glass panel shut.

'Make the call.'

Rupert dialled a number on his mobile and said, 'It's on.' He frowned. 'How the hell do I know what time? You wait, okay?' He switched off and shook his head. 'I've said it before. Good help is so hard to find these days.'

'Poor Rupert.' She took out a cigarette, he lit it for her, and she leaned back.

*   *   *

Harry's Place was another of Salter's warehouse conversions on Hangman's Wharf. The old yard had been converted into a car park. There were new window frames in mahogany and the exterior brickwork had been cleaned and a few steps had been added to make the front entrance more imposing. Next to it flowed the Thames, with plenty of traffic on the river, the lights sparkling on the other side as darkness fell.

There was a queue at the door, mainly young people hoping for a cancellation for the restaurant or admittance to the lounge bar. Joe Baxter and Sam Hall stood at the top of the steps wearing tuxedos and black tie.

The Bentley drew up and Rupert got out and opened the door for Kate.

Baxter said to Hall, 'That's her,' and went to meet them. 'It's a pleasure to see you again, Countess.'

'These are Mr Baxter and Mr Hall, Rupert. I have very nice pictures of them on my computer.'

There were two young men at the front of the queue sporting black silk bomber jackets with a scarlet dragon on the back and Chinese characters underneath. They both wore gold earrings, and their hair was long and black. The one who spoke up had a cockney accent.

'Here, how are they getting in and we can't even make the bar?'

'I'll tell you what you'll make,' Joe Baxter said. 'The back of the queue if you don't shut up.'

The man subsided, muttering under his breath, and Hall held the door wide to let them through, then followed. He escorted them up the stairs to where the headwaiter stood at the booking desk, a dark, energetic Portuguese in a white tuxedo.

'Fernando, these are Mr Salter's guests.'

Fernando smiled. 'A pleasure,' and led the way into the restaurant, which was beautifully designed in Art Deco style, tables dotted around a small dance floor, booths behind. There was a cocktail bar straight out of the thirties, and a trio played dance music. All the waiters wore white monkey jackets.

Fernando led the way to a large booth, and two of the boys pulled the table out so they could sit.

'What may I offer you to drink?'

'Jack Daniel's for me, with branch water,' Rupert

told him. 'A champagne cocktail for the lady. When are you expecting Mr Salter?'

'He's on his way.'

'Then we won't order yet,' Kate said. 'Just the drinks.'

Rupert took out a pack of Marlboros and shook out two. He lit them both and offered her one. 'Just like in the movies.'

She laughed. 'Whatever else you are, darling, Paul Henreid you're not.'

'Though Bette Davis played a number of ladies who remind me of you.'

'What a compliment, Rupert.'

The drinks came. 'You're enjoying this, aren't you?'

'Absolutely.' She toasted him. 'Cheers, darling.'

Shortly afterwards, Harry Salter and the others came in. 'Are you being looked after okay?'

'Perfectly,' Kate Rashid said.

'Good. We'll join you then.'

Joe Baxter had followed and stood against the wall, his arms folded, Billy beside him looking grim. Dillon sat at the end of the booth, a cigarette smouldering from the right-hand corner of his mouth. Ferguson and Harry sat opposite.

'As it's my shout, I'll order for all of us,' Harry

said, and turned to Fernando. 'Cristal all round, still water, none of that sparkling stuff, scrambled eggs, smoked salmon, chopped onions, tossed salad all round.'

Fernando retreated hurriedly and Kate said, 'A man who knows his own mind.'

'That's why I'm here and a lot of others are long gone.'

Ferguson said, 'So, what's it all about, my dear?'

'Here we go, Rupert, the General playing the bluff and honest English gentleman. What it's all about, General, is that I want you off my case. I know you've been checking up on me. So has Daniel Quinn. And I know you wouldn't be sitting here with me if you'd found anything good. We had an interesting meeting in Washington the other night, you know. Strong words were spoken, views exchanged. I'm sure Blake's passed all that on to you.'

'Of course,' Dillon said. 'It was just after a couple of guys tried to mug Quinn on his way to the White House.'

'Really? How unfortunate. I assume he handled himself well. But speaking of mugging, what about you and your little foray to Loch Dhu?'

'Ah, well, just a little recreation. We stayed at

Ardmurchan Lodge a few years ago, and thought we'd try it again. Very pleasant. Ferguson and I went shooting.'

'I just bet you did,' Kate said.

'Deer,' Dillon told her, and smiled. 'Just deer.'

'Brown had to have nine stitches in his face. I seriously disapprove of thugs pistol-whipping my employees. Try it again and you'll regret it, Dillon.' Her face was a mask of restrained anger. 'And what was the purpose of going all the way up there just to let me know you'd been there? You could have phoned me.'

'To get the official line on your Act of Class Warfare kiddies?' Ferguson asked. 'All that bunkum about country pursuits for school parties? You're not teaching them to play patty fingers up there.'

'We have nothing to hide, General, and you know damn well you can't prove otherwise.'

'What about all those organizations of yours in the Middle East?' Ferguson asked.

'I'm a very wealthy Arab. I feel privileged to be able to help my people. Some organizations there have political aims, but we're interested in social and educational programmes. We pay for teachers and build schools and small hospitals all over Arabia, from Iraq to Hazar.'

'And Beirut?' Dillon put in.

'Of course Beirut.'

'The Children's Trust, which is a front for Hezbollah,' Ferguson told her.

She sighed. 'Prove it, General. Again, prove it. Everything my Trust does is above board.'

'What about your trip to Hazar tomorrow? Is that above board, too?'

She shook her head. 'Enough. General, as you well know, Rashid Investments derives most of its billions from oil in Southern Arabia, the Empty Quarter and Hazar. I go there all the time. I'm weary of this, Rupert, and suddenly I seem to have lost my appetite. Let's go.' She stood up. 'Thanks for the hospitality, gentlemen. But I warn you, stay out of my affairs, or you'll regret it.'

'Come on,' Billy said, his eyes burning. 'Come on and try, any time you want.'

'Cool it, Billy,' his uncle told him.

'Good night.' She nodded to Rupert and he followed her out.

At that moment, Fernando and a posse of waiters arrived with the scrambled eggs and smoked salmon.

'Well, it looks good to me,' Harry said. 'So let's eat. I've had enough of that bloody woman for the moment.'

* * *

Outside, the queue had disappeared. Rupert and Kate Rashid drove off, but as they approached the end of the wharf, Rupert said, 'Pull in.'

Kate said, 'What are you up to?'

'I think I'll hang on to watch the fun. I'll catch up with you later.' He got out.

'Take care, darling,' she said as he closed the door and walked away.

When they'd finished eating, Harry Salter ordered brandies all around and told Billy to cheer up. 'You've got a face on you like death itself. Don't worry, Billy, we've got her number.'

'She's a nutter.' Billy tapped his head. 'Who knows what she'll do next. I bet even she doesn't bleeding well know.'

'I take your point,' Dillon told him. 'But she does have an agenda and we're part of it.'

'I said we'll sort her,' his uncle told him. 'Trust me.'

'I'd listen to him, Billy,' Dillon said. 'He said the same thing before the two of you sorted the Franconi twins the other year. Rumour has it they're in cement on the North Circular Road.'

'Yes, well, that was business,' Salter said. 'You know what happened there, don't you? They got some IRA explosives expert to stick a bomb under my Jaguar. Lucky for me and Billy, he got the timer wrong and the car blew up just before we got there.' The brandies arrived and he shook his head. 'Terrible times we live in, General. Anyway, here's to all of us 'cos we're still here.' He swallowed his Hennessey in a single gulp. 'Come on, Billy, let's walk them out.'

They stepped out of the front door and Rupert Dauncey watched from the darkness as they reached Ferguson's car, his chauffeur at the wheel. Suddenly, there was a shrill cry, and five men erupted from between the cars, carrying baseball bats. They were all Chinese, all wearing black silk bomber jackets with the Red Dragon insignia, and the two in front were the two from the queue.

One of them rushed in and swung at Billy, but Billy raised his right foot into the man's crotch. Dillon avoided a similar blow, grabbed for a wrist, and rammed his assailant head-first into a Volvo. The others pulled back and circled.

The one with the cockney voice said, 'We've got you now, mate. You're going to get yours.'

Harry Salter showed not the slightest fear. 'Red Dragons? What is this, carnival night in Hong Kong?'

The one Billy had kicked had dropped his baseball bat and Billy picked it up. 'Come on, let's be having you.'

The leader said, 'He's mine,' moved in close and swung. Billy fended off the blow, let him get close, tripped him, and put a foot on his chest. The others started forward and Dillon took out his Walther and fired in the air.

'This is getting boring. Get your arses out of here, and leave the bats behind.' There was dismay on their faces, and yet hesitation, so he fired at the second man who'd been in the queue, shooting off the lobe of his left ear. The man screamed and dropped his bat and the others followed suit.

'Now get out of here,' Salter said, and they ran. He said to Billy, 'Not him.' He nodded at the one on the ground. 'I want words with him.' He turned to Ferguson. 'This might not be something you should see, General.'

Dillon said, 'I'll report in later.'

'I'll look forward to it,' Ferguson replied.

He got into the Daimler and drove away as Joe Baxter and Sam Hall arrived on the run. Billy still had a foot on the Chinese man, and Joe said, 'Did we hear shots?'

'You certainly did, my old son,' Harry told him. 'Bruce Lee here and his merry men tried to give us a going-over.' He stirred the man with his foot. 'Have him up, boys.'

Billy removed his foot, and Baxter and Hall raised the man by an arm each. He didn't seem afraid but simply glared as Harry moved close.

'Big man,' growled the attacker. 'How good are you on your own?' And he spat in Salter's face.

'No manners.' Harry took out a handkerchief and cleaned himself. 'He needs a lesson in etiquette. Billy?'

Billy punched the man in the stomach until he doubled over, then kneed him in his face. Salter took a handful of hair and raised his head.

'Now be a good boy and tell me who put you on to me.'

The man shook his head, though he seemed less tough now. 'No, I can't.'

'Oh dear. All right, Billy, on his back and stamp on his shin. Put him on sticks for six months.'

The man gave a grunt. 'No! All right . . . It was a man called Dauncey. That's all I know. Gave me a grand to see to you.'

'Where is it?'

'Inside pocket.'

Billy found it, a bundle of ten-pound notes with an elastic band around them. He passed it to Salter, who slipped it in a pocket.

'Now, that wasn't too hard, was it? Of course, you've seriously upset me, and that won't do.' He picked up a baseball bat. 'Right arm, Billy.'

The man tried to struggle, but Baxter and Hall held him fast and Billy pulled the arm straight. The baseball bat rose and fell. There was a crack, and the man cried out and slumped to his knees.

Salter crouched. 'There's a hospital a mile up the road. You need the Casualty department, my old son, but you should be able to make it. Just don't come back here again. If you do, I'll kill you.' He stood up. 'I think I could do with another brandy.'

He walked away. The rest followed, but Dillon paused to call Ferguson on his mobile. The General was still in the Daimler.

'What a surprise – they were hired by Rupert Dauncey.'

'Well, at least we know where we are now. What happened to the Chinese gentleman? Not in the river, I trust?'

119

'One of the walking wounded. I'll see you tomorrow.' Dillon clicked off his phone and went inside.

It was quiet outside, the only sound that of the injured man hauling himself off his knees. Rupert Dauncey slipped out of the shadows. 'Are you all right, old man?'

'He's broken my arm.'

'I'd say you're lucky he didn't break your neck.' He took out a cigarette and lit it with his AK lighter. 'In fact, you're lucky I don't break your neck, you idiot.' He blew a stream of smoke at him. 'Let me just leave you with this thought. Step out of line, open your mouth just once – and I'll kill you myself. You understand?'

'Yes,' the man moaned.

'Excellent.'

Rupert Dauncey walked away, and after a while the other man began to stumble up the street.

HAZAR

7

Northolt, on the outer edge of London, was an RAF base much used by the royal family, the Prime Minister and major politicians. Because of this, it had become increasingly popular with users of executive aircraft and proved a lucrative sideline for the Royal Air Force.

It was ten o'clock the following morning when Kate Rashid and Rupert Dauncey passed through security and drove round to the apron where the Gulfstream was standing. The engines were already turning over as they arrived, and a few minutes later they had started their climb to fifty thousand feet.

When they levelled out, a young woman in a navy blue uniform approached them. 'Tea as usual, Countess?'

'Thank you, Molly.'

'Coffee for Mr Dauncey? We have an American

in the family now!' Molly went to the kitchen. Kate said, 'Give me a cigarette and go over it again, Rupert.'

He did as ordered and described the events of the night before. He shook his head. 'I can't understand it. The Red Dragons came highly rec-ommended.'

'Those incompetents in Washington came highly recommended, too.'

'Yes, I'm obviously going to have to get better sources. Now, what's the agenda for today?'

'We land at Hamam airport, then we'll take a helicopter to Shabwa Oasis in the Empty Quarter, then further into the Empty Quarter, to the oasis at Fuad. I have a camp there. I'd like you to see it.'

'What goes on there?'

'You'll see.'

'Mystery on mystery, hmm? Do we go to Hazar Town?'

'Oh, yes, I'd like to see Tony Villiers.'

'Are you going to have him bumped off?'

'I'd rather not. I like Tony. He's a superb com-manding officer, and since the Sultan forbids him to go into the Empty Quarter, he's really not much threat.' She shrugged. 'We'll see. I've taken certain steps which should give him pause for thought.'

'Such as?'

'Oh, let that be another little mystery for now, Rupert. Pass me *The Times*.' She opened it to the financial pages.

Villiers had left most of the Scouts in Cornet Bobby Hawk's hands and was proceeding down the desert road to Hazar Town. This was hill country, filled with rocky defiles and great cliffs the colour of ochre. There was no traffic, not a sign of another human being, not even a goatherd.

He had two Land Rovers with eight men, including himself, a light machine gun mounted in each vehicle. It was incredibly hot and dusty, and Villiers was looking forward with pleasure to his room at the Excelsior Hotel, a bath and a fresh uniform.

They stopped by a pool at a spot called Hama at the foot of some cliffs. The water was deep and cool, and one of the men stood at a machine gun on watch while the others took off their bandoliers and sandals, walked into the pool in their robes, and splashed each other like children. Villiers lit a cigarette and watched, amused. But the smile quickly vanished as a spattering of stones came down the cliff in a shower. He glanced up, and his men started to plunge through the water to their weapons. A shot rang out and the leading man went down, a bullet in his head.

The machine gunner raked the cliffs up above for a full minute, as the men reached their rifles and fired up, too, but there was no reply. Villiers brought it to a stop. There was silence now.

Selim crawled to him beside one of the Land Rovers, and Villiers waited for a while, then stood up.

'No, *Sahb*,' the Sergeant said.

The silence was eerie. 'It's all right. Whoever it was has gone already. I don't know why, but it was hit-and-run.'

'Maybe *Adoo* bandits from the Yemen, *Sahb*. Or maybe Omar there offended someone?' They gazed at the floating body.

'No, it could have been any one of you.' He turned to his men. 'Go on, get him out of the water.'

Three of them waded in and pulled the body out. They had a couple of body bags in one of the Land Rovers amongst the general supplies and got Omar into one.

'Put him on the bonnet of number two Land

Rover,' Villiers ordered. 'And tie him on tight. The next few miles are rough.'

Someone produced a coil of rope and they placed the body as instructed, running the rope across and beneath the vehicle. The other Scouts watched in silence, subdued.

'Right, we'll move out now,' Villiers said.

Selim sat beside him, looking troubled. '*Sahb*, one thing puzzles me. If the man who did this thing simply wanted to kill only one of us, why not the *Sahb*, why not the most important of us?'

'Because they didn't want me dead,' Villiers told him. 'They just wanted to send a signal, Selim.'

Selim looked even more troubled. 'Can this be so, *Sahb*? Who would want this?'

'Someone from the Empty Quarter. One of those people who shouldn't be here and perhaps shouldn't be there, Selim. We'll find out soon enough.' He smiled. 'As Allah wills.'

Selim, deeply disturbed, looked away, and Villiers lit a cigarette and leaned back.

The Port of Hazar was small, with white houses, narrow alleys and two bazaars, but the port area was busy, filled with shabby coastal ships, Arab dhows and fishing boats. The two Land Rovers stopped at the largest mosque, where Villiers delivered Omar's body to the Imam.

Afterwards, they drove down to the Excelsior Hotel, where he told Selim and the other five Scouts to take a couple of days off and gave them twenty dollars each in fives. They were American dollars, an old custom that delighted them, for US dollars were greatly appreciated in Hazar. He told them he knew where to find them if necessary and dismissed them.

The Excelsior dated from colonial days and still had a whiff of British Empire about it. The bar had the look of an old movie, with cane furniture, fans turning on the ceiling and a marble-topped bar, bottles ranged behind. The barman, Abdul, wore a white monkey jacket from his days as a waiter on cruise ships.

'Lager,' Villiers told him, 'and as cold as it gets.'

He went out through the French windows and sat in a large cane chair, the awning above his head flapping in the wind. Abdul brought the lager. Villiers ran a finger down the glass, beaded with moisture, then drank slowly, but without stopping, washing away the sand and the heat and the dirt of the border country.

Abdul had waited, an old ritual. 'Another one, *Sahb*?'

'Yes, thank you, Abdul.'

Villiers lit a cigarette and looked out to the horizon, a dark mood on him. Maybe it was the death of Omar, and the puzzle why he himself had been spared. On the other hand, maybe he'd stayed in Hazar too long. He'd been married once, more years ago than he cared to remember: Gabrielle of the blonde hair and the green eyes, the love of his life. But he'd been away from home too much, they'd drifted apart, and finally divorced just before the Falklands War. What made it worse was that she'd married the enemy, an Argentine Air Force fighter ace who later became a general.

No one could ever replace her. There had been women, of course, but never one to move him enough to marry again. For Villiers, it had been a life of soldiering in strange places, his only anchor the old family house in West Sussex, and the home farm, worked by his nephew, who was married with two children and also doubled as the estate manager. They were always begging him to give up soldiering while he was still in one piece and come home.

Abdul interrupted his reverie with the second

lager. Someone called, 'I'll have one of those,' and Villiers turned to see Ben Carver walk in wearing flying overalls and a Panama hat. He flopped down in the chair opposite Villiers and fanned his face with the hat.

'Christ, it's hot out there.'

'How's the air taxi business?'

'Lucrative, with all those oil leases out there on the border country. I've replaced the Three-Ten your friend Dillon crashed last year.'

'He didn't crash it, he was shot down by Bedu, as you well know.'

'All right, so he was shot down. I've still got the Golden Eagle, and I've got a couple of South African kids flying over in my new Beechcraft. Well, it's not exactly new, but it'll do nicely.'

'Are they going to stay?'

'They're giving it six months. I need someone. There's a lot of Rashid work around.'

'I hear she's coming in today.'

'The Countess? Yeah, she's flying in with someone named Dauncey. Not staying long, though. Got a slot back to London the day after tomorrow.'

'Dauncey is her cousin. Tell me, Ben, when you fly to oil sites out there in the Empty Quarter, do you see much action?'

'Action? What do you mean?'

'Well, since the Sultan won't let the Scouts cross the border anymore, I just don't know things the way I used to. Who do you see?'

Carver wasn't smiling now. 'A few caravans, will that do?' He swallowed his lager and stood. 'I see nothing, Tony.'

'Which is what you're paid to do?'

'I'm paid to fly to exploratory oil wells, land in the desert, then fly back.' He walked to the door and turned. 'And I'm paid to mind my own business. You should try it.'

'So that means you don't fly that new toy of hers, the Scorpion? I've seen that helicopter crossing the line dozens of times when we've been on patrol. That isn't you at the controls?'

Carver glared as he walked out, and as Villiers stood, he realized Abdul was carefully cleaning a glass-topped table close to the open French window. He'd obviously heard every word.

'Another lager, Colonel?'

'No, thanks.' Villiers smiled. 'I'll be down for dinner later,' and he walked out.

*　　*　　*

He had a long hot shower to get really clean, then relaxed in a tepid bath for half an hour, thinking about things, particularly his encounter with Ben Carver. A good man, Ben, DFC in the Gulf War, but with an eye on his bank account. He wouldn't want to rock the boat, especially the Rashid boat. There were certain things Villiers could take for granted about Kate Rashid, though. She would stay at the Rashid Villa in the old quarter, a Moorish palace. At some stage, she would proceed to Shabwa Oasis by helicopter. And she would dine at the Excelsior restaurant that night, because she always did.

Evening was falling, orange streaks colouring the horizon beyond the harbour. He towelled his long hair vigorously, remembering his years with the SAS, when you were never sure what would happen next, if you'd suddenly have to assume a civilian identity, an Army haircut wouldn't do. All that Irish time that would never go away.

As he stood at the mirror combing his hair, he thought about how to handle dinner, then decided to go all the way: no linen suit tonight, something to impress. He took a tropical uniform from the wardrobe, khaki trousers and bush shirt, the medal ribbons making a brave show. He held it up and smiled. That would do nicely.

Rupert was much impressed with the Rashid Villa. He stood in the great hall, looking up at the vaulted ceiling. There were wonderful rugs scattered on the marble floor, Arab antiques on all sides, and the walls were painted with frescoes.

'This is really quite a show.'

'Thank you, darling. There are offices at the back, computers, the works. This is headquarters for Rashid Investments in Hazar and the whole of Southern Arabia.'

The head house boy, who had greeted them at the great copper door, said, 'Abdul, from the Excelsior, has been waiting to see you, Countess.'

'Where is he?'

'With Abu.'

Abu was her body servant, a fierce Bedu warrior from Shabwa Oasis. He was always there to greet her when she arrived in Hazar and stayed at her side for the length of the trip.

'We'll have tea and coffee on the terrace. Bring him to me.'

She led the way up marble stairs with Rupert following, passed along an airy corridor, and came out on a wide terrace, the awning flapping in the early evening breeze. The view was stupendous, for they were high up above the rooftops.

'Magnificent.' Rupert sat down and offered her a cigarette.

'It'll be dark soon. Dusk doesn't last long here,' Kate said.

Behind them, Abdul was ushered in by Abu, who was tall and bearded with a hard face, and wore a white head cloth and robe.

'Abu, it is good to see you,' she told him in Arabic.

He smiled, a thing he rarely did, and salaamed. 'And for me to see you, Countess, is a blessing as always. This creature wishes to see you.'

'Then let him speak.' She said to Rupert, 'Abdul is the barman at the Excelsior.'

'Countess, I have news,' Abdul said in Arabic.

'English, please, my cousin has no Arabic.'

'Colonel Villiers came in from the border earlier this afternoon. Two Land Rovers and six Scouts. He was ambushed when they halted at the pool at Hama. One of his men was shot dead. Omar. There was a sniper on the cliffs.'

The house boy came in with the tea and coffee, served it unobtrusively and withdrew.

Kate Rashid said, 'How do you know this?'

Abdul shrugged. 'The Scouts are in the bazaar and they've been talking.'

She nodded. 'Is Villiers *Sahb* eating at the hotel tonight?'

'Yes, Countess, but I have more. The colonel was drinking lager on the terrace and Mr Carver joined him. I managed to hear their conversation.'

She turned to Rupert. 'Ben Carver is an old RAF hand who runs air taxis out of Hamam. He does a lot of work for Rashid.' She nodded to Abdul. 'Go on.'

Abdul told her everything, for he had an excellent memory and prided himself on it. When he was finished, she opened her purse and took out a fifty dollar bill and handed it to him.

'You've done well.'

He backed away and raised a hand. 'No, Countess, this is for you, my gift.'

'For which I thank you, but do not dishonour me by refusing mine.' Abdul bowed and smiled, took the bill hurriedly, turned and went out.

Rupert said, 'So Villiers is pumping people for information?'

'On Ferguson's behalf, we can assume.'

'Who ambushed him?'

'Who do you think?' She spoke to Abu. 'You've done well. The one you killed, who was he, this Omar?' The answer was important. Since the Scouts were all Rashid Bedu, the family links with those in the Empty Quarter were immensely strong.

'My second cousin.'

'I want no blood feud over this.'

'There will be none, Countess.'

'And Villiers *Sahb* will not be touched until I give the word.'

'As you say, Countess, I would only kill him face-to-face. He is a great warrior.'

'Good. My cousin here is a great warrior, too. He fought many battles with the American Marines and is precious to me. Guard him with your life.'

'As you say, Countess.' He went out.

She explained to Rupert what Abu had told her, and suddenly, darkness started to fall and the house boy came in and switched on the lights. Moths fluttered instantly.

'So what now, cousin?' Rupert asked.

'I think a glass of champagne.' She nodded to the house boy, who was hovering, and gave the order. A moment later, Abu appeared.

'It grieves me to disturb you, Countess, but Selim asks to see you.'

'Selim? Really? How interesting. Bring him in.' She said to Rupert, 'Another man has turned up – and this one is a Sergeant in the Scouts.'

'And, of course, a Rashid. It still puzzles me how this all works, both sides made up of the same people.'

'That's because you're a Yank and you don't understand the Arab mind.'

The house boy appeared with a bottle of Bollinger in an ice bucket and two glasses. He thumbed the cork off expertly and poured.

'I thought alcohol was forbidden in Arab countries,' Rupert said.

'It varies. Hazar has always had a rather liberal attitude.'

'And you go along with that? After all, you are a Muslim.'

'I also don't wear a *chador*,' she said, referring to the obligatory headscarf for Muslim women. 'I'm also half English, Rupert. I serve both sides of the coin.'

As she sipped champagne, Abu ushered Selim in. The Sergeant looked very worried.

'You speak good English, Selim, so we'll speak

English now. Does Villiers *Sahb* know you are here?'

'No, Countess.' Selim was instantly alarmed. 'I am here because I felt I must speak to you.'

'Why?'

'We've been in the border country, the Scouts, with the Colonel. We no longer cross into the Empty Quarter.'

'I know this.'

'Villiers *Sahb* asked me many questions. He wanted to know if there was anything going on over the border.'

'And what did you tell him?'

'That I knew nothing. But he made me feel uncomfortable. I don't think he believed me.'

'Which shows his intelligence, for you were lying to him, weren't you?'

'Countess, please.'

'Light me a cigarette, Rupert.' He did so and passed it to her. 'But you must not lie to me, Selim.' She leaned forward. 'So tell me what you have heard whispered.'

'The camp, Countess, the camp at Fuad Oasis. Foreigners come and go, and there is sometimes much gunfire. Those who roam the desert, the *Adoo* bandits, have heard of such things.'

'Many people talk mysteries, and loose tongues abound. But they can be cut out, Selim. Why have you come to me? You are the Colonel's man.'

'But I am also Rashid.' Selim was bewildered. 'My loyalty is to you first, Countess. You are our leader, all Rashid agree.'

'Even the Hazar Scouts?'

'Well, there are those who are old-fashioned in their ways who look to the Colonel.'

'Men who keep their oath, you mean, unlike you? You also swore the oath. You tasted salt with Colonel Villiers, and ate his bread. There is a matter of honour here, and loyalty. You say you are loyal to me, but can I depend on loyalty and honour from a man who has none?'

'Countess – please,' Selim said wildly.

'Go from my sight. Never return.'

Abu gripped Selim's arm and pushed him out of the terrace. Rupert said, 'What was that all about?'

'Honour is everything to my people. Men die for it – and Selim will die for his lack of it.'

Abu returned and, to Rupert's total astonishment, said in excellent English. 'The man is a dog, Countess. What would you have me do?'

'See to him, Abu.'

'At your orders.'

He went out and she smiled slightly at Rupert. 'When Abu was eighteen, his uncle, a rich trader, sent him to London University. He got a degree in economics, but on his return, he found that he preferred being a warrior. He is a very good one.'

'Then God help Selim.'

She finished her champagne and stood up. 'Time for a shower and a change of clothes. I'll show you your suite.'

Selim hurried from one narrow alley to another, making for the old quarter, and yet the truth was he had no idea where to go. He had thought to find favour with the Countess. Instead, he had received a death sentence. Nothing was more certain. He paused and stood in a doorway to consider the situation.

There was nowhere to hide, not in Hazar, not in the high country of the border or in the Empty Quarter. The word would go out amongst his people, and every hand would be against him. His mind raced and came up with only one possible solution: the harbour. There were boats there that called at every port in Southern Arabia. Perhaps he could get to Aden or even Mombassa on the east coast of Africa. There was a larger Arab population there and it was far from Rashid territory.

He hurried away, taking a different direction, and came out on the waterfront. It was very dark, but there were lights on the moored shipping. If he could slip on board one of the ancient coastal steamers, all would be well.

He turned on to one of the boardwalk wharfs, which had several boats tied up. It was very quiet, with only the sound of distant laugher, and then a board creaked behind him and he turned and saw Abu. Selim turned to run, but Abu was faster. He caught him by the robe, a knife in one hand, pulled back Selim's head, and drew the knife across his throat. Selim sagged, the life going out of him, and Abu wiped his knife on the man's robe and pushed him over the side of the wharf. The body fell some fifty feet, there was a splash, then only the silence again.

Abu walked away quickly. When he had gone, another Arab came out of the darkness wearing the crossed bandoliers of the Scouts, an AK slung from his left shoulder. He peered over the edge of the wharf and saw Selim's body floating facedown in the faint light at the stern of a coastal steamer. After a moment, he turned and walked away.

Villiers made a striking figure in his tropical uniform as he went into the bar at the Excelsior. There were only half a dozen people, all alone, and all European, with an air of business about them. One or two looked at him, curious. There was no sign of Kate Rashid or Rupert Dauncey. Villiers moved to the bar, where Abdul polished glasses.

'I'd have thought the Countess would be in tonight. I know she's in town.'

'Later, *Sahb*, she comes later.'

'Did she tell you that?'

Abdul looked nervous. 'Would you like a lager, Colonel *Sahb*?'

'Not now.'

He walked out, lit a cigarette and stood at the top of the steps leading down to the garden. One of his men squatted at one side of the steps, his AK across his knees.

Villiers said in Arabic, 'I see you, Achmed.'

'And I you, Colonel *Sahb*.'

'So why are you here?'

'Selim is dead. He floats in the harbour.'

'Tell me,' Villiers said, offering a cigarette and a light.

'We were to go with the women in the bazaar, have whisky sups. *Sahb* knows we can do that there.'

'And?'

'Selim was troubled, not himself. He said he had to see a friend. I thought it strange, so I followed.'

'And where did he go?'

'The Rashid Villa. It was almost dark. I stood in the palms on the other side of the street and looked up to the terrace. The Countess was there with a man, English, I think.'

'No, American. I know who this man is.'

'Then Abu brought Selim on to the terrace, and he and the Countess talked. A little later, Selim came out. He stood there looking worried, as if he didn't know where to go.'

'What do you mean by worried?'

'He had the stink of fear on him, *Sahb*. He started down the street, and I was about to follow when Abu came out and went after him.'

'And you followed.'

'Yes, *Sahb*, down to the harbour. He turned on to one of the wharfs. He seemed to be examining the ships, then Abu ran up behind him, cut his throat and pushed him into the water.'

Villiers said, 'Why would Abu do this thing?'

'For the Countess, *Sahb*.'

'But what would be her reason?'

'Allah alone knows this.'

Villiers offered him another cigarette. 'I'm grateful, Achmed, that you've told me this, but why? You, too, are Rashid, the Countess is your leader.'

He knew the answer before it came. 'But *Sahb*, I have tasted your salt, sworn the oath, and I am your man. This the Countess would agree on. It is a matter of honour.'

'And perhaps Selim had none.'

Achmed shrugged. 'He was a weak man.'

'But a good Sergeant.'

'I would be better, *Sahb*.'

Villiers smiled. 'Well, you must prove that to me.' He took out his packet of cigarettes and gave them to him. 'Go on, you rogue, but no mention of this to the others.'

'It will come out, *Sahb*, these things do.'

'Let it be in its own time.'

Achmed faded into the darkness and Villiers went inside and approached the bar. *A matter of honour.* That was supremely important to the Bedus, and perhaps Kate Rashid also saw it that way.

'Cigarettes, Abdul,' he said. 'Marlboros.'

Abdul passed a pack across. 'A lager now, Colonel?'

Before he could reply, a voice said, 'Why, Tony, how nice,' and he turned to find Kate Rashid entering the bar, Dauncey with her. She wore a simple white shift, and magnificent diamond earrings and necklace. He wore a linen suit and a pale blue shirt.

'Countess.' Before he could say more, she reached up and kissed his cheek.

'I've told you before, it's Kate to my friends. This is my cousin, Major Rupert Dauncey, Marine Corps. And this, Rupert, is the famous Colonel Tony Villiers.'

They shook hands. 'My pleasure, Major,' Villiers told him.

'No, mine. I've heard a lot about you.'

'Champagne on the terrace, Abdul – you must join us, Tony, and for dinner,' Kate said.

'How can I refuse?'

Her eyes glittered and there was an excitement in them, for as she and Rupert had been leaving the villa, Abu had appeared.

145

'Are all things well?' she'd asked.

'It is done, Countess.'

'Good. It's a nice night for a walk. You will accompany us.'

He'd fallen in behind them, his hand on the hilt of the *jambiya*, the curved Arab knife at his belt, although not a soul in Hazar would have gone against him.

'The dog died, is that it?' Rupert shook his head. 'God, but you're a hard woman, harder than I ever could have believed.'

'This is a hard land, darling, and being hard is the only way to survive.' She slipped a hand in his arm. 'But no sad songs. I want to enjoy myself this evening.'

8

The night wind blowing in from the sea was warm and perfumed, a touch of spices there. Kate was sitting on a swing seat, Rupert and Villiers opposite her across a cane table. Abdul was serving champagne.

'You look absolutely splendid, Tony. All those medals. He's got everything except the Victoria Cross, Rupert.'

'So I can see.'

'You and Rupert have things in common,' she told Villiers. 'The Gulf War, Serbia and Bosnia.'

'Really?' Rupert said. 'That's very interesting. Which unit?'

'SAS.' Villiers decided to push it. 'I'm surprised you didn't know. Kate certainly knows everything about me.'

'Now then, Tony, you're getting fractious. On the other hand, I know you've had a hell of a day.

To paraphrase Oscar Wilde, to lose one man might be considered careless, but to lose two . . .'

Villiers turned to Rupert. 'One thing you'll discover about this place is that news travels fast. Nothing stays secret for long. I did lose a man when we stopped at the pool at Hama on the way in.'

'Tough luck,' Rupert said.

'Yes, but the second man, my sergeant, Selim, was murdered only a short while ago down on the docks.' He smiled at Kate. 'You must have remarkable sources.'

'It's the secret of my success, Tony. But enough of this. Let's order.'

The meal was excellent, for the chef had a French mother, and had trained in Paris. Rupert Dauncey and Villiers, as soldiers do, discussed their personal experiences in the Gulf War and the former Yugoslavia.

'So you were behind Iraqi lines with the SAS?' Rupert asked. 'How long?'

'Oh, before the war started. We knew it was coming and exactly what Saddam Hussein intended.' Villiers shrugged. 'People like me with a working knowledge of Arabic were at a premium. Like Kate's brother Paul.'

'Did you know him?'

'We were in the same regiment, the Grenadier Guards, but he was long after my time. I knew him there, though. He had his men kill my second-in-command, Cornet James Bronsby. The Rashid have a very effective technique. They slice the skin down from the chest. It takes a long time. The loss of masculinity is the final touch, but then Kate will have told you all this.'

'Actually, I hadn't,' she said.

'Why? Were you ashamed?'

'No. My people expected it. It's their way.' She shrugged. 'And you got your revenge, Tony. Dillon killed four of my men the following morning. And one of them was my brother, George.'

'If he couldn't take the consequences, he shouldn't have joined.'

Abdul appeared with three glasses of cognac on his tray. Kate sipped a little of hers. 'I hear you have a new second-in-command, another House-hold Cavalryman?'

'Yes, a Lifeguard this time. Cornet Bobby Hawk. A nice boy. You'd like him.'

'Perhaps *he* shouldn't have joined.'

The threat was implicit and he was angry now, tired of playing games, so he swallowed the cognac down.

149

'Oh, you can do better than that, Kate. Tell me, why didn't Abu go for a head shot on me out there at Hama?'

'Why, Tony, I'm shocked. You're far too important, not only to Hazar, but to me. You're the best commander the Scouts have ever had. And you follow the Sultan's instructions.'

'Which means your instructions.'

'I rule the Empty Quarter, Tony, and I don't need the Scouts there. I don't want them. Police the border country, the high country, but stay on your side of the line.'

'Why? Do you have something to hide over there?'

'That's my business. Next time you speak to Charles Ferguson, tell him to mind his.' She nodded to Rupert. 'We'll go now. We have an early start in the morning.'

He pulled back her chair and said to Villiers, 'It's been an interesting evening, Colonel.'

Villiers stood up. 'You could say that. Good night, Kate.'

She smiled and led the way out, and Villiers said, 'Another cognac, Abdul,' and went back to the terrace to think things over.

Kate Rashid and Rupert walked back to the

villa, Abu behind. 'He's quite a man,' Rupert said. 'But he's right. Why don't you have him killed?'

'That might come later, but not for the moment. As I said, his work in the high country with the Scouts is useful to me, and good for Hazar.'

'But what about his link with Ferguson?'

'Villiers can't tell him anything if he doesn't know anything. That's all that matters.'

'Well, you're the expert. What's our schedule tomorrow?'

'The helicopter will be ready at seven. We'll call in at Shabwa, it's expected of me, then we'll fly on to Fuad Lake.'

'How far?'

'Another hundred miles deeper into the desert.' They had reached the steps leading up to the door of the villa and she turned to Abu. 'Where are the Scouts at the moment?'

'They've been operating out of El Hajiz. There's good water there, but they may have moved.'

They were speaking in English. 'Villiers *Sahb* will join them soon, I think. You stay and watch him. When he leaves, follow. Take one of our Land Rovers.'

'What are your orders?'

'I think he needs another lesson. He's proving difficult.'

'The new officer?'

'Perhaps a fright will be enough. It is all as Allah wills. I leave it with you. Good night.'

The copper door opened as if by magic, the house boy appeared, and she passed through, Rupert following.

'Remind me never to give you cause to become annoyed with me,' he said.

'As if you would.' She smiled. 'You're perfectly safe, darling. After all, you are a Dauncey.'

Abu went straight down to the bazaar, a neck cloth obscuring his face, and went to the café that he knew the Scouts used regularly when in Hazar. They were seated at a table drinking coffee, Achmed and his four comrades. There were people all around, some squatting against the wall. Abu pulled the neck cloth higher over his face, covering it almost completely, squatted there, head down, and listened to Achmed and his friends talk.

Achmed had not told them of Selim's death, had not even hinted at it. For the moment, he told them that Selim had received a message about some family trouble and had decided to go home.

At that moment, Villiers appeared and they all scrambled to their feet. Achmed told him, 'Selim was upset. I think it was bad news from the family. He's not been around, *Sahb*. He must have gone.'

'Then you are now sergeant,' Villiers told him. 'We leave at dawn for El Hajiz. Get the Land Rovers ready and pick me up at the hotel.'

'As the *Sahb* commands.'

Villiers turned and went. Achmed and his comrades moved out. Only then did Abu get to his feet and walk away.

Knowing the Scouts' destination, Abu left the villa before dawn in a Land Rover. Kate Rashid and Rupert were driven by the house boy to a small landing pad she'd had constructed on the outskirts of Hazar, where a Scorpion helicopter waited with room for eight passengers. The pilot was Ben Carver, who was crouched beside it in blue RAF flying overalls.

'Good morning, Ben,' she said. 'This is my cousin, Rupert Dauncey. How's the weather?'

'Well, it's going to be bloody hot, but there's nothing new in that. Shabwa's fine, but there's a chance of a sandstorm in the Fuad area.'

'We'll just have to tough it out. Let's get moving.'

There was an airstrip at Shabwa, an enormous oasis with palm trees and a pool the size of a small lake, plus many, many tents, horses, camels, herds of goats, and several Land Rovers. The Scorpion landed, and as Kate Rashid got out, people surged forward, not only warriors with rifles but women and children. Several rifles were fired into the air, children cried out in delight, and the crowd milled around, trying to touch her.

The warriors pushed them away and formed two lines. Two young boys ran forward, each with a robe, and helped Kate and Rupert into them.

She raised an arm to the warriors, fist clenched. 'My brothers.'

They roared their approval and more rifles were fired into the air. She led the way to where a huge awning had been prepared, with a carpet and cushions to sit on. Two of the sub-chieftains squatted crosslegged beside her and engaged in a lively conversation in Arabic. Rupert lit a cigarette and was served thick sweet coffee in a metal cup, and seed cakes. The two old chieftains were also busy with coffee, and many people sat and watched.

'Unbelievable,' Rupert said. 'I've never seen anything like it.'

'These are my people, Rupert.'

'And yet this is only half of you. When you took me down to Dauncey the other month, the villagers were just the same, in a strange way. Dammit, when we went in the Dauncey Arms for a drink, everybody who was sitting down stood up.'

'That's because they are also my people, and they're as dear to me as those here. Dauncey roots go deep, Rupert, and they're your roots, too.'

'Something to live up to, all that,' Rupert said, and somewhat to his own surprise, realized that he meant it.

Women appeared with various dishes: rice, lentils, plenty of unleavened bread, and a hot stew.

'What the hell is in that?' Rupert asked.

'Goat, darling, and don't say no or you'll give offence.'

'Dear God,' Rupert said.

'No knives and forks. We eat by hand here and make sure you use your *left* hand.' She smiled. 'Now eat it up like a good boy, then we'll carry on to Fuad.'

They left an hour and a half later. Rupert said, 'What am I going to find at Fuad?'

'In effect, an army camp. We have young Arabs from all the main Arab states. We teach them basic weaponry skills with rifles and machine guns, plus more sophisticated weapons such as shoulder-fired missiles.'

'What about bomb-making and explosives?'

'Yes, that, too, though it's pretty basic. Mostly how to use explosives effectively with timer pencils. There's a limit to what we can do. It isn't exactly up to Provisional IRA standards. We usually have around fifty in the camp, mostly men, but a few women pass through. They do eight weeks here and then go back home and pass their knowledge on.'

'Who are the instructors?'

'Mostly Palestinians.'

'Are they up to it?'

'Good help is hard to find. The chief instructor is first class, though, Colum McGee. He was in the IRA for years.'

'So what's the purpose of all this?'

'To have lots of reasonably trained young revolutionaries scattered throughout the Middle East, youngsters who would happily overthrow their governments, who hate capitalism and the wealthy.'

'But, Kate, *you're* a capitalist and you are unbelievably wealthy. And yet you want to destabilize the lot. It doesn't make sense.'

'It does if you want revenge, darling, it does if you want revenge.'

'And how do you achieve that?'

'Later, Rupert. When the time is right.' She glanced down below where sand boiled in a great cloud. So Ben Carver had been right. A desert storm was brewing.

Villiers and his men were well into the hill country, passing between those great ochre cliffs, making for the pool at Hama. For some time, as the wind increased in force, he had been aware of the fine particles of sand being carried with it, and he and his men had covered their noses and mouths with scarves.

As they approached the pool, he said to Achmed, 'We'll stop and replenish the water bags.'

'As the *Sahb* commands.'

Achmed got out with two Scouts, but Villiers stayed in his seat, sheltering behind the windshield, lighting a cigarette in cupped hands. Achmed and the two Scouts filled the goatskin bags, and were turning to bring them back to the Land Rovers, each man carrying two, when there was the crack of a shot, and a bullet hole appeared in the bag Achmed carried in his left hand and water spilled out. The three men dropped the bags and ran for the shelter of the Land Rovers and crouched, weapons ready.

'No return fire,' Villiers said.

The wind moaned, more sand carried with it. Achmed said, 'Look, *Sahb*, there are tyre marks in the sand, a Land Rover for sure. Someone has passed this way before us. Maybe Abu.' Villiers started to get up and Achmed pulled him back. 'No *Sahb*, not you.'

'I think it is Abu, but if he could hit the goatskin he could have hit you. He can't shoot me because the Countess wants me alive. This means he's just been playing with us. I'll prove it to you.' He stood up and called in Arabic, 'Abu, have you no honour? Are you afraid to face me?' He walked out into the open. 'Here I am, where are you?'

The visibility was greatly reduced now. They heard the sound of an engine starting up and a vehicle drawing away.

'He has gone, *Sahb*,' Achmed told him.

'And we should go, too, and reach shelter. It may be a while before this blows over.'

At the end of the pass was a crumbling fort left over from the old days. The stables still had a roof on them, the Land Rovers drove inside and they all dismounted.

Villiers said to Achmed, 'Get the spirit stove going. Coffee for you and tea for me. A can of food for each man. They can choose what they want.'

'As the *Sahb* orders.'

Villiers looked out as the sand was whipped up into a fury and wondered how Abu was getting on out there, but even more, wondered what he intended.

* * *

The Scorpion made Fuad before the sandstorm reached full intensity. Rupert was aware of the palm trees of the oasis below and his trained vision took in the crude blockhouse, the firing range beyond it, and many Bedu tents of the kind evolved over the centuries to handle the vagaries of the Empty Quarter, including sandstorms.

There were many men waiting down there, faces covered against the sand. Kate turned to Rupert. 'The breath of Allah, that's what the Bedu call it.'

'Then he must be in an angry mood.'

Carver put down between two clumps of palm trees, and men ran forward with ropes, fastened them around the skids, and tied the other ends to trees.

Ben Carver switched off. 'Jesus,' he said, 'that was a stinker.'

'You did well,' she told him.

Carver got out first and held the door, and she wrapped her scarf around her head and mouth and took the lead. Someone offered her a hand, a large man in jeans and a leather bomber jacket, a scarf wrapped around his face. Rupert followed and they hurried toward the tents.

The tent they entered was large and well

appointed, with carpets on the floor, cushions, and a low table. It was all quite luxurious. Drapes against the tent walls flapped a little as the wind buffeted them, and yet in there, the sound was subdued and somehow far away.

The man in the bomber jacket removed his scarf, revealing a tangled black beard flecked with grey. It was Colum McGee, and he was smiling.

'Good to see you, Countess.' She introduced Rupert, and a moment later Carver arrived.

'How long will it last?' she inquired.

'I've checked the weather report from Hamam airport. It should die down in two or three hours.'

She checked her watch. 'Eleven o'clock. That would leave time for an inspection and we could still make it back to Hazar by nightfall. We might as well have something decent to eat, Colum.'

'Well, I can't offer a full Irish breakfast, Countess, but the women in the kitchen bake fairly decent bread even though it's unleavened. If you want lamb stew or goat, fine. Otherwise, I can offer various things from cans. Corned beef, new potatoes, carrots, peas.'

'I think that should do nicely. Did you bring the refrigerated box in, Ben?'

'One of the men took it to the kitchen for me.'

'Good, we'll have a drink.'

Carver went out along a tented tunnel and entered the kitchen. There was a round stone fireplace in the entrance, three cooking pots hanging from spits, half a dozen women working at various tasks. The blue plastic refrigerated box was on a low table.

In the main tent, Kate Rashid said, 'All Ben Carver knows is what he sees, Colum, the camp and the occasional training. I don't want him to know anything else. Leave the serious business until after the meal.'

'As you say. I'll go and give the women their orders, but an old RAF hand like Ben won't miss much.'

As he went out, Ben appeared with the box. When he opened it, there were three bottles of champagne and several plastic wine glasses. He uncorked a bottle and started to pour.

'Four glasses, Ben.'

'All the comforts of home,' Rupert told her.

'Look upon it as a picnic,' she said as the Irishman returned. 'So, how's the training programme, Colum?'

'Much as usual.' They all sat down on cushions with their drinks. 'Mind you, those Palestinian kids are full of fire, but against Israeli troops they wouldn't last very long.'

'I'm sure you're doing the best you can. But let's eat and we can discuss it later.'

Back at the old fort, the storm was already abating. Villiers and his men waited, and finally he got out his Codex Four and called up Bobby Hawk.

'Where are you?'

'About twenty miles east from El Hajiz oasis. What about you?'

Villiers told him. 'Are you on the move?'

'No, sheltering in a cave.'

'Good. It'll blow itself out in an hour or so. We'll rendezvous at El Hajiz. We've lost two men by the way, Omar and Selim.'

'Good God, how?'

'I'll tell you when we meet.' He switched off his mobile and called to Achmed, 'More tea,' then he called Ferguson in London and brought him up to date.

*   *   *

After the meal, Kate said, 'I've had worse. You've done well, Colum.'

'We aim to please.'

'I'm glad to hear it. Let's talk.' She turned to Carver. 'If you'll excuse us, Ben, this is business.'

Carver couldn't get out fast enough. The money she paid him for his services was enough to satisfy his greed. He couldn't help knowing about the existence of Fuad, but he very much preferred that whatever they were doing there remained a mystery.

Back inside, Kate was saying, 'So you're managing all right with the Palestinian instructors?'

'Just about.'

'So if I wanted a serious project taken care of, one that would require expertise in the bomb department, where would I go? I asked you this when we last met, remember, and asked you to think about it.'

'The best internationally is still the IRA, although the Prods are moving into the market. What about those people you hired when you wanted a hit on the Council of Elders on their way to the Holy Wells? Aidan Bell, wasn't it, along with Tony Brosnan and Jack O'Hara?'

'All long gone. Sean Dillon killed Aidan.'

'Ah. A bastard, Sean, though he was a good comrade in the old days.' He smiled. 'And him working for the Brits now.'

'So what would you suggest?'

'Strangely enough, Aidan's cousin on his mother's side, Barry Keenan. Drumcree is his patch these days. The Provos are out of it. He thinks they're a bunch of old women. His affiliation these days is to the Real IRA, and they're back with old-fashioned Republicanism. There's an Irish saying, which roughly translated means those kind of people would shoot the Pope if they thought it would advance the cause.'

'That's a good one. Can you arrange for me to see Keenan?'

'Not in England, there are outstanding charges against him there.'

'Ireland?'

'Oh, yes, even in the North the RUC won't touch him, not since the peace process began.'

'I'll see him in Drumcree. Arrange it for me.'

'It'll take time.'

'I'm not in a rush.' She stood up. 'Let's see if the wind has dropped enough for Rupert to have a look at the camp.'

Colum said, curious, 'Do you know about this sort of business, Mr Dauncey?'

'You could say that.' Rupert smiled lazily.

They were escorted to a large tent on the outskirts of the encampment. Half a dozen young Arabs were in there, faced by an instructor across two trestle tables, on which various items necessary to the explosives business were laid out. There were timer pencils, other kinds of fuses, clockwork, timers, and various samples of explosive. It was all very basic, and Rupert was not impressed.

'Let's move on,' he said to McGee, 'before I lose my enthusiasm.'

They went to the shooting range, where recruits were lying down, propped on their elbows, cut-out targets of men standing four hundred metres away.

'Pass me your glasses,' Rupert told McGee, and he focused on the targets. 'Not so good. A few random hits, but most of your men are missing.'

'And you could do better? If you were familiar with the AK, you'd know it's at its finest as a close-quarter automatic weapon. Four hundred metres is a stretch for anyone.' He tried to kill the sarcasm and failed. 'But then you know the AK intimately, I suppose?'

'Well, I have been shot in the left shoulder by one, but luckily that was in the last week of the Gulf War.' Rupert went forward. 'Personally, I've always found it an excellent single-shot weapon.'

Colum McGee went and got one from a wooden rack, picked up a magazine, and rammed it home. He held it out. 'Show us.'

'My pleasure.' Rupert handed the glasses to Kate. 'Let's just take the first five from the left and the last five on the right.'

Colum blew a whistle and made a signal. Everyone stopped firing, unloaded, and stood up. The instructor shouted at them and they moved back. Rupert went forward. He didn't lie down but stood, then raised the AK to his shoulder, and started to fire slowly and carefully. There was a moan from the crowd as he finished, and Kate lowered the glasses and turned to McGee.

'Ten headshots. I only know one other man that good, and he killed my brother George and three men at four hundred metres – Sean Dillon.'

'I've never seen anything like it,' Colum said.

'Well, you wouldn't,' Kate told him. 'What next?'

'Unarmed combat. They tend to do well at that. Most of them are off the streets anyway.'

The required area was on the other side of the oasis behind the palm trees, where the sand was soft. Young men squared up to each other in pairs. The instructor was a powerfully built man with a bald head and a heavy moustache. His English was very reasonable and his name was Hamid.

Kate said, 'My cousin would like to see something of your work.'

He looked Rupert over and was not impressed. 'Ah, something for the tourists.' He beckoned two youths forward. 'Try to take me.' They looked distinctly worried. 'I said, try to take me,' he shouted.

They ran in at him together. He avoided the first boy's punch easily, grabbed him by the jacket, then fell backwards, a foot on the boy's stomach, and tossed him high in the air. The youth crashed to the ground, Hamid rolled on his front and kicked backwards at the other boy, dislodging his left kneecap. The boy lay crying on the ground.

Hamid confronted Kate, Rupert, and McGee, hands on his hips, smiling triumphantly. 'Is that good enough?' There was a kind of contempt in his voice.

'Hell, you're too good for me. I pass.' Rupert put a hand up placatingly.

Hamid laughed, head thrown back, legs apart, and Rupert kicked him between them, dead centre. Hamid went down hard and started to assume the fetal position. Rupert put a foot on his neck.

'Very careless, fella, very. I could break your neck easily, but I won't, because I imagine help is hard to find out here.' He turned to Kate. 'Is that it? Can we go now?'

'You bastard,' she said, but she was laughing.

Carver was doing something inside the Scorpion. When he saw them approach, he got out. 'Ready to go?'

'We'll spend the night in Hazar, then we'll leave at seven for Northolt.' She turned to McGee. 'I'll leave Keenan and Drumcree to you.'

She climbed inside, Rupert followed her, and they took off a few moments later.

When Villiers and his men reached El Hajiz, Bobby Hawk and his troops were already there with three Land Rovers.

'Good to see you.' Villiers held out his hand. 'Decent trip?'

'Better than yours, by all accounts. What happened?'

'I'll fill you in later. Let's set up camp.'

They laagered up the five Land Rovers in a semi-circle against a bluff, the scattered palms of the pool of the oasis behind them. Some of the men cut fuel from nearby thorn bushes with their *jambiyas* and lit a fire. Soon, water was heating in two pots and Villiers spoke to the assembled men.

'For those of you who were not there, Omar was shot dead by a sniper at the pool at Hama.'

There was an excited buzz of anger.

'Settle down. Later, Selim was murdered in Hazar, his throat cut. I know who did these things. It was Abu, the bodyguard of the Countess. He could have killed me, but did not. At Hama he struck again, hitting a water bag Achmed was carrying. Obviously, he could have killed him, too, but chose not to. I exposed myself, called him to face me. Again he could have shot me but didn't, because the Countess wants me alive. I will only die if we venture over the line, so we stay in Hazar for now. I just wanted all of you to know all of this.'

He turned to Achmed. 'Put three men at the machine guns, everyone else can eat.'

Later, Villiers and Bobby were presented with a stew, courtesy of Heinz, composed of baked beans and a cock-a-leekie soup, with plenty of unleavened bread to go with it.

'Not quite the officers' mess at Windsor,' Villiers said.

'Not bad, though,' Bobby Hawk said. 'It's given me a taste for honest plain food, all this canned stuff we're eating.'

He was only twenty-two, and had already done a tour in Kosovo with the Lifeguards in Challenger tanks and armoured cars. The chance for a posting to the Hazar Scouts was something he'd been unable to resist, although it had put back his promotion to second lieutenant. Villiers, of course, could have told him the opposite. His time with the Hazar Scouts would count for a great deal for his future military career.

They finished eating, and one of the men took their mess tins and another brought them enamel mugs and a kettle of the bitter black tea that even Bobby was developing a taste for. Dusk was falling, and the men moved to squat by the Land Rovers and left them to the fire.

'Do you think he's out there, sir – Abu?'

'I'm sure of it.'

'Do you think he'll have another go?'

'Yes, but I don't think he plans to kill anybody else. It'll just be another warning – a reminder that Kate Rashid has her hand on my neck.'

'I hope you are right, sir,' Bobby said, feelingly.

They sat and talked for an hour. A Scout came forward and tossed more thorn branches on the fire, refilled the kettle with fresh tea and boiling water, and put it close to them.

Bobby picked up the kettle to pour the tea, when there was a single shot, and a puncture appeared, hot liquid spurting as the kettle flew from Bobby's hand.

'Jesus Christ.' Bobby jumped up and pulled the Browning from his holster. He stood there, gun extended.

'No,' Villiers cried. 'It's Abu all over again. If he could hit the kettle, he could have hit you.'

The Scouts reached for their rifles, one of the machine gunners opened up into the darkness. Villiers jumped up and waved.

'Stop shooting. He won't fire again.'

There was silence. Bobby holstered his Browning and managed a shaky laugh. 'I hope you're right, sir.'

And then there was a second shot, a heart shot that lifted the boy off his feet and hurled him backwards. The Scouts roared with anger and they started to fire indiscriminately into the darkness. Villiers crouched beside Bobby, who heaved convulsively and died.

Villiers experienced such rage as he had never known. He called to his men. 'Stop firing *now*!' They lowered their weapons reluctantly, and he turned, back to the fire, and spread his arms wide. 'Abu, I am here. Where are you? Do you kill boys now? Come try a man!' But the only reply was the sound of a Land Rover starting up and moving away.

Abu drove one-handed and held a scarf against his right cheek. It had been a lucky escape. A stray machine gun bullet, part of the return fire to his kettle shot, had creased his right cheek. He was angry with himself for doing what had not been necessary. His strategy in shooting at Achmed at Hama and the young officer had been sound; he had just wanted to show them that he could have killed them. His second shot at Bobby Hawk could not even be excused as a reflex action. He'd taken his time, and hesitated, but then rage and pain had proved too much for him. He could have shot Villiers, but at least he was sane enough not to have done that. The Countess would understand. At least he hoped so. He pulled in at the side of the dirt road, opened the medical box and found the plaster dressings, with which he covered his wound. Then he carried on, driving through the night toward Hazar.

The men were putting Bobby Hawk in a body bag. Villiers sat by the fire drinking from a half bottle of whisky, kept in the medical box for medicinal purposes. He drank deeply from the neck of the bottle and smoked a cigarette.

He'd asked Kate Rashid why Abu hadn't gone for a head shot on him and she'd said he was too important and meant it. He'd allowed that to cloud his judgement and had got it wrong, totally and hopelessly wrong, and Bobby Hawk had paid for it with his life.

Achmed came and said, 'Do you wish to look at Cornet *Sahb*?'

'Yes, thank you, I will.'

He stood over the body bag, which was unzipped

at the top so that Bobby's face showed, the eyes closed in death. The corruption in the heat of the day would be very quick, the thought of it too hard to bear. And then a thought struck him and he turned to Achmed.

'Close the bag, then tie *Sahb* to the bonnet as we did with Omar. We'll leave in ten minutes, and drive down to Hazar through the night.'

'As the Colonel *Sahb* commands.'

Villiers sat down again and got out his Codex. He tried Ferguson on the special line at the Ministry of Defence and found him in the office.

'It's me again, Charles. Something bad has happened.'

Hannah Bernstein and Dillon happened to be in the office and Ferguson waved a hand and switched his red phone to audio. 'Tell me, Tony.'

Which Villiers did. 'I got it wrong and the boy is dead.'

'It's not your fault, Tony. It's Kate Rashid's fault.'

'You'll have to speak to the commanding officer of the Life Guards. Bobby has a widowed mother and two sisters at university. They'll have to be told.'

'I think the Life Guards will take care of that.'

'You know how long a body lasts out here, Charles, so I'm calling in a favour.'

'What is it?'

'If you sent Lacey and Parry here in the Gulfstream, got them out of Farley within the next hour or so, they could make the flight in, say, ten hours. I'll get the right kind of coffin in Hazar, force the documentation through, and they can take him back to London.'

'You don't need to ask, Tony.' He nodded to Hannah. 'Take care of it at once, Superintendent.' She hurried out. Ferguson said, 'Anything else?'

'Yes. I want you to know you can count on me from now on. There's something out there and I'll do anything I can to find out what it is. Anything I can do to pull her down, I will.'

'That's good to know. We'll call and let you know Lacey and Parry's departure time.'

Villiers clicked off. The men were waiting. 'Right, let's move out,' he said, got in beside Achmed, and they drove away.

Abu reached the Rashid Villa at five o'clock in the morning. The house boy told him the Countess was up and taking a shower. He gave

Abu coffee and went to announce his presence to his mistress. She appeared in a house robe at the head of the stairs, and as Abu stood up, Rupert, wearing trousers and a khaki bush shirt, joined her.

She came down the stairs, Rupert following. 'Your face looks awful. Is it bad?'

'The kiss of a bullet, no more.'

'How did this happen?'

He told her, omitting nothing. 'I have made bad trouble for you, Countess. The Colonel will not let this go.'

'What's done is done.' She frowned. 'But Villiers will come straight to Hazar with the body. I want you out of here now. Call at Dr Yolpi's on the way out of town for treatment, then straight to the Empty Quarter and Shabwa. Wait there until you hear from me.'

She held out her hand, he kissed it, then went out without a word. Rupert said, 'So now what?'

'I'll get dressed, you pack, and we'll make the airport as fast as possible.' She turned to the house boy, who was hovering. 'Have the limousine brought round to front door.'

As they went back upstairs, Rupert said, 'Why the rush?'

'I've a nasty feeling where Tony Villiers is concerned. I'd rather not see him at the moment.'

'What? Is the hard woman afraid?'

'Go to hell, darling.'

Fifteen minutes later, they went downstairs again, Rupert carrying two suitcases. The house boy opened the door, they walked out and found the five Land Rovers of the Hazar Scouts lined up across the street, all machine guns manned. Tony Villiers stood beside the lead Land Rover, his arms folded.

She hesitated, then came down the steps, Rupert behind her. 'Why, Tony, what a surprise.'

He didn't beat about the bush. He pointed to the body bag. 'I'm sure Abu got here ahead of us. Bobby Hawk is in there. It's not Abu's work, really. It's yours, Kate.'

'Is that so? And what do you intend to do about it?'

'I declare *jihad* on you, Kate Rashid, war to the knife. And I intend to cross the line into the Empty Quarter any time I want.'

'I'll look for you there.'

'Good. Now get out of here before I shoot you myself.'

She hesitated, then got in the limousine with

Rupert and drove away. Villiers watched her go, then walked to Achmed and got into the rear of the lead Land Rover.

'So, my friend, take me to the undertaker.' Achmed gave the order and they drove away.

OXFORD
———
LONDON
———

9

On the Gulfstream, Kate Rashid sat thinking, and Rupert drank black coffee.

'It's very unfortunate,' he said. 'Abu's enthusiasm getting the better of him like that.'

'Yes, it's very provoking. Now I may have to deal with Villiers in a way I hadn't intended.'

'You mean, if he crosses the line into the Empty Quarter?'

'Yes. I'd have to declare open season on him and the Scouts.'

'Why not simply put the word out that they should all leave him, fade away into the night? After all, they're Rashid and you're the boss.'

'You still don't get it, Rupert. They've taken the oath. They belong to Tony, until death if necessary.'

'Hell, I'll never understand the Arab mind.'

'You've said that before. Now let's turn to other

things. I've been thinking about this Liberty in Europe Day.'

'Yes, Saturday. What about it?'

'I've been thinking that it might not be too good an idea for us to be seen to be too closely connected with it, not right now when we're under investigation. We have to maintain our nonviolent front. When heads start getting cracked, I want us to be perceived as the voice of reason. So this is what I want you to do: I want you to go to Oxford and see Professor Percy. Make it clear that the Rashid Educational Trust is only interested in matters of welfare and education, that we're totally against violent protest of any kind, and that we expect him to tell the students that.'

'You know what they're like. They'll go anyway.'

'Well, of course they will! But we'll be on record as opposing it. And in case you have any problems with him, I happen to know that there's a discrepancy of some fifty thousand pounds in the accounts of the Act of Class Warfare at Oxford . . . so Percy has some explaining to do.'

'Do you really think heads will be cracked?'

'My dear, I'm counting on it, especially with little Helen Quinn toddling along like the good little dilettante she is. With any luck, she'll get arrested. That really would look bad in the papers. The gossip columns would love it – the revolutionary who's a Senator's daughter.'

'You bitch. You don't miss a trick, do you?'

'No, darling. Just make sure that you don't.'

Saturday morning found him in Oxford at the Lion. The pub was crammed with students and Percy was already there, a pint of beer in front of him.

Rupert paused beside him. 'I'll just get a drink.'

He pushed through the crowd and saw Helen Quinn and young Grant at the end of the bar. He smiled and went over to order a large Jack Daniel's from the barman.

'Hello, there,' he said. 'You're going to the rally, then?'

Grant stopped smiling and became aggressive. 'What's it got to do with you?'

'Alan, shut up.' She smiled at Dauncey. 'Yes, we're going on the bus.'

'I wish you wouldn't. It could get very nasty. The more I've read about it, the more likely it sounds that there'll be violence, and we simply couldn't condone anything like that.'

Students nearby were listening and Percy, coming forward, had also heard. Grant said, 'You don't approve?'

'Not of riots, and police trying to crack your skull with a baton.'

'Afraid, are you? A ponce like you would be. Rupert Dauncey. What kind of a name is that?'

Students standing around laughed and Helen said, 'Stop it, Alan.'

He ignored her. 'I know what it is, it's a ponce's name.'

Rupert smiled gently. 'If you say so.' He picked up his drink and returned to Percy.

The professor said, 'I'm sorry about that.'

'That's okay. He's young. But I meant what I said. I think it's all too dangerous. I want you to get on that bus and tell them not to go.'

'Get on the bus? But I told you. I've other plans. I –'

'You can forget them. Listen to me. The Countess and the Rashid Educational Trust acted in good faith in supporting Act of Class Warfare. We believed in its philosophy – but we do *not* believe in violent protest.'

'But I can't control their behaviour.'

'I realize that. But you can tell them how you feel when they're on the bus.'

'No, I –'

'Professor.' Dauncey leaned close. 'We've put a lot of trust in you. Also a lot of money. Wouldn't it be a shame if it should come out that there is a discrepancy of fifty thousand pounds in the ACW accounts?'

Percy seemed to shrivel up. 'I don't know anything about that,' he whispered.

'Oh yes, you do. Imagine what it would be like at Wandsworth, someone like you, sharing the showers with murderers and sex offenders. Not a pretty picture, Professor.'

Percy had turned white. 'For God's sake, no.'

'We wouldn't appreciate the scandal ourselves. It would damage our reputation. But it would damage you much more, wouldn't it?'

'All right,' Percy moaned. 'Whatever you say. But they'll go anyway, no matter what I say.'

'Oh, I'll back you up. You can introduce me as representing Rashid. Nobody can say afterwards that we didn't do our best.' He looked across the room and saw Grant making for the men's room and got up. 'I'll be back.'

When he went into the toilet, Grant was just

finishing. He turned, pulling up his zipper. For the moment, they were alone.

'What do you want, ponce?'

Rupert kicked him on the right shin, doubled him over with a blow to the stomach, then grabbed the left wrist and twisted the arm straight. He raised a clenched fist.

'How'd you like me to break it for you?'

Grant moaned with pain. 'No, please, stop.'

Rupert exerted more pressure. Grant cried out and Rupert swung him around and slapped his face. 'Now listen to me. I happen to know you're here at Oxford only because all your expenses are paid by an outside scholarship. Do you know who's behind that scholarship? Do you?'

Grant moaned again and shook his head.

'*We* are. The Rashid Educational Trust. And we can take it away so fast it'll make your head spin. So, step out of line with me again and you'll be out of Oxford and working at McDonald's. Understand?'

'Yes,' Grant rubbed his arm, tears in his eyes.

Rupert lit a Marlboro. 'So this is what I want you to do.'

Alan Grant fumbled in his pocket for a tissue, and his fingers brushed against the pen his brother had sent him. Something, a bad feeling, made him switch it on now.

Rupert took a paper bag from his pocket.

'There are three pieces of candy in there, chocolates. Each has an Ecstasy tablet inside. I want you to offer the girl one during the demonstration.'

'Why – why should I do that?'

'Because there's a fair chance you'll be busted by the police when the riot starts, which it will. A drug bust would be very embarrassing for her father, you understand?'

'What happens if the shit doesn't hit the fan? If she takes the pill and doesn't get arrested?'

'There'll be other times. Just get her back to that bus in one piece.'

'We aren't coming back tonight.'

'Why?'

'My brother's working in Germany. He's got a one-room flat in Wapping. He said I could spend the weekend there.'

'And she agreed?'

'Yes.'

Rupert shook his head. 'She must be hard up. What's the address?'

'Ten Canal Street. It's just up from Canal Wharf on the Thames.'

'Do you have a mobile phone?'

'No, just the house phone.'

Rupert took out his diary and pencil. 'Give me the number,' which Grant did. 'Right. Now look after her. I'll check you out this evening. Remember, give her the pill *during* the demonstration. And make sure she doesn't mix it with alcohol. I don't want her sick, Grant, just high. Are we clear?'

Grant mumbled yes.

'And if you say anything – *anything* – about this to anyone, you will be very, very sorry. Is that clear, too?'

Grant nodded.

'Good. Now you can go.'

He gave Grant time to leave, then followed him. Most of the students had gone, but Percy still waited in the booth.

Rupert said, 'Come on. Get ready to make your speech,' and led the way out.

The coach waited outside the school hall. About forty people were on board and half a dozen students stood on the pavement, chattering in anticipation. Rupert and Percy climbed up into the bus.

'So you're coming with us, sir?' someone called.

'Yes, but against my better judgment. I believe

this whole thing could turn very nasty,' Percy said.

Someone shouted, 'Get stuffed.'

'No, seriously. Act of Class Warfare isn't about violence. We're about change, peaceful change. I fear this is a dreadful mistake. We shouldn't go, none of us should go.'

Rupert took over. 'Listen, my name is Dauncey and I represent the Rashid Educational Trust. As some of you know, we help sponsor Act of Class Warfare, but we can't condone violence of any kind, and believe me, it's going to get violent today. Professor Percy is right – it's the right cause, but the wrong time and place.'

The reaction was just what he expected. A chorus of 'Why are we waiting?' burst from the back of the coach, and Rupert shrugged. 'It's on your own heads, then.'

He sat next to Percy. Helen was across the aisle from him. Grant averted his gaze and looked out of the window. The girl smiled.

'It's quite exciting, really,' she said to Rupert.

'Your first riot.'

'Oh, I don't believe all that. It'll be fine, I'm sure of it.'

'Let's hope you're right.'

She turned away, her face troubled.

Bobby Hawk's funeral was at eleven o'clock that same morning at a small village called Pool Bridge in Kent, an hour out of London. Ferguson went down and Dillon accompanied him. It was still bad March weather, with only the hope of spring to look forward to.

Dillon lit a cigarette and opened his window. 'Nice countryside.'

It started to drizzle. Ferguson said, 'I wonder what she's been up to since they got back?'

'I have no idea. The events in Hazar over the last few days must have given her something to think about, though.'

'Anything new from Roper?'

'Not a thing. He says he's been through all available leads. He can't explore her mind. He can only try and find a pattern to her actions, which means she's got to make the next move.'

'I take your point.'

'Anyway, I'm seeing him this afternoon, just in case.'

'Good.' Ferguson leaned back. 'I wonder how Tony's making out.'

'She shouldn't have annoyed him,' Dillon commented. 'That was a serious error on her part. She'll live to regret it.'

'Let's hope so,' Ferguson told him, and they entered Pool Bridge.

The village was typically old English, with cottages, an ancient church, a pub, and a country hotel that looked Georgian. There was a line of cars parked at the side of the church, and Ferguson cursed softly.

'Damn it, we're late. Come on, Dillon,' and he got out and hurried to the large oak door.

The service had just started, and the church was so full that they had to stand at the back. They saw the coffin, and the rector in his vestments on the steps of the sanctuary above it. Mrs Hawk and her two daughters, all in black, occupied the front pew. The commanding officer of the Life Guards was there, and his opposite number from the Blues and Royals, supporting each other, as always.

Late in the service, the Life Guards' colonel joined the rector on the steps, and outlined Bobby Hawk's brief career, praising him for his service and character.

Yes, but what does it all mean? Dillon asked himself. What's the point? The boy was only twenty-two years old, and then the organ started and the hymns began.

Outside at the graveside, the drizzle turned to heavy rain and the General's chauffeur appeared and discreetly offered an umbrella.

'Why does it always rain at funerals?' Dillon asked.

'Some kind of tradition, I suppose,' Ferguson said.

And then it was over, and the crowd started to make their way to the country hotel. There was a selection of wines, a buffet. Most people seemed to know each other. Dillon asked one of the waiters to get him a Bushmills and stood back.

Mrs Hawk approached Ferguson and kissed his cheeks. 'Good of you to come, Charles.'

'I'm surprised you'll talk to me. To a certain extent, your son was working for me.'

'He was doing his duty, Charles, and that's all that matters.'

She moved on, and the Life Guard colonel approached. 'Nice to see you, Charles. It's a bad business. That's two cornets Tony Villiers has lost out there.'

'You think he'll find difficulty in replacing young Hawk?'

'Not while there are enough mad young fools just out of Sandhurst.'

He glanced curiously at Dillon, and Ferguson said, 'Sean Dillon. He works for me.'

The Colonel's eyes seemed to widen. 'Good Lord, *the* Sean Dillon? I was trying to catch you in South Armagh more years ago than I care to remember.'

'And thank God you didn't, Colonel.' Dillon turned to Ferguson. 'I'll see you at the car.'

It was just after three when the coach unloaded by the river, and the students joined the steady stream of people walking up Horse Guards Avenue to Whitehall. Rupert and Percy drifted along at the back, unknowingly passing the corner where, during the Gulf War, an IRA professional named Sean Dillon had mortar-bombed Number Ten Downing Street from a white Ford Transit.

They heard a lot of noise, the babble of many voices, and when they turned the corner into Whitehall, it was already crowded with people. A line of police vehicles stretched across the road to prevent access to the gates of Number Ten, the police all in riot gear and some of them on horseback.

The crowd surged forward, more and more people arriving and applying pressure from the back. The Oxford contingent was already splitting up, scattering throughout the crowd. Helen Quinn and Alan Grant were forced to one side and swallowed up, Rupert and Percy pushed elsewhere.

Up front, young men, faces obscured by balaclava helmets or ski masks, presented a new and sinister element: And then it happened. A petrol bomb soared from somewhere inside the crowd, hit the ground just in front of the police line, and burst into flames. There was another and yet another, as the police retreated a few yards.

The crowd roared as two more petrol bombs were thrown, and yet there was also an element of panic, a lot of people realizing they'd got into something worse than they had expected. Some turned and tried to work their way back, and at that moment, the mounted police charged.

They were met by a hail of missiles, but the police kept coming and burst into the front ranks, batons rising and falling. Total panic now reigned everywhere, people crying out, women screaming.

Henry Percy turned desperately, terrified. 'I can't take this. I must get out.'

For what it was worth, Rupert himself had no intention of staying. The police, after all, didn't ask questions at such affairs. The fact that you were there was enough. He was just as likely to get clubbed on the head and thrown into the back of a van, and that wouldn't do.

He said to Percy, 'Don't panic. Just follow me,' and he started back, kicking and punching his way through.

They made it to Horse Guards Avenue and joined a throng of people who were doing the same thing, most of them running. Finally, they turned out onto the main road beside the Thames and made it back to the coach. They weren't the first; at least half a dozen students were ahead of them.

Percy scrambled inside and Rupert followed. Two of the students were girls, and they were crying. The boys didn't exactly look happy, either. Percy sat, head in hands.

Rupert said to the students, 'I warned you, and you wouldn't listen.' He turned to Percy. 'God knows what's happened to the others. But that's your problem, isn't it?'

He got out, walked along the Embankment in the direction of Vauxhall Bridge, managed to hail a black cab, and told the driver to take him to South Audley Street. Kate would be pleased that it was all working so well.

It was half past four in Whitehall, people running everywhere, and Alan and Helen had been forced to shelter in a doorway with several others. He hadn't given her the drugs yet – there hadn't been time. Besides, he had other things on his mind. Helen was afraid but excited at the same time. She clutched Grant's arm, and he took half a bottle of vodka out of his pocket and unscrewed the cap. He had a very long swallow. The police were charging again, and she clutched his arm even harder. Grant felt himself getting hard. He was going to score today, he could tell – but he might as well make sure of it.

'Take it easy. Here, have a drink.'

'You know I only like white wine.'

'Come on, it'll calm you down.'

Reluctantly, she took the bottle and swallowed. It seemed to burn all the way down. 'God, that's strong.'

'Not really, it's just the taste. Have another pull.'

'No, Alan, I really don't like it.'

'Don't be silly, it'll make you feel better.'

She did as she was told.

There was another roar from the crowd as the police forced their way forward relentlessly, clubbing their way through, and now very large numbers of people were turning and fleeing.

Grant said, 'Time to go,' took her hand and pushed his way through the crowd.

They moved down Horse Guards Avenue and made it to the Embankment. The coach was still there on the other side of the road, waiting for stragglers.

'Maybe we should go back to Oxford,' she said, feeling light-headed from the drink.

He put an arm around her reassuringly.

'Come on, baby, it'll be all right. Okay, it was a piece of shit back there, but let's not let it spoil the weekend.'

'All right,' but there was a reluctance in her voice.

'Come on, we'll get a cab.' Which they did a few moments later.

* * *

At South Audley Street, Rupert Dauncey switched off the live coverage on television and turned to Kate.

'There they are, all running like scared rabbits.'

'I wonder what happened to the Quinn girl?'

'I'll call the place where Grant's staying and see.' He did, but the phone simply rang and rang.

He replaced the receiver and frowned, looking out at the gathering darkness of the March evening, uneasy and not really sure why.

He said to Kate, 'I think I'll go down to Canal Street and see if they're there. I'll use your Porsche, if that's okay.'

'Why, darling, you're taking this personally.'

'I love you, too,' he told her, and left.

In the cab, Grant remembered the Ecstasy chocolates and gave her one. He knew it was too late for Dauncey's purposes, but, hell, now she'd really be ready. He intended to screw her brains out. And screw Dauncey, anyway. Big, self-important bastard, with his threats. Grant wasn't afraid of him – he had it all on tape! And on the way to the bus after leaving Dauncey, he'd run into a friend who wasn't going to the demonstration. It had been the perfect opportunity. He'd given him the pen for safe-keeping and told him to stick it in Grant's mailbox. No sense risking it getting lost in the excitement.

No, Mr Dauncey, Grant thought, grinning to himself, we'll just see who's going to be very, very sorry.

At the house in Canal Street, he began the wrestling with Helen Quinn on the couch. She was thoroughly drunk now and struggling, trying to avoid his kisses.

'No, Alan, I feel awful. My head's splitting.'

'You'll be all right. I'll be back in a minute.'

He went upstairs to the bathroom, trembling with excitement. He splashed his face with water, dried it and combed his hair, and was just coming back down when he heard a sudden cry. He ran down the rest of the stairs and went into the living room.

She was writhing convulsively on the couch, her entire body shaking. 'What is it?' he cried.

When he put a hand to her face, it was burning; he saw that her eyes were bulging and then froth appeared on her mouth. It was every horror story he'd ever heard about people who got an adverse reaction to Ecstasy.

He couldn't walk out. Everyone knew they'd been together. There was only one thing for it, St Mark's Hospital half a mile up the High Street. If he got her there, they'd fix her. He ran to the front door, opened it and then the garage door, got into his brother's Escort and reversed out. He went back inside, helped her to her feet and looped her bag around her neck. Strangely enough, she was able to shuffle along, and he got her out of the house and into the rear seat of the Escort.

Rupert, in the Porsche, had just turned into Canal Street. He saw Grant leading her out, and knew instantly from the way she was walking that there was something seriously wrong. He drove past the Escort, turned the Porsche, and was on their tail as Grant drove away. They were at the hospital in minutes.

Rupert followed them into the main car park and watched as Grant got her out. She was really suffering now, walking like a zombie, as Grant took her up the steps to the entrance to the Casualty department. Rupert got out and followed.

Inside, it was crowded, as was typical of most National Health Service hospitals; all seats were taken, with some people standing. Rupert stayed back by the entrance. Grant glanced around, wondering what to do, and Helen cried out and started to struggle. He couldn't hold her and she fell to the floor. Some people jumped up in alarm.

A passing nurse ran over and knelt beside her. There was a huge amount of foam on her mouth now.

The nurse looked up at Grant. 'What is it?'

He lied through his teeth, panicking now. 'Don't ask me. I was passing outside. She was obviously ill and trying to get up the steps. I thought she was on some drug. I just gave her a hand.'

The nurse called to those at the desk. 'Emergency!'

As two other nurses ran over, Helen's heels started to drum on the floor, and her body shook and then went still. One of the nurses felt for a neck pulse, then looked up.

'She's gone.'

Grant said stupidly, 'She can't have gone.'

A male nurse put a hand on his shoulder. 'She's dead, son.'

'Oh, my God!' Grant turned and ran away, and Rupert went after him.

Grant was nearly out of his mind, he didn't know what to do. When he got back to Ten Canal Street, it was nearly dark. He parked the Escort, found the half bottle of vodka, and sat at the kitchen table drinking it, swallow after swallow very quickly. When the front door bell rang he was already drunk. He ignored it, but it rang again. Angry, he went to open it.

He stood there, swaying, and Rupert pushed him back. 'I was here earlier. I followed you to the hospital.' He turned Grant and ran him into the kitchen. 'I saw what happened. She's dead.'

'I had nothing to do with it.'

'You had everything to do with it.' Rupert got him by the tie, took the Colt .25 from his inside pocket, and put it against the boy's left temple. 'Did you give her one of the pills?'

Grant was shaking a great deal, as much from the large amount of vodka he'd drunk as from fear. 'Just as you said. I can't understand it. I've taken Ecstasy. I've never had a reaction like that.'

'Some people do. It's a kind of allergy,' Rupert said, but he was looking closely at Grant. 'But that wasn't what caused it, was it? You're completely drunk, Grant.' He spied the empty bottle on the table. 'You gave her vodka, didn't you? You got her drunk and then you gave her drugs, and after I *told* you not to mix them. You really screwed up this time, didn't you?'

Grant started to cry. 'I didn't mean to. I didn't want to, she took the bottle. I couldn't stop her. And anyway, *you* gave me the Ecstasy. It's just as much your fault as mine.'

As a piece of self-justification it was monumental, but all Rupert did was straighten Grant's collar. 'You know what, Alan? You're right. But you don't look good. I think you need some air,' and he pushed him out of the kitchen to the front door.

'What's down here?' Rupert asked.

'Canal Wharf.'

'Why are the other houses boarded up?'

'They're going to redevelop. Everyone's gone except my brother. The Council's going to rehouse him when he comes back from Germany.'

It was almost fully dark now, and they turned onto the wharf, passing under a single street lamp.

There were lights on the other side of the river. A pleasure boat passed, the sound of music drifting across.

Grant stood at the edge, maudlin now. 'There's a beach when the tide's out. I used to play down there when I was a kid, all my mates swimming, but not me. I could never get the hang of it.'

'That's good,' Rupert said, stepped back and stood behind him. Then he pushed hard with both hands and Grant went over with a cry.

He surfaced, floundering, his arms thrashing. 'Help me,' he called, and went under again.

He seemed to have gone, but then he surfaced again, with very little movement now. Rupert peered down. 'Are you all right, my friend?' There was a choking sound and Grant slipped away for the last time. 'Yes, I thought you were.' He shook his head and said softly, 'She was a nice girl. You shouldn't have done that.'

He turned and walked back to the Porsche.

Back at South Audley Street, Kate Rashid was still sitting at the fire and it was as if nothing had occurred in between.

'Well, did you find them?'

He didn't have a drink, simply went and opened the French window at the small terrace and lit a cigarette.

'I believe once, in an excess of enthusiasm, I said I'd do anything for you, even kill for you.'

'I remember, darling.'

'Well, I just did.'

She looked stunned, then began to smile. 'What happened?'

And he told her.

The charge nurse at St Mark's who'd received Helen Quinn's body examined her bag and found many items in it to establish her identity, the most obvious being her American passport. There was also a card for the Oxford Students' Union, another for St Hugh's College.

Blood tests at the hospital had established the presence not only of alcohol but of Ecstasy. As was the usual practice, the hospital administrator informed the police and then phoned the principal of St Hugh's College with the sad news. He canvassed other students in the residence hall and discovered that some of them had been on the bus with her and Alan Grant. The principal then phoned the American Embassy in Grosvenor Square, and it was the American Ambassador who, because of Daniel Quinn's status, had the unhappy task of phoning the President on his direct line.

At the White House, Jake Cazalet was in the Oval Office. He listened in horror, then put the phone down and rang Blake Johnson in the Basement and told him to come upstairs at once.

Blake arrived in shirtsleeves, with a sheaf of papers. 'I had stuff for you anyway.'

'Never mind that,' and Cazalet gave him the grim news.

Blake was staggered. 'I can't believe it, especially the drug suggestion. I've met Helen many times. She just wasn't the sort.'

'I can't comment. Students on a day out, who can say?' Cazalet sighed. 'Drugs are the curse of modern life. Where is Daniel now?'

'He reported in yesterday from a place called Prizren. It's in the multinational sector of Kosovo. You were busy, so I spoke to him.'

'What's he doing in this Prizren place?'

'There's been an outbreak of fighting, Albanians ambushed by Serbs, or something like that.'

Cazalet said, 'I'll tell him myself. It's the least I can do.'

'Thank God it's not me. How do we handle it?'

'He'll want to be in London as soon as possible. Using Presidential authority, how soon can that be arranged?'

'A helicopter north from Prizren to Pristina. Then a direct flight to the UK. I should have it arranged within an hour.'

'Do it then. But first get him on the phone for me.'

Quinn was outside Prizren with a small detachment of French paratroopers, part of the multinational force. Four Serbs had been killed, and they waited in their body bags in the village square for a helicopter to arrive.

One of the men gave Quinn a cup of coffee, and their captain, a young man named Michel, was on a mobile. Quinn was drinking his coffee when his own special mobile sounded and he switched on.

'Quinn.'

'Daniel? Jake Cazalet.'

Quinn was astonished. 'What can I do for you, Mr President?'

Cazalet hesitated. 'What are you up to now?'

'Oh, sheltering from heavy rain at the arsehole of the world outside Prizren. I'm with the French. We've got a few Serbs in body bags to get out of here, and we're just waiting for a helicopter. What's this about, sir?'

Cazalet said, 'Daniel, I've got heartbreaking news for you.'

Quinn said, 'What would that be, Mr President?'

And Cazalet told him.

A short while later, Quinn switched off the phone, experiencing a feeling he had never known before in his life. Michel clicked off his mobile and came to him.

'Hey, *mon ami*, I'm told they're diverting another helicopter to here just for you. It's taking you to Pristina. You really must have some kind of influence, eh?'

'No. It's a personal thing.' He stared almost blindly at the Frenchman. 'My daughter, Helen. I've just been told she's dead.'

'*Mon Dieu*,' Michel said.

'Twenty-two years old, Michel. I mean, who dies

at twenty-two years old?' He buried his head in his hands and wept.

Michel snapped his fingers at his sergeant, a half bottle of cognac was produced, and Michel unscrewed the cap. 'You'd better take a large one, and another if you need it, *mon ami*. Just take your time.' There was the sound of a helicopter in the distance.

'They're coming for you now.'

The President spoke to the chief of staff at the London Embassy, who was eager to please. They spoke in conference, Blake listening.

'You're an old London hand and you're also a lawyer, Frobisher,' the President said. 'You've looked at the facts in the case. How will it be handled?'

'It's a police matter, Mr President, because of the drug connection and the fact that the young man who delivered her ran away. Someone got the licence number of his car, though – one of the nurses who followed him out.'

'So the police will run him down?'

'Absolutely. The licence number will lead to the owner's address.'

'Then what?'

'There'll be an autopsy, followed by a coroner's inquest. Once that's over, the body will be released.'

'Right,' Cazalet said. 'I've arranged to get Senator Quinn to the UK as soon as possible. I'll have Blake Johnson liaise with you on this. The senator gets our best shot. Anything he wants. If there are any roadblocks with the British police or legal system, use all your Embassy's muscle to overcome them.'

'At your command, Mr President.'

'Fine. I know you'll do your best.'

'Of course, sir.'

Blake cut in. 'Hello, Mark, Blake here. I'll notify you when and where Daniel will get in and you can arrange to pick him up.'

'I'll do it myself. Leave it with me, Blake.'

The line went dead and Cazalet drummed his fingers on the desk, thinking. Finally, he said, 'Listen, whatever Frobisher is able to do, he's still at a disadvantage. It's a different country, different police procedures, different legal system.'

'So what are you saying?'

'I think we need Charles Ferguson on this.'

'I'll speak to him at once.'

*　　*　　*

When the news reached Henry Percy, he was horrified. Dauncey's accusation about the funds had been true enough. He'd been mesmerized by the sums passing through his hands, and then temptation had set in. A few thousand here, a few thousand there. Who would notice? But the chickens had come home to roost. Now this.

He telephoned Rupert Dauncey in London. 'Thank God you're there. Something terrible has happened.'

'And what's that?' Dauncey said, pretending ignorance.

Percy told him. 'Such a nice girl. She's the last one I'd have suspected of being on drugs. And what worries me, too, is the position of our organization. That dreadful riot, the violence.'

'Yes, it spoils all our good work,' Rupert said. 'But no one can fault the Trust, Professor. You behaved with great responsibility when you warned the students on the bus and tried to dissuade them.'

'That's true.' Percy hesitated. 'And, of course, so did you, Mr Dauncey. No one could have done more.'

'Yes, and if the matter is raised at the inquest,

any student who was present would have to confirm what we both said.'

Suddenly, Percy felt much brighter. 'Of course.'

'You have my personal support. As to the other matter, I've spoken to the Countess, who feels there may have been a genuine error on your part.'

'That's very kind of her.' Percy was overjoyed.

'We'll speak again,' and Rupert smiled as he put the phone down.

A police car was outside the Canal Street house. Two constables, a man and a woman, checked the Escort and found the keys inside.

'That's a trifle careless these days,' the female officer said.

'Still, it's the right car,' her colleague replied, as he checked the number plate.

There was a dim light at the back of the hall. They tried the doorbell but got no response, then went up a narrow footpath to the rear and found the kitchen light on. The man tried the door, but it was locked.

Two young men turned the corner at the end of Canal Wharf by the wharf itself. They stopped at the edge to urinate and, at the same moment, looked down to where the tide was receding, and saw Alan Grant's body, half in the water, half out.

'Jesus Christ,' one of them said, just as the two police officers returned to their car. The young man saw them. 'Down here,' he called. 'There's a body on the beach,' and the police hurried towards him.

At Pristina, the first plane out to London was a Royal Air Force Hercules from Transport Command. Word had gone out and the crew was subdued, but saw to Quinn's every need. He was sensible enough to eat some food, have a couple of coffees, and allow the RAF Sergeant looking after him to pour a little brandy in each.

The skipper came down to see him, looking absurdly young in spite of being a squadron leader. 'Terribly sorry about your great loss, sir. Anything you need, just ask.'

'That's kind of you.'

Quinn lit a cigarette and thought about it. '*Your great loss*.' How apt that was, how painful. Death was so final; he'd learned that at an early age with the barbarity of Vietnam.

And the one thing that wouldn't go away was this suggestion of a drug connection to the whole rotten business. It couldn't be true. That wasn't the Helen he'd known and loved.

He lay back in the canvas chair in which they'd put him, stretched out his legs, folded his hands, and slept the sleep of exhaustion.

10

Charles Ferguson was enjoying breakfast in front of the fire at Cavendish Place the following morning when Blake Johnson called him. Ferguson listened, his face grave.

'This is a bad one, Blake. What do you want me to do?'

'Daniel Quinn will want answers. The President thinks you can help find them.'

'So you don't believe the most obvious explanation? A young woman on the loose, too much to drink, the wrong pill?'

'No. And I think Daniel will find that difficult to believe. Do what you can, Charles. Hannah can help him deal with Scotland Yard and the coroner's court. Dillon's been pretty creative on occasion.'

'That's an unusual way of putting it, but, yes, we should be able to do something. Leave it with me, Blake.'

He called Hannah Bernstein on her mobile. She was on her way to the office. 'Listen carefully.' He told her what had happened.

'That's terrible,' she said. 'What do you want me to do?'

'Talk to your friends in Special Branch. Use your muscle. Find out what the police are doing and what they've got.'

'Right, sir.'

He clicked off, then tried Dillon, who was running around the streets close to Stable Mews in a blue tracksuit, a towel on his neck. His mobile sounded and he slowed and took it out.

'Where are you?' Ferguson asked.

'Morning run. Where are you?'

'At home. I want you to see Roper.'

'Why?'

Ferguson told him.

At Regency Square, the buzzer sounded, the door opened, and Dillon went in. Roper was in his wheelchair working at the computer. He turned.

'You want something, I can tell.'

'You could say that. Daniel Quinn's daughter, Helen, is dead. The word is that it's drug-related.

She was admitted to Casualty at St Mark's Hospital last night and died there.'

'Oh dear.' Roper started to hack his way in and very quickly came up with the details. 'Helen Quinn, twenty-two, American citizen, address St Hugh's College, Oxford. Preliminary blood tests show a high alcohol content and traces of Ecstasy. They're doing an autopsy at twelve.'

'Dammit to hell,' Dillon said. 'So it's true. Her father won't like that. What else have you got?'

'I can access her personal records at Oxford.'

'Do that.'

Dillon lit a cigarette and Roper tapped away. 'Here we go. Usual background details. Reading politics, philosophy, and economics. Member of the Oxford Union, Music Society, Oxford Literary Workshop.' He frowned. 'Well, I'll be damned. Oxford has a branch of Act of Class Warfare. She was a member.'

'Helen *Quinn* was a member of Act of Class Warfare?'

'I'll see if they have a website. Yes, here we are. Huh. Well, now we know why she was in London yesterday. They sent a delegation to that Liberty in Europe fiasco.'

'That figures,' Dillon said.

Roper sat back. 'Yes. Funny, isn't it? Daniel Quinn keeps tabs on Kate Rashid. Rashid funds a bunch of questionable organizations. One of them is Act of Class Warfare, and guess who's a member? Daniel Quinn's daughter.'

'Are you suggesting Kate Rashid had something to do with the girl's death?'

'No, no, but still – quite a coincidence. And I abhor coincidence. I like life to be orderly. One and one must always make two.'

'This from the man who spent seven hours defusing the largest IRA bomb ever, then put himself in that wheelchair from practically a firecracker.'

'All right,' Roper shrugged. 'Some days one and one make three. Anything else you need?'

'That twelve o'clock autopsy, as soon as you can.'

'Fair enough. Do you want me to see what the police are up to?'

'Hannah's working on that, but it can't hurt to see what you can find, too. I've got to get going. Let me know if you turn up anything.'

Dillon left and Roper cut into Scotland Yard's Central Records Office. He examined what was there and frowned. There was an ancillary link to the case of one Alan Grant, Canal Street,

Wapping, believed drowned and believed to be the person who had delivered Helen Quinn to the hospital. Roper sat back, still frowning. The name Alan Grant was familiar, and then he remembered where he'd seen it. He went back to the Act of Class Warfare website, and there he was: Oxford, also a second-year student at St Hugh's College reading physics.

Another coincidence he didn't believe in. He picked up the phone to Ferguson.

At Cavendish Place, Dillon looked out of the French window in the drawing room, then turned. Ferguson was sitting by the fire.

'So, we not only know why she went to London, we know that this Grant delivered her to the hospital, did a runner, and ended up dead by drowning.'

'And I've got more.' Hannah Bernstein bustled in from outside. 'Both Quinn and Grant went to London on a special bus hired by a professor named Henry Percy, and guess who came along for the ride?'

'Who?' Ferguson said mildly.

'Would you believe Rupert Dauncey?'

Dillon laughed harshly and Ferguson said, 'What on earth was he doing there?'

'Percy gave Scotland Yard what would usually be termed a full and frank statement. Rashid funds ACW, as we know, and Dauncey came down to try and call off their participation in the rally. Said it was too dangerous. Both he and Percy even made speeches to the busload of students pointing out the dangers of the rally.'

'Did Dauncey end up going?'

'With Percy, but they left when it got rough. Percy went back to the bus and Dauncey said he was going home.'

'Very convenient, Dauncey just showing up like that,' said Dillon. 'Making noble speeches.'

'And get this,' said Bernstein. 'Percy actually introduced Dauncey to Helen Quinn. Said he wanted to meet a fellow American. Percy says he heard him urging her not to go to the rally but that her boyfriend, this Alan Grant, mocked him in front of everybody. They ended up going to the rally, but then people lost sight of each other, and that was the last Percy saw of either of them.'

'Hmm,' Ferguson said. 'So on the face of it, they went to Canal Street after the riot, probably for sex, had a few drinks, some drugs, and she had an adverse reaction. Grant takes her to the hospital, she dies on the instant, and he runs for it, doesn't know which way to turn . . . and commits suicide.'

'Which might be believable . . . if it weren't for the damn smell of the Rashids.'

The phone rang. Hannah answered it and found Roper on the other end. 'I'm faxing the autopsy through now. They're doing Grant next. I'll send those details when they come in.'

She got the fax from Ferguson's study and read it as she went back to the living room. She looked up. 'Confirmed, sir. She was heavily over the line on alcohol, had certainly taken Ecstasy. Otherwise healthy, well nourished. Not a virgin, but no evidence of sex before her death.'

She handed the fax to Ferguson, who read it through. 'Poor girl. God knows what her father will make of it.' He looked up. 'I still don't know what I make of it.'

'Well, I do,' Dillon said. 'If you'll excuse me, I've got things to do.'

'Such as?' demanded Hannah.

'That's my business. Talk to you later, Charles.'

He left, got a taxi to the Ministry of Defence,

booked a limousine, and told the driver to take him to Oxford. There was something he wanted to check.

Traffic was light and they were there in an hour and a half. As they reached the outskirts, he called Roper on his mobile.

'Can you pull me in Henry Percy's address from that police report perhaps?'

'Hang on.' He was back in two minutes. 'Has an apartment, 10B Kaiser Lane. What are you up to?'

'I'll let you know later.'

They found Kaiser Lane with no trouble; 10B was at the top of a gloomy stairway in a Victorian semi-detached. Dillon pulled a cord and an old-fashioned bell jangled. After a while, he heard the shuffle of steps, the door opened, and Percy appeared. He was bleary-eyed and looked as if he'd been sleeping.

'Professor Percy?'

'Yes.'

'I was asked to call on you by Rupert Dauncey.'

Percy managed a smile. 'I see. You'd better come in.' He led the way along the corridor and entered a parlour. 'Now what can I do for you?'

'First of all, I'd like to introduce you to a friend

of mine, my Walther PPK.' He took it from his special pocket. 'And this is his friend. He's called a Carswell silencer.' He screwed it on the muzzle of the Walther. 'Now I can shoot you through the kneecap and nobody will hear a thing.'

Percy was terrified. 'Who are you? What do you want?'

'I've seen your statement to the police about Helen Quinn's death. You say Rupert Dauncey was against the students going to the rally because he anticipated violence?'

'Yes.'

'And that you both made it clear on the bus that you were against going?'

'Yes, yes. There were over forty students there. They can confirm it. The Oxford police have interviewed some of them.'

Dillon grabbed him, pushed him back over a table, and rammed the Walther into his knee. 'So you're telling me Dauncey's as pure as the driven snow, is that it?'

Percy totally freaked. 'No, no, no. I mean, yes, but – it's just that he changed his attitude.'

'What do you mean?'

'At first, he was all for positive action. He thought it good for the students.' He hesitated and carried on. 'He arranged for some of them to go to training courses in Scotland.'

'Did Helen Quinn go?'

'No, but her boyfriend did, Alan Grant.'

'You know he's dead.'

'Yes, the police have been in touch. They said he committed suicide.'

Dillon stood back. 'Don't believe everything you hear. So that's all you can tell me, is it? Dauncey used to be bloodthirsty, but now he's changed.'

'That's right.'

Dillon rammed the Walther in again. 'And you expect me to believe that fairy tale? When did you last see him?'

'We spoke on the phone late last night.'

'What did he say?'

'That it was a good thing he and I had spoken to the students as we had, since we'd probably be called to the inquest.'

'Yes, that was very convenient, wasn't it, Henry?' Dillon stood there for a moment, looking at him, then he began to unscrew his silencer. 'You're not leaving anything out now, are you, Henry? Anything that might change this little tale of yours?'

Percy thought about the fifty thousand, but

decided on discretion. 'I've told you the truth, as God is my witness,' he said piously.

'Yes, well, I wouldn't call God into this if I were you, Professor. I'll see you at the inquest. And when you speak to Dauncey next – tell him Sean Dillon was here.'

He walked into the hall. Percy hesitated, then picked up the phone. 'Dauncey? It's Percy.'

In the hall, Sean Dillon smiled and let himself out.

Daniel Quinn had Frobisher take him to the American Embassy first, and wait. He went up the steps and identified himself to the security guards. In two minutes, a Marine Captain in uniform was greeting him.

'My name's Davies, Senator. It's a privilege to meet you. Ambassador Begley is waiting.' Quinn, unshaven and still in combat gear, shook hands with him.

'If I may say so, you look as though you've had a hard time out there.'

'Well, I wouldn't recommend Kosovo for your next vacation, Captain.'

'This way, Senator.'

A couple of minutes later, he opened the door to the Ambassador's office and ushered Quinn in.

'Hello, Elmer.'

Begley was wearing a Savile Row suit, his grey hair perfectly groomed. There couldn't have been a greater contrast. He came round the desk and took Quinn's hand. 'Daniel, I'm so sorry. If there's anything we can do – anything – the resources of the Embassy are at your disposal. Sit down.'

'If you don't mind, I won't, Elmer. I just wanted to touch base. I'd like to get to my house, shower and change, then I have an appointment with General Ferguson.'

'Charles? He's a friend. You'll be in good hands there. But remember – anything we can do.'

'Thank you, Elmer.'

Quinn's house in Park Place was in a turning off South Audley Street, a pleasant Regency building with a small courtyard. Luke Cornwall, his chauffeur, a large black man from New York, was hosing down a Mercedes town car. He stopped at once, his face grave.

'Senator, what can I say?'

'There's nothing to be said, Luke, but thank you.

Right now I feel like shit, though, so I'm going to shower and change, and then I want you to take me to Cavendish Place.'

'You've got it, Senator.'

Quinn went up the steps, the door opened, and Mary Cornwall appeared. She'd been a maid for years at the Boston house, had seen Helen grow up, and there were tears in her eyes. He kissed her on the cheek.

She was crying. 'Sometimes I wonder whether there's a God in heaven.'

'Oh, there is, Mary, always hang on to that.'

'Can I get you anything to eat?'

'Not now. I'm going to change. I have an appointment.'

He went along the panelled hall, hurried upstairs, and opened the door to his bedroom suite. It was light and airy, with maple panelling, his favourite paintings on the walls, and Turkish carpeting. On his return he'd always experienced conscious pleasure on entering this room, but now it meant nothing.

In the bathroom, he stripped, dropping all his clothes to the floor, turned on the shower, and soaped himself all over, trying to wash away the stench of Kosovo and death.

Half an hour later he came downstairs, perfectly groomed, wearing a brown Armani country suit and brogues. Mary was in the kitchen and he didn't bother her. He simply opened the front door and went down the steps to where Luke, in a dark blue chauffeur's uniform, waited.

Rupert Dauncey was waiting, too. He'd calmed Henry Percy when Percy had called him in a panic, but he disliked the idea that Dillon was still on the case. He also wondered where Daniel Quinn was, so he'd checked with a friend at the Embassy, who told him Quinn had arrived and was on his way to Park Place.

Park Place! That was a bit of luck. Dauncey had driven around the corner without knowing the number of the house, but then he had seen Luke standing waiting by the Quinn Mercedes. Rupert pulled in further along the street and saw Quinn emerge from the house. As Luke drove away, Rupert was already turning and he went after him.

It was Hannah Bernstein who answered the door at Cavendish Place and found Quinn standing there.

She recognized him from the photo in his file, just as he recognized her from the material Blake Johnson had shown him in Washington.

'Superintendent Bernstein.'

'Senator Quinn. Please come in.'

She led the way into the sitting room. Dillon was drinking Bushmills by the French windows, and Ferguson got up.

'I wish I could say this is a pleasure, Daniel, but it doesn't seem appropriate. We all feel for you.'

'That's appreciated.'

'Do you know Sean Dillon?'

'Only by reputation.' Quinn shook his hand. 'If you know anything about me, you'll know my grandfather was born in Belfast and fought with Michael Collins. He was chased out to the States in 1920.'

'So he'd be Irish Republican Brotherhood,' Dillon said. 'Worse than the mob, that lot.'

Quinn managed a smile. 'You could say that.'

'Will you join me in a Bushmills?' Quinn hesitated, and Dillon added, 'I'd recommend a large one. The Superintendent's put a file together that won't exactly cheer you up.'

'Then I'll take that as sound advice.'

231

Dillon gave him the whiskey in a shot glass and Quinn drank it in a single swallow. He put the glass on a table and took the file from Hannah.

Ferguson said, 'That file gives you a full history of our dealings with the Rashids, and everything we know so far about your daughter's death, including the details of her post-mortem and the police inquiries. In fact, we've just added details of the post-mortem of her boyfriend, too, Alan Grant.'

'Who? I've never heard of him.' Quinn was astonished. 'I didn't know she had a boyfriend.'

'I'm afraid she did,' Hannah Bernstein said.

'Afraid?'

'It's all there, Senator,' she told him quietly.

'Show the Senator into my study,' Ferguson told her. 'He can read the file in peace.'

She led Quinn out. Dillon said, 'What a sod.'

'I agree, and I'm not looking forward to when he's done. You'd better pour me one of those, too.'

Twenty minutes later, Quinn came back into the room. His face was very pale and the right hand shook slightly as he raised the file.

'Can I keep this?'

'Of course,' Ferguson said.

Quinn said, 'Right, I'll go along to the mortuary now. I'll need to identify her.'

'Then drink this.' Dillon poured another Bushmills. 'Get it down. You're going to need it. In fact, I'll come with you.'

'That's kind of you.' Quinn turned to Hannah. 'What about the inquest?'

'It's tomorrow morning. We managed to get them to bring it forward.'

'Good. The sooner the better.' He drank the Bushmills and said to Dillon, 'Let's get it done.'

Rupert had sat patiently in his Mercedes just down the street from the apartment. Finally, Quinn and Dillon came out, got into the limousine, and were driven away.

'Dillon,' Rupert said softly. 'Now, that's interesting.' A moment later, he was following them.

The mortuary was the sort of ageing building that, from the outside, looked more like a warehouse than anything else. Inside, it was different. There was a pleasant reception area, well decorated with fitted carpets. A young woman at a desk looked up and smiled.

'Can I help you?'

'My name is Quinn. I believe you have my daughter here?'

She stopped smiling. 'Oh, I'm so sorry. We had a call a short while ago saying you were coming to identify the body. I've notified the local police station. It's only five minutes away.'

'Thank you.'

'And I've notified Professor George Langley. He's our regular forensic pathologist, and fortunately he's in the building right now. I thought you'd want to speak with him.'

'Thank you. We'll wait.'

He and Dillon sat down, but only moments later, a small grey-haired, energetic man entered. The girl whispered and he came over.

'George Langley.'

'Daniel Quinn, and this is Sean Dillon, a friend.'

'You have my deepest sympathy.'

'May I see my daughter?'

'Of course.' He said to the woman, 'Send in the police officer when he arrives.'

The room he led them into was walled with white tiles, and had fluorescent lighting and a line of modern-looking steel operating tables. Two bodies were covered with some sort of white rubber sheets.

'Are you ready?' Langley asked.

'As I ever will be.'

Helen Quinn looked very calm, her eyes closed. A kind of plastic hood was on her head and a little blood seeped through. Quinn leaned down and kissed her on the forehead.

'Thank you.'

Langley replaced the sheet and Quinn said, 'I've seen your report to the coroner. The alcohol, the drug? There's absolutely no doubt?'

'I'm afraid not.'

'It's so unlike her. That's just not the girl I knew.'

'That's sometimes the way of it,' Langley said gently.

'And the boy? Is that him?' He nodded to the other body. 'I didn't even know he existed.'

'Well, yes, that is Alan Grant.' Langley hesitated, then said, 'I shouldn't do this, but it's an unusual business.'

He lifted the sheet and Quinn looked down at Grant, who seemed even younger in death. 'Thank you.' Langley replaced the sheet. 'And do you think he committed suicide, the way the police are hinting?'

'I only deal in certainties, sir. He had consumed

a vast amount of vodka, but there was no trace of Ecstasy. No sign of any kind of bruising. Did he fall by accident off that wharf, did he jump? I can't help you there.'

There was a knock at the door and a uniformed police officer appeared. 'Ah, there you are, Professor.'

The sergeant had a form on a clipboard. 'I regret the circumstances, Senator, but would you please formally identify the deceased?'

'She is my daughter, Helen Quinn.'

'Thank you, sir. If you'd sign the form,' and he nodded to Dillon, 'Perhaps you'd be kind enough to witness it.'

They did as they were asked and he withdrew. Langley said, 'I'll see you at the inquest.'

'Of course. Many thanks,' and Quinn led the way out.

They got in the Mercedes, and as Luke drove away, Dillon said, 'A hell of a business.'

Quinn said, 'We'll drop you off,' then leaned back and closed his eyes.

And Dauncey followed.

11

Quinn arrived at the coroner's court at ten the following morning. There were few people about, the odd police officer passing through. A young man was sitting on one of the benches, wearing a trench coat, a travelling bag on the floor beside him. He looked tired and unshaven.

Quinn shook a cigarette from a packet of Marlboros and lit it. The young man seemed to wince. Quinn held out the pack. 'Can I offer you one?'

'I'm supposed to have stopped, but what the hell.' He took a cigarette, fingers shaking, and accepted the light. 'I'm knackered. I just flew in from Berlin and there was a delay at Tempelhof. You know what airports can be like when you're sitting around for four or five hours. I thought I'd miss the hearing.'

And Quinn, having gone through Hannah

Bernstein's file several times now, knew instinctively who he was.

'Is your name Grant?'

'That's right, Fergus Grant.'

'Alan Grant's brother.'

Grant looked bewildered. 'Who are you?'

'Daniel Quinn. Helen Quinn's father.'

Grant looked dismayed. 'Oh, my God. Look, I know almost nothing about any of this, except that they're both dead. The police spoke to me by phone and just gave me the bare facts. That he was found drowned, that his girlfriend was dead. I never even knew he had a relationship.'

'And I didn't know she did. What about your parents?'

'My old man cleared off when I was twelve and Mum died of cancer five years ago.'

'I'm sorry.'

Grant shrugged and stubbed out his cigarette. 'They've told me hardly anything.'

'Well, this inquest should cover it all.' At that moment, Hannah Bernstein came in, followed by Ferguson and Dillon, and Quinn said to Grant, 'Excuse me,' and joined them.

'The man I've been talking to is young Grant's brother, Fergus. Just in from Berlin.'

'Yes,' Hannah said. 'I heard this morning that this was to be a joint hearing.'

Before she could elaborate, the doors opened and an usher appeared. 'Court Three is now in session.'

They filed in, followed by Grant and half a dozen members of the public, the kind of people who came for the entertainment value more than anything else. There were several functionaries, a police sergeant in uniform, and the Clerk of the Court. Hannah went and spoke to him, then returned to the others and joined them at the benches.

A moment later, George Langley came in and reported to the Clerk of the Court. Dillon said to Ferguson, 'The pathologist.'

Rupert Dauncey and Henry Percy came in straight afterwards, with an usher who escorted them to the Clerk. As they turned away, Dauncey looked directly at Quinn and his friends, smiled slightly and sat down on the other side of the aisle with Percy.

The Clerk of the Court got things moving. 'The court will rise for Her Majesty's Coroner.'

The Coroner, a scholarly-looking man with white hair, came in and sat high above the court on the bench, the officials below. A door opened to one side and an usher led in the jurors, who squeezed along their benches. The Clerk of the Court administered the oath and the proceedings got started.

The Coroner had a dry and precise voice. He said, 'Before we begin, I wish to make a statement. Circumstances being what they are, and with the permission of the Lord Chancellor's Office, this inquest will consider the facts surrounding the deaths of both Helen Quinn and Alan Grant, each appearing to have a bearing on the other.' He nodded to the Clerk. 'We'll start with the police evidence.'

The uniformed Sergeant was called and quickly went through the basic facts, how Helen Quinn was delivered to the hospital, how Alan Grant was traced to Canal Street, and then the discovery of his body. The Sergeant was dismissed and the Clerk called Henry Percy, who went to the stand nervously and confirmed his identity.

The Coroner picked up a paper from the stack in front of him. 'So, Professor, you knew Helen Quinn and Alan Grant well?'

'Oh, yes.'

'And can you confirm they had a relationship?'

'It was common knowledge amongst the other students.'

'Were you aware of any ill feeling between them?'

'On the contrary. They seemed to live in each other's pockets.'

'On the day in question, the coach trip to the rally in Whitehall, you were on the coach, I understand?'

'Yes. We'd heard that the rally might get violent, and we feared that the students would become embroiled, and so we begged them not to go.'

'Did they listen?'

'Only half a dozen.'

'You said we?'

'Rupert Dauncey was with me, representing the Rashid Educational Trust. They fund Act of Class Warfare, the group I belong to.'

'A curious name. What does it signify?'

'A dislike of capitalism. We aim to re-educate people, change their thinking.'

'You mean catch them young,' the Coroner said dryly. There was laughter in the court. 'You may go.'

The Clerk called Rupert Dauncey, who moved to the stand. He looked imposing in an excellent navy blue flannel suit. The Coroner didn't keep him long.

'I've read the list the corporation sent over of the charities supported by your Trust, Mr Dauncey. All very laudable, I'm sure.'

'The Countess of Loch Dhu and Rashid Investments have spent millions worldwide on these enterprises.'

'But you weren't happy about the trip to London?'

'Not at all. When I heard that the United Anarchist Front was behind it, I was horrified. I went to Oxford to back Professor Percy in asking the students not to go.'

'And you saw Helen Quinn and Alan Grant there?'

'I sat next to them. I'd been introduced to her on a previous visit by Professor Percy. I urged her in the strongest terms not to go. Grant told me they were spending the weekend in London at his brother's house, so I suppose that was a reason for them to go anyway. However, I deeply regret my failure to persuade Helen to listen.'

'You had no personal responsibility, Mr Dauncey.'

'Yes, but it was an organization backed by Rashid that ended up at that rally and she went along for the ride. If she hadn't been in London, things might have turned out differently.'

'I doubt that, sir, but your self-questioning does you credit. Stand down.'

Rupert returned to his seat, having obviously made an excellent impression, and Professor George Langley was called.

The Coroner said, 'I have before me autopsy reports on both the deceased. You performed them yourself?'

'Yes.'

The Clerk of the Court was passing copies to the jury. The Coroner said, 'I suggest a quick look, ladies and gentlemen, to familiarize yourselves. I'll give you five minutes.'

'That's good of him,' Dillon murmured.

'Behave yourself,' Hannah told him.

'Don't I always?' He turned to Quinn. 'Are you all right?'

'So far.'

They waited while the Coroner examined more papers and looked up. 'We'll proceed. Professor Langley, what are the essential facts here?'

'That Helen Quinn drank a sizeable amount of vodka and took an Ecstasy tablet at a later stage.'

'Not first?'

'Oh, no, the chemical breakdown would have been different if she'd taken it before the vodka.'

'You don't say alcohol, you specify vodka.'

'Yes. We can differentiate. We can even ascertain the brand, the type.'

'And is that important in this case?'

'Absolutely. It links Helen Quinn to Alan Grant.'

'So, let us come to him. Once again, what are the essential facts?'

'That Alan Grant had drunk a very great deal of the same vodka consumed by Helen Quinn. I identified the brand and, at my urging, the police searched the house at Ten Canal Street and found an almost empty bottle.'

'And the Ecstasy?'

'A small paper bag was discovered in Grant's left hand jacket pocket containing two chocolates, each containing an Ecstasy tablet. I had a lab analysis done.'

'And?'

'They were the same batch as the one taken by Helen Quinn. No question.'

'Now let us come to the manner of his death.'

'By drowning. There was no suggestion of foul play, no bruising. I visited the scene and examined the wharf.'

'And what was your conclusion?'

'There is no rail at the end of the wharf. If there had been, and it was broken, one might have suspected a drunken accident. It could still have been an accident, a man as drunk as Grant could easily have lurched over that open edge. Or . . .' He shrugged.

'Or what, Professor?'

'Or he could have stepped off deliberately, drunk, and perhaps guilt-ridden by the death of the girl.'

'But that, of course, is conjecture on your part, Professor, and this court must only concern itself with facts. You may stand down.'

'As you say, sir.'

Langley did as he was told and the Coroner turned to address the jury. 'Ladies and gentlemen, this is a tragic matter indeed, two young people on the threshold of life, members of an ancient and honourable university, their lives snuffed out. However, we must, as I've just reminded Professor Langley, stick to known facts, not supposition. So, let me remind you of what seem to be the salient facts.'

He seemed to be collecting his thoughts, and there was silence as everyone waited.

'That both drank large amounts of the same

vodka is beyond dispute. That Alan Grant, to be frank, dumped the dying girl at St Mark's Hospital is beyond dispute. As to the Ecstasy, there are questions you must ask yourselves. Why didn't he take one? Why only the girl? You may conjecture that hiding an Ecstasy tablet in a chocolate was a device to dupe the girl, but I must warn you there is no proof of this. Perhaps the girl obtained the tablets and concealed them in the chocolates for safety reasons. It is perfectly reasonable to argue that his action in running away was panic, even if the girl had taken the tablet of her own free will.'

He looked at the ceiling, fingertips pressed together. 'As to the matter of Grant's death, it was death by drowning, we know that, but whether caused by himself because of fear or guilt, we shall never know, and this makes a verdict of death by misadventure inadmissible.

'A final point in this whole sorry matter. Mr Dauncey, on behalf of the Rashid organization, seemed to feel some guilt in the matter, because the students were actually in London for the rally in Whitehall. My own opinion is rather different. Vodka can as easily be consumed in Oxford, and certainly this also applies to Ecstasy. I fail to see that the coach trip had any bearing on events.

However, Mr Dauncey's concern does him credit.'

He shuffled his papers into an orderly pile and swivelled in his chair to face the jury fully.

'So, how may I advise you in such a case and with no witnesses? Did Alan Grant slip the girl the Ecstasy tablet by subterfuge or did she take it herself? We don't know and never shall. Did he fall off the wharf in a drunken state or, in despair, take his own life? Again, we don't know and never shall. In the circumstances, I can suggest an open verdict, which is both legal and proper. You may, of course, retire to consider your verdict.'

But they didn't bother. Everyone leaned together, there was a ripple of conversation, and they sat up. The foreman stood. 'The open verdict seemed sensible to us.'

'Thank you,' said the Coroner. 'Let it be so entered.' He turned to the court. 'I now come to the question of the next of kin. If Fergus Grant is in court, please stand.' Grant did so, looking bemused. 'I will now issue you with a burial order, as Alan Grant's brother. You may retrieve your brother's body at your convenience. You have my sympathy.'

'Thank you, sir.' Grant sat down.

'Senator Daniel Quinn.' Quinn stood. 'I will

issue you with a burial order. You also have my sympathy.'

'Thank you,' Quinn said.

The Clerk cried, 'The court will rise for Her Majesty's Coroner.'

And it was over, the jury moving and the court clearing. As Rupert Dauncey passed, he nodded and said to Quinn, 'You have my sympathy, too, Senator.'

Hannah had gone to the Clerk of the Court's desk, where Grant was standing. The Clerk gave them each a burial order. Grant walked down the aisle with her and Quinn stopped them.

'Listen, I'm truly sorry. What the Coroner said was true. We'll never know the truth. We can't go back, so let's go forward.'

Grant was close to tears and half embraced him. 'God help me.'

'Maybe he will.'

They watched Grant go and moved out through the foyer to the pavement. Ferguson said to Quinn, 'Now what?'

'Well, if you could give me the address of a crematorium, that would be good. I'd like to take her ashes home. If you've any influence in that area, General, I'd appreciate it.'

'Superintendent?' Ferguson asked.

'Leave it with me, Senator.'

'Why don't you join me in my car, Superintendent, and we can get started. I'm not looking for a funeral – I'll arrange that back home – but a Catholic priest would be appreciated.'

'Consider it done,' Hannah said.

'I'll come with you, too.' Dillon turned to Ferguson. 'We'll see you later.'

'Running things now, are you?' Ferguson asked.

'Don't I always?'

They drove to Park Place, Hannah huddled in the corner, making one call after another. She was still at it when they arrived. Mary opened the door and Quinn led the way into the drawing room.

'Coffee, Mary.'

'And tea for me,' Dillon said.

She went out and Quinn said to Dillon, 'He was good, friend Dauncey, very good.'

'Yes,' Dillon said. 'But he'll trip up yet. There's something there. We just have to find it.'

Hannah clicked off. 'I've arranged for an undertaking firm we use to pick up your daughter. The ceremony will be at North Hill Crematorium at two o'clock. A Father Cohan will meet you there.'

'Meet *us* there,' Dillon said. 'I'm going with you.'

'Then I'll come, too,' Hannah said. 'If that's all right with you.'

'Of course it is,' Quinn told her. 'I'm very grateful.'

'That's what friends are for, Daniel,' said Dillon.

Father Cohan was a London Irishman and the only good thing about North Hill Crematorium. The whole thing was a bad experience, and the taped celestial choir in the background didn't help, but Cohan was as robust and sincere as anyone could want.

'I am the resurrection and the life, saith the Lord. He that believeth in me, though he were dead, yet shall he live.'

I wonder, thought Quinn. A total waste of a young life and to what end, to what purpose? No, I can't believe, not any longer. Let those who will do so, but not me. And yet, for some strange reason, he thought of Sister Sarah Palmer and Bo Din all those years ago in Vietnam.

Father Cohan sprinkled the coffin, it moved on

the conveyor belt into the darkness beyond, and it was over.

One of the undertakers said, 'We'll deliver the ashes this evening, Senator. Park Place, I understand?'

'Number eight.' Quinn shook hands. 'I'm grateful.'

They moved outside and Father Cohan went with them. 'You have a car, Father?' Hannah asked.

'Yes, I'll be fine.' He grasped Quinn's hand. 'Give it time, Senator. There's always a reason. You'll find it one day.'

They moved to the Mercedes, where Luke waited. 'That's it, then,' Dillon said.

Quinn shook his head. 'No, there's one more thing I want to do before I leave. I'm going to drive up to Oxford and retrieve Helen's things from her room at St Hugh's. I'll drop you two off.'

'Her room?' Dillon lit a cigarette and thought. 'You know, I never looked at her room, or Grant's. You don't mind if I come, too, do you?'

They made Oxford in an hour and a half. Quinn gave Luke directions, and they turned in through the gates at St Hugh's and paused at the lodge. The porter emerged. 'Can I help?'

'You may remember me, Daniel Quinn? I'm here to collect my daughter's things.'

The porter stopped smiling. 'Of course, sir. May I say how sorry I am. She was a lovely girl. I'll phone the principal to let him know you're here.'

'That's good of you.'

They drove on and Luke dropped them at the entrance. Quinn led the way into the entrance hall. 'We'll check in with the principal and then get on with it. His office is this way, just beyond the Junior Common Room. That's where the kids hang out.'

By the entrance there were rows of pigeonholes. Each one had a slot with the student's name, in alphabetical order. They paused and Quinn found his daughter's. There were three letters. He examined them and sighed, holding one up. 'My last letter to her from Kosovo.'

Dillon ran a finger along the names and found Alan Grant's pigeonhole. There was no mail in it, but the box wasn't empty. Dillon reached in and pulled out a pen. He looked at it curiously, then dropped it in his pocket. There was something about it . . .

The door to the principal's office opened and he came out. 'There you are, Senator.' He held out a hand. 'I can't tell you how distressed we all are.'

They shook hands.

'You'll have come for your daughter's clothes and belongings. I asked some members of the staff to pack her suitcase. I hope we did right.'

'That was kind of you.'

'Do you need me to come with you?'

'That won't be necessary.'

'There's the key to her room.' The principal handed it over, hesitated and then said, 'Your daughter was a wonderful young woman, well liked by the staff and other students. What I heard of the circumstances, it's beyond belief. It simply is so out of character that it doesn't make sense.'

'To me, neither, but I'm grateful you said it.' Quinn turned away and Dillon followed.

The room was on the first floor. There was a single bed, two suitcases beside it, a carrying bag open and empty on the bed, a wardrobe, desk and chair. Books were on two shelves, a photo of Quinn with his arm around Helen stood on the desk. It was very quiet, very simple, and yet the room was filled with her presence. He leaned on the desk, wracked by a dry sob.

Dillon put a hand on his shoulder. 'Take it easy. Just breathe slowly.'

'I know. I'll be okay. I'll pack the carrying bag with her books and the odds and ends.'

He started taking them down and Dillon moved to the window and took out the pen and examined it.

'What have you got there?'

'I noticed it in Alan Grant's pigeonhole. It looks familiar somehow, like I've –' He snapped his fingers. 'Of course!'

'What?'

'I've seen one of these before. This isn't an ordinary pen. It's a recording device.'

Quinn paused as he put books into the bag. 'What? Are you sure?'

'You twist and put the top down. It has a surprising amount of volume.'

'But what was Alan Grant doing with that?'

'Let's find out,' and Dillon turned it on.

And he was right. The sound was particularly clear as Rupert Dauncey said, 'There are three pieces of candy in there, chocolates. Each has an Ecstasy tablet inside. I want you to offer the girl one . . .'

Dillon pressed down with his thumb. There was

silence. Quinn stared at him, his face drained, the skin stretched tightly over the cheekbones.

'I know that voice,' he whispered.

'Rupert Dauncey.'

Quinn sat on the edge of the bed. 'Let's hear the rest of it.'

Afterwards, he sat with his head in his hands for a while. Finally, he looked up. 'That bastard was responsible for my daughter's death.'

'I'm afraid so.'

'But why did Grant go along with it?'

'I don't know. Dauncey may have had something on him – it's clear from the recording he was under pressure. And he might not have thought it was any big deal. Lots of students try that stuff. A pound to a penny, he'd experimented himself.' Dillon shook his head. 'He didn't mean for Helen to die.'

'Which is why he killed himself?'

'If he killed himself. The more we look into this, the more we see Dauncey's fingerprints. I've a hunch we'll find even more before we're through. Dauncey's capable of anything.'

'Well, so am I.' Quinn got up. 'Let's get back to London, Sean. Can the recording on that pen be copied?'

'I believe so. I have a friend who could probably handle it for us.'

'Then let's get moving.' He picked up the two suitcases, Dillon got the carrying bag, and they left.

At Regency Square, Dillon made the introductions and Roper examined the pen. 'Yes, I know how these things work. I can put it onto a cassette tape. That would enhance the sound.'

'Just the one,' Quinn said. 'No other copies.'

'As you wish. I'll need to run it through first.' He pointed Dillon toward the kitchen. 'After your comments about my wine, Sean, I got a bottle of Irish whiskey in. It's not Bushmills, but I presume it will do. On the shelf next to the fridge.'

Roper moved to a bench piled with electronic devices and got to work. Dillon found the whiskey bottle and two glasses and poured him and Quinn one each. They sat side by side on the windowseat.

Dillon said, 'What do you intend to do?'

'I intend to meet with Rashid and Dauncey.'

'Are you certain about that?'

'Oh, yes.' Quinn was calm. 'Don't worry, Sean, I won't have a gun in my pocket, however much I'd like to. There are other ways.'

Roper turned his wheelchair. 'One pen and one tape.' Before Dillon could move, Quinn took them. 'Mine, I think. Many thanks, Major.'

'My pleasure.' He said to Dillon, 'Let me know what's happening, won't you?'

They found Ferguson at Cavendish Place, and when they went in, Hannah was seated at his side, going through a batch of papers.

Ferguson said, 'Things okay at Oxford?'

'Well, you could say it was a revealing experience,' Dillon told him.

Hannah frowned. 'What's that supposed to mean?'

'I'll leave it to the Senator.'

It was Ferguson's turn to frown. 'Quinn?'

'Before I explain, I'd like to raise a question. Superintendent, you're a serving police officer. What you're going to hear now is evidence of criminal conduct, but it's *my* business. If you can't treat it in confidence, then I'd prefer you to leave – and no offence intended.'

Hannah looked shocked, but Ferguson stayed calm. 'The Superintendent is seconded to my department and is subject to the restrictions of the Official

Secrets Act. What's said in here stays in here.' He turned to Hannah. 'Please confirm that.'

Hannah looked troubled but said, 'Of course, sir.'

Ferguson turned back to Quinn. 'So, what have you got?'

'We found a pen in Alan Grant's mailbox.'

'A secret recording pen,' Dillon put in.

Quinn held the tape up. 'Major Roper has just made a copy for me that enhances the sound quality. You'll find it interesting.'

Ferguson said, 'Superintendent?'

Hannah got up, took the tape from Quinn, and went and inserted it in the cassette player on the corner of the sideboard. When she switched it on, it was loud and clear.

'There are three pieces of candy in there, chocolates,' Rupert Dauncey said. 'Each has an Ecstasy tablet inside . . .'

When they were done, Hannah said, 'That's one of the most cold-blooded things I've ever heard.'

'A bastard of the first water,' Ferguson said.

Hannah carried on. 'With that evidence, the police will be able to arrest him at once.'

'And charge him with what? Murder? No. Manslaughter? No. A good lawyer would claim that all Dauncey intended was to get my daughter into trouble to embarrass me. At the worst, he might be charged with contributing to her death, but I'm not even confident of that.'

'But there's much more to it, Senator, you know there is.'

'Of course I do. But with Rashid's resources, how do I know he'll get more than a slap on the wrist? Dauncey could say he was sorry, that his personal antipathy had taken things too far, and what kind of sentence would he draw? Come on, you tell me.'

'I will,' Dillon put in. 'And you're right. The tape's damaging, but it's not enough.'

'And I couldn't put any of the background into evidence, any of the history of the Rashids and the President. All the events involving you people are classified.'

Hannah said, 'So Dauncey and Rashid get away with it?'

'I didn't say that. If necessary, I'd have no hesitation in taking Rupert Dauncey's life myself.' There was silence, and then he added, 'But I have other ideas. I'm going to South Audley Street to confront them now. Dillon, are you coming with me?'

'I'm your man,' Dillon said.

Ferguson sighed and got up. 'Then I suppose I'd better come, too, as the voice of sanity.' He turned to Hannah, 'Not you, Superintendent. I have a hunch it would be better if you weren't there, Official Secrets Act or not.'

Luke delivered them to the Rashid house, where a maid in a black dress and white apron answered the door.

'Is the Countess at home?' Ferguson asked.

'Yes, sir.'

'Be kind enough to tell her that General Ferguson, Senator Quinn, and Mr Dillon would appreciate a word.'

They waited in the hall while the maid went upstairs. She was back in a moment, stood at the top, and called, 'Please come up, gentlemen.'

She showed them into the drawing room, where Kate Rashid sat by the fire, Dauncey standing behind her.

'Well, well,' she said. 'What do we have here? The Three Musketeers? All for one and one for all?'

'That's not funny, Kate,' Dillon said. 'And I

don't think you'll find it funny yourself when you hear what we have.'

'Such as?'

Quinn took out the pen. 'We found this at Oxford. It belonged to Alan Grant. I know you know who he is, so don't pretend you don't.'

'Of course we know,' said Kate Rashid. 'Don't be melodramatic, Senator.'

'Well, this is what you don't know. This pen is really a recording device. And Alan Grant turned it on when your cousin started threatening him.'

Kate Rashid looked taken aback. Then she rallied. 'Nonsense. Where would someone like him get a thing like that?'

'His brother's in the security business,' Dillon said. 'It was a present.'

Quinn took the tape from his pocket and held it up. 'We took the liberty of making a copy. The quality is much better. You'll see.'

There was a sound deck in the corner and he switched it on and slipped the tape in place. There was a moment's silence, then Rupert Dauncey started to speak . . .

Afterwards, Dillon said, 'Any way you try to spin it, it's bad for you, Kate.' He looked at Dauncey. 'And you.'

'Guaranteed prison time, I'd say,' Ferguson said.

But, remarkably, Rupert was unfazed. He lit a cigarette, face calm. 'Do what you like,' he said. 'You won't get far. You must realize that, Ferguson, don't you?'

'No, that's the wrong way of putting it,' Quinn said. 'What you mean is, we won't get far enough. You'll get some stupid piddling sentence, of which you'll only serve half anyway. And you know what? You're right. You know what this is worth?' He held up the pen. 'Nothing. Its only useful function is to tell me you were responsible for my daughter's death.'

And he tossed the pen and the tape into the fire.

Ferguson said, 'For God's sake!' as the tape flamed and the pen melted. Even Dillon looked surprised.

Quinn continued. 'I'll be flying to Boston tomorrow morning with my daughter's ashes. When she's laid to rest, I'll be back. Then we'll get started.'

'And what's that supposed to mean?' Kate Rashid asked, visibly rattled.

'Countess, I intend to go to war on you and your company. I intend to ruin you. And ruin you I will, if it's the last thing I do.'

'And you,' he said, turning to Rupert Dauncey. 'You are a dead man walking.'

He turned and led the way out.

After they'd gone, Kate Rashid said, 'Well. That was rather nasty, darling. Though you have to admire that gesture. Do you think it's true, that those were the only copies of the tape?'

'I've never been more certain of anything in my life.' He lit another cigarette. 'I'll have his house watched, so we know when he's back.'

'Then what?'

'Then I'll handle it.' He smiled. 'The "last thing I do" will come somewhat sooner than he expects.' He turned. 'And what about you? What about this bomb thing of yours?'

'I'm still waiting to hear from Colum McGee. Once he's arranged things with Barry Keenan, we'll fly to Belfast and drive down to Drumcree.'

'Do I finally find out why?'

'Of course. Just not yet. Everything comes to he who waits, darling.' She seemed to have regained her spirits.

'So what would you like to do while we wait?'

'Oh, let's have a little fun. I was thinking of going

down to Dauncey Place. I keep my plane there at the air club, my Black Eagle. I was thinking we could fly over to the Isle of Wight and have a picnic.'

'But what about Ferguson and his crew?'

'My dear Rupert, that's exactly the point. They'll *never* believe we're going over there just to have a picnic. It'll drive them crazy!'

At Ferguson's suggestion, Luke drove them to the Dorchester. They went in and sat in a corner.

'Champagne hardly seems in order,' Ferguson said.

'No, but a brandy would be,' Quinn said, and held up his right hand, which shook slightly. 'I've got to learn to control myself from now on.'

'I thought you did a remarkable job of doing just that,' Ferguson said. 'But, look, Senator, we have to tread carefully here. Before your daughter's death, we had nothing concrete, nothing that in law would allow us to take on Kate Rashid and her organization in an appropriate way. That recording gave us a foothold, but you chose to destroy it, which leaves us back where we started.'

'It was my decision.' Quinn swallowed his brandy.

'But an unwise one if you intend a violent response.'

'No, General. You misunderstood. My action left me with my options wide open. And I do intend a violent response.'

'In which case,' Dillon said, 'you can count on me.'

'Dillon, I must remind you who you work for.'

'That could be remedied, General,' Dillon told him easily.

Ferguson gave him a long look. 'I'd be sorry to hear that.' He turned to Quinn. 'It's your welfare I'm concerned about.'

'I know that.' Quinn got up. 'I must go. I've got things to do.'

'You'll need to speak to Blake Johnson. The President has an interest in this,' Ferguson reminded him.

'Now there you can help me.' Quinn nodded. 'You bring Blake up to date for me, General. Tell him everything.' He smiled. 'Thanks, Sean,' and he went out.

'Underneath the calm, he's an angry man,' Ferguson said gloomily. 'That's not good.'

'It never is,' Dillon told him, and they finished their brandies.

LONDON

BOSTON

WASHINGTON

LONDON

12

The following morning, Kate Rashid and Rupert Dauncey left the house in a maroon Bentley. Dillon was parked a little way along the street, wearing a helmet and black leathers, pretending to be working on his Suzuki motorcycle. He got on and followed them.

There was no particular reason for the trip, and he hadn't told Ferguson or Hannah he wasn't reporting in. It was a fine bright morning with plenty of traffic, so he was able to stay back, and the Bentley was conspicuous enough. They took the motorway for most of the time until Hampshire, then country roads, where he had to take more care.

He was surprised when they didn't take the turning to Dauncey Place. He was able to stay behind a couple of farm trucks, the Bentley up ahead, and then it turned left and Dillon saw the sign DAUNCEY AERO CLUB.

It was the sort of place that had probably been an RAF station in the Second World War and then developed over the years. He saw a central building, a control tower, and something like thirty planes parked at the edge of two grass runways. Several vehicles were there, as well, and the Bentley was one of them.

Dillon parked down toward the first runway and got out his binoculars. As Ferguson often liked to boast, Dillon could fly anything, and most of the planes he knew.

There was a rather nice Black Eagle taxiing along the side of the nearest runway. It stopped not too far away and a man in white overalls got out. Rupert Dauncey and Kate Rashid appeared from the main building and walked toward him. She wore dark Ray Bans and a black jumpsuit. Rupert was in a bomber jacket and trousers. They paused to speak to the other man, then got into the Eagle. It taxied to the far end of the runway, turned, and took off.

Dillon moved to the end of the railings as the man in the white overalls approached and said cheerfully, 'Nice Eagle, a real beauty. It's a collector's item these days.'

'Owned by the Countess of Loch Dhu,' the man said. 'Flies it herself, and she's good.'

'Where to today?' Dillon asked, and offered him a cigarette.

The man accepted. 'She sometimes likes a day out in France, but she told me she was going to the Isle of Wight today. First, she was going to drop in at the big house, Dauncey Place. She has an airstrip there.'

'Is that legal?'

'It is if you own half the county.' The man laughed. 'There's a café inside if you want anything.'

'No, thanks, I'd better get going.'

Dillon got on the Suzuki and drove away. He rode back up to London, thinking.

The next time he parked was at the Dark Man on the wharf at Wapping. Harry Salter, Billy, Baxter and Hall were eating shepherd's pie, and everyone, except Billy, was drinking beer.

Salter looked up with a frown. 'Here, what's this?' and then Dillon took his helmet off. 'Jesus, it's you, Dillon,' and Salter laughed. 'You up for a part in a road movie or something?'

'No, I've been for a run in the country, Rashid country. Dauncey village and beyond.'

Harry stopped smiling. 'Trouble?'

'You could say that.'

'Then you'd better have a drink on it.' He nodded to Billy, who went behind the bar and came back with half a bottle of Bollinger and a glass.

Dillon thumbed off the cork and poured. 'What do you think, Billy? There's an aero club six miles from the house down there and she flies out of it in a Black Eagle, similar to the plane Carver flew when you and I went down to Hazar that time.'

'You mean she flies it herself?'

'It was news to me, Billy – I never knew she was a pilot.'

'Well, you learn something new every day,' Harry said, 'but that's not what you came to tell us, is it?'

'No, it isn't,' and he gave them the full story: Quinn, his daughter, Alan Grant, everything.

When he was finished, there was silence for a few moments, and Billy said, 'What a bastard.'

'That doesn't even begin to describe him,' Harry said. 'I knew he was trouble the minute I set eyes on him. What happens now?'

'Quinn will be back in a few days. Then we'll see.'

'He was crazy to destroy that pen and tape,' Harry said. 'Dauncey would have gone down the steps for what he did.'

'And for how long?' Billy demanded. 'No, Quinn was right. He wants more than the law can give him, and I say more power to him.'

'So you'll be helping him go to war when he gets back?' Harry asked.

'That's about the size of it.'

'And the General?'

'Doesn't approve.'

Billy said, 'What in the hell are we talking about here? Kate Rashid sentenced us all to death, didn't she? And that includes Ferguson. I think we should be in this together.'

'And so do I.' Harry held out his hand. 'Count us in, Dillon, whatever Ferguson says.'

Before leaving London, Daniel Quinn had spoken to his old friend from Vietnam days, Tom Jackson, at Quinn Industries in Boston, shocking him greatly with the news of Helen's death. Quinn didn't go into the details of what had really happened. He didn't see the point.

'Is there anything I can do?' Jackson asked.

'Yes. I'm bringing Helen's ashes with me. I want you to get in touch with Monsignor Walsh. I want a funeral tomorrow, and I want it very low key, with very few people.'

'Of course.'

'I want to stave off for as long as possible any newspapers that might want to make something out of the suggestion of drug involvement in her death.'

'I understand.'

'To that end, I'm not informing the extended family. I'd like you to be there, Tom, but I'll be frank. It's mainly because I may need your good offices.'

'Anything.'

'Telephone Blake Johnson at the White House. Let him know what's happening. He has my permission to inform the President. I'll leave it with you.'

Tom Jackson, an astute and clever attorney, said, 'Daniel, is there more to this?'

'One of these days I'll tell you, old buddy.'

The following afternoon, he sat in the church at Lavery Cemetery, where the Quinn family had a mausoleum. There was Monsignor Walsh, who had been the family priest for so many years that he had christened Helen. He was assisted by a much younger priest, a Father Doyle. Two attendants from the cemetery staff waited in sober black at the rear of the church.

Monsignor Walsh was doing his best in trying circumstances. In a way, it was reminiscent of the crematorium in London, and Quinn let the usual familiar words drift over his head. I am the resurrection and the life, saith the Lord.

But it's not true, Quinn thought. There is no resurrection here, only death.

Behind him, the church door opened and banged shut, steps approached along the aisle, there was a hand on his shoulder and he looked up to see Blake Johnson, who managed a smile and sat in the opposite pew.

They stood for the Lord's Prayer and Walsh sprinkled the ornate cask containing the ashes. The taped organ music was subdued now. The young priest picked up the ashes and nodded to Quinn, who went forward and received them.

A procession formed, the two cemetery attendants at the front, then the two priests, Quinn following with the ashes, Tom Jackson and Blake

Johnson bringing up the rear. True to form, it started to rain as they came out. The two attendants produced umbrellas for Blake and Jackson, one held an umbrella over Quinn, the other over the two priests.

The little procession wound its way through the cemetery, which was very old. There were pines and cypresses, winged angels and Gothic monuments, the sentiments on the gravestones recording an implacable faith in the possibility of life in the hereafter.

The attendants stopped at a large pillared mausoleum, with angels on either side of a bronze door. One of them produced a key and pulled the door open.

Quinn walked between the two priests. 'If no one minds, I'd like to do this on my own.'

Inside, there were several ornate coffins: his mother and father, his wife, and three other members of his extended family. Flowers had been placed beneath a niche in the wall. The cask with her ashes fitted quite well. He knew, because Jackson had told him, that her name would be chiselled into the granite beneath the niche, enhanced with gold leaf.

He stood there quietly, his head not bowed in

prayer, for he was beyond prayer. 'Goodbye, love,' he said softly, then went out.

One of the attendants shut the door and locked it. Monsignor Walsh moved close. 'Daniel, don't close out the world, don't close out God. There is a purpose in all things.'

'Well, you'll forgive me if I'm not buying that this afternoon, but thanks for coming. She was always very fond of you. You must excuse me,' and Quinn walked off, followed by Jackson and Blake.

They reached the car park by the church and he paused. 'Sorry, Blake, it's not my best day. I'm grateful you've come.'

'The President himself wanted to be here, Daniel, but it would have turned into a circus, which he knew was the last thing you would have wanted.'

'I appreciate his thoughtfulness.'

'You're going back to London?'

'As soon as possible.'

'The President wants to see you.'

'Why?'

'General Ferguson spoke to us. He's concerned. We all are. I'm sorry to have to remind you that you're bound to the President by the Presidential Warrant. You can't say no.'

Tom Jackson said, 'Presidential Warrant? I thought that was an old wives' tale.'

'Well, it isn't,' Blake said.

Quinn said, 'Okay, I'll go home, pack a few things for the return journey, and I'll see you at the airport. You can give Tom a lift.'

Jackson said, 'For God's sake, what's going on?'

Quinn said to Blake, 'Did Ferguson tell you everything?'

'Yes.'

'Good. You can tell Tom on the way back. Like I said, I'll see you at the airport.'

He climbed in beside the chauffeur, gave him an order, and they drove away.

Blake had arrived in a Presidential Gulfstream. Quinn spoke to his own pilots, told them to follow to Washington and book a slot for London. Jackson was there to see him off.

'Daniel, if you want that bastard dead, let me do it, but not you. He's not worth it.'

'It's my affair, Tom, don't worry about me. I'm kicking you out of the Legal Affairs department, by the way.'

Jackson looked shocked. 'But, Daniel, what have I done?'

'Nothing but do a good job at everything to which you turned your hand. Bert Hanley spoke to me. That heart of his is worse than ever. The doctors want him out. So, you're president, effective immediately. I'll still be around as chairman, but you'll manage pretty damn well without me.' He hugged Jackson. 'God bless, Tom, but I've got things to do.' He smiled bleakly. 'Bo Din all over again.'

'No, Daniel,' Tom Jackson called, but Quinn was already passing through security.

Later, on the plane, Blake said, 'He thinks the world of you.'

'He's a great guy and I'd go to hell for him, but what I've got to do, I've got to do. I'm determined about it.' He tipped his seat back and closed his eyes.

Clancy Smith opened the door for them and they entered the Oval Office. Cazalet, in shirtsleeves, was wearing reading glasses, signing one letter after another. He glanced up, got to his feet, and came around the desk.

'Daniel. I'd like to say it's good to see you.'

'Mr President, let's take it as read and get on with things. What can I do for you?'

'Let's sit down,' which they did, and Cazalet carried on. 'General Ferguson has spoken to us, Blake and myself, on a conference call. I'm truly shocked at what he told me about Rupert Dauncey's conduct in this matter.'

'It wasn't really aimed at me, you realize. Dauncey didn't intend my daughter's death. He simply wanted her on drugs at that rally, hoping she might be arrested and become a serious embarrassment to me personally and to you politically.'

'And the whole thing went hideously wrong,' Blake said.

'Ferguson explained your reasons for destroying the recording,' Cazalet said. 'And I must be honest and say I'm dismayed. You could have nailed Dauncey in court.'

'He'd have got off lightly, Mr President, and that's not good enough. He didn't murder my daughter, but he's responsible for her death, not that wretched young man, and I intend to see that he pays.'

'But legally and properly, Daniel. We must operate within the confines of the law.'

'That wouldn't even put a dent in the Rashid empire. And tell me this – what happens if the law doesn't work? Aren't I entitled to justice?'

'No,' the President said, 'because justice is nothing without the law. It's what binds us all together, it's the framework of all our lives. Without it, we're nothing.'

'Which is exactly what the bad guys count on. I'm tired, Mr President, and a lot of people would say the same thing. Tired of the wrongdoers getting away with it.'

'What I say still holds true.'

'Then on this matter, we must agree to differ.'

He stood up and Cazalet said, 'If you're determined to follow this course, Daniel, I can't protect you. You realize that, don't you?'

'I would expect it.'

'Then I have to tell you, you no longer have any official status for me in London. The Embassy will no longer offer you any kind of assistance.'

'And I am no longer bound by Presidential Warrant?'

'I suppose that, too, yes.'

'May I go now? I have a plane waiting to take me to London.'

'One last thing. General Ferguson feels as I do.

He will not involve himself or his people in this course of action. That means you won't be able to rely on any assistance from Sean Dillon.'

'Mr Dillon has indicated differently, and he strikes me as a man of strong views.'

'I regret to hear it. Goodbye, Senator.'

Blake ushered Quinn out. 'I hope you know what you're doing.'

'Never more so.'

Quinn walked away and Blake went back in the Oval Office. Cazalet was back behind the desk. 'Do you think I was wrong?'

'No, sir, you weren't. But he's right about one thing. Nobody is going to break Kate Rashid and her organization using the law or any other straight up-and-down methods. This is one of those scenarios that calls for the Dillons of this world.'

'But Daniel Quinn isn't a Dillon. There isn't a devious bone in his body.'

'Perhaps he'll turn out to be a fast learner, Mr President.'

Late that night in London, Rupert Dauncey had a phone call from one of the security people he'd put on duty outside Daniel Quinn's house, in a telecom van. There were two of them, Newton and Cook, both ex-SAS.

'He's back, sir,' Cook said.

'When did he arrive?'

'An hour ago. I tried you, but your phone wasn't on.'

Dauncey said, 'I was out for a run.'

'Well, I thought you'd like to know that that chauffeur of his has come out in full uniform and he's standing by the Mercedes. I'd say Quinn's about to move.'

'I'll be there in three minutes.' Dauncey slammed down the receiver, picked up his mobile, and was out of the flat in seconds. A moment later, he drove Kate's Porsche out of the garage. As he approached the corner of Park Place, the Mercedes turned out and he had a quick flash of Quinn sitting beside Luke. He followed and called Newton and Cook.

'I've got him and I'm close behind. You stay where you are.'

The traffic was light because of the lateness of the hour. Quinn lit a cigarette and leaned back in the seat. He'd always liked cities at night, particularly late at night. Rain-washed deserted streets, that feeling of loneliness. *What the hell am I doing?* he asked himself, and the thought had been immediately overwhelming.

They moved down toward the river, the Tower of London, St Katharine's Dock, and finally came to Wapping High Street and pulled in at St Mary's Priory. He'd last been here a year before, on one of his London trips for the President. It was a grim building in grey stone, with a great, well-worn oak door which stood open. A bell tower could be seen, and the roof of a chapel beyond the high walls.

'I won't be long,' Quinn told Luke, and got out and crossed the road.

A sign said ST MARY'S PRIORY, LITTLE SISTERS OF PITY: MOTHER SUPERIOR, SISTER SARAH PALMER.

'We never close,' Quinn said softly, and passed inside. In a cubbyhole, the night porter sat drinking tea and reading the *Evening Standard*. He glanced up.

'Good evening.'

A notice on the wall said: *The chapel is open to all for private worship.*

'Is the Mother Superior in?'

'I saw her go into the chapel a little while ago, sir.'

'Thank you.'

Quinn crossed to the chapel door, which stood open, and passed inside.

Rupert, parked some distance behind the Mercedes, had seen him cross the road and followed him, pausing only to read the sign before venturing in.

He adopted the simple approach and said to the porter, 'Where did my friend go?'

'The chapel, sir, he was looking for the Mother Superior.'

'Thank you.'

Rupert moved to the open chapel door and could hear voices. He peered in. It was very dark, the only light the candles up by the altar. He went and sheltered behind a pillar and had no difficulty in hearing what was being said.

When Quinn stepped into the chapel he paused and looked towards the image of the Virgin, the candles burning in front of it so that it seemed to float in the darkness beside the altar. Sister

Sarah Palmer was on her knees scrubbing the floor, a menial task usually performed by novices but in her case designed to teach her humility, in spite of being Mother Superior. It was cold and damp and there was the unmistakable chapel smell.

'Candles, incense, and holy water,' he said softly. 'You'll have me crossing myself next.'

She paused and looked up at him calmly. 'Why, Daniel, what a surprise. Where have you come from?'

'Kosovo.'

'Was it bad?'

'Too many bodies in the streets.'

She dropped the scrubbing brush in her pail and mopped the floor with a rag. 'As bad as Bo Din?'

'Different, but as bad in its own way.'

She squeezed out the rag. 'What is it, Daniel?'

'Helen's dead.'

She stayed there on her knees, staring at him. 'Oh, dear Lord.' She got up as he dropped into one of the pews, and sat in front, half-turned toward him. 'What happened?'

He started, then, and told her everything.

Afterwards, she said, 'God has placed a burden

on you, Daniel. What has happened is a terrible thing, but you must not allow it to destroy you.'

'And how would I do that?'

'By seeking refuge in prayer, by reaching out for God's support . . .'

'Instead of seeking revenge?' Quinn shook his head. 'But that's all I feel. It's a strange thing, suffering. I've discovered that there is the possibility of solace in making the other person suffer. It's as if nothing is enough. By letting Rupert Dauncey off the hook, I've extended his suffering, his punishment.'

'Such thoughts will destroy you.'

'If that is the price, I'll pay it.' He got up, and so did she.

'Why did you come here, Daniel? You knew I couldn't condone your intention.'

'Yes, but it was important that you hear the facts from me and perhaps understand my future conduct.'

'So what do you expect, a blessing?'

'It wouldn't come amiss.'

There was steel in her voice, a kind of anger, and for a moment she seemed the young nun at Bo Din again.

What she did then was the hardest thing she'd

ever done in her life. She said, 'Go, Christian soul, from this world, in the name of God the Father Almighty who created thee.'

'Ah, very apt.' Quinn smiled gently. 'Goodbye and God bless you, Sarah.' And he turned and went out.

Filled with despair, she dropped to her knees in the pew and started to pray. There was a movement nearby, and she opened her eyes, half-turned, and found a man squatting beside her. The blond hair, the handsome face. It was the Devil's face, she knew that at once.

'It's all right, Sister, I mean you no harm. I followed him here and, of course, saw your name at the door. I know who you are. You're the remarkable young nun from Bo Din.'

'And who are you?'

'Many things. A bad Catholic, for one. Don't worry, I'd never harm you. God wouldn't forgive that.'

'You're crazy.'

'Possibly. I'm also the man he blames for his daughter's death.'

'Rupert Dauncey,' she whispered.

'That's me.' He stood. 'I liked your idea of a blessing. A prayer for the dying. That could well be appropriate.' He smiled. 'Don't forget to give him a call. Tell him I was here.'

His footsteps echoed away and she pushed herself up and sat again in the pew, more afraid than she had ever been.

Back at Park Place, Newton and Clark saw the Mercedes drive into the yard. Quinn and Luke got out, and Quinn said, 'I won't need you first thing, Luke. I'll go for a run in Hyde Park around seven-thirty, so tell Mary breakfast at nine.'

The two men across the street heard it, and Cook phoned Dauncey, who had just got in, and relayed the information.

Rupert said, 'Very good. Go home, but be back in the morning, dressed for running. When he leaves the house, follow him to the park.'

'Then what?'

'Do what you have to do.'

He didn't go to see his cousin and bring her up to date. Sister Sarah Palmer was too personal, and Kate would never understand his feelings. He poured a Jack Daniel's, found the evening paper, and sat down to read it. A moment later, his phone rang and he picked it up.

'It's Quinn. I've had Sister Sarah Palmer on the phone. I swear to God, if you harm that lady . . .'

'Don't be stupid, Senator, she's the last person in the world I'd harm, a marvellous woman like that. So goodnight and sleep tight.' He hung up.

Quinn replaced his receiver, conscious that he actually believed Dauncey. He stood there thinking about it and, on impulse, rang Sean Dillon at Stable Mews.

'It's Quinn.' He told him the story. 'I believe it when he says he wouldn't harm her. I don't know why, but I do.'

'All right. The important thing, though, is that he followed you to this St Mary's Priory, obviously from your house. I'd say you have watchers. Anything unusual in your street?'

'Hang on a minute.' Quinn went to the window and peered out. 'There's a British Telecom van.'

'Telecom, my arse.'

'Thanks for the tip.'

'How did things go in Boston?'

'Much as you'd expect. It was Washington that was the disappointment.' He told him about it, finishing, 'And he made it clear Ferguson agrees with him.'

'Well, we'll see about that. I'm my own man,

and always have been. I'll see you in the morning and we'll discuss it.'

'I'm going for a run in Hyde Park at seven-thirty. Have breakfast with me at nine.'

'It's a date,' and Dillon put down the phone.

Dillon woke early the next morning and, looking at the clock, realized he had time to join Quinn on the run. He got up, dressed in a tracksuit, went downstairs, found his helmet, opened the mews garage, and drove away on the Suzuki.

On the way to Park Place, he thought about the Telecom van that Quinn had mentioned and wondered about the best way to handle it. Possibly an anonymous call to the police. Simple and direct.

He turned into South Audley Street from Grosvenor Square, and as he moved toward Park Place, Quinn emerged and darted across the road. A moment later, Cook and Newton, in tracksuits, showed up and followed him. Dillon cursed, swerved into Park Place, and turned in through Quinn's gates. He pulled the Suzuki up on its stand, reached into the right-hand saddlebag, lifted the secret flap at the bottom, and found his Walther. He slipped it into the right-hand pocket of his tracksuit and went after them, running fast.

Quinn crossed Park Lane using the underpass, ran up the steps on the other side, and entered Hyde Park, followed by Newton and Cook. Dillon, pressing hard, was not far behind.

It was a misty morning, with a light drizzle. Half a dozen soldiers of the Household Cavalry cantered by, exercising their mounts, and there was the odd solitary rider. Quinn cut across the grass toward the trees. The mist was thicker there and there was no one about.

He heard a sudden rush of feet behind him and, as he turned, Newton shouldered him, sending him staggering. He fell to one knee and Cook kicked him in the chest. Quinn rolled over and managed to get to his feet as Cook ran in again. It all came back, the tricks of the trade, and he blocked Cook's punches, wrestled and threw him over his hip. Newton moved in from behind and slid an arm around his neck. Quinn dropped to his knees and turned over, tossing Newton over his head.

And then they were on their feet, both of them

facing him. 'Right, mate,' Cook said. 'This is where you get done.'

And then there was a shot, the sound flat on the damp air, and Dillon arrived, Walther in hand. 'I don't think so.' He moved close. 'Who put you up to this? Dauncey?'

'Get stuffed,' Cook said.

Dillon kicked him between the legs, sending him down, turned to Newton, grabbed him by the front of his tracksuit and held the Walther against his left ear.

'You have two choices. Number one, I blow your ear off. Number two, you tell me who sent you.'

Newton panicked. 'Okay, okay, it was Dauncey.'

'There, wasn't that easy? I'd see to your friend if I were you, then report in and tell him Dillon was here.' He chuckled. 'Though I wouldn't want to be in your shoes when he finds out you've blown it.' He nodded to Quinn. 'Let's get out of here,' and they jogged away.

At about the same time Newton and Cook were reporting the sad news to Dauncey, Quinn and Dillon confronted Ferguson at Cavendish Place. Hannah had just arrived, in response to a call from Ferguson, and was in time to hear what had taken place, both at the Priory and in the park.

Dillon finished his story and smiled. 'So we know where we are. War to the knife.'

'That's as may be,' Ferguson told him, 'but we still can't prove a thing. Dauncey will deny any relationship to those men.'

'I couldn't care less,' Quinn said. 'This isn't about the law, Charles. It's about what we know and what we do about it.'

'The President has spoken to me, you know.' Ferguson shrugged. 'You're on your own in this.'

'No, he's not. He's got me,' Dillon said.

'Then you no longer work for me,' Ferguson told him calmly. 'I'd think it over.'

'I have.' Dillon turned to Quinn. 'Let's go, Senator.'

Afterwards, Hannah said, 'Are you sure about this, sir?'

'Only that Dillon will go to work with his usual ruthlessness.'

'And that suits you?'

He smiled at her. 'Admirably.'

13

Later in the day, Dauncey lunched with Kate Rashid and told her with annoyance about the events of that morning.

She shook her head. 'What is this, the third time, Rupert? Either Quinn leads a charmed life or we're seriously going to have to re-examine our way of doing business.' She gave him a pointed look, but then she smiled. 'But right now, I really don't care. Quinn was just the sideshow. The main event is about to begin.'

'What do you mean?'

'I've heard from Barry Keenan. Colum McGee has arranged a meeting.'

'Where?'

'Drumcree, in three days' time. We'll go over Thursday afternoon, stay at the Europa, and drive down to Drumcree Friday morning. If things go well, we should be able to fly back from Aldergrove that evening.'

'And is that when you're finally going to tell me what you're up to?'

'Absolutely, darling.'

At the same time, Dillon and Quinn were ringing the bell at Regency Square. The door clicked open, and they found Roper at work as usual.

'I was just going to get in touch with you,' he told Dillon. 'Rashid and Dauncey are flying to Belfast on Thursday afternoon. They're staying at the Europa, and coming back on Friday evening.'

'You think this is important?' Quinn asked Dillon.

'I don't know. It could just be business, but the last time I was in Ireland with Kate Rashid, she was hiring the IRA. We'll fly out before her and see where she goes. Maybe I'll even show you the delights of Belfast City.'

'Now that you've finished, could I get a word in?' Roper said.

'About what?'

'It so happens I *know* where she's going. I know I'm a simple soul, but it seemed logical to me that they would have some company cars, and I found it in their database: A chauffeur, name of Hennessy, and his Volvo. He'll be driving them around.'

'You clever bastard.'

'No, I'm a brilliant bastard. I remembered about your involvement with Rashid and Aidan Bell and the IRA last year . . . and that the name Drumcree figured largely.'

'Jesus,' Dillon said. 'Don't tell me . . .'

'Oh, but I *am* telling you. Hennessy picks her and Dauncey up at the Europa at nine-thirty Friday morning and proceeds to the Royal George at Drumcree. That's a strange name for a pub in the IRA heartland.'

'Well, I'm from County Down myself, and people have a sense of history where I come from. It's always been called that. Anything else?'

'Of course. As you'll recall, Drumcree was originally Aidan Bell's patch, before you killed him and his two henchmen, Tommy Brosnan and Jack O'Hara.'

'To be accurate, I killed Aidan and Jack. It was Billy Salter who shot Brosnan.'

'I stand corrected. Anyway, I thought I'd access both the RUC and Army Intelligence at Lisburn, just to check on the Drumcree situation at the moment.'

Quinn, who had stood by in silence, said, 'You can do that?'

'I can do anything,' Roper said, and smiled. 'Even the White House.'

'Never mind that,' Dillon said. 'Drumcree?'

'Oh, yes. Well, according to Lisburn, a chap called Barry Keenan runs things there now. Do you know him?'

'A long time ago. Aidan Bell's nephew.'

'He has two minders, named Sean Casey and Jack Kelly. But they're not with the Provos anymore, they're Real IRA.'

'Barry was always tops in the explosives business. Big with the bombs.' Dillon nodded. 'She's at it again.'

'But at what, exactly?' Quinn asked.

'I'd say she's hiring Keenan to do what he does best – blow something up. Only not just any old thing, otherwise why go to the trouble of hiring the man considered by many the finest bomb maker in the IRA?'

'How do we find out the target?' Quinn asked.

'If she followed the pattern from last time, she'll meet Keenan in the snug at the Royal George. It's a kind of back parlour. She isn't about to speak to him in the bar.' Dillon said to Roper, 'A listening device, preferably with a recorder. We'd need to stick it somewhere in the snug.'

'Will we have time to plant it?'

'They should be there by eleven, certainly not any earlier. If we leave at seven-thirty, we'll be there at nine. They do breakfast at the pub, an Irish fry-up. One of us can dump the recorder in the snug.' He turned to Roper. 'But can you supply the right article?'

'Nothing run-of-the-mill would do. They might talk a long time. As it happens, I've got just the thing. It'll give you two hours.' He held up a small gadget, silver in appearance and no bigger than the palm of his hand.

'From when?' Dillon asked.

'From when you turn it on.' He produced a black plastic box with a scarlet button. 'Remote control. Just press the button when you see her go in the pub.'

'That should do it?'

'As long as we can recover the recorder afterwards,' Quinn said.

'We travel hopefully on that one,' Dillon told him.

He took the recorder and the remote control and slipped them into one of his pockets. Roper said, 'There's just one thing, Dillon. Your face isn't exactly foreign to the IRA, and certainly in Drumcree, where you've been before.'

'True, but the British Army knew my face, too, and couldn't lay a hand on me in thirty years.' He turned to Daniel Quinn. 'I did a bit of theatre work before I answered the call of the glorious cause.' He laughed. 'I once walked down the Falls Road dressed as a bag lady, and no one suspected. I can fix myself up.'

'Taking the Gulfstream?' Roper asked.

'No, I'll fly myself on this one.'

Roper looked at him questioningly.

'I'll explain later, old son. Let's go, Daniel.'

Back in the Mercedes, Dillon said, 'There's an aero club at Brancaster out in Kent. They have a nice Beechcraft there.'

'Will we have any problems?'

'No. I still have top security clearance.'

'Even though Ferguson has disowned you?'

'Don't worry about Ferguson. He's playing silly buggers. Non-involvement simply means deniability for him. He still wants the results.'

'You're sure of that?'

'Absolutely. Now let's go book that Beechcraft.'

There was no problem with the plane except that the available slot was after lunch the following day, later than Dillon had wanted. They had something to eat in a roadside café on the way back, and Luke took him to Stable Mews.

Dillon went into the kitchen, poured a Bushmills, and sat at the table. Everything was in motion now, he could feel it. He didn't know exactly what Rashid was up to, but the time for waiting was over, and that felt good. Only one thing bothered him. After all, Ireland was Ireland. If things got out of hand, would Quinn be able to do what was necessary? Could he pull the trigger without question? He'd handled himself well so far, but killing a man was different from beating up a couple of thugs.

Dillon sighed. He needed somebody to protect his back and that meant only one person.

He drove to Park Place, and when Quinn answered the door, he said, 'I've got to see some friends of mine. Come on, it'll complete your education.'

They drove down to Wapping and parked outside the Dark Man. Dora was behind the bar, polishing glasses. There was no sign of Harry or Billy.

'They're down on the boat,' she said.

Dillon led the way along the wharf and it started to rain a little. 'Amongst other enterprises, Harry has a few riverboats. He's had one of the smaller ones, the *Lynda Jones*, refurbished. It's his pride and joy. Wait till you see.'

There was a desolate air to the river at this point, which was strangely attractive: some decaying boats, two half-sunken barges. The *Lynda Jones* was at the end and reached by a gangway. Baxter and Hall were varnishing on the prow, Harry and Billy sat at a table under the stern awning, reading: Harry, a newspaper and Billy, a book.

'Philosophy, Billy?'

They both looked up and Harry said, 'Well, look what the cat dragged in.'

'Harry, Billy, I'd like you to meet a friend, Senator Daniel Quinn.'

Harry frowned, then got up and held out his hand. 'We know all about you, Senator, sit down.' He turned to Dillon. 'I assume this isn't a social visit, Dillon. What's up?'

'In a minute, Harry. First – Billy, why don't

you show me that new panelling you've put in the saloon?'

They left Harry and Quinn at the table, and Billy led the way in. Dillon closed the door and Billy turned. 'What is it?'

'Kate Rashid's going to Belfast, and I'm following her. Quinn's coming with me because he's hell-bent on some sort of revenge for what happened to his daughter. But here's the thing. He was a great war hero in Vietnam, but that was a long time ago. A lot of people over there know me, Billy. I need someone to watch my back.'

'Well, you've found him. I'm bored here, anyway. It's always a laugh a minute with you, Dillon, isn't it? Let's go and break the news to Harry.'

When they told him, Harry's reaction was quick. 'Maybe I should come, too.'

'No need,' Dillon said. 'With luck, we'll be in and out of Drumcree in an hour or two.'

'And hopefully find out what that bitch intends,' Harry said.

'It must be something special,' Dillon agreed.

'But if she sees you, the game's up, Dillon. Come to think of it, she's met the Senator, too.'

'And Billy. So he and Quinn will just have to

make sure she doesn't see them. It's different for me. Watch.'

He went into the saloon and closed the door. When it opened again, he shuffled out, head slightly to one side, his left arm stiff, shoulder down. The face seemed twisted, the entire body language had changed.

Harry recoiled in his chair. 'Unbelievable.'

Dillon straightened and said drily, 'Yes, I was a great loss to the theatre. There's one thing you both should know, however. For various reasons, this trip isn't sanctioned by Ferguson. I'm doing it on my own, so whatever you do, you'll be doing it for me, Billy.'

'So how will you get tooled up? You won't be able to take arms through to Belfast,' Harry said.

'I still have my contacts over there, Harry. A phone call will do it.'

'Well, bring this little bugger back in one piece. It grieves me to say it, Dillon, but since we met you, he's developed a taste for this sort of caper.'

And Billy Salter, a London gangster, four times in prison, a man who had killed in his time, a lover of moral philosophy, smiled coldly.

'Well, you know what Heidegger said. "For

authentic living, what is necessary is the resolute confrontation of death."'

'You must be cracked,' Harry said.

'Let's just say I have a better chance of finding what is necessary in Belfast than at the Flamingo Club in Wapping on a Saturday night.'

Twenty-four hours later, Harry delivered Billy to the Brancaster Aero Club, Joe Baxter at the wheel of the Jaguar. Billy was wearing a black leather bomber jacket and Joe Baxter carried his bag. Billy leaned on the rail, looking at the planes.

'I wonder which is ours?'

A small man was leaning on the rail nearby. He had a bag at his feet and was also wearing a bomber jacket and a cloth cap, from which black hair escaped. His glasses were tinted and he had a dark moustache.

He said in a faultless upper class English accent, 'That's yours over there, old chap. Beechcraft. Smashing plane. The red and cream job.'

'Looks good to me,' Harry said.

'Well I'm happy you're happy.' Dillon turned to greet Daniel Quinn. 'Morning, Senator. If you're ready, we'll get out of here.'

Harry said, 'I wouldn't have believed it if I hadn't seen it myself.'

Dillon picked up his bag. 'Right, gentlemen, let's get going,' and he went through the gate in the fence and led the way to the Beechcraft.

The flight to Aldergrove airport outside Belfast was smooth and uneventful. They went through customs and security and Dillon led the way to the long-term car park.

'Shogun four door, dark green,' he told the other two and gave them the number. 'Somewhere on the fourth floor.'

It was Billy who discovered it. Dillon reached under the rear and found a magnetized key box, with which he opened the rear door. He lifted the trap inside, where tools and odds and ends were kept. There was a tin box, and when Dillon opened it, it proved to contain three Walther PPKs, each with a Carswell silencer and spare magazine. There was also a field medical kit with Royal Army Medical Corps on the lid.

He took one Walther and said to the others, 'Help yourselves.'

Billy hefted his in his hand. 'Feels good, eh, Senator?'

Quinn gazed down at his Walther. 'Strange, Billy, it feels strange.'

'Where are we staying?' Billy asked as they drove away.

'Well, not the Europa. There's a nice enough hotel just up the road from it, the Townley. If you like, I'll show you around a little. But remember, Senator, at all times you're a bluff, honest Yankee tourist, right? As for you, Billy, if we're going down the Falls Road, keep your mouth shut. They don't like the English much.'

'You know it well?' Quinn asked.

'Particularly the sewers. I used to play hide-and-seek in there with British paratroopers more years ago than I care to remember.'

'And that's a bleeding show-stopper if I ever heard one,' Billy said.

Later, Dillon was driving along the Falls Road. They'd eaten at a small restaurant in a side street, visited a couple of bars, and then he'd taken the other two on the grand tour.

'So this is the famous Falls Road. Hell, it looks so normal, just another city street,' Quinn said.

'Well, this one's run with blood in its time,' Dillon said. 'Plenty of pitched battles between the

Provos and the British troops.' He was quiet for a moment. 'It was a hard way to live.'

'So why did you?' Quinn said. 'Why did you do it?'

Dillon lit a cigarette, one-handed, and didn't reply. Billy said, 'Leave it, Senator.'

'But why?'

Billy leaned toward him. 'Say you're an actor in London. You get a phone call to say your father's dead, caught in the crossfire of a firefight between Brit Paras and the IRA. What do you do? You come home and bury him, then you join the glorious cause. It's the kind of thing you do at nineteen.'

There was silence, then Quinn said, 'I'm sorry,' but before things could go any further, Dillon's Codex rang.

'Who is it?'

'Ferguson. Roper told me you went to Belfast, which I assume you meant him to do. Where are you?'

'The Falls Road.'

'Just the place for you. Anyway, the minute you know what she's up to, let me know.'

'Why, Charles, I thought I was on my own now. I thought I no longer worked for you. Isn't that what you said?'

'Don't be coy, Dillon, you know exactly what's going on.'

'Well, what if I don't want to work for you anymore?'

'Don't be stupid, either. Where else would you go?' And Ferguson put his phone down.

'Who was that?' Billy inquired. 'Ferguson?'

'Welcoming me back into the fold.'

'Unctuous bastard.'

'Why, Billy, you've been reading another book. We'll drop in at a real Irish bar I know on the way back to celebrate, and then an early night.'

Drumcree was typical of the villages on the Down coast. A small harbour, grey stone houses, fishing boats – that was about it. They pulled up outside the Royal George, an eighteenth-century inn, nicely refurbished, the sign, a portrait of King George III, obviously recently repainted.

'I'm starving.' Dillon got out and they followed him. He said over his shoulder to Quinn, 'Don't forget, you're the Yank abroad.'

A bell tinkled as they went in. Three young men, one in a reefer coat, two in anoraks, were sitting in the window seat eating sizeable breakfasts. There was no one behind the bar.

Dillon assumed his version of a southern accent and said genially, 'Hey, what you boys are eating looks real good. How's a man get service round here?'

The three stopped talking amongst themselves, and one of them, a hard-faced youth with cropped red hair, looked Dillon and his friends over with a certain contempt.

'Tourists, are you?'

'That's right,' Dillon said, and indicated Quinn. 'My friend's grandpappy was born in Belfast. Emigrated to the good old US of A years ago.'

'Well, that must have been nice for him,' Red Hair said. 'Ring the bell on the bar.'

Which Dillon did, and a moment later, the publican came out, one Patrick Murphy, who Dillon remembered well from his last visit. He didn't recognize Dillon for a moment but was obviously surprised to see them.

'Can I help?'

'You can indeed. A large Bushmills whiskey, a pint of Guinness, and an orange juice.'

One of the three men, the one who sported a fringe beard, burst into laughter. 'Have you ever heard the like? Orange juice.'

Dillon put a restraining hand on Billy's arm and ignored them as Murphy got the drinks and said, 'Will there be anything else?'

'Yes,' Dillon told him. 'We'll have some breakfast. Where's the gents'?'

'Just along the corridor.'

Dillon knew very well where it was, next to the snug, but, of course, he wasn't supposed to. He brought the drinks to the table.

'I need the toilet,' he announced. 'Anyone else?'

'I'm fine,' Quinn said.

Dillon went along the corridor, paused outside the gents', aware of sounds from the kitchen, then opened the snug door and moved in. There was a fire on the open hearth, chairs arranged beside it, a coffee table in between, a smell of polish and a general tidiness that argued that Murphy had made a special effort. A row of books stood on the window ledge beside the fire. Dillon placed the recorder behind them, turned, and went out.

The breakfast was excellent and Dillon kept up the performance. 'Hey, this is damn good.'

'It sure is,' Quinn told him. 'A hell of a good idea dropping in here.'

Murphy appeared with a large pot of tea, milk and three cups. Dillon said, 'Fantastic. Is there anything round here worth looking at? That old castle up on the hill, for instance?'

'There's not much there,' Murphy said. 'However, Drumcree House is half a mile up the road. That's National Trust, it's open from ten o'clock. It's worth a look, if that kind of thing takes your fancy.'

'Thanks for the tip. Say, do you do lunch, my friend?'

'Yes.'

'Well, we'll do the tourist bit and be back.'

The three men at the window whispered together again, then got up. The one with the beard paid Murphy at the bar and followed the others out.

Quinn said, 'Not exactly friendly.'

'They wouldn't be. All strangers are under suspicion in areas like this. That's why it's essential to keep the American touch. I'll pay the bill, and let's go and act like tourists.'

They explored the village, what there was of it, and paused at the Shogun, where Dillon found a pair of binoculars. They went to the end of the jetty and took turns checking the fishing boats out at sea, then they climbed up the hill to the castle. It wasn't much except for the view, and then the Volvo they were waiting for came down the road below, entered the village, and pulled up at the pub.

'And here they are, right on time,' Dillon said, as Hennessy got out and opened the door for Kate Rashid, and Rupert moved round to join her.

'Now what?' Billy asked.

'Hang on. There's no sign of Keenan yet.' But almost immediately an old Ford wooden-framed station wagon appeared from a back lane and pulled up behind the Volvo. Dillon focused the binoculars. 'There you go: Barry Keenan, Sean Casey, Jack Kelly.'

They watched the three men enter the pub, and Billy said, 'So, what do we do?'

'They'll be a while, too long for us to hang around watching. We'll go up the road for an hour or so and take a look at Drumcree House. We'll come back later.'

Barry Keenan had the look of a scholar more than anything else – of medium height and wearing a tweed suit, his black hair peppered with grey – and yet he was a man who had been responsible for many deaths. Casey and Kelly were typical IRA foot soldiers, straight off a building site or a farm.

Kate and Rupert had already been shown through to the snug by Murphy, and the three men joined them. Outside, Dillon and his friends were walking toward the Shogun. He operated the remote control and a tiny red light came on.

'We're in business.' He smiled and opened the driver's side of the Shogun. 'Let's go.'

'A pleasure to meet you,' Keenan told her. 'What do I call you?'

'Countess will do.'

'Then Countess it is, and your friend?'

'My cousin, Rupert Dauncey.'

'Right, Countess, let's get started. What do you want from me?'

'What did Colum tell you?'

'He said you needed a bomb expert and that Hazar was the destination. That was all he knew, except that it would be a big payday.'

'He's right there.' She pushed the briefcase she'd brought with her across the coffee table. 'A hundred thousand pounds, evidence of my good faith.'

Keenan opened it, revealing the stashed banknotes. 'Jesus,' Sean Casey whispered. Keenan showed no emotion and closed the briefcase.

'That's an advance against one million pounds,' she said.

Kelly and Casey looked at each other with wide eyes. Keenan said, 'And what would you expect me to do for money like that?'

'Blow up a bridge for me.'

'In Hazar?'

'No, the Empty Quarter. That's north of it. It's disputed territory, so even if you should get caught, you couldn't be tried in a court of law. It makes some activities . . . easier.'

'I know all about the place,' Keenan said. 'I know you and your brother hired my uncle, Aidan Bell, to blow some people up last year, but it got all cocked up, and the three men he brought with him all died. I even know who killed them: Sean Dillon and that old bastard Ferguson.'

Kelly said, 'A damn traitor, Sean, and him working for the Brits.'

'Tell me, I used to hear from Aidan for a while, but then he stopped. Do you know how he is?'

'What he is, Mr Keenan, is dead. Dillon shot him.'

'But we'd have heard,' Kelly said.

'No, Ferguson has a disposal team. Cremation off the record. His outfit does it all the time.'

Keenan stayed calm, and yet the skin seemed to have stretched over his cheeks and the eyes were dark. 'Have you anymore good news for me?'

'About Dillon?' She nodded. 'He killed my three brothers as well.'

There was a long silence. 'Will he be involved in this business?'

'Not that I know of. Does that make a difference?'

He shook his head. 'I'll settle with him later, after I've sorted this bridge. Tell me about it.'

She opened the briefcase and removed a file from a flap inside the lid. 'It's all there. Photos of the bridge, specifications, everything.'

'I'll look later. Just tell me.'

'The bridge at Bacu spans a five-hundred-foot gorge and is four hundred yards wide. It was constructed during the Second World War for military purposes and was never needed. It carries a single railway track. The rolling stock is Indian, and it's very old-fashioned. It still uses steam.'

'Anything else?'

'Oil pipes run along it as well, from fields in Southern Arabia all the way to the coast. The pipes are controlled by my company. That was part of the original leasing agreements with both

American and Russian interests. Quite simply, they are my pipes. If that bridge is blown and the pipes go with it, the international oil market will be thrown into chaos. They represent one third of the world's supply. I've had engineering reports from experts that tell me that it would take two years to replace the Bacu.'

'And why would you want to blow up your own pipelines?'

'I told you: I want to create chaos. Understand this, Mr Keenan. I have more money now than I could ever possibly need. What I do not have is my mother and my three brothers. I hold Dillon responsible for that, and Ferguson, and some others, but most especially I hold responsible the President of the United States. I *will* have my revenge on him, if not by killing him outright, then by throwing America into the worst economic depression it has known in several decades. Cazalet's presidency will be ruined, history will record him as a failure – and *that*, for a man like Cazalet, is something worse than death. Yes, this will do nicely, I think. Will you do it?'

Keenan whistled. 'Remind me never to get you mad at *me*. Yes, I'll do it.'

Kelly said, 'Are you sure, Barry? It could be a hard one.'

'So when have we been afraid of hard ones? What are we, a bunch of old women like the Provos, making peace?'

'I want fast action here. Can you be at Dublin Airport at nine o'clock tomorrow morning? I'll have a plane pick your men up and fly you straight to Hazar.'

'By God, woman, you move fast.'

'That's the way I prefer to work. I've also just got word that a train is leaving our freight yard at Al Mukalli in the Oman to go north into the Empty Quarter by way of the Bacu bridge. It's carrying forty tons of high explosives meant for use in exploratory work in the American fields.'

'Jesus,' Keenan said. 'A hell of a bang that would make, especially if the train happened to be on the bridge at the time and helped by a touch of Semtex. When does the train leave?'

'Three days from now, the seventh. You'll have two clear days in Hazar Town to get ready, and my helicopter can take you down to Al Mukalli to join the train. It leaves at four o'clock in the morning. You'll have four hours before you reach the Bacu, plenty of time to do what you have to.

There'll only be the driver and fireman up front, and a guard at the rear. When you're finished at the Bacu, I'll pick you up in the helicopter.'

'Suits me. I'll read the file and make a list of what we'll need.' He turned to his men. 'Dublin Airport in the morning, then.'

She and Keenan got up. 'We're flying back from Aldergrove this afternoon, then we'll refuel and carry straight on to Hazar. We'll be waiting for you when you arrive. You'll find my coded mobile number in that file.'

'It's been a sincere sensation, Countess. I'll see you off.'

Outside, he and his men watched the Volvo drive away. Casey said, 'What a body on that woman. I'd love to give her one.'

'You know your trouble, Sean?' Keenan said. 'You don't know a great lady when you see one,' and he kicked him in the right shin. 'Now let's talk about this job.'

14

Both vehicles had gone when Dillon and the other two got back to the pub. 'In we go,' he said. 'And we'll have a drink at least.'

Four old men were sitting in the corner drinking Guinness and laughing together. The red-haired young man who'd been having breakfast with his two friends was back in the window seat, also drinking Guinness and reading a newspaper.

Murphy was at the bar. 'What's your pleasure, gentlemen?'

'Same as before,' Dillon said. 'I'll be back in a minute.'

He went along the corridor, opened the snug door, and was out again in seconds, returning to the bar. They sat at a table and Murphy brought the drinks over.

'Will you be having lunch then?'

'No, thanks,' Dillon said. 'We've decided to get back to Belfast.'

The red-haired man swallowed the rest of his Guinness and left. Quinn said, 'You got the recorder?'

'Yes, everything's fine.'

'Great, we can listen to it in the Shogun.'

'If we get a chance.'

Billy said, 'What do you mean?'

'Keep your shooter ready is what I mean, and you, Senator. Come on, drink up and let's get moving.'

He paid the bill and said to Murphy, 'Thanks, old buddy, see you again.'

As he got behind the wheel, Billy said, 'What makes you think we could be in trouble?'

'Just a bad feeling about those three fellas earlier. I could be wrong, but I've told you before, this is Indian territory.'

Billy was beside him and Quinn was in the rear seat. 'What do we do?'

'If we're stopped, I'll keep my hands on the wheel to make them feel good. You and Billy have your guns ready under your coats, and get out on the passenger side so the Shogun's between them and you.'

A black Ford car appeared from behind them, the man with red hair at the wheel.

'Why am I always right?' Dillon asked.

At that moment, a red Toyota skidded out of a farm track up ahead and braked to a halt, blocking the road. Dillon got close, quite deliberately, as he braked. The one with the beard slid from behind the wheel, and his passenger, wearing a reefer coat, produced a .38 Smith and Wesson.

'Can I help you?' Dillon asked.

'Yeah, by turning out your pockets and producing well-filled wallets. This is Real IRA country, boyo. As enthusiastic members, we're always in the market for funds for the organization.'

'Why, that sounds like highway robbery to me,' Dillon told him.

'Exactly. Out of the car.'

The red-haired man had eased from the Ford and took an old Webley from his pocket. 'Come on,' he called.

Billy and Quinn got out, each with a hand under his coat. 'Hands on heads,' the bearded man shouted.

'Now,' Dillon called, and reached for the Walther tucked against the small of his back under his coat, drew it and rammed the muzzle against the bearded man's ear and fired.

Billy's hand came up, his arm extended, and he shot the man in the reefer coat in the left hand. The man screamed and dropped his Smith and Wesson. The red-haired man, totally shocked and covered by Quinn's Walther, stepped back in alarm, lowering his gun. Quinn froze, and his hand and the Walther shook. Seizing the opportunity, the red-haired man's arm swung up and he shot Quinn in the right shoulder, sending him staggering. Billy half-turned, his Walther extended, and shot the man through the right thigh. He lurched back and fell over.

Dillon slid from behind the wheel, went round the Shogun, got an arm around Quinn, picked up the Walther he'd dropped and put it in his pocket. 'You take the wheel, Billy. I'll see to the Senator.'

He opened the rear door of the Shogun, found the army medical kit, and put it in beside Quinn, who was clutching his shoulder.

Dillon squatted down beside the bearded man, who was holding a handkerchief to his shattered ear, his face twisted in agony.

'I'd say you and your friends need some medical

assistance, old buddy,' he said, still maintaining his American persona. 'I could call the RUC for you, but I don't think you'd like that.'

He got in the back of the Shogun. 'Move it, Billy, and just keep going.'

He got Quinn's jacket off and then unbuttoned the shirt, eased it down, and checked the wound. 'How is it?' Quinn asked.

'Still in there. Not gone through. Don't worry, this is an army kit, there's everything necessary to treat a gunshot wound.'

'What he needs is a bleeding hospital,' Billy said.

'No, Billy, what he needs is to get the hell out of Northern Ireland.'

He found a scalpel in the box and cut the sleeve away. It was surprising how little blood there was. He got an antibiotic ampoule out and stabbed it into Quinn and did the same thing with a morphine ampoule. Only then did he apply a field service dressing pad and tie it firmly in place.

He got what was left of the shirt off him, then leaned over the backseat. Thanking God they'd booked out of the hotel, he opened Quinn's suitcase and found a checked flannel sports shirt, which he helped him into.

Afterwards, he found a sling in the kit, eased Quinn's right arm into it, then got his jacket back on. The rent in the sleeve hardly showed, and he could always put his raincoat over his shoulder on the way to the plane.

He eased Quinn back into a more comfortable position. 'Okay, Senator?'

'I let you down,' Quinn said. 'I can't believe it. I just couldn't pull that trigger. I don't understand – a man like me.'

'I've said it before, Vietnam was a long time ago. Just take it easy.'

He got out his Codex and called Ferguson at the Ministry. 'Oh, do I have a tale of woe.'

'Tell me.' Dillon did, sticking to the bare facts. Afterwards, Ferguson said, 'What do you want me to do?'

'Get us a slot out of Aldergrove. We should be there in an hour. They've got the Beechcraft out of Brancaster registered in my name. It'll be two hours to Brancaster, so have an ambulance there in three to pick Quinn up and take him to Rosedene. I'd also contact Henry Bellamy if I were you.'

'I'll get back to you.'

Quinn said, 'Rosedene?'

'A special little hospital we use.'

'And Henry Bellamy?'

'Professor of Surgery at Guy's Hospital, the finest surgeon in London, many people think.'

Quinn closed his eyes and opened them again. 'What about the recording?'

'That's a thought. Let's hear it.'

He switched on the tape and it came through, clear as a bell. 'A pleasure to meet you,' Keenan said. 'What do I call you?'

Afterwards, Quinn said weakly, 'She's crazy, of course.'

'A raving loony. She must be,' Billy said.

Dillon nodded. 'She always was a bit that way, Billy.' His Codex rang. It was Ferguson, who said, 'Your slot's arranged and the ambulance will be at Brancaster. And I've fixed up Henry Bellamy. Are you certain the Senator's up to the plane trip?'

'He has to be. If I deliver him to the Royal Victoria Hospital in Belfast, they'll call in the RUC. Does he need that kind of publicity? I think not, and the three badly damaged specimens we left beside the road outside Drumcree would agree.'

'All right, we'll keep our fingers crossed. So Kate

Rashid was having a meeting with Barry Keenan? How did you find out?'

'Some inspired computer trawling by Roper. I won't bore you with the details. The only important thing is I knew she was going to the Royal George in Drumcree, and Roper discovered that it's Real IRA country and Keenan runs things, and remember what he's famous for? One of the best bomb makers in the business. It seemed logical to assume Kate was up to her old tricks.'

'And is she?'

'She certainly is. We planted a recorder in the snug at the George and retrieved it later. You've got the whole meeting on tape. Anyway, I have to go. We're just coming up to Aldergrove.'

'Just tell me what her target is.'

'The bridge at Bacu in the Empty Quarter. It spans a huge gorge. Carries an old railway line and the main pipelines linking the interior oil fields to the coast. Keenan's agreed to blow it up for her.'

Ferguson was horrified. 'She can't do that, it would cripple world oil supplies.'

'I think that's exactly the point, Charles.'

*   *   *

The flight went smoothly. Quinn, dulled by the morphine, slept most of the way and safely arrived at Brancaster. Dillon and Billy went with him in the ambulance to Rosedene, where they found Henry Bellamy waiting in reception, having a cup of tea with a pleasant middle-aged woman in matron's uniform. Dillon had removed the moustache and tinted glasses.

She kissed him on the cheek and said in an Ulster accent, 'Your hair looks dreadful. I suppose you've been up to fun and games again.'

'Absolutely, Martha.' The trolley came in, pushed by two paramedics. 'Be good to this one, Professor,' he said to Bellamy. 'He's a Medal of Honor winner. He received a gunshot wound in the right shoulder approximately four hours ago.'

'What treatment has he had?' Dillon told him, and Bellamy nodded. 'Prepare him for theatre, Sister, and you and your friend can check back later.' He smiled. 'And shampoo your hair, Dillon, just for me.'

They got a taxi, and he and Billy shared it to Stable Mews. Billy said, 'She's got to be stopped, hasn't she?'

'I'd say so.'

'And that means us?'

'I'd say so again, Billy, if you're game.'

'You know I am, Dillon. But I won't tell Harry until the last minute. He'd only worry. When do you think it will be?'

'Well, you heard her tell Keenan and his boys to be in Dublin tomorrow morning. The job itself is scheduled for three days from now.'

Billy nodded. 'That's good. I'd like to get on with it.'

The taxi rolled up to Stable Mews and Dillon got out with his bag. 'Oh, and Billy,' he murmured, 'I also wouldn't tell Harry you've just been using a shooter now. As you say, it gets him worried.'

'He'll know,' Billy said gloomily, and left.

Within minutes, Dillon was in the shower, shampooing his hair vigorously, the black dye trickling everywhere. Only when his blond hair was spotless again did he step out and towel vigorously.

He pulled on black cords, a black Armani shirt and his old flying jacket, combed his hair, and checked himself in the mirror.

'Not bad, you old sod,' he said softly, and his Codex rang.

Ferguson said, 'Where are you?'

'Stable Mews. I'm on my way.'

'Make it Roper's. I'll see you there, I've had him check this Bacu place. And don't forget the recorder.'

Dillon put it in his pocket, left the cottage, went to the end of the street and hailed a cab.

Dillon found Roper at his computers, but no sign of Ferguson as yet. Roper was working away at the keys and downloading a mass of material. He stopped and looked Dillon over.

'You're looking well, but I suppose action and passion suit you. Ferguson filled me in about the gunplay. What about Quinn?'

'Having surgery at the moment with Henry Bellamy at Rosedene. A bullet in the right shoulder delivered by a rather old-fashioned Webley thirty-eight.'

'Webley? God, they must be hard up for weaponry. What went wrong?'

'Quinn simply froze when he was face-to-face with them. He could have shot the man involved, but couldn't pull the trigger. Billy had to do it for him.'

'I imagine he's taken it badly.'

'Exactly. Especially as they weren't any real challenge. There were three of them and not very good. Billy got two, I took care of one. Amateurs, really. We left them damaged, not dead.'

'So, a successful trip.'

Dillon took out the recorder. 'Thanks to you. We've got everything Keenan and Kate said to each other.'

'I look forward to hearing it. Ferguson told me the target, and I went into Rashid Investments' projects for Hazar and the Empty Quarter.'

The doorbell sounded, he pressed the electronic switch, and a moment later Ferguson and Hannah came in. 'There you are,' he said.

'As ever was.' Dillon smiled at Hannah and kissed her on the cheek. 'God bless, Hannah.'

'You've been in the wars again, Sean.'

'For a good cause.' He held up the recorder. 'You want to hear it, General?'

'I damn well do.' Ferguson sat down and Dillon switched it on.

Afterwards, Ferguson said, 'It's even worse than I thought. How the hell do we handle it?'

'You could always ring her up,' Dillon said cheerfully. 'And say, "Hello, Countess, I have a tape of a certain conversation between you and a notorious IRA bomber. We know what you intend."'

'Yes, but what does she intend?' Roper said. 'To blow up a railway bridge – her own bridge – in disputed territory where no international law holds sway. And by the way, she also owns the railway, the rather ancient Indian rolling stock and the track, even the continuance of it from the Empty Quarter down through Oman to the coast. She even owns the oil pipes.'

Ferguson looked at Hannah. 'What on earth kind of legal case would there be, Superintendent?'

'Not much of one – even if there was a legal system in her part of the Empty Quarter.'

'By the way, General,' Dillon said, 'you couldn't even ring her up. From what she said, she's on her way to Hazar right now. Keenan and his boys arrive tomorrow. The bomb's set for the seventh. Hardly gives you time to send for the SAS or the Marines.'

'So what's the solution?'

'Give me a moment.' Dillon turned to Roper. 'Show me what you've downloaded about the bridge itself and the area around it.'

'I can show you on the screen.'

He did so and Dillon had a look and stabbed a finger at a point about fifteen miles south of the Bacu. 'Tank Five, what's that? There's a little sign beside it.'

'Remember, this is a steam train. They need a lot of water in that kind of heat, and they usually have to stop and fill up along the way. According to the map, it's a steep gradient,' Roper added.

'That's it,' Dillon nodded. 'A good spot to board the train.'

'Who's boarding the train?' Ferguson was bewildered.

'I am, it's the only solution. Board the train at Tank Five and dispose of Keenan and his two friends.'

'On your own? You must be mad.'

'Actually, Billy's already volunteered his services. Of course, it means you've got to get your arse into gear, get hold of Lacey and Parry and tell them to get our plane ready for a quick departure to Hazar.'

'But, Dillon,' Roper said, 'how in the hell would you get to Tank Five? There are Rashid Bedu all over the place, goatherds, caravans, God knows what.'

'Billy and I will do a parachute drop, early morning when it's still half-dark. We've done it before.'

'Sean, are you sure?' Hannah said.

'There's no time for anything else, no other way. Now do me a favour. As well as Lacey and Parry, speak to the Quartermaster at Farley Field, tell him what I'm up to and say I'll need the usual equipment.'

She turned to Ferguson. 'Sir?'

He took a deep breath. 'Get on with it, Superintendent.'

'Excellent,' Dillon said. 'One more thing. Speak to Tony Villiers. His input could be crucial. I'm going home to pack.' He grinned at Roper. 'If I need you, I'll phone you.'

Ferguson said, 'I'll drop you off,' and they went out, Hannah following.

Billy was sitting in his usual booth at the Dark Man when his phone rang. Dillon said, 'Just listen.' When he was finished, he added, 'Are you in or out?'

'I haven't got time to waste, Dillon. I've got to pack. I'll see you at Farley.'

Harry said, 'Farley? Pack? What the hell's going on?'

Billy told him.

* * *

In Hazar, Villiers was encamped with five Land Rovers and nineteen Scouts at the Oasis at El Hajiz, where Bobby Hawk had been killed. The line was only a mile away and he had every intention of crossing it and driving under cover of darkness to Fuad. Achmed, who had proved an excellent Sergeant, had volunteered to go with him, the intention being to blow up the ammunition and arms store at Fuad, aided by a large block of Semtex and a timing pencil.

He answered his Codex and found Ferguson on the other end. 'Charles, what can I do for you?'

'Just listen.' Villiers did, while the General went through everything they'd learned.

'What do you want from me?'

'Any input you think useful. You don't seem surprised.'

'Nothing Kate Rashid does surprises me anymore. As for input, Dillon's idea of dropping in by parachute at Tank Five makes sense, since he and young Salter have done that kind of thing before. However, let's say it works, they dispose of Keenan and his men and foil the plot. It leaves them with a problem.'

'What's that?'

'How to get out in one piece. That's hostile terrain, Bedu country, and mainly Rashid Bedu, Kate's people. I also imagine her helicopter will be in the area hoping to pick up Keenan and his men.'

'What would you suggest?'

'I suppose I'll have to go for Dillon and Billy myself. Actually, it's a good thing you phoned me.'

'Why?'

'I was going to drive to Fuad with my sergeant under cover of darkness and blow up their ammunition and explosive store, but I can't do that with this other thing coming up. Kate Rashid would be alerted.'

'You're right.'

'I'll check on her movements. The other problem is the possibility that Dillon and young Salter might be recognized from the last time, and the news might reach her. But she may have gone up country. I'll let you know.'

'What if she hasn't?'

'Well, we have the RAF compound at the airport now. Make sure your plane has RAF roundels, and have the crew wear uniform. I can pick Dillon and

Salter up. In Arab gear, and with a scarf across the face, they'd make acceptable Scouts for the time that's necessary. Are you coming?'

'I hadn't thought of it.'

'I'd need bigger robes for you. I'll speak to you later, Charles.'

At Farley Field, Dillon arrived as the Gulfstream was taxiing up to the apron, and noticed the RAF roundels at once. The engines were switched off, the door opened, the steps came down and a Flight Sergeant emerged in RAF uniform, a man called Pound whom Dillon knew well.

'Mr Dillon, sir. I see we're bound for foreign parts again.'

'And a rather hot one.' Lacey came down the steps, also wearing full uniform. 'Very pretty,' Dillon said. 'It's the first time I've seen you with that Air Force Cross ribbon.'

'The General wants us to have an official smokescreen at Hazar. You and young Billy have got to be kept under wraps. Colonel Villiers is turning you into Scouts.'

'Mr Dillon.' A voice called, and Dillon turned and saw the quartermaster standing in the entrance of the admin block. 'I've got our stuff ready.'

Dillon followed him in and found various items laid out on a trestle table: two silenced AK-47s, two Brownings with Carswell silencers and titanium bullet-proof vests. Last, but not least, the parachutes.

'Anything else, sir?' the quartermaster asked.

'No, I think we'll start the Third World War nicely with that little lot.'

The quartermaster called, 'Sergeant, give me a hand.'

Pound came in and they transferred everything into two RAF-issue hold-alls and carried them to the plane. Dillon lit a cigarette and walked out to the steps. The Daimler drew up and Ferguson got out. His chauffeur followed, carrying a suit bag.

'Put it in the plane,' Ferguson told him.

'What's all this?' Dillon asked.

'I'm going with you. No arguments.'

'You'll look rather striking in Bedu robes.'

At that moment, Harry Salter's Jaguar drew up, Baxter at the wheel. Harry and Billy got out, Baxter opened the boot and produced two bags.

Harry said, 'Damn you, Dillon, but if Billy's going, so am I.'

Dillon grinned at Ferguson. 'No arguments?'

'Oh, get on board and let's get moving.'

They went up the steps and settled in. Lacey and Parry were already in the cockpit, and Pound closed and locked the door. The engines turned over, the Gulfstream eased down the runway, turned and took off. It climbed higher and levelled off at fifty thousand.

'I've spoken to Tony.' Ferguson told them what Villiers had said.

'Nice to know he's on our case.' Dillon lit a cigarette. 'What about Quinn?'

'Oh, he'll be fine. He isn't going to die on us or anything, but Bellamy says he'll be laid up for a while. Oh, and I tried the White House, but the President is on an official visit to Argentina, so I had to make do with Blake Johnson. He was horrified to hear about Quinn and about Kate Rashid's plans.'

'What did he say?'

'That he would inform the President.'

'Was he suitably alarmed?'

'What he actually said was: "Tell Dillon and Billy to go in and kick ass."'

Dillon turned to Billy. 'Now there's a compliment. So here we go again.'

'Saving the free world. Why does it always have to be us?'

'We're too good at it, that's the problem,' and Dillon called to Sergeant Pound, 'I'll have a Bushmills now.'

HAZAR

15

When the Rashid plane landed at the airport outside Hazar, the Scorpion was waiting at the end
of the runway, Ben Carver beside it. Kate, Rupert,
and the three Irishmen boarded it, and a couple of
porters transferred the luggage. Within minutes,
the Scorpion was taking off, and an hour later,
as evening was falling, it landed at the airstrip
at Fuad.

There was the usual scattering of Bedu – women,
children and a number of the trainees – curious
as to what was happening, and Colum McGee
came forward to greet them. He grasped Keenan's
hands.

'It's good to see you, Barry.'

'And you, you old bastard.'

McGee nodded to Casey and Kelly. 'Christ, but
he must be hard up if you two are the best he
can do.'

'Get stuffed,' Casey said.

McGee turned to Kate. 'Supper's waiting.'

'You go ahead. I want a word with Ben.'

The Irishmen went off together and she turned to Carver. 'Go back now. We're staying here. Be back here tomorrow evening. I want you to take our Irish friends to Al Mukalli. How long will it take?'

'An hour and a quarter.'

'Good. You'll return here tomorrow evening, leave at one-thirty in the morning, drop them at the goods yard at Al Mukalli, and return here again. Later that morning, you'll take me, the Major and three men to the Bacu Bridge, where we'll pick up Mr Keenan and his friends. How long is that?'

'About the same as the other trip. It's just in a different direction.'

'Good. We'll leave at six-thirty.'

'Will fuel be a problem?'

'No, we've stacks of it here in jerry cans.'

Carver was sweating a lot and he was worried. He'd looked the other way regarding the activities at Fuad, but Keenan and his men made him uneasy.

'Look, am I getting into something here I shouldn't?' he said awkwardly.

'Yes,' she said calmly. 'You're into piloting my helicopter when I want you to, for which you are considerably rewarded. Of course, if this gives you a problem, I can have Carver Air Transport's licence to operate in Hazar transferred to someone else.'

Rupert said gently, 'I think she's got a point, my friend, don't you?'

'No problem. I was only asking.'

She said, 'On your way, then, Ben,' turned away, and walked toward the tents, Dauncey at her side.

Carver wiped sweat from his face with a handkerchief. 'I'm getting too old for this,' he said softly, climbing into the Scorpion, and took off.

Kate Rashid and her cousin joined the others, who were already sitting cross-legged in the great tent, the evening meal spread before them. On this occasion there was just the six of them, and women brought goat stew to augment the fruit, dates, and unleavened bread.

Casey and Kelly eyed the stew dubiously and Casey said, 'What is it?'

'It's food,' Keenan said. 'Just get on with it.'

'But where are the knives and forks?'

'You just use your hands,' Colum McGee told them, and dipped in using a piece of the bread.

Kate Rashid said, 'Is everything Mr Keenan wanted ready?'

'Sure. Plenty of Semtex, timers, both clockwork and pencil. Lots of det cord. Put that together with the forty tons of high explosives that train is carrying, and it's goodnight Vienna.'

'Excellent,' Kate Rashid said. 'What do you think, Rupert?'

'The great virtue is the simplicity of it.'

She smiled. 'Yes, well, I always did like things simple.'

'There is one thing, Countess,' Keenan said. 'What happens afterwards? How do you explain it?'

'Well, it's hardly my fault if Arab terrorists decided to blow up the Bacu Bridge, is it?'

'Of course.' Keenan smiled. 'Now why didn't I think of that?'

When the RAF Gulfstream was halfway to Hazar, Ferguson spoke to Villiers on his Codex and explained the situation. 'So, Harry and I decided to come along for the ride, so that makes four of us. Will that be a problem?'

'Not to me. Kate Rashid arrived with Dauncey

and the three Irishmen, by the way. I had one of my Scouts at the airport looking out for them. They transferred to her Scorpion, with Ben Carver piloting, and went up country.'

'Shabwa?'

'I would say Fuad, so Keenan can pick up his supplies.'

'So we could stay at the Excelsior?'

'I wouldn't recommend it. Even the barman and the hotel manager are on her payroll. I've set up camp about twelve miles out of town. I'll pick you up at the RAF compound with suitable gear.'

'What was that all about?' Dillon asked when Ferguson switched off.

Ferguson explained, and Harry Salter said, 'So we're going to look like the London Palladium cast of *Ali Baba and the Forty Thieves*.'

'You'll love it, Harry, you and the General back with the Scouts, sitting beside a fire of dried camel dung, sleeping under the stars.'

'Yes, well, you can enjoy it if you want. I'll just endure it.'

The Gulfstream landed, Lacey at the controls, and taxied up to the RAF compound and straight inside a hangar, where they found Villiers leaning against one of two Land Rovers, smoking a cigarette. He'd driven one himself and Achmed was at the wheel of the other.

'Good to see you.' He shook hands all round.

'That's a great tan you've got, Colonel,' Billy said. 'Been on holiday, have you?'

'Cheeky young bugger,' Villiers told him. 'You'll find robes and head cloths in the back. Sort yourselves out and we'll get moving.'

Which they did. Harry said, 'Jesus, do I look as bad as you lot?'

'Worse,' Dillon told him. 'Believe me, Harry, worse.'

'I'll take you and Harry, General,' Villiers said. 'You two go with Achmed and we'll get out of here.'

The encampment was by a pool, an outcrop of rock sheltering it, and a few scattered palm trees. There were three bivouac tents beside a roaring fire, five Land Rovers in all.

They had a meal – canned soups, Heinz beans, and new potatoes all mixed into a kind of stew – but the bread was the local unleavened kind.

Billy wiped his plate with a piece. 'That was good. I thought you'd be giving us goat.'

'Not you, Billy.' Villiers called to Achmed. 'One of my bottles of whisky and the tin cups. Scotch, I'm afraid,' he said to Dillon.

'It'll do to take along.'

It arrived, and Villiers unscrewed the cap and poured a generous measure into each cup, Billy declining as usual. Villiers handed the bottle back to Achmed.

'The night is cold, but if you take a whisky sup for yourself, do it in my tent that the others may not see.'

'Allah is merciful and so you are, *Sahb*.'

He slipped away and Villiers said, 'So let's go over it again. Barry Keenan, bomber extraordinaire, and his friends Kelly and Casey, will be delivered to Al Mukalli to board the freight train leaving at four a.m. It proceeds north to the Empty Quarter at approximately eight a.m. I presume Keenan will have done everything he needs to do by then with the explosives.'

'I would think so,' Dillon said.

'So, we're at Tank Five, where you and Billy board and have the fifteen miles to the Bacu to do the business. After which, the train still works, the bridge is intact, and Kate Rashid's Scorpion is hovering around, hoping to pick up Keenan and company.'

'With Rashid Bedu all the way back to Hazar and the airport,' Dillon said.

'I know, so I'll come and get you with my Scouts. It should take about four hours. I can't promise, mind you. These roads can be hell and it is desert country.'

'Ah, well, something to look forward to, Billy,' and Dillon smiled.

In London the following afternoon, Hannah called at Rosedene, since Henry Bellamy had told her he intended to be there. She waited in reception, talking to Martha, and finally Bellamy joined them.

'How is he?' Hannah asked.

'Poorly, running a fever, and not happy with himself. Look, I don't know the details of what happened and I don't want to, but it's left him depressed.'

'Can I see him?'

'Of course, but don't overdo it.'

Quinn lay against high pillows, a robe covering his bandages, his eyes closed, but he opened them when she pulled a chair up.

'Superintendent. Good of you to come.'

'How do you feel?'

'Lousy.'

'I can sympathize. I was once shot three times. It hurts like hell, but it passes.'

'Not what's going on in my brain. I let Dillon and Billy down. I faced that guy and froze. The gun shook in my hand, I couldn't pull the trigger. He'd have probably finished me off if Billy hadn't shot him.'

'Well, Billy would. He and Dillon have at least one thing in common. They're killers by nature.'

'And I'm not?'

'No, in spite of your war record. None of this is anything to be ashamed of, Senator.'

'I haven't seen Dillon. Will he be coming in?'

'No, he's in Hazar.'

'Damn. I should be there,' Quinn said. 'Tell me what he's doing there.'

At Fuad, Keenan and his men spent the day meticulously checking the material that Colum McGee had provided. Keenan even made them unscrew the casing several times and check the insides.

'Jesus, is this necessary, Barry?' Casey asked.

'Only if we want to look busy. I'd like the Countess to think she's getting her money's worth. I've checked the specifications of that bridge again.

I figure that with forty tons of high explosive on board, all I need do is use one big block of Semtex as an igniter linked to the other stuff with det cord.'

'The old-fashioned way?' Kelly said.

'The old-fashioned, simple way.' Keenan smiled. 'And I'm always in favour of that.'

At the Scouts' camp, it was early evening. Villiers appeared with Lacey and Parry and everyone sat around the fire.

Lacey said, 'I've worked out that we can make the Tank Five area in thirty minutes. I'd say we should leave at six. You'll want to get yourselves established at the Tank, maybe do a recce.'

'That sounds fine by me,' Dillon said.

'The only thing is,' Villiers put in, 'I'll have to leave with my men around three-thirty. We'll drop you off at the RAF compound and you'll have to sit it out until your six o'clock takeoff.'

Dillon turned to Lacey. 'We'll see you then.'

Ferguson said, 'So will I. Besides Dillon and Billy, you'll have two passengers, Squadron Leader.'

Lacey smiled. 'Of course, General,' and he and

Parry got in a Land Rover and Villiers drove them away.

After midnight, at Fuad, Carver gave the Scorpion a thorough check and topped up the tanks from jerry cans, helped by a couple of Bedu. Keenan and his men carefully packed hold-alls with Semtex, timers and the det cord, and stowed them carefully away, then they went back to the block house that was the communication, weapon, and explosive store.

'What's your pleasure?' Colum McGee asked.

Keenan had a look at the rifle racks. 'An AK-47 will be fine for each of us, and a bag of magazines.'

'What about pistols?'

'Okay, three Brownings.'

McGee laid them out on the trestle table. The three men armed themselves and returned to the Scorpion. Kate Rashid had appeared with Rupert and was talking to Carver. He checked his watch.

'Ten past one. We might as well go. The weather report's good. No wind to speak of. Should be a smooth run.'

Kate Rashid said, 'On your way, then. Make history.'

'No, thanks, I spent years in Ireland doing that. This time I prefer to make a buck. I'll see you at the Bacu.'

Carver was already at the controls. Keenan climbed in after Casey and Kelly and slid the door closed. A moment later, they started to lift off.

The flight was as smooth as Carver had predicted, and the sky was luminous with stars scattered like diamond chips around a half moon. Al Mukalli wasn't much of a place, only the odd light was showing. It seemed more like an old-fashioned whistle stop than anything else. There were flat-roofed buildings, a small web of railway lines, wagons parked to one side, and two railway engines, one of them linked to a long line of freight cars, some open to the sky.

As the Scorpion started to descend, two men dropped out of the train and looked up and another man got out of the guard's van at the rear. The Scorpion landed, and Keenan opened the door and got out with Casey, and Kelly passed out the hold-alls and rifles.

Carver called. 'Right, I'm out of here. I'll see

you at the Bacu,' and he took the Scorpion up and away.

The three Arabs stood waiting as Keenan and his men approached. They all wore the usual head cloths, but only one wore a robe. The others were in white oil-stained overalls.

'You were expecting us.' Keenan made it a statement.

The one in the robe said, 'Yes, *Sahb*, I am Yusuf, the guard.' He pointed to the older, bearded man. 'This is Ali, the train driver.'

His English was good. Keenan nodded to the younger man, who was powerfully built. 'Who's he?'

'Halim, the fireman. They speak no English.'

'I understand you are all Rashid?'

He could see the pride on Yusuf's face. 'Yes, *Sahb*, we are of the clan.'

'And the Countess?'

'Our leader, the blessed one, praise be to Allah.'

'So you have been informed what is expected of you?'

'Indeed, *Sahb*.'

'Good.' Keenan walked to the engine, aware of the gentle hum of escaping steam, the unmistakable smell. He looked inside. 'My granddaddy drove one of these back home. When I was five, he took me up there on the footplate. They're firing up, getting ready for the run.'

'A right old stink on it,' Kelly said.

'You've no soul, no poetry,' Keenan told him, and said to Yusuf, 'Take us to your van.'

Yusuf led the way, mounting the iron steps at the very rear of the train to a railed platform. He opened a door and led the way in. Two oil lamps hung from the ceiling. There was a desk, long leather-covered benches, a small stove with a kettle on it and a gas cylinder underneath. At the other end was a washbasin, a narrow door beside it labelled *Toilet* and another door. Casey and Kelly put the hold-alls with the Semtex and timers down.

'Anything to eat?' Casey asked.

'Dates, *Sahb*, dried meat, bread.'

'Jesus,' Casey said.

Yusuf added, 'There is tea in the cupboard, *Sahb*, English tea.'

Keenan turned as Kelly produced a half bottle of whisky from one of the bags. 'I'll have a go at that.' Kelly unscrewed the cap and handed him the bottle. Keenan took a long pull and handed it back. He said to Yusuf, 'We still leave at four o'clock?'

'Yes, *Sahb*.'

Keenan glanced at his watch. 'Forty-five minutes. Right, we'll check the freight cars and you can show me where the explosives are.'

The open ones were loaded with oil pipes. The explosives were in the two enclosed cars in the centre of the train, stacked in boxes and clearly visible when Yusuf slid back the doors. Ladders gave access to the roofs at each end of the cars, and down through trap doors inside.

Keenan said, 'That's fine. I can get in while we're travelling.' He turned to Yusuf. 'Tell me, what happens to you on the other side of the Bacu, afterwards, I mean?'

'We have friends in the hills, *Sahb*, we will be safe.'

'That's all right then. Let's go back and try that tea of yours.'

At six o'clock, when the Gulfstream taxied out of the hangar at the RAF compound, Dillon and Billy were ready to go in black jumpsuits and titanium waistcoats. The parachutes and weaponry were on the floor by the door. Parry closed it, then returned to the cockpit.

Dillon and Billy sat opposite Harry and Ferguson, while the Gulfstream turned at the end of the runway and awaited takeoff instructions. It was already less dark, but the moon still made a fine display.

Harry looked very tense. 'Bleeding crazy. How can you jump from a thing like this? It's suicide.'

'We did it in Cornwall two years ago,' Billy said. 'My first jump. I'm still here, aren't I? You worry too much.'

At the airport at six-thirty, Kate Rashid, Dauncey, and Abu and two Bedu, all armed with AKs, climbed into the Scorpion. Carver, in the cockpit, looked over his shoulder. 'The weather's changed. There's a bit of a headwind. It might take us a little longer.'

'Just get on with it,' Rupert Dauncey told him and turned to Kate. 'Here we go then, cousin. What was that remark of yours? To make history?'

She was wearing a black jumpsuit and a burnoose, the hooded Bedu cloak. 'I'm all in favour of that, darling. Give me a cigarette.'

He lit two, passed her one, and they started to rise.

*   *   *

At the same time, the Gulfstream, approaching the target area, descended from five thousand feet to one thousand. Parry came from the cockpit, wearing headphones skewed a little so that his left ear was free.

'Four minutes, gentlemen.'

Dillon and Billy strapped on their parachutes and suspended the AKs across their chests. Dillon looped a pair of Nightstalkers around his neck. They were standing now and waiting. Lacey started to reduce power. 'Open the door,' he told Parry over the headphone.

Parry did as he was told and dropped the steps. There was a mighty rush of wind as Lacey throttled back almost to stalling speed.

'Now!' he shouted. 'One thousand feet.'

Dillon went out on the first step and dived, Billy close behind him. Parry wrestled with the door and Ferguson turned to help him. Lacey boosted speed and turned away, climbing for the return to Hazar. It was quiet again.

Ferguson returned to his seat, and Harry said, 'God help them.'

* * *

In the light of the half moon, with dawn touching the horizon, the desert below was clearly visible and the line of the railway unmistakable, the huge oil pipelines running on both sides. The wind was stronger now, and Dillon found himself drifting. Billy was close at hand and a little higher.

Dillon got the Nightstalkers to his eyes and checked the line to his right, but there was nothing. He turned to the left, and there was Tank Five about a mile away, a blockhouse of some kind and a water tower.

The ground was coming up fast, and a moment later he landed in soft sand between two enormous dunes and rolled over. He divested himself of his 'chute and started to cover it, when his name was called. He turned and found Billy halfway up the side of one of the dunes.

He finished burying his 'chute. Above him, Billy was doing the same and then started down. Dillon lit a cigarette and waited.

'Piece of cake,' Billy told him as he arrived. 'But I couldn't see any sign of the target.'

'I did, thanks to the Nightstalkers. A mile down the line that way.' He looked at his watch. 'A quarter to seven. We'd better get moving,' and they started down the side of the track.

*　　*　　*

There was much more light now as they reached Tank Five, the trip having taken a good half hour because of the difficulty of walking in the soft sand, which was being whipped up by the increasing wind.

The blockhouse, when they reached it, was a poor sort of thing constructed from concrete breezeblocks. There were a couple of windows, the frames long gone, and a wooden door which opened with difficulty, sand drifted against it. Inside, the pumping mechanism was rusted with age.

'That's not worked in years,' Billy said. 'Where do they get the water from? Maybe we got it wrong, Dillon, maybe it isn't a water halt any more?'

They went outside and looked up at the tank, high on four rusting iron legs. A canvas tube was suspended from the underside of the tank, hanging beside an iron ladder. There was some sort of brass fitting on the end and Dillon examined it.

'It's certainly damp. There's a little seepage. I'll take a look.'

He climbed the ladder and reached the top of the tank, which was covered, but there was an inspection hatch. It creaked open, and when he looked inside, the water level was almost to the top. He went back down the ladder.

'It's full. Obviously, the pumping system isn't working. Maybe the well ran dry. They probably couple a water tank to the train every so often and refill this tank that way.'

'So it's still working. Thank God for that. Now what?'

'I'm going to check in with Tony Villiers.'

Who was pushing hard, seated in the front Land Rover, the other four in a line behind him. They were in a small sandstorm, which could have been worse but was bad enough, for he and his men had had to cover their faces. In fact, he was lucky to hear his Codex and get it out of the left breast pocket of his bush shirt.

'Dillon here. I'm just touching base. Billy and I have made it to Tank Five. What about you?'

'We might reach the other side of the Bacu by eight-thirty, but I can't guarantee it. We've got a touch of sandstorm here.'

'Yes, it's a bit like that here,' Dillon told him. 'Do your best. I'll call again to confirm the train's arrival.'

'Good hunting,' Villiers said.

Next, Dillon tried Ferguson, but got a no-response signal. All this he had done while sheltering inside the blockhouse with Billy.

'What happens when the train arrives?' Billy asked. 'Do we stay in here?'

'I don't think so, just in case someone decides to take a look.' Dillon went out and examined the terrain at the rear of the tower. There was a steep slope, large rocks and boulders here and there, sand drifting against them. 'We'll take cover up there. When the train starts moving again, the blockhouse and tower will give us some cover as we come down the slope.'

'We'll have to be damn quick. How do we board?'

'The guard's van at the rear.'

'What if there isn't one?'

'There always is, Billy.' Dillon glanced at his watch. 'A quarter to eight. Time for the moment of truth.'

There was a sound, a kind of whisper in the distance, and then a long, drawn-out whistle.

'Here she comes, Billy, let's get under cover.'
They started up the slope and bedded down.

The door by the toilet in the guard's van opened to
a metal ledge. There was a coupling to one of the
open cars loaded with oil pipes, a wooden plank
walkway giving access across four open wagons
in all. Then came the enclosed cars containing
the explosives, the ladder to each of them leading
to the roof. Finally, the water tank and the coal
tender. The point was that the engine was totally
reachable and there were small access doors at each
end of the enclosed wagons.

All of which suited Keenan's purposes. During the
trip from Al Mukalli, he and Casey and Kelly had
laid their charges, opening the access doors between
the two explosive wagons, linking them with det
cord. The block of Semtex was in the front wagon,
and the det cord also linked to chemical fuses Keenan
had stuck in some of the explosives packages.

It hadn't taken long. He'd decided on a couple of
timer pencils, after all. They were ten-minute jobs
and already in place in the Semtex block and ready
to be broken at the appropriate moment when the
train was halted on the bridge.

In fact, for the past hour or so, Keenan had enjoyed himself more than he had in years. Casey and Kelly had returned to the guard's van and the whisky bottle, but Keenan had made his way up to the engine and joined Ali and Halim on the footplate.

Ali had allowed him to handle the controls, drive the old engine, savour the wind in his face, the smell of steam, and Keenan had found it wonderful. As the train started up the steep gradient to Tank Five, he sounded the whistle. Yusuf had explained the necessity for the stop, and now Ali tapped him on the arm and took over. He started to slow the train down and up ahead was Tank Five.

Crouched behind the rocks halfway up the slope, Dillon and Billy waited, and suddenly Dillon's Codex rang.

He answered instinctively. 'Who is it?'

'Ferguson. I wondered what was happening.'

'We're at Tank Five and the train's just toiling up the slope, that's what's happening, so I'd get off the line if I were you, General.'

The train ground to a halt below amid a hissing

of steam. Ali and Halim got down from the foot-plate, followed by Keenan.

'The man himself,' Dillon said softly. 'That's Barry Keenan, Billy, and that's Kelly and the other is Casey,' he added, as they arrived, each with an AK slung from his shoulder. Yusuf trailed at the rear.

The voices below were muted, as Dillon and Billy watched, and Halim brought a length of canvas tubing linked to the train, which he clipped onto the end of the outlet tube at the bottom of the tank. He started to work a lever, which was obviously a hand pump. Dillon debated whether to call Villiers and decided to leave it until they were on the train. Kelly and Casey were laughing at something.

'We could knock them off now,' Billy whispered. 'Why not?'

'Because we can't be certain what Keenan's done on the train. He'll have everything ready to blow, probably timers. I suspect the explosives will be in the enclosed freight cars, but we need one of those bastards to show us.'

'I see your point.'

At that moment, Halim uncoupled the canvas water tubes, Keenan got back on the footplate, and Kelly climbed up a ladder to the top of the front car and squatted there. Casey did the same, sitting behind him on the rear car. Ali and Halim followed Keenan and Yusuf moved to the rear of the train.

'The guard,' Dillon said.

They watched him enter the guard's van and shut the door. Keenan, under Ali's supervision, was at the controls. He sounded the whistle, the train juddered, and there was a great cloud of steam.

'Move it, Billy,' Dillon said and led the way, sliding down the slope at the rear of the block-house.

The train was moving now with a great clanking, and as it passed they ran out onto the track, reached for the rail of the platform to the guard's van, and heaved themselves up. Keenan kept pulling the whistle line. Billy and Dillon, AKs ready, stood on either side of the door.

Dillon got his Codex out and called Villiers. He got an answer almost immediately. 'Is that you, Dillon?'

'As ever was. They've taken on water. Billy and I are on the platform at the rear of the guard's van. We're going in hard, so do your best and let Ferguson know.'

He clicked off, put the Codex in his pocket, and grinned at Billy. 'I'm an older guy, so you can have the honour.'

'Bastard.'

Dillon turned the brass handle and opened the door and Billy was through in a second, AK ready. At the desk, Yusuf turned in alarm as the two demons, dressed in black, appeared. Billy had him back against the desk, the muzzle of the AK under his chin.

'He'll kill you without hesitation,' Dillon said in Arabic. 'And the weapon is silenced. No one will know.'

Yusuf was terrified. '*Sahb*, please don't.'

'You speak English?'

'Yes.'

'Then use it now, my companion has no Arabic. Answer my questions and live. Where are the explosives you carry?'

'On the two enclosed cars in the centre of the train.'

'The three men, the Irishmen, what have they done since you left Al Mukalli?'

'I don't know, *Sahb*.'

'You lie. Kill him, Billy.'

Billy stood back and took aim and Yusuf cried wildly. 'No, *Sahb*, I speak the truth.'

'You still lie. You are Rashid Bedu, you and the engine driver and fireman. I know this because the Countess boasted you were her people. As this is so, you must know the train stops on the Bacu Bridge, where the Irishmen will blow it up. Is this not so?'

'Yes, *Sahb*.'

'So tell me the truth. What have they done, the Irishmen, since leaving El Mukalli?'

Yusuf was in despair. 'I only know that they have worked in the explosive cars for most of the time, but I was instructed to stay here, *Sahb*. I have not seen what they have done.'

It was obviously the truth, and Dillon lit a cigarette and passed it to him. 'Is it easy to get to those cars?'

'Yes, *Sahb*, through the door, and there are walkways across the open cars.'

'So you can go all the way to the engine?'

'Yes, *Sahb*.'

Dillon turned menacing. 'Is there more to tell me or have you told me all?'

'I swear it on the life of my eldest son.' He was

obviously trying hard, sweat on his face. 'They worked in the car for an hour or an hour and a half. Afterwards, two of them sat in here and drank whisky. The leader joined Ali and Halim on the footplate. He's been driving the train.'

'Driving it?'

'Yes, *Sahb*, when we were taking on water, Ali told me he is like a young boy. He loves trains.'

'Did he tell Ali this?'

'No, *Sahb*, he has no Arabic and Ali no English. It's just the way he behaves.'

Billy said, 'So what's the big deal, Dillon?'

'The big deal is he's busy up there, Billy, and that's good.' He took Yusuf by the arm and pushed him to the back of the van. At that point, looking up the gradient, the train was doing perhaps twenty-five miles an hour. 'I'll keep my word,' he said to Yusuf. 'I promised that if you told me the truth, I would let you live.' He opened the rear door.

'But, *Sahb*, I . . .'

'*Sahb*, nothing. Jump and perhaps you live, stay and you certainly die.'

Yusuf went down on the metal steps and jumped to one side of the track, where banks of sand covered the oil pipes. He rolled over several times and then the train went round a corner and he was lost from view.

'What now?' Billy said.

'We need either Casey or Kelly, either will do. That's why it's useful that Keenan is busy on the footplate. Let's go.'

He opened the door and looked out across the open cars, able to see Kelly on top of the front explosives car and Casey on the one behind. The train was rattling along now, blowing up sand and emitting clouds of steam.

'Now what?' Billy demanded.

'I'll cross to that rear wagon and you stay here. When I get there, shoot Casey in the head. Knock him off the roof for me. Kelly's looking the other way. He won't see.'

'Then what?'

'I'll entice Kelly down. It's a chance we'll have to take that he'll behave as I expect.'

'Okay, you're the boss.'

Dillon stepped out on the walkway, started across the swaying cars, and reached the rear door of the explosives car, the ladder up to the roof beside it. He turned and waved to Billy. Casey was trying to light a cigarette, the AK across his knees as he sat there. Billy took careful aim and shot him in the head, the muted crack of the silenced AK drowned in the noise of the train. Casey keeled over, slid down the slightly curved roof and went over the edge, rifle and all.

Dillon looked back to the body at the side of the track, waited until the train went round another curve, then mounted the ladder and peered over the edge. Kelly squatted there on the other roof, unaware that Casey had gone.

Billy had stepped back inside the guard's van out of sight. Dillon eased slightly down the ladder and called, 'Kelly, help me.' He went down the ladder all the way now and stood waiting, his AK ready.

The voice, muffled by the train noises, was difficult to hear, but Kelly looked round and Billy watched, ready to shoot him if necessary. Kelly got up, slung his rifle over one shoulder, crossed to the end of the front car, and jumped to the second. He stood there, swaying, then came on.

'Casey, where are you?' he called as he reached the edge.

'Dead and gone, but you've got me, your old friend Sean Dillon.' Dillon trained the AK on him. 'Come on down or you're a dead man, too, and if

374

I don't get you, my friend will,' and Billy stepped out of the guard's van.

'Holy Mother of God, you, Dillon! It can't be.'

'I said get down here.'

Kelly did as he was told. Dillon took the AK from him and threw it down to the side of the track. He opened the door to the inside of the car as Billy joined them.

'Get in there,' and he shoved Kelly in. 'Open the outside door, Billy.'

Billy did as he was told, and the interior was flooded with light. 'Right, show me what Keenan did.'

'Jesus, Dillon, he'll kill me.' It was an instinctive and stupid reply.

Billy decided to take a hand and played the bad guy. 'It's a waste of time, Dillon. Just let me throw him out.'

'But he'd break his neck,' Dillon said. 'I mean, we're doing about forty miles an hour.'

'So what?'

Billy rammed the muzzle of his AK into Kelly's stomach, forcing him back to the open door, and he cracked.

'No, Dillon, I'll show you.'

'Get on with it, then.'

Kelly turned to the boxes of explosives. 'Barry put chemical fuses in this lot. They're linked by the det cord to the next car.'

'And what's in there?'

'Semtex. They're on ten-minute timer pencils.'

'Good. Now get a grip on that det cord and yank out the fuses.' Kelly did as he was told. 'There you go. That was easy, wasn't it? Now, next door and you can tackle the Semtex.'

It was at the same moment that Keenan happened to turn, and saw, to his surprise, that there was no sign of his men. They were very close to the bridge now, he could see it a mile ahead, as the defile through which the train ran widened. Uneasy, he mounted the walkway over the coal tender and water tank and reached the first car. The trap door in the roof was open. He'd done that deliberately to alleviate the heat inside – it wasn't good for Semtex, which could become unstable. He heard voices and peered in.

Billy had opened the sliding door, and Kelly, who had ripped out the chemical fuses and det cord, was removing the pencil timers from the

Semtex. He turned to throw them out through the open door, and Keenan, in a blind rage, drew his Browning from his pocket.

'You stupid bastard!' He shot Kelly twice in the back, driving him out through the open door.

Billy fired up at him and Keenan stepped back. 'Keep firing, Billy,' Dillon called, ducked out, and went up the ladder to the roof.

The train was rocking and Keenan was having difficulty keeping his feet under him. He fired wildly, the bullet going several feet to one side of Dillon. He tried to take aim again, then a look of amazement crossed his face.

'Christ, Dillon, it's you.'

'God bless all here, Barry,' Dillon said, and fired the AK on automatic, driving him back over the front end of the wagon to fall beneath the wheels of the train. A moment later and Billy joined him.

'Dillon, we did it.'

'Saved the world again, Billy.' Dillon got out his Codex and called up Villiers. 'Mission accomplished, Tony. Keenan and his friends are stiffed and all the explosive charges are defused. We're almost at the bridge. Where are you?'

'Two miles the other side, but you'd better

keep going. You could have trouble. The Rashid Scorpion passed over me.'

'Is that so? Thanks for the warning. See you soon and we'll stop the train then.'

Billy said, 'Now what?'

'Tony says he just saw the Rashid helicopter, so we keep going hard until we meet up with them. You go down on the footplate with the driver and fireman and keep them at it. I'll talk to them. Get on with it.'

Billy did as he was told and dropped down to Ali and Halim, who looked greatly shocked. Dillon shouted down in his bad Arabic. 'Everyone else is dead. If you want to live, keep the train moving and do as you're told, otherwise my friend will shoot you.'

Ali looked cowed, but Halim, as it sank in, looked angry now. Dillon went back to the roof of the first wagon, got the Codex, and rang Ferguson. There was an almost instant reply.

'Ferguson.'

'Dillon. I'm standing on top of a train just about to cross the Bacu Bridge. There've been no nasty explosions, so the oil can continue to flow to an ungrateful world, which will never know how close it came to disaster.'

'And Keenan and company?'

'Dead, I'm afraid, gone to that great IRA rest home in the sky.'

'As usual, you astonish me.'

'God save us, General, I astonish myself sometimes, but I must go. I think I heard the Rashid helicopter approaching.'

They were on the way in to the bridge, the Scorpion at six hundred feet, when Rupert Dauncey first saw the column of Land Rovers over to the left. Kate Rashid picked up a pair of binoculars and focused on them.

'It's Tony Villiers and the Scouts. What's he doing here?'

'More importantly,' her cousin said, 'how did he know to be here?'

The Bacu Bridge loomed ahead, an awesome sight, and the train started to cross. 'What the hell is going on? It isn't stopping,' Kate said.

Dauncey had taken the binoculars from her and focused them. He passed them to her. 'Even more interesting is how an old friend of yours happens to be down there dressed in a Special Forces combat uniform.'

It was her turn to focus the binoculars. 'My God,' she whispered. 'Dillon, but how?'

As the Scorpion made its pass, Dillon waved cheerfully.

'Damn you,' she said.

The train continued to cross, Dillon still waved. It reached the other side and she said, 'Abu, shoot him.'

'Waste of time, sweetie,' Rupert told her. 'That's not the way this thing operates.'

Abu pulled open the door, leaned forward and fired, but the helicopter bucked and he dropped his rifle and grabbed at a seat belt, almost going headfirst through the door.

On the footplate, Billy looked up at the sound of the shot, and Halim grabbed at Billy's AK, forcing the barrel up. Billy fired, alerting Dillon, but even as he did so, the fireman, with his great strength, hurled Billy backwards out of the engine.

As Dillon shot Halim in the back, too late, driving him also to the side of the track, Dauncey took the binoculars and focused on Billy. 'It's young Salter.'

Kate Rashid shouted at Carver, 'Land beside him. Go on, do it.' She turned to Rupert. 'Give me your Walther.'

'Now look, Kate, Villiers will be here at any moment. Let's get out of here.'

'Give me your Walther!'

Abu glared at Dauncey and held his AK ready. Rupert sighed, took out the weapon, and gave it to her. 'As you say, cousin.' The Scorpion turned, hovered, and went down.

Dillon dropped onto the footplate and rammed his AK into Ali's side. 'Stop the train,' he said in Arabic. 'Now.'

Ali did as he was told and Dillon jumped to the ground, turned and ran back.

Billy, dazed, was hauled to his feet by Abu and the two Bedu. There was blood on his face from a bad cut.

'You bastard,' Kate said. 'You little Cockney swine. I told you all that you were dead when I was ready. Well, your time has come. Go on, run for it.' She said to Abu in Arabic, 'Make him run.'

Abu sent Billy staggering away, and she fired at him repeatedly, most of her bullets hitting the titanium waistcoat, but two struck the top of his right thigh and another passed through the left side of his neck.

Dillon dropped to one knee and fired, catching one of the Bedu, then swung as Rupert pulled Kate inside, and shot Abu in the back of the head as he tried to follow them. The other Bedu simply ran away, making for the sand dunes.

As Carver took the Scorpion up, Dillon ran to Billy and fell on his knees beside him, and it was at that moment that Tony Villiers and the Scouts arrived.

They laid Billy across the rear seats of one of the Land Rovers while Villiers checked him out, a combat medical kit open on the driver's seat. They'd taken off the titanium waistcoat, which had four bullets embedded in it.

'Has he had it?' Dillon demanded.

'Well, I'm no doctor, but I've treated plenty of gunshot wounds. Here, the bullet's gone straight through the neck. If it had damaged an artery, the blood would have been pumping out, and it isn't, so we can do a temporary job on that with wound packs. Pass me one.'

He quickly bandaged Billy's neck, who moaned softly, eyes staring. 'Thank God for titanium,' Dillon said.

'Yes, but he's been shot twice at the top of his right thigh.' Villiers took a scalpel from the kit and sliced open the material, exposing two bullet wounds. There was very little blood and he felt round to the other side. 'They're still inside. God knows how much damage they've done. All I can do is bandage again and give him morphine. There are drips in the medical kits in all the Land Rovers. Someone can sit close and hold one for him.'

'That's me,' Dillon said.

He helped sit Billy up as Villiers used the wound pack, tying it securely round the waist. Finally, he covered the gash in the face with a large bandage and carefully inserted the needle from one of the drip bags into the left arm. The Bedu had watched impassively, and now Achmed came forward and held the plastic bag high.

'Four hours to Hazar and a hospital, on this road. Does he have a chance?' Dillon asked.

'I don't know, but I can improve his chances. I'll call Ferguson.'

He found him enjoying the comforts of the Excelsior, there no longer being any reason for them to maintain their presence in Hazar secret.

'Where are you?' Villiers asked.

'In the bar at the Excelsior, celebrating with Harry. I've spoken to Blake Johnson. He's over the moon.'

'Well, hold the celebration. Billy's been badly wounded. Kate Rashid shot him several times in the back.'

'Dear God.'

'We need to get him to Hazar Hospital as soon as possible. The train's no good. It carries on north into the Empty Quarter, which leaves us with a four-hour trip by road.'

'But can the boy survive that?'

'Well, his chances would improve if you arranged to have an ambulance come to meet us halfway. The head of surgery at the hospital is a man called Daz, an Indian. He's done a lot for me in the past. Get in touch with him and arrange it. They can't miss us. It's the only road.'

'Leave it with me.'

Villiers said, 'Let's get out of here. You sit beside Billy, Dillon, I'll go in front with Achmed. My lads will have to sort themselves out.' He turned to his men and said in Arabic, 'Let's move out. We push for Hazar hard.'

* * *

In the Scorpion, Kate Rashid called Captain Black on his mobile and found him at the airport. 'What can I do for you, Countess?'

'We'll be landing in about an hour. I want an immediate departure slot for England. Take care of it.'

'Of course, Countess. There was a message for you from your houseboy. He said that if you were in touch, to tell you he's heard General Ferguson and a Mr Salter have moved into the Excelsior.'

'Thank you.'

She switched off and passed the information to Dauncey. 'It's a good thing we have our personal luggage on board. We can get straight off.'

'Are we running, Kate?'

'Don't be silly. From what? The Bacu Bridge is still in one piece, and so is the train. Everybody down there is dead. They can't prove a thing.'

'Interesting though, that they were all here. I wonder how they knew?'

'It's something to do with Dillon, it always is. God knows what, not that it matters now. At least I've settled the score with one of them.'

'But not Dillon.'

'My day will come, darling, just wait and see.'

* * *

An hour and a half after leaving the bridge, Villiers received a call from Daz. 'Ah, Tony, the General explained your predicament. Describe the young man's symptoms.' Villiers told him quickly what had happened and what he'd done.

'And how is he now?'

'Unconscious, but still with us. It's a rough ride.'

'I know. I decided to come myself. It could make big difference. It won't be long now, Colonel.'

Villiers told Dillon, who said, 'Thank God. There's no colour in him at all.'

'Just keep the faith,' Villiers said. 'That's all we can do.'

The wind sprang up again, spraying sand everywhere, and Dillon leaned over Billy, trying to protect him, despair in his head now. My younger brother, that was how he liked to describe himself, Dillon thought.

'God damn you, Kate,' Dillon said softly. 'If he dies, there'll be no place you can hide from me.'

A moment later, a large ambulance emerged from the murk in front of them. Daz, a tall, cadaverous Indian wearing a hooded burnoose, emerged with two paramedics carrying a stretcher. They had Billy on it in a moment and turned back to the ambulance.

'We'll get straight back,' Daz said. 'I don't want to waste time.'

Villiers said, 'Go with him, Dillon. I'll see you soon.'

Dillon ran after Daz and climbed in the rear of the ambulance. Suddenly, it was a calmer, more ordered world, the sound of the wind and the sandstorm remote, and he sat there watching Daz and his paramedics working on his friend.

In the lounge at the hospital three hours later, Dillon and Harry Salter sat drinking whisky from a half-bottle obtained from the Excelsior bar.

'What a bastard,' Harry said.

Dillon nodded. 'You've no idea how sorry I am.'

'Oh, yes I have. It's not your fault, Dillon.' He shook his head. 'I couldn't love that boy more if he was my own son.' Suddenly, he held out his paper cup. 'Give me another.' His hand shook a little. 'He could die on us, Dillon, and that bitch shot him in the back.'

'You know what they say, Harry. Absolute power corrupts absolutely. It gives some people the idea they can do anything and get away with it. Kate Rashid's like that, but what happens when you find out you can't get what you want, can't have your own way? It's enough to drive you mad, if you're not mad already.'

'Well, she bleeding is. If I ever get my hands on her . . .' He didn't finish, because Tony Villiers and Ferguson entered.

'Any news?' Ferguson asked.

Dillon shook his head. 'Not yet.'

'Well, I have. I've just checked with Lacey at the airport. Apparently, Kate Rashid and her cousin left for London more than two hours ago.'

'Flying the coop,' Dillon said.

'You could say that,' Ferguson replied. 'But look at it another way. What do we really have on her? The Bacu Bridge didn't happen. She's still the leader of the Rashid Bedu, the most powerful figure in Southern Arabia.'

'What about the tape – the recording?'

'It doesn't mean a thing, because none of it happened. What would you ask the Director of Public Prosecutions to do? What would they be trying to get the richest woman in the world for, a flight of fantasy? No, the DPP's office wouldn't touch it with a bargepole, and if they did, a posse of London's most gifted QCs would make mincemeat of them.'

'So she gets away with it?' Harry said.

At that moment, Daz entered the lounge, still in his operating clothes. Harry was on his feet in seconds. 'How is he?'

'I've done all I can here. He was lucky that the bullet in the neck missed a major artery, otherwise he'd have bled to death. Eighteen stitches in the face will leave him with an interesting scar, but the trouble is the other two bullets. They've fractured the pelvic girdle. He's going to need a top orthopaedic surgeon when he returns to London, but in my opinion, it's nothing that can't be put right.'

'Where is he now?' Harry asked. 'Can I see him?'

'I'd rather not. He's in intensive care. Tomorrow morning would be better.'

'When will he be fit for a trip to London?' Ferguson asked.

'I'd say four days from now, assuming no complications.'

'Excellent.' Ferguson turned to Harry. 'You'll want to stay with him?'

'Too bloody right.'

'Good. I've got to get back to London, but we'll stay in touch. I'll have the Gulfstream come for you four days from now and I'll discuss the case with Henry Bellamy. If anyone knows who the best orthopaedic surgeon in London is, he will.'

'Great,' Harry said.

'We've got an early start in the morning, Dillon,' Ferguson said. 'Unless you want to stay with Harry.'

'No,' Dillon told him. 'I might as well go with you. I have things to do in London.'

'Right. We might as well have dinner at the Excelsior. Will you join us, Colonel?'

Tony Villiers said, 'Thanks, but no, General. I also have things to do.'

The following morning, before they left, Ferguson and Dillon stopped by to see Billy. Harry was already sitting in the lounge, having stayed overnight in a guest room.

A staff nurse went to check if it was all right for them to go in. At the same moment, Tony Villiers entered. He was in a head cloth and tropical uniform, a Browning belted to his waist. He looked tired, his face finely drawn and covered with dust, as was his uniform.

'Good God, Tony,' Ferguson said. 'What have you been up to?'

'General mayhem. Have you seen Billy yet?'

'We're hoping to any minute.'

Salter led the way in. Billy was propped up high, a cage over his legs, tubes everywhere. He was obviously very weak but managed a smile. Salter leaned over and kissed him on the forehead.

'Bleeding hell,' Billy said. 'What's got into you?' He looked up at Dillon. 'We really screwed them, didn't we? Even when she tried, the bitch still couldn't kill me.'

'Thanks to the Wilkinson Sword Company and their titanium waistcoats.'

'Yeah, let's invest, Harry, buy a few shares.'

Dillon cut in. 'She's gone, Billy, she and Dauncey, back to London.'

'Good riddance.' Billy winced in pain. 'Let it go, Dillon, she's not worth it.'

The staff nurse, standing at the back, said, 'I think you'd better leave now, gentlemen.'

Villiers said, 'One more moment.' He moved closer to Billy. 'I have a present for you.'

'And what would that be?'

'I missed dinner last night because I went up country with my Scouts, camped at El Hajiz. I took a couple of bags of Semtex with me, left my men, and crossed into the Empty Quarter. Just me and my sergeant, Achmed. The conditions were terrible, with the storm, but we hit Kate Rashid's terrorist camp at Fuad at one in the morning, scattered a few blocks of Semtex around with ten-minute pencil timers, and then blew most of the camp to hell – vehicles, ammunition and explosives store, the lot.'

'You bastard,' Billy said. 'You wonderful bastard. I'd laugh, but I'd burst my stitches. Oh, that'll give Her Highness something to think about.'

Later, as the Gulfstream climbed to fifty thousand feet, Dillon called to Sergeant Pound for a cup of tea. They sat in silence for a while.

Finally, Ferguson said, 'You were right, absolutely right on this one.'

'What do you mean?'

'When you said there was no time to send in the Marines or the SAS. This one required the Dillon touch.'

'Yes, it worked, but we were lucky. It might not work the next time.'

'Oh, have it your own way, Sean. Just do me a favour.'

'God help me when you call me Sean. What would the favour be?'

'Let it alone now. I saw what you looked like, back there with Billy. I don't want any vigilante nonsense. There's no profit in it.'

'You're talking in riddles, and me just a simple Irish boy.' Dillon turned and called to Pound. 'A Bushmills down here, Sergeant, so I can drink to the Devil Herself.'

LONDON

DAUNCEY PLACE

16

The Gulfstream landed at Farley Field at seven in the evening, London time, and found the Daimler waiting. Dillon and Ferguson said goodbye to Lacey and Parry and drove away.

Ferguson said, 'Drop you home?'

'Yes, then I'd like to see Daniel Quinn.'

'I'll meet you there, after I touch base with Hannah.'

Dillon checked his watch. 'Fine. Let's say nine o'clock?'

'Suits me.'

He dropped Dillon and the Daimler drew away. The Irishman got the front door open. He'd noticed the Telecom van parked a little way up the street and found his Nightstalkers, went upstairs to his bedroom, and focused them on the windshield. Newton and Cook were clearly visible.

'Jesus,' he said softly. 'Don't they ever learn? You never give up, do you, Kate?'

A phone call had told her about the attack on Fuad and the plane's departure from Hazar and she'd given Dauncey his instructions. He listened to what she had to say.

'Are you sure about this? Don't you think it's better to let things calm down for a little while?'

'On the contrary. I killed Billy Salter and he saw me do it. He'll be after me sooner or later, and I'd prefer to be after him first. To handle it virtually as soon as he's back could catch him off guard.'

'Catch Dillon off guard?' Rupert laughed. 'That'll be the day.'

She was angry, not that it surprised him. Since the events at the bridge, there had been a change in her. There wasn't the control he was used to, the icy calm, but a wildness, and a glitter in her eyes that made him uncomfortable.

'Are you with me on this or not?' she demanded.

'Of course I'm with you. You want him dead. I'll help you.'

'Yes, I want him dead, but only if I can do the job myself. He killed my brothers, he's ruined so much that was important to me. It's time he paid. We'll go down to Dauncey this evening, just you and me. You can drive. I'll phone ahead and give the servants the night off. Those two goons you employ, the so-called security men. They're ex-SAS, aren't they?'

'Yes.'

'Then they should be able to handle a simple snatch-and-grab.'

'They didn't do too well in Hyde Park.'

Her anger was fierce. 'Well, tell them they have to do better, or I'll ruin them. Do you understand? They'll never work again. I have that power, Rupert, you know I have.'

In a strange way, it was as if she was demanding that he agree, and he raised a hand defensively. 'Of course you do. I'll arrange it.'

'Good. Now get me a drink.'

Dillon showered and changed, put on black cords, a matching shirt, his old flying jacket, and a pair of jump boots. A three-inch throwing knife was concealed in a pocket on the inside of the right boot. He took it out and checked it. Both edges of the blade were razor sharp and he replaced it carefully.

He went down to the hall and opened a secret door under the stairs that swung out to his touch. There was an assortment of handguns there: a Browning, two Walthers, a Colt .25 short-barrelled job in an ankle holder. He took one of the Walthers, the one with a silencer on the end, slipped it in the special pocket under his left arm, and went into the garage by the interior door from the kitchen. He got in the Mini Cooper, opened the door with the remote control, drove straight out and away.

A timer on the garage door closed it if it was left open, so he kept on going, aware of the Telecom van's lights coming on behind him. All his precautions had been intended to prevent an immediate confrontation. That would come later, at a time of his own choosing.

Ferguson and Hannah were already in the reception area at Rosedene, talking to Martha, when he went in.

'How's he doing?' Dillon asked.

'Not too well. There was an infection of some sort, which hasn't helped.'

'I saw him this morning,' Hannah said. 'He was talking about going home.'

'Does he know what happened at the Bacu?' Dillon asked.

'Not yet. The General didn't tell me about it until he phoned to say what time you'd be arriving. I knew you'd be seeing the Senator, so I thought I'd leave it to you.'

'All right,' Ferguson said. 'Let's go in.'

Quinn was sitting up, still wearing the sling and reading a book. 'You're back.' He laid the book down. 'What happened? Good news, I hope?'

'Good news and bad,' Dillon said, and told him.

Afterwards, Quinn said, 'I'm really sorry about Billy. But you guys sure got the job done: Kate Rashid must be livid.'

'I imagine so. We put a major spoke in her grand scheme. What about you? How are you feeling?' Dillon asked.

'You mean my health or my head?'

'Both,' Ferguson put in.

'Bellamy's a fine surgeon. I'll heal eventually, so I'm not worried about that. But I've been thinking a lot while I've been lying here and I've come to a decision. I'm not up to the hard stuff anymore.'

'What about vengeance is mine, saith the Lord?' Dillon said.

Quinn shook his head. 'I spent a lot of time working it through. I decided that Helen was worth more than that. And so is her memory.'

It was Hannah who said gently, 'And Kate Rashid and Rupert Dauncey?'

'Oh, they'll get theirs. From the sound of it, they've already started to. It's a downward slope for them now – they'll destroy themselves. Just as I almost destroyed myself. It's a powerful drug, revenge – and just as deadly.'

'I'm glad to hear it, for your sake,' Ferguson told him. 'Try and get some rest now.'

'Just one more thing. I wouldn't like to think any of my friends thought they were doing me a favour by taking things further.'

He looked directly at Dillon, who said, 'Now do I look like that kind of fella? On the other hand, Kate Rashid did shoot Billy in the back seven times. If his bulletproof waistcoat hadn't stopped four rounds, he'd be a corpse now.'

'So you're the one talking vengeance?'

'No, I'm the one under suspended sentence of death, together with the General and Harry Salter. You could say I'm concerned to know whether I should wear my titanium waistcoat at all times. Goodnight, Senator.'

Ferguson and Hannah followed him out. She said, 'Sean, you're not going to do anything silly?'

'Did you ever know me to? Go on, be off with you, the two of you.'

'I'll see you at my office at nine in the morning. Meanwhile, no funny business, and that's an order,' Ferguson said, and he and Hannah left.

They went down the steps to the Daimler. Ferguson said, 'Why does Dillon do it? It's as if he's looking for death.'

'No, sir, that's not it. In fact, he doesn't care whether he lives or dies anymore.'

'God help him, then.'

Dillon stood on the top step and watched them go. The Telecom van was across the street. He went down the steps to his Mini Cooper, got behind the wheel, and drove away quickly.

Newton was in the passenger seat, as Cook drove. He took a sawn-off shotgun from under the seat, opened it to check the cartridges, and snapped it shut.

'When do we hit him?' Cook asked.

'He's got to go home sooner or later. We'll try him getting out of the car.' He patted the shotgun. 'He may be hot stuff, but not with one of these pointing between his eyes. That's what separates the men from the boys.'

Not far from Stable Mews and on the other side of the square was Dillon's local pub, the Black Horse. There were many vehicles parked there at that time of night. Dillon turned in, parked at the end of a line of cars and went into the saloon bar. He didn't order a drink, simply stood at the window and looked out to see the Telecom van reversing into a parking space.

He left the saloon bar, went into the lounge, which was crowded with people, and let himself out of a side door. He moved down the line of parked cars, bending low, and reached the rear of the van. Newton was smoking and had the window down. Cook said, 'Maybe one of us should go in and see what he's up to?'

'Don't be stupid. He'd recognize us, and what he's up to is having a drink.'

'Alas, no.' Dillon took out his Walther and touched Newton on the side of the skull. 'What he's up to is considering whether to blow your brains out, and this is a silenced weapon. You'd sit here, the both of you, for quite a long time before anyone realized you'd shuffled off this mortal coil. That's poetry, by the way, but then, I'm Irish.'

'What do you want?' Newton's voice was harsh.

'That, for a starter.' Dillon reached inside and took the shotgun, which he placed on the roof. 'Now yours,' he told Cook. 'You must have something.' Cook hesitated, then took a Smith and Wesson .38 from an inside pocket and offered it butt first. 'Strange how people are always giving me guns,' Dillon said.

'Can we go now?' Newton asked.

'Not until you tell me what Dauncey intended. What was going to happen to me? A bullet in the head and into the Thames?'

'No, it wasn't like that.'

Dillon yanked open the door and put the muzzle of the Walther against Newton's knee. 'As I said, this is silenced, so no one will hear a thing while I kneecap you. As you may know, I was IRA for years, so putting you on sticks doesn't give me a problem.'

'No, not that. I'll tell you. Dauncey said the Countess wanted us to jump you, sling you in the back of the van, and drive you down to Dauncey Place. He was very specific. She wanted you in one piece.'

'There, that wasn't so hard, was it?' Dillon shut the door and stood back. 'If you two were SAS, then God help the country. I'd say you need a different line of work.' He fired into the front offside tyre, which collapsed at once. 'I'll just make it the one. Changing it will give you something to do. Please give Dauncey my best. Tell him I'll see him soon.'

He picked the shotgun and the revolver off the roof, went to the Mini Cooper, and drove away. Newton got out. 'All right, let's change the bloody tyre.'

'What about Dauncey?'

'He can go fuck himself. But I'll call him anyway. I'd like to think he can sort that bastard out if he visits them.'

'Then what do we do?'

'You heard the man. Find a different line of work.'

Dillon parked the Mini Cooper outside the cottage, went in and straight upstairs. He wasn't angry, but remarkably cool. It was no longer a question of letting it go, as Ferguson and the others had wanted, even Billy. He knew one thing with absolute certainty: Kate Rashid would never let it go, not where he was concerned.

But for the moment, he was bushed, the effects of the last few days rolling up on him, and that would never do. He needed to be at his best. He punched the security system on by the front door, went up to his bedroom, and undressed. He put the silenced Walther on the small table beside the bed, got in and left the lights on. In spite of that, he immediately plunged into a profound sleep.

A while later, he came awake with a start, checked his watch, and found that it was half past three. He felt fine, clear-headed, his brain sharp. He got up, pulled on his black cords, then put on the titanium waistcoat, the shirt over it, and finally the flying jacket. He found an old and favourite white scarf to finish things off, then went downstairs and opened the secret door again. He took out the Colt .25 and checked it. A lightweight weapon, but not with the hollow point cartridges with which it was loaded.

He replaced it in the ankle holster, pulled up his trouser leg, and strapped the holster in place just above the top of the left jump boot. He already had the silenced Walther under his left arm, and now he took out the other Walther and slipped it into his belt against the small of his back.

He went and found his silver cigarette case, filled it from a box, slipped it into his inside right pocket, and also found his old Zippo lighter. All this he had done calmly and meticulously. It was like preparing for war.

There was a mirror in the hall by the door. He took a cigarette from his case, lit it, and smiled at himself.

'Well, here we go again, me old son,' he said, and left.

In the library at Dauncey Place, Kate Rashid sat by the great fireplace, a black Dobermann called Carl on the floor beside her. A log fire burned on the hearth, and she was ablaze with jewellery and wearing her usual black jumpsuit. She and Rupert hadn't been to bed, had simply sat there waiting. The door opened, and Rupert came in with coffee things on a silver tray, which he placed on a table close to her.

'I don't think he's coming, sweetie.'

'But your man Newton told you he was coming.' She poured coffee into two cups.

'Not quite true. What he actually said was that Dillon had told him to tell me he'd see me soon. Why should that have meant tonight?'

'I know it does, because I know Dillon like no one else,' she said serenely. 'He'll be here.'

'For what? Breakfast?'

He went to the sideboard and found a bottle of Rémy Martin. 'Do you want one?'

'I don't need it. Perhaps you do.'

'Nasty, sweetie, nasty.' He poured a large one, returned to the table, and put it in his coffee. 'Your diamonds are amazing tonight. Why are you wearing them?'

'I wouldn't want to disappoint him,' and there was that half-smile again, the glitter in the eyes.

My God, she really is mad. He swallowed the coffee and cognac down and glanced at his watch. 'Almost six. He's certainly taking his time.'

He went to the French windows, opened them, and peered out over the terrace and beyond the balustrade to the trees. It was still dark, but dawn was beginning to break and it was raining heavily.

'Bloody awful weather.' He lit a cigarette and went back to the fireside.

Dillon reached the outskirts of the village after just over a two-hour drive, passed the massive gates to Dauncey Place, and turned into the parking area at the church a quarter of a mile down the road. There were a dozen or so vehicles there already, probably owned by villagers from the cottages on either side of the narrow road. He took an old Burberry trench coat from the boot of the Mini and a cloth cap, put them on, and set off through the rain.

He had no fixed plans. Something was in motion and he was just going with the flow. He thought back to the Heidegger quote again. *For authentic living, what is necessary is the resolute confrontation of death.* Was that what it had always been about? A mad game, constantly seeking death? Any half-baked psychiatrist could have told him that. He turned in through the gates and started up the drive through the heavy rain. The darkness was lightening perceptibly, and halfway along the drive he saw something a hundred yards to his right beyond some beech trees that surprised him. He hesitated, then went to explore. It was Kate Rashid's Black Eagle, which he'd seen at the Dauncey Aero Club.

'Now there's a thing,' he said softly, turned, went back to the drive and continued toward the house. He saw the light in the library at once and turned off the drive and worked his way through the trees, staying in their cover when he reached the edge of the lawn.

He saw Rupert open the French windows and stand there for a few moments and then turn back into the room. Dillon let him go and then started across.

In the library, Carl whined, then growled deeply. 'Seek, boy, seek him out,' Kate Rashid said, and the dog vanished through the French windows. She turned to Rupert. 'You know what to do.'

He produced a Walther, moved to one side of the fireplace, and pulled back the heavy tapestry, revealing a door. When he opened it, there was a toilet inside. He stepped in, leaving the door slightly open, and dropped the tapestry.

The Dobermann ran across the lawn, barking, and Dillon whistled, a strange and eerie sound, and the Dobermann stopped dead. Dillon whistled again, all the loneliness in the world in it, and the Dobermann whined and sidled up.

'See, you're just a pussycat at heart. You didn't know I had the gift, did you? Neither did your mistress. Be a good boy and we'll go and see her,' and he started across the lawn, the dog following.

In the library, Rupert called softly, through the

tapestry, his voice muffled, 'What the hell's happened to Carl?'

'I don't know,' she replied.

Dillon moved in through the French windows, the Dobermann at his side. 'God bless all here. Jesus, it's a wet one.' He took off the Burberry and rain hat. 'What's his name?'

'Carl,' she said calmly.

'Don't blame him, Kate, I have a way with dogs, have had since childhood. Would there be a drink in the place?'

'On the sideboard. I can't guarantee Irish whiskey, though.'

'Sure, and I'll find something.' He helped himself to Scotch, and Carl went with him to the sideboard, sitting.

'Remarkable,' she said. 'Those things are supposed to be the fiercest guard dogs in the world.'

'It must be my winning personality. Where's the good Rupert?'

'Around.'

'Terrible people he employs. Newton and Cook.' He shrugged. 'Total rubbish.'

'I agree.'

'I see you've got the Eagle parked here.'

'You know about that?'

'You usually keep it at the Dauncey Aero Club six miles away, but you use your own airstrip here when it suits.'

'Yes, I had one of the staff at the club fly it down for me yesterday.'

'Where would it be this time? Isle of Wight again?'

'Is there anything you don't know? Where Rupert is, for example?'

'I'm sure he'll tell me at the right moment.'

The tapestry parted and Rupert emerged, gun in hand. 'Which is now.'

Carl slipped beside Dillon and the rumble in his throat was infinitely menacing. Dauncey turned his Walther on him and Dillon raised a hand. 'Shoot the dog and I'll kill you myself.'

'Leave it, Rupert,' Kate said.

Dillon fondled Carl's head. 'There's a good boy,' and the dog rubbed against him. 'Go on to your mistress now.' He pointed, and Carl went and sat by her.

'Now what?' Dillon asked.

'Oh, something special, I think. Shooting's too good. That's for people like Billy Salter.' She smiled.

'If I can interject,' Dillon said. 'Billy's still alive.

Sorry about that, Kate. Everything's going wrong, isn't it?'

There was a kind of rage in her eyes, but only for a moment. 'So I'll have to shoot him again.'

She slipped her hand between the cushion on which she was sitting and the arm of the sofa and took out an old German Luger.

'This has been in the family since the First World War. Paul taught me how to shoot with it in the woods when I was quite little.'

Dillon had his hands on his hips. He could have reached for the Walther in his belt and shot Rupert Dauncey that instant, and her, too, for he saw she had the safety catch on, and yet he held back. In a way, it was mesmerizing, being face-to-face with the most beautiful woman he'd ever known, a woman he now realized was totally unbalanced. And yet, like a bad dream, he had a part to play, had to see it through.

'You owe me, Dillon, you owe me for the three brothers you killed.'

'Ah, well, I always pay my debts.' He was a little mad himself now. 'By the way, the safety catch is on.' She examined the Luger and remedied it. 'Will that do?' he asked.

'Not really. Rupert?'

She turned the Luger on Dillon and Rupert laid his gun on the library table, opened a dresser, and took out a roll of masking tape. 'Turn around.'

Dillon did as he was told and Rupert bound his wrists behind him.

'Get his gun,' Kate Rashid told him.

Rupert took it from the pocket under Dillon's left arm and laid it down. 'That's better,' she said.

'Not if he carries another one. I bet I know where it is.' He felt under the back of Dillon's flying jacket and found the second Walther. 'There you go, sweetie.'

'So now what?' Dillon asked.

'I think I'll take you for a flight,' she said. 'Show you what a good pilot I am.'

'That should be interesting.' Dillon nodded. 'I'm a great pilot myself, but I'm always willing to learn. Are we going to France for lunch?'

'For Rupert and me, perhaps, but it'll be a somewhat shorter flight for you.'

'Ah, like that, is it?'

'Absolutely. Let's get moving.'

She left the Luger on the coffee table and Rupert prodded Dillon in the back. 'Just do as you're told and I promise we'll make it painless.'

They went out and Kate Rashid draped Dillon's Burberry around her shoulders, put on the rain hat, closed the French windows on Carl, and followed.

It was light now, the sky sombre with heavy grey clouds, and visibility was poor. The rain was relentless as they followed a path through the beech trees and came out to the meadow and approached the Black Eagle.

'Lousy flying weather,' Dillon said. 'Are you sure you want to do this?'

'Oh, yes.' She took the keys from her pocket and unlocked the Airstair door and opened it. The steps came down and she went up. Rupert gave Dillon a push.

'Up you go.'

Dillon moved awkwardly because of his bound hands. Rupert pushed him down the aisle and sat him in one of the rear seats by the window. There was a toilet and luggage space behind him and an inflatable life raft.

'Now be good.'

He moved to the Airstair door and closed it one-handed, facing Dillon and still menacing him with his gun. At the same moment, the port engine burst into life, followed a little later by the starboard. The plane started to roll forward, Kate Rashid increased speed, then lifted up into the rain no more than fifty feet above the row of beech trees at the end of the runway.

She climbed very quickly to three thousand feet. Way below, there was grey cloud, in some places black and heavy with more rain and mist, as they crossed an area of marshes and coastal beaches and headed out to sea.

All this Dillon could see from the window at the same time that he was extracting the knife from the inside of his right jump boot. He got his hands round the handle, positioned the knife, and the razor sharp edge sliced through the masking tape immediately. He replaced the knife in his boot, pulled away the tape, and sat waiting.

She turned and said over her shoulder, 'Now, Rupert,' went down to about two thousand and reduced speed.

Rupert lifted the locking bar and opened the Airstair door. There was a rush of air. He leaned over, the Walther in his left hand, and pulled Dillon up and forward.

Kate Rashid glanced over her shoulder again and she was laughing. 'You can rot in hell, Dillon.'

Dillon said, 'For God's sake, no,' and half-slipped to the floor.

'Now don't be silly, old friend, make it easy on yourself. Just get up.' Which Dillon did, at the same time he was drawing the Colt from the ankle holster, ramming the muzzle into the side of Rupert Dauncey's head, and pulling the trigger.

There was an explosion of bone fragments and blood, the hollow point cartridge doing its work, and Dauncey dropped the Walther and fell back against the side of the door. Dillon pushed and sent him out into space. He grabbed at the Airstair door and closed it.

He turned and found that Kate Rashid had put the Eagle on automatic and was reaching for her purse. She took out a small pistol, but he lunged, wrestled it from her and tossed it to the back of the plane. She was hysterical with rage and clawed at him. Dillon slapped her face.

'Stop it! Pull yourself together! It's over.' She was in the left-hand seat of the dual-controlled plane and he clambered into the right. 'Take us back.'

'To hell with you.'

'All right, I'll do it.'

Dillon switched from the automatic pilot to

manual control, banked to port, and started towards the coastline, two or three miles away.

Unlike most planes, the Black Eagle sported an ignition key. She reached for it now and switched it off, then pulled out the key. The engines stuttered to a halt. She pushed open the quarter-light in the window beside her and tossed the ignition key out.

'There you are, Dillon. We'll go to hell together.'

'That was very stupid. But it's surprising how far you can glide in one of these things.'

She looked out at the mist as they descended and to the distant shore. 'We'll never make it. We're going into the water, and even if you could land this thing on water, a light aircraft like this will only float for a minute and a half.'

'Very true, but there's a life raft back there – and I do happen to know how to land on water. Do you?'

'Damn you, Dillon!'

They were down to six hundred feet, and he said, 'Let me tell you. Keep your landing gear up, full flaps. Light winds and small waves, land into the wind; if it's a heavy wind and big waves, land parallel to the crests.'

And then they were close, there were small waves, and he landed into the wind. They bounced across the waves and settled.

'Come on,' he ordered, and scrambled out of his seat, made it to the door and opened it. He moved to the luggage compartment, got the life raft and tossed it out. It started to inflate automatically.

He turned to call her again, and saw her leaning out of the cockpit and picking up Rupert Dauncey's Walther, which had slid along the side because of the incline of the plane.

'I told you I'd see you in hell,' she cried.

As Dillon ducked, she fired wildly. The round plucked at his right sleeve, and he flung himself out of the door into water of mind-numbing coldness and struck out, grabbing for the raft's line. He hung on and turned. The Eagle had tilted more now, the tail up, the port wing under the water.

She was still there in the cockpit, screaming at him, one hand gripping the open quarter-light, and then the tail lifted high and the Eagle simply slipped beneath the surface.

He made it to the life raft and hauled himself inside. There were two paddles and a couple of survival boxes he didn't bother to open. He slid the paddles through the oarlocks, no other emotion left in him except a stubborn need to survive.

He started to row toward the shore, distant in the mist and rain. It was a long way off, but not as far as Kate Rashid had gone.